Praise for
Elizabeth Mansfield

"Renowned for delighting readers."
—*Affaire de Coeur*

"One of the enduring names in romance."
—*The Paperback Forum*

"Another classic treat . . . notable for its polished writing and gleaming wit." —*Booklist*

"Delicious contretemps." —*Rendezvous*

"One of the best-loved authors of Regency romance."
—*The Romance Reader*

WESTFIELD WASHINGTON
PUBLIC LIBRARY
333 West Hoover Street

SIGNET

REGENCY ROMANCE

COMING IN SEPTEMBER 2004

The Vampire Viscount and
The Devil's Bargain
by Karen Harbaugh

Together in one volume, two new stories of ingenues who get more than they bargained for with their darkly mysterious lovers.

0-451-21287-8

The Countess and the Butler
by Elizabeth Brodnax

Michael was a prince, but exile has forced him to seek employment in the home of the Countess of Amesworth. The young widow was content alone until this handsome butler renews her passion.

0-451-21340-8

The Madcap Heiress
by Emily Hendrickson

Adam Herbert yearns for adventure. What he finds is heiress Emily Lawrence. Together they discover a love worth more than any fortune.

0-451-21289-4

Available wherever books are sold, or
to order call: 1-800-788-6262

Poor Caroline

and

Matched Pairs

Elizabeth Mansfield

Rom
m

SIGNET
Published by New American Library, a division of
Penguin Group (USA) Inc., 375 Hudson Street,
New York, New York 10014, U.S.A.
Penguin Books Ltd, 80 Strand,
London WC2R 0RL, England
Penguin Books Australia Ltd, 250 Camberwell Road,
Camberwell, Victoria 3124, Australia
Penguin Books Canada Ltd, 10 Alcorn Avenue,
Toronto, Ontario, Canada M4V 3B2
Penguin Books (NZ), cnr Airborne and Rosedale Roads,
Albany, Auckland 1310, New Zealand

Penguin Books Ltd, Registered Offices:
80 Strand, London WC2R 0RL, England

Published by Signet, an imprint of New American Library, a division of Penguin Group (USA) Inc. *Poor Caroline* and *Matched Pairs* were originally published in separate editions by Jove Books, a division of Penguin Group (USA) Inc.

First Signet Printing (Double Edition), August 2004
10 9 8 7 6 5 4 3 2 1

Poor Caroline copyright © Paula Schwartz, 1995
Matched Pairs copyright © Paula Schwartz, 1996
Excerpt from *A Grand Deception* copyright © Paula Schwartz, 1988
All rights reserved

 REGISTERED TRADEMARK—MARCA REGISTRADA

Printed in the United States of America

Without limiting the rights under copyright reserved above, no part of this publication may be reproduced, stored in or introduced into a retrieval system, or transmitted, in any form, or by any means (electronic, mechanical, photocopying, recording, or otherwise), without the prior written permission of both the copyright owner and the above publisher of this book.

PUBLISHER'S NOTE
These are works of fiction. Names, characters, places, and incidents either are the product of the author's imagination or are used fictitiously, and any resemblance to actual persons, living or dead, business establishments, events, or locales is entirely coincidental.

BOOKS ARE AVAILABLE AT QUANTITY DISCOUNTS WHEN USED TO PROMOTE PRODUCTS OR SERVICES. FOR INFORMATION PLEASE WRITE TO PREMIUM MARKETING DIVISION, PENGUIN GROUP (USA) INC., 375 HUDSON STREET, NEW YORK, NEW YORK 10014.

If you purchased this book without a cover you should be aware that this book is stolen property. It was reported as "unsold and destroyed" to the publisher and neither the author nor the publisher has received any payment for this "stripped book."

The scanning, uploading and distribution of this book via the Internet or via any other means without the permission of the publisher is illegal and punishable by law. Please purchase only authorized electronic editions, and do not participate in or encourage electronic piracy of copyrighted materials. Your support of the author's rights is appreciated.

Poor Caroline

Prologue

Winter 1802

"There she is," Lady Whitlow said to her brother, the Viscount Crittenden, in what was supposed to be a whisper. "Poor Caroline."

Little Caroline Whitlow, twelve years old and benumbed by the sudden death of her parents and the abrupt disappearance of the comfort and security she'd known all her life, stood frozen in the doorway of the enormous drawing room of the Grange, the viscount's country seat. Her mouth was set in a tight, stubborn line, and her head was held abnormally high. She carried her infant brother Gilbert in her right arm and clutched the hand of her three-year-old brother, Arthur, in her left hand—three penniless orphans uncertain of their future. She'd overheard her aunt Martha, and something inside her sickened. She hated those words, *Poor Caroline*. She'd heard them whispered behind her back repeatedly since her parents died, and she knew she would do anything—*anything!*—not to hear them again.

Lady Whitlow glanced over at Caroline worriedly. She was very fond of the child, but she wondered what Clement would think of her. The girl's attitude was prickly at best, an attitude not designed to endear her to a stranger or win his goodwill. And goodwill was necessary for a child in her penniless situation.

The three orphans were the children of her husband's brother, Benjamin Whitlow; and she, the childless and widowed Martha Whitlow, was their only living kin, their aunt by marriage if not by blood. She wished the best for the poor children, but she herself did not feel capable of bringing them up. Though she was anguished over their diminished prospects, she felt helpless to do anything for them. She had no experience with children, and her modest town house in London was not adequate. She'd brought them here to the viscount, her brother, in desperation. She didn't expect him, a confirmed bachelor, to take them in, but perhaps he might contribute to their support or have some suggestions as to what to do with them.

Caroline, meanwhile, stood in unflinching immobility under the gaze of the two adults. At a mere twelve years of age, she already had three pronounced characteristics that would stay with her into adulthood: a head of thick, curly auburn hair that she kept cut short; a pair of large, gold-flecked, speaking eyes; and an unshakable pride. Those qualities were immediately apparent to the aging Clement Meredith, Viscount of Crittenden. He leaned forward from the depths of his large wing chair and studied her with admiration. "Proud little thing, ain't she?" he cackled admiringly to his sister.

"Yes, poor child." Martha, Lady Whitlow, sighed. She stood beside his chair, still wearing her travel bonnet and cloak. "Too proud, I'm afraid, for her diminished position in life."

"Nay, don't say so. I like pride. You have it, and so have I."

"Yes, it's true. But you should know better than most that pride can be damaging. It has cost you dearly, hasn't it?"

"I don't know what you're prattling of," he muttered, his mouth hardening.

"You most certainly do!" his sister exclaimed. "Pride cost you the companionship of our brother and the nephew you were so fond of."

"Never mind. Don't speak of them," the viscount said curtly. "I no longer think of them."

"I'm only saying, my dear, that one can sometimes be too proud. In Caroline's case, perhaps it would be better to have humility. The poor child, and the two baby brothers she won't let out of her grasp, were not left a feather to fly with. My brother-in-law, Benjamin, had no head for business. It took every penny I could salvage from the sale of his house to pay off his debts. So what good is pride to these poor children?"

The viscount peered intently across the room at the girl standing in the doorway. Then a slow smile suffused his wrinkled face. "I like the little chit," he chortled. "Look at the way she tilts up her chin. And how she glares at me, as if daring me to pity her. I like her. I'll take her in, damme if I don't! That'll give her a proper position in life."

Little Caroline, who'd heard every word, lifted her chin even higher. "If you want me," she said loudly, "you'll have to take my brothers, too." Only a tiny tremor on the last syllable revealed how frightened she was.

"Come here, child," the viscount ordered, beckoning from his easy chair with one bony finger. "Let me have a closer look at you."

Caroline shifted the sleeping infant higher on her shoulder, grasped the three-year-old's hand tighter, and taking a deep breath, started across the room, dragging the little boy behind her. As they approached the viscount's chair the boy began to cry. "Hush, Arthur!" Caroline hissed.

Martha Whitlow frowned down at her. "Well, don't just stand there, girl. Make your bow."

The child curtsied. "How do you do, my lord?" she said with well-trained politeness.

The viscount, using a cane to help him, rose from his easy chair. The three-year-old, ducking behind his sister and grasping her leg, howled in fright, and the baby, wakening, began to whimper. The viscount ignored the disturbance. He patted the girl's shoulder to put her at ease. "So, Miss Caroline Whitlow, even though you haven't a free hand to offer me, I'm pleased to make your acquaintance. This little fellow is called Arthur, eh? That's a good name. What's the baby called?"

"Gilbert." She fixed her wide, frightened eyes on the viscount's face. "They don't usually cry . . . much."

"You needn't look like that, child. I won't separate you from your brothers. You've had enough of separation, God knows."

Martha gave a little cry of gratitude. "Oh, Clement!" she exclaimed, throwing her arms about his neck. "How very good of you!"

"Nonsense. They'll bring some life into this old house." He hobbled over to the corner and yanked at the bellpull. "I'll send for some maids to take the boys upstairs and set up a nursery," he said to Caroline kindly. "Then you and Martha and I can have a nice, peaceful tea."

"Thank you, my lord, but—"

"Who don't you just call me Uncle Clement?"

"Yes, Uncle Clement, but I think it would be better if I went with the maids to help set up the nursery."

The viscount shrugged. "As you wish, my dear."

A few minutes later, two neatly dressed housemaids appeared. One took the still-sobbing Arthur in her arms. The other reached for Gilbert, but Caroline would not release him. With a quick bow to her "uncle," the girl turned to follow the maids out of the room.

"Aren't you going to thank your new uncle?" Martha chided.

Caroline turned, looked from one to the other, and tried to speak. But something stilled her tongue. She could only stand there and hang her head.

The viscount crossed the room and smiled down at the silent girl. "You know, little Caroline," he said as softly as his hoarse voice permitted, "once you become accustomed to me and this place, you and your brothers will all like it here. I have gardens and woods and a lake and a stable full of horses."

"Th-thank you, my lord," the girl said, her head lowered.

He put his hand on her chin and lifted her face. "You find it hard to say thanks, eh? You don't like to be beholden."

"No, my lord, I don't," she admitted bluntly.

He threw back his head and gave a hearty laugh. "Neither do I, my girl, neither do I. I think we shall deal famously together."

And so they did, for twelve untroubled years. And during all those twelve years, no one ever again referred to her as Poor

Caroline. What's more, she had every expectation that they never would again.

Expectations, however, often have an irritating way of going wrong.

1

Twelve Years Later
October 1814

The letter from England, addressed to *Captain Christopher Meredith of the 4th Dragoons, Somewhere on the Peninsula,* had taken five months to find its way to the proper hands. How it managed to track him to a lonely hacienda on the side of a sparsely populated Spanish hill he was never to discover. But it arrived at a most opportune moment. Kit Meredith, erstwhile captain of the 4th Dragoons, was now an unemployed, bored, almost destitute civilian, and very tired of licking his wounds. He was more than ready for a change.

On this particular day, the day that was to bring him the change he so desired, he was desultorily digging out stones from the dry earth on the south side of the Spanish house, vainly hoping he could turn the small arid area into something resembling an English kitchen garden. While he worked, his mind dwelt upon his grim prospects. He wondered, as he always did these days, how he could possibly manage to improve the state of his finances, at least enough to get back to England.

He'd been badly mauled at Salamanca, where he'd taken bullets in his chest and upper right arm and had his left leg crushed by his horse when it had been shot from under him. For two years he'd been recuperating in this tiny hacienda in the hills east of Bejar. Thanks to the hospitality of the elderly Spanish couple who'd taken him in (in return, of course, for a generous monthly stipend), and the devoted ministrations of his batman, Morris Mickley, he'd almost completely recovered.

But two years on a desolate hillside of a foreign land—years spent, at first, contending with excruciating pain and later with the struggle to regain the use of his limbs—had taken their toll. He was often subject to feelings of irritability, or depression, or hopelessness. These moods were exacerbated by the constant uproar created by his host and hostess, whose dreadful harangues in loud, rapid, incomprehensible Spanish assailed his ears daily. The noise of their bickering, cutting through the somnolent, hot Spanish air, made him long for the quiet, cool green of England.

Only two things had kept him sane. The first was his batman, an utterly loyal, sensible, ingenious fellow whose companionship was food for a lonely soul and whose rich cockney humor was, to Kit, a cheery reminder of England. The second was his satisfaction at having managed to acquire, during these difficult months, four beautiful Spanish horses. The trouble was that he had no funds left with which to transport them—or his batman or even himself—back to England.

Now that his leg (the slowest of his wounded parts to heal) was finally strong enough to allow him to move about with a barely noticeable limp, he yearned to return home. But the recovery had cost him dearly. Every penny he'd managed to save of his captain's pay and the small legacy his father had left him were almost gone. As were two years of what should have been his prime. At twenty-nine, he believed, he should have more to show for his life than four horses, a limp, and empty pockets.

Pausing in his labors to wipe his brow, he saw his batman, Mickley, come strolling round the corner of the house, the letter in his hand. "What have you there?" he asked.

"Dunno 'ow this ever found ye, Cap'n," the batman answered, holding it out to him. "It's been everywhere from Vimiero to Ciudad Rodrigo."

Kit took the letter and studied it with mild curiosity, noting that the seal had somehow remained miraculously intact. "Can't be anything important," he muttered, seating himself on the stone wall that surrounded the hacienda. "Now that I've sold out, there's no reason for anyone to contact me."

Mickley watched as Kit broke the seal. His captain was finally beginning to look well. The Spanish sun had darkened his invalidish pallor, and in the past couple of months he'd at last added some weight to his tall, lanky frame. The batman was about to say something about it when a glance at the captain's expression stilled his tongue. The man looked stunned.

Kit had taken only one quick look at the letter, but that look caused his back to stiffen, his brows to lift in surprise, and the fingers of both hands to tighten on the single sheet. "What . . . ?" the batman began to ask.

But Kit held up a hand for silence. His eyes gleamed with excitment as he read the letter for the second time—much more carefully now. "Good God!" he exclaimed at last.

The batman eyed him curiously. "Whut's it say?"

"My uncle's dead," Kit said gleefully.

Mickley snorted. "That don't sound like somethin' to cheer the soul."

"Well, it cheers mine. I'm his heir."

The batman looked mildly surprised. "Is 'at a fact? Well, it seems to me that ye should give the poor dead bloke a passin' sigh afore ye start countin' yer gains."

"I hardly knew him," Kit explained, his eyes fixed on the letter. "He and my father never got on. I haven't seen him since I was a child."

"Then why'd the fellow make ye 'is heir?"

"He had no offspring. Neither did his two sisters. My father was the only one of the four Merediths of that generation to have a son. So you see, I'm the next male in the line." He looked up at his batman and grinned. "Can you believe it? I've become the Viscount Crittenden! From now on you'll have to call me Your Lordship."

"Huh! That'll be the day," the batman sneered. "I 'ope ye came into somethin' more substantial than a title."

Kit glanced down at the paper still clutched in his hands. "I think I have. This letter suggests that there's a sizable estate."

"Estate, eh? Well, that's somethin' like!" Mickley tried not to show how impressed he was, but he couldn't help adding, "Sorta like winnin' a lottery, ain't it?"

"Yes," Kit said, somewhat numbed by the surprise of it all, "I suppose it is."

"What sorta estate?"

"The letter doesn't give details. But I know there's a manor house. My father used to talk about it. It's called the Grange. Crittenden Grange. It's in Shropshire." Kit's eyes took on a faraway look as he tried to picture the green hills of Shropshire and the ancestral lands that were now his.

Suddenly, the full import of the news burst upon him. He jumped to his feet, grasped his batman by the shoulders, and whirled him about in a wild burst of exuberance, stirring up a cloud of dust from the sun-dried earth. "Mick, you clodcrusher, *smile*!" he shouted ecstatically. "We're going home!"

2

Gilbert Whitlow was only twelve and knew nothing about love and courtship. His brother Arthur was fifteen and knew everything. "You may as well face it, Gil," Arthur said to the younger boy, who was hanging precariously over the second-floor banister in the hope of getting a glimpse of his sister's suitor. "She'll have him. So there's no need to crane your neck. I tell you she'll have him."

The words were said with an air of such smug certainty that they irked Gilbert to the soul. "So *you* say," he retorted, wrinkling his freckled nose in disgust.

"Yes, so I say." Arthur, darker in coloring and more serious in aspect than his mischievous brother, pulled the younger boy from the banister by the scruff of his neck to the safety of the landing. "She'll wed him whether we like him or not. Would you like to wager against it?"

Gilbert shook off his brother's hold. "Caro will never marry Mr. Lutton. He never laughs."

"She'll do it anyway," the older boy said glumly.

"How do you know she will? She wouldn't have him the last time he asked."

"That was more than a year ago. Uncle Clement was still alive. Caro didn't have to marry *anyone* then."

"I don't see why she has to marry anyone now," Gilbert grumbled, dropping down on the top step and twisting a lock of his disheveled blond hair in despair. "Why can't we go on as we've always done?"

Arthur sighed. "You know why as well as I do. The letter."

"Oh, right!" Gilbert, remembering, looked more despairing than ever. "The letter."

* * *

They'd learned about the letter only a week before. It had been six months since Uncle Clement's funeral, and the two boys were feeling particularly cheerful to see that their sister had at last given up wearing mourning. The two brothers and their sister Caroline were sitting at the breakfast table in the morning room of Crittenden Grange. Wide beams of sunlight spilled from the tall windows, sparkling on the tea service, the breakfast china, and their three faces. Caro seemed to have finally shaken off her doldrums. Arthur, studying his sister's face, was relieved to see it had lost some of the pallor that months of bedside nursing, followed by months of worry about their future, had brought to it. She was looking particularly fetching this morning, he thought, in her pretty blue dress and with her short auburn curls highlighted by the sunshine.

She was merrily teasing Gilbert for eating an entire muffin in two bites. "You look like a squirrel"—she giggled—"with all that bread stuffed in your cheeks."

Gilbert swallowed it all with a gulp. "You're laughing," he remarked, pleased.

Caro looked surprised. "Is that so unusual?" she asked.

"You haven't laughed much lately," Arthur said.

"I suppose I haven't. The past few months have been . . . difficult."

"Why?" Gilbert asked. "Because Uncle Clement died?"

A cloud seemed to cover Caro's face. "Yes, that," she said. "And . . . other things."

"What other things?" Gilbert persisted.

"You know what other things," Arthur muttered under his breath to his brother, trying to keep the younger boy from spoiling the cheerful atmosphere.

"No, I don't," Gilbert insisted.

"It's all right, Arthur," Caro said gently. "Gilbert has a right to know. You see, dearest, I've been worried because I don't know what Captain Meredith will do about us when he comes to be the new viscount."

"But why does it worry you, Caro?" Arthur asked. "The

fellow is a captain of the dragoons, after all. The dragoons are top-of-the-trees. You don't believe, do you, that someone like that would arrive without warning and throw us out in the snow?"

"I'm sure Captain Meredith is a fine gentleman," Caro said, stirring her tea thoughtfully, "but he is under no familial obligation to us. We are only related by marriage to his aunt Martha, a tenuous connection at best. Just because Uncle Clement—who, you know, was not really an uncle to us at all—took us in when Mama died doesn't mean that his heir is obliged to do the same."

"But it's been six months and no word," Arthur said. "Maybe he won't ever come."

"That's what I'm hoping," Caro said, throwing them a smile. "No one has heard from him since he went off to the Peninsula years ago. It's wicked to wish him ill, and I don't, of course, but it would be lovely if he's never found."

"Do you think he might have been killed in the war?" Gilbert asked, wide-eyed.

"No, for we would have been notified. What I hope is that he met a lovely Spanish señorita and is happily ensconced somewhere in Spain with his wife and a dozen children and will never wish to come home."

But at just that moment, Uncle Clement's solicitor made his appearance. Mr. Halford had driven up from the city for the express purpose of acquainting Caro with the contents of the letter—the letter that was to change everything.

The gray-haired, potbellied solicitor with the pince-nez perched on his nose was shown in by Sowell, the butler. He'd started out very early that morning (for the trip from London to Crittenden Grange required three hours of rapid transport), and having been nauseated by the rocking of his aged coach, he arrived tense, nervous, and dyspeptic. "Good day, ma'am," he said sourly from the doorway.

Caro felt her heart sink. There could be only one reason for the fellow's presence—that he was bearing the news she'd been dreading. "Do sit down, Mr. Halford," she said, forcing herself to be calm, "and let Sowell bring you some breakfast."

"No, thank you, ma'am, nothing to eat."

He dropped down upon a chair at the foot of the table and placed a large leather writing case before him. Refusing her offer of tea, he attempted to still the tremors in his stomach by taking deep breaths. When at last he felt able to speak, he dug into the leather case and pulled out a much-handled, much-folded sheet of paper. "I've had a letter from Spain," he said, peering across the table at each of them in turn, the eyes behind his pince-nez blinking with serious intent. "From . . . *him*."

"Him?" Caro'd asked, trying vainly to hide her alarm. "You don't mean . . . ?"

"Yes, the new Viscount Crittenden himself, Captain Christopher Meredith that was."

"He's in Spain?" Caro asked, a look of relief brightening her eyes at the thought that the new viscount might be living the very life she'd envisioned for him.

"He was at the time he wrote this. I believe he is now on his way home."

"Oh." The relief faded from her eyes as quickly as it had come. "He's coming *here,* then?"

"Within a fortnight, I believe."

"As soon as that?" Everyone at the table could see her spirits sink.

"Yes, I'm afraid so." The solicitor adjusted his spectacles nervously. "Having received the notification of his inheritance, and having no encumbrances to prevent it, His Lordship made immediate plans to take over his . . . er . . . duties."

"No encumbrances, you say? Does that mean he has no family?"

"None. He'd been wounded at Salamanca, but he's quite well now. According to the date on this letter, he set out from a place called Bejar more than a week ago and expects to be in England by the tenth. The letter contains the instructions he wishes to be carried out in time for his arrival."

Caro stiffened at once. "Instructions?"

Arthur understood his sister's reaction to that word. Caro was a very independent sort. She didn't respond well when given orders. Their father had died shortly after Gilbert was born, and their mother a mere eight months after that. It was Caro who'd been responsible for the two boys' upbringing—and her own—ever since. Even though Uncle Clement had taken them in, he'd been too preoccupied with his ill health to pay much attention to two underage boys. Caro had made all the decisions regarding their care; she'd supervised meals, hired tutors, mended trousers, chosen books, arbitrated quarrels, and, in general, guided their lives. As for Uncle Clement, he soon found himself relying on her to run the household, take care of his correspondence, and watch over his health. But even Uncle Clement, viscount though he was, did not give Caro orders. He'd learned very early that one didn't order Caroline Whitlow about. Caro didn't take "instructions."

But of course the solicitor couldn't know all that. Unaware of Caro's stiffening, he opened the letter and began to read aloud the orders that the new viscount had sent. These were quite explicit, ranging from his wishes for the location of his bedroom (facing south) to the number of household staff he required (four). Among the other items on his list of requirements were a bedroom adjoining his for his batman; an English—not a French!—chef in the kitchen; and room enough in the stables for the four horses he was bringing with him from Spain. *If necessary,* he wrote, *sell four of the estate's horses to make room for mine.*

"Dash it, Caro," Arthur cried out, "he won't sell my Windracer, will he? Or your Brandywine?"

"Hush, Arthur," Caro said, white-lipped. "How can I say? Let Mr. Halford finish."

"There's not much more," the solicitor said. "He concludes only with the request that no ceremonies or social events be held to mark his arrival. 'After my years in Spain,' he writes, 'I require nothing more than a time of absolute quiet and peace.'"

"Absolute quiet?" Caro muttered angrily under her breath.

"And what about us? We, I suppose, will be expected to hide in the attic and thus be out of his way!"

The two boys exchanged looks. Their sister was in a fury, and they knew it. They watched uneasily while she paced twice about the room, trying to regain control. "Tell me, Mr. Halford," she asked finally, her mouth tight, "is the man mad?"

The solicitor felt it incumbent upon him to defend his client, although he could not meet Caro's eyes while he did it. "It is not madness, is it, ma'am, for a man to wish for peace and quiet after serving in a war?"

"Should fighting a war make one inconsiderate of others?" she shot back. "There's not a word in that . . . that . . . document to show that the fellow has given a single thought to *us*! Have we not been part of this household more than twelve years? What are his intentions toward us, pray? And what of the staff? He *must* be mad if he expects to run this house with a staff of four. What does he think we should do with the other twelve, most of whom have been employed here more years than I? Discharge them?"

Mr. Halford's eyes fell. "I fully understand your concern, Miss Whitlow," he murmured, biting his lip unhappily, "but you do realize, I hope, that I must do as I'm ordered."

"Yes, of course," Caro murmured with a helpless flutter of her hands. "I mustn't vent my spleen on you. You are not to blame for any of this."

An unlawyerly expression of sympathy crept into Mr. Halford's eyes. He had felt for years that Clement Meredith, the late Viscount Crittenden, had been remiss in his duty. He'd made these three young persons his wards, but he'd never formalized the arrangement. Nor had he ever taken the trouble to rewrite his will to make provision for them. Whenever the solicitor had tried to suggest making revisions, the viscount had put him off, saying he would get to it when he felt "more the thing," and that there was plenty of time. But there hadn't been much time after all, and now it was too late.

Mr. Halford took off his pince-nez and rubbed the marks the glasses had left on his nose. "Perhaps, when His Lordship arrives, and you both can speak face-to-face, you and he can come to some amicable agreement about such matters as the size of the staff and the disposition of the horses."

"Judging from the man's 'instructions,' it seems to me that His Lordship, the former Captain Meredith, is much too arrogant to come to amicable agreements," Caro snapped.

"Now, now, ma'am, we don't know that, do we?" the lawyer said placatingly. "We mustn't leap to unwarranted conclusions."

"Oh, mustn't we? Well, I, for one, find my conclusions perfectly warranted. I therefore intend to vacate this house well before His Lordship appears on the scene. Let him have his peace and quiet and be damned!" With those unladylike words and an equally unladylike stride, she flounced from the room.

That was why, a mere week later, the two boys were waiting on the stairs to learn if their sister truly intended to wed the vicar who never laughed. "I still don't understand why the letter means that Caro has to marry someone," Gilbert said.

Arthur sat down beside him and put an arm about his shoulders. "The letter implied that the new viscount doesn't want us here. Caro needs to find another place for us."

"That damned letter," Gilbert muttered, still not fully understanding how and why everything had so quickly changed.

Arthur sighed. "You'd better learn to curb your foul tongue if we're going to be living with Mr. Lutton."

Gilbert shuddered at the thought. "Living with a vicar, ugh! Sermons at breakfast."

"Homilies with luncheon," Arthur agreed glumly.

"Prayers at dinner. Damn."

"Watch it, Gil. From now on, every time you say *damn*, you'll be treated to a sermon on profanity," Arthur warned, not unkindly.

"As if you never swear," Gil threw over his shoulder at the older boy. "You say damn ten times more'n I—"

But the sound of the knocker at the front door stilled his tongue. Both boys immediately flew to the banister and looked down to the entry hall four flights below. They watched the butler cross the marble squares of the hallway and throw open the door. "Good evening, Mr. Lutton," they heard him say as he took the visitor's hat. "Miss Whitlow is awaiting you in the library."

The two men below them crossed the floor and disappeared from view. The boys exchanged foreboding looks. "*Now* do you want to wager on it?" Arthur asked. "My top boots for your arrowhead?"

"No," the younger boy said glumly. "You're probably right. She'll have him." He stalked off down the hallway to his room, muttering as he went, "Damn Mr. Lutton. Damn the damned letter. And damn Captain Meredith, even if he was a dragoon!"

"Watch it, Gilbert," Arthur called after him. "I warned you about the need to curb your vile language."

"I may as well use vile language while I still can," the boy retorted before slamming his door.

3

Mr. Henry Lutton, the vicar, followed Sowell down the hall. He was a small man, but his lean frame made him appear taller than he was. He had dark eyes and hair but a scholar's pallor. His lips were thin, his nose sharp, and his eyes piercing. He was balding on both sides of his forehead, which left a peculiar triangle of dark hair in the middle, the apex pointing down to his nose. This pattern of baldness was, however, not disfiguring. Rather, it enhanced his appearance of sober, almost cold, intellect. Nor did his appearance contradict his character. Mr. Lutton was not known among his congregants as a man who was particularly friendly or convivial. They consoled themselves with the awareness that what his sermons lacked in warmth they made up for in depth.

Once over the library's threshold, Mr. Lutton closed the doors in Sowell's face and turned with a smile to the girl sitting on the sofa. "So, Caro, my dear, is it true? You've reconsidered?"

Caro, perched primly on the edge of the seat, her hands folded in her lap, looked up at him. "That's what I wrote in my note," she said softly.

The vicar studied her with satisfaction. She would make the perfect vicar's wife, he thought. Her face, with its slightly pointed chin, high cheekbones, and wide, gold-flecked brown eyes, was quite lovely, but the short, naturally curled, auburn hair that framed it indicated that she was a woman not given to vanity. Those abundant curls that fell so charmingly over her forehead had never felt a curling iron or the attentions of a hairdresser. The same lack of vanity was apparent in her form. She was as slim of waist and shapely of bosom as a man might wish, but her gown was not designed to show her off. It was modestly cut and trimmed with only a simple white lace collar, perfect attire for a churchman's wife. Yes, he said to himself complacently, the men will envy me, but the ladies will not resent her for it.

He crossed the room in three quick strides and took a place beside her. "Dearest!" he exclaimed, taking her hand. "You've made me more happy than I can say!"

"No, Henry, please, restrain your happiness for a moment. We must talk this matter over honestly." She looked into his face, her brows knit worriedly. "My feelings have not changed since the last time we discussed this matter. I do not love you."

"But your note. Your change of heart . . ."

"It was not a change of heart but of mind."

"I see." He leaned back against the sofa cushions calmly. "May I ask what changed it?"

"Necessity. I must leave the Grange. I need a home for my brothers and me."

"But, my dear, you needn't look so upset. I guessed as much."

"Did you?" She turned her whole body round to face him squarely. "Nevertheless, it must be painful for you to hear."

"Not at all. It has the virtue of honesty."

"Yes, but you cannot wish to wed someone who comes to you out of selfish need."

He smiled at her fondly. "I can and I do."

"But why?" she insisted. "Surely you desire more of marriage than the little I can give you."

"You can give me a great deal. Your lively companionship . . . the exciting challenge of your mind . . ."

Her eyes fell, and she turned her head away. "But not . . . intimacy."

Henry Lutton reached out, took her chin in his hand, and forced her to meet his eyes. "I am not a person much interested in, shall we say, the physicality of wedlock. I am quite content living a life of the intellect."

This surprised her. "Don't you wish for children?"

"Having children is not, for me, a strong desire," he replied without emotion, although his hand fell from her face.

"But . . ." Her brow wrinkled in sudden distress. "What you are describing is . . . is a marriage of convenience!"

He smiled. "But, my dear, isn't that what you yourself had in mind?"

She blinked, aghast. "Good heavens! I didn't think of it that way before, but it *is*!"

"Then we're in perfect agreement."

She stared at him. "But a marriage of convenience is, essentially, a dishonest arrangement, is it not?"

"Dishonest? Well, I suppose, in a way . . ."

"In *every* way. The very *vows* are taken with . . . with reservations."

"But when you wrote me that you'd reconsidered, knowing you did not love me, didn't you realize all this?"

She rose from the sofa and began to pace about the room. "I think I . . . I believed that I might . . . that you might . . . that someday, with the years, we might *come* to love each other."

He thought about that for a moment and then said gently, "I suppose that prospect is not inconceivable."

She came to a stop in front of him and looked down at him frankly. "But you don't really believe it will happen that way, do you? Or even want it."

"To be honest, Caro," he murmured, not meeting her stare, "I would be quite content with the arrangement you call a marriage of convenience."

"You, a man of the cloth? You can't mean it! Do you actually propose taking vows with reservations in your heart? How can you possibly assuage your conscience while living such deceit?"

"It's a small deceit. I think I can live with it, if you can."

She looked at him sharply, aware of a keen disappointment in him. Then she turned away. "But I don't think I can," she said dully. "I should have realized before that this solution to my problem is immoral."

"It seems to me, my dear, that your judgment of your plan is too critical," Mr. Lutton said.

She shook her head. "It's dishonest. You've admitted that." Honesty, to Caro, was the most prime of all virtues, as, conversely, dishonesty was the worst of all the vices. She had assumed that Henry Lutton, being a man of the cloth, would surely feel the same. "I don't believe either one of us would be comfortable with dishonesty."

"Dishonesty is too harsh a word for the marriage I envision," the vicar suggested, still hopeful.

But Caro would not be swayed. She began to pace again, realizing that she'd come to a firm conclusion. "Dash it, Henry, this is all that horrid Captain Meredith's fault! If it weren't for him, I would never have sent you that note. But I won't let him push me—push *us*!—into a dishonest marriage. I won't!"

Mr. Lutton, recognizing defeat, sighed and looked down at his hands. "That means, I take it, that you won't have me after all."

She couldn't face him. "I'm dreadfully sorry, Henry."

He rose and crossed the room to her, taking her hands in his. "Then what will you do?"

"I don't know." She pressed his hands affectionately, smiled sadly, and walked away from him to the door. As she disappeared down the hall her voice floated back to him, strong and determined. "I shall simply have to think of something else."

4

“We must do something for poor Caroline,” the elderly Lady Whitlow announced to her sister in her strong, surprisingly youthful voice. But the butler’s entrance with the tea tray stilled her tongue. She remained silent while he handed out the teacups, unwilling to go further into the details of poor Caroline’s dilemma until she and her sister were alone. Lady Whitlow, who in her youth had been the famous beauty Martha Meredith, was now a heavyset, overbearing octogenarian whose straight back and uplifted chin were evidence of her ongoing rebellion against the encroaching infirmities of age. Everyone who knew her agreed that Martha, Lady Whitlow, was remarkably sharp and agile for her eighty-two years. However, at this moment, her usual strong-mindedness had given way to anxiety. She’d received a disturbing letter from Caroline this morning. A very disturbing letter.

She picked it up from her lap and, opening it, glanced over at her sister, who was sitting on the sofa opposite her armchair, huddled over her teacup. Letitia Meredith, although three years younger than Martha, was thin and stooped, and looked almost emaciated in her black, high-necked dress that, even in its neck ruff and cuffs, held not the least suggestion of color. Like a black crow, Lady Whitlow thought, pushing a vagrant gray curl back into her widow’s cap. If she weren’t so troubled about poor Caroline, Martha would have smiled at the ridiculousness of her sister’s garb, especially the black silk rose that adorned the crown of her black bonnet. But she could not allow her thoughts to be distracted. It was her niece on whom she must concentrate. “We must do something for poor Caroline,” she said again.

"Yes, of course we must," murmured Letitia absently, her shaking, high-pitched voice quite unlike her sister's rusty growl.

Lady Whitlow eyed her sister in disgust. Letitia, who'd never married (having refused all her offers because, she'd claimed, they hadn't lived up to the suitor of her dreams), was considered by the world to be of a softer, more agreeable nature than her elder sister. But Martha knew Letitia could be as stubborn and contrary as any member of the family, except of course when she was daydreaming. Unfortunately, she was often given to daydreaming and, in that condition, was wont to agree to whatever was being said, even—as in this case—if she didn't know quite what she was agreeing to. "How can you say 'of course,' Letty, when you don't yet know what the girl's written? I do believe you're growing senile."

Letitia Meredith, roused from her woolgathering, rose angrily from her chair, fumbling for the cane she always carried. "If you're going to insult me, Martha," she said, her voice rising in pitch, "I shall take my leave. I came the moment I got your note, but now I'm very sorry I obeyed your summons. I was in the midst of reading in the *Times* about Napoleon having left Elba and landing on French soil. It was bad news enough for me today. If I'd stayed home, I wouldn't have had to endure the added discomfort of your insults and your freezing drawing room." She pulled a handkerchief from the cuff of her long sleeve and sniffed into it. "Dash it, I *knew* I should've kept my shawl with me instead of surrendering it to your insistent butler."

"You always surrender to insistence," Martha said, putting the letter aside and rising. "Here, take mine." And she tossed her blue wool shawl to her sister.

The act was a kind of peace offering, and Letitia, who understood her sister's crochets, accepted it. "I don't know why you're so parsimonious with your fires," she said, pulling the shawl over her shoulders. "Really, Martha, if *I* were expecting guests, I would have had the fire going in the drawing room from morning on."

"I feel perfectly comfortable," Martha lied. "You keep your rooms much too warm."

As if to contradict her, the wind came up at that moment and sent a spatter of rain against the windows. Letitia shivered. It was a dreadful day, even for London in March, with a chilling rain that showed every intention of falling all afternoon. "Only for the sake of dear Caroline would I have ventured out on such a day," she muttered.

Martha fixed a cold eye on her. "Then for Caroline's sake, stop whining about Napoleon and the weather and everything else we can't do anything about, and sit down to discuss what we *can* do!" She stomped over to the tea table and helped herself to a scone. "Really, Letty, you look like a crow and sound like a titmouse."

Letitia had heard this sort of insult too many times to let it bother her. "A crow indeed," she objected mildly as she sat back down. "You know very well I'm wearing mourning."

"There's absolutely no difference between your ordinary garb and your mourning clothes," her sister retorted. "You simply love black."

Letitia made a dismissive wave of her handkerchief. "Did you send for me to mock my clothes or to talk about Caroline?" she asked.

"You're right. Caroline is our subject, not your ridiculous appearance. Though even *you* should realize that the black rose on your hat is the outside of enough."

"So are your insults. Keep to the subject, if you please."

Martha, her expression changing from disgust to worry, drew in her breath. "You'll find this hard to believe, Letty, but Caro writes that young Meredith is going to drive her out of house and home!"

Letty stared at her in disbelief. "Going to drive her out? Whatever do you mean?"

"It's plain English. Drive her *out*. Out in the cold, and with Arthur and Gilbert, too!" As she uttered the words their implication struck her full force. Her ramrod back suddenly sagged against the cushions of her chair. "My beloved Whitlow, and Clement, too, must be turning over in their graves!" she muttered, wincing.

Letty's light blue eyes widened. "Good heavens, Martha, you don't mean *Kit* Meredith! He wouldn't!"

"Whom else could I mean? He's the heir, isn't he?" Martha waved the letter at her. "Only see what Caroline writes! She says he's notified Halford that he intends to take over the Grange, lock, stock, and barrel, and he wants no one else around to get in his way."

"But that doesn't sound *at all* like Kit! He would never do such a thing, would he? I've always found him such a very sweet-natured, generous young fellow—"

"Nonsense. You hardly know him, any more than I do. I don't believe we've met him more than twice since Josiah, our short-tempered brother, estranged himself from the family."

"Perhaps it *was* only twice, but the boy was delightful each time." Her eyes grew glassy, as if her mind had gone to some other place and she no longer saw what was right there in front of her. It was a habit of hers that drove her sister wild. "Why, the last time I saw him—at the Farringtons' ball, I think it was—he sat beside me for almost the entire evening, and—oh, my dear, he was *so* kind! When he realized I'd come alone, he insisted on seeing me home!"

"Dash it, Letty, pay attention! The Farringtons' ball was six years ago! He'd not even bought his commission. Perhaps the years of war have changed the boy. Hardened him."

Letty's wrinkled lips quivered. "Do you really think so? That he's become hard?"

"What else am I to think? Isn't that what happened to his father? Why, after Josiah and Clement quarreled, Josiah hardened his heart against the whole family, didn't he? Perhaps it's proof of the adage 'like father like son.'"

"I don't believe it. I always felt that Kit was more like his mother than like Josiah."

"But Caroline is not the type to complain without reason. And I'm not saying it just because she's my brother-in-law's daughter, or because she and the two boys are all that's left of my dear Whitlow's family. I say it because she's not the sort to complain at all. In all the years she'd tended Clement—and given his nature, we can guess she had a great deal to put up with—she never uttered one word of complaint, did she?"

"No, never. Not once."

"Then we must assume she has good reason for what she says in the letter."

Letty sighed. "Yes, I suppose we must. Poor Caroline!"

"Yes. The question is, what shall we do about her? I suppose I shall have to offer her shelter here with me."

"Here?" Letty gave a small snort. "You're not serious."

Martha looked over at her in surprise. "Why not?"

"Because you're too set in your ways and too short-tempered to put up with long-term guests, especially two young boys. Besides, you'd freeze them to death."

Martha ignored the gibe, being preoccupied with the unpleasing prospect of the disruption of her quiet household. "I don't relish the idea of a house full of youngsters, I admit, but my dear Whitlow would have wished me to take in his brother's children." She looked over at Letty speculatively. "If you would agree to take one of the boys—"

"Is that what you've been getting at all this while? That you want me to offer to house one of the boys?"

"Well, yes. That would make things a bit easier for me."

"Heavens, Martha, you can't wish to separate the family! Gilbert is only a child, and a change from the country to London will be hard enough on him without his having to be torn from his brother and sister." She paused for a moment, her eyes taking on that faraway look, and then she said suddenly, "Why don't I take them all?"

Martha gaped at her. "You can't mean it!"

Letty gave a cackling laugh. "Ha! I've startled you, haven't I? You look as if you're going to swoon."

"You know I never swoon. Never in my life! But you *have* surprised me. Why are you making this offer? Caro and the boys aren't even related to you."

"They weren't related to Clement either, yet he made them

his wards. And I've grown to love the girl over the years, just as you have."

"But, Letty, you barely have room for yourself in your tiny house."

"It is smaller than this one, I admit, but I wouldn't call it tiny. I have two unused rooms on the second floor, and a perfectly decent apartment in the attic."

Martha blinked thoughtfully. "Yes, I suppose that would serve," she murmured, her spirits rising at the possibility of being able to help Caroline without putting herself out. But it would not be fair, she told herself sternly, to put this all on Letty's thin shoulders.

While she debated with herself, Letty reached for her cane and struggled to her feet. "My place will serve very well," she said with unusual decisiveness.

Despite the obvious advantages of Letty's offer, Martha didn't like to have decisions taken out of her hands. "What makes you think you can put up with the confusion and chaos better than I?" she demanded.

"Because I can be agreeable, while you are usually contentious. It is my nature to avoid argumentation, while it is yours to seek it."

Martha, who ordinarily would have made a sharp retort, was startled into silence, both by the generosity of her sister's offer and the truth of her last remark. "Would you really take them in, Letty?" she asked after a long moment's consideration. "You're not just acting on impulse, are you?"

"No, I'm quite willing to do it." She dropped the borrowed shawl on the sofa and started toward the door. "Someone has to. I am the logical one."

Martha followed her sister down the hall. "You have no idea how you've relieved my mind," she said. "I'll write to Caro at once."

Letty, after being helped into her outer garments by the butler, paused in the doorway and went into another one of her daydreams. "Heavens, Letty, keep your mind on what you're doing!" Martha barked. "Your coachman is holding the door for you."

Letitia blinked up at her sister, her eyes filling with tears. "Oh, dear, I just can't help it. All this talk of family disruption has made me dreadfully discomposed."

Martha stiffened. "You're not going to tell me you changed your mind!"

"About taking in Caro and the boys? No, of course not." She wiped a tear from the corner of an eye with one gloved finger. "But it's all so sad."

"What is? That poor Caro has to leave her home?"

"Yes, that, of course. And that Kit Meredith has become so hard-hearted."

Martha shrugged. "I've observed more than once that matters of inheritance often bring out the worst in people. Whatever is greedy and selfish in human nature seems to come to the surface after wills are read."

Letty shuddered and stepped out into the rain. "My dear Kit Meredith, greedy and selfish?" She shook her head as she limped slowly to her waiting carriage. "I find it almost impossible to believe."

5

Kit Meredith could not leave Spain simply as a consequence of having acquired a title. He needed money. Travel was expensive, and his most recent payment to his landlord for the rooms he and Mickley occupied had left him down to his last farthing. Thus, when he wrote to Mr. Halford, the executor of his uncle's estate, to acknowledge receipt of the news of his inheritance, he was forced, despite considerable embarrassment, to explain his predicament. *I cannot undertake to return home at this time,* he wrote, *unless the estate is solvent enough to defray the costs of the return to England for myself, my man Mickley, and my four horses.*

Mr. Halford responded promptly (though somewhat cryptically) with the information that *the estate is quite solvent enough for any expenses that Your Lordship may incur.* The solicitor went on to say that he hoped the enclosed check would be adequate to take him and his man to London in a style *appropriate to His Lordship's position,* and that he would be happy to receive His Lordship in his chambers in the City, at which time he would fully apprise him of the extent of his wealth.

The check had been amazingly generous; not only was it large enough to permit the new viscount to ship his horses home and to provide excellent accommodations on an English merchant vessel for himself and Mickley, but there was enough left over to enable Kit to purchase a very fine new phaeton. That purchase was his very first act after landing in Southampton.

But he did not use the phaeton to make for London, as Mr. Halford had instructed him to do. Instead, he set out for

Crittenden Grange as soon as the phaeton was delivered to his keeping. Now that he was back on English soil, he explained to Mickley, he was burning with eagerness to see his new English abode. Going to London would have necessitated a detour to the east. He was determined to head straight north to Shropshire.

Not wishing to arrive at a household that was unprepared to receive him, Kit sent a letter to the Grange, addressed *to whom it may concern,* containing the information that he and his man would be arriving in two days. Then Mickley strapped their few possessions onto the back of the new phaeton, and they were on their way.

Kit let Mickley take the reins on the drive north. He wanted to be free to feast his eyes on the early-spring landscape, so different from the dry, brown Spanish terrain he'd become accustomed to. But though he reveled in the views, he permitted no dawdling. The only pauses they made along the way were two brief hours in Oxford (paying a sentimental visit to the rooms where Kit had stayed years ago when he was a student), and a mere four hours at an inn near Stratford-on-Avon to get some sleep. In less than two days of riding they reached their destination.

It was early afternoon when they entered the outer gates. As Mickley turned the new phaeton onto the curved drive that led to the Grange, Kit felt his pulse race with excitement. He barely noticed the shabby old landau that lumbered past his carriage, making its way out. Mickley, however, gave the equipage a quick glance as it passed by. He noticed a young lady within who appeared to be consoling a weeping, towheaded little boy with a freckled nose, while an older boy peered forlornly out of the carriage's rear window. "Did ye see that?" he remarked to Kit. "Two boys an' a lady, lookin' fer all the world like they was comin' from a funeral."

Kit turned to look after the disappearing carriage. "What business could they have had at the Grange?" he wondered.

But he gave the incident no other thought once he arrived at his new home. He was too overwhelmed by what he saw to think of anything else. Crittenden Grange was much lovelier than anything he'd imagined. Though he'd visited the Grange once or twice in childhood, before his father and his uncle had had their rift, he had only vague memories of those visits. He did remember, however, that his father had often spoken of the Grange with an unmistakable nostalgia. The Grange had been his father's boyhood home. Kit sensed that it pained him afterward to be so forcibly separated from it. Nevertheless, those wispy memories were incapable of preparing him for what he now saw.

The house looming up before him was old and, though enormous, not particularly grand. It was hard to say what made it so very beautiful. The center structure, a four-story building with an old but impressive limestone facade, was flanked by two long wings. The wings were much lower to the ground than the center building, but they extended out like two long arms embracing the lush green landscape. House and land had grown old together and now seemed so much a part of one another that it was difficult to tell where one ended and the other began. Lushly flowering shrubs clung to the old stone foundations, and tall, thickly branched trees waved over the magnificent split-stone tiles of the sloping roof. His heart clenched with the joy of first love; this, the family home, surpassed not only his memories but his dreams. Though he had not known it until this moment, this was just the sort of place where he'd wish to spend the rest of his life. "Good Lord!" he breathed, awestruck.

"Ye cin say that again," Mickley mumbled, staring. "Here I was reckonin' that a grange was on'y a sorta farmhouse."

"The center building probably *was* a farmhouse once. A granary, at any rate," Kit said as his gaze took in the rows of arched windows, the pedimented doorway, and the huge number of chimneys rising in irregular intervals along the roof. "The wings must have been added when the place was converted to a manor house."

He had to tear his gaze from the building, however, to take note of what appeared to be a more pressing matter—a crowd of people standing in front of the massive doorway watching the approach of the carriage. "I wonder what *that's* all about," Kit muttered. "Didn't I write that I wanted no ceremonies?"

As he and Mickley climbed down from the phaeton, two figures detached themselves from the crowd and came toward them. One was a plump fellow dressed in stiffly formal attire, whose pompously dignified movements told Kit—quite rightly—that he was the butler. The other was a tall, thin fellow with a clerical collar. The butler approached them first, bowed stiffly, and uttered some polite words of welcome, but Kit noted that his expression was icy. Then the other man stepped forward. The butler introduced him. "May I present the vicar of Crittenden Church, Mr. Henry Lutton?"

"How do you do, my lord?" the cleric said with a polite bow.

"I'm happy to meet you," Kit responded, shaking his hand.

Mr. Lutton gave him a thin smile. "Mr. Sowell here has warned me that you wish to have no ceremonies to mark your arrival, but in my capacity as head of our congregation, I could not permit you to take your place among us without a word of welcome."

Kit returned the smile with a much warmer one. "I appreciate your taking the time from your duties just to give me this greeting," he said.

Mr. Lutton's smile died. "It was not just for this greeting," he admitted. "It was for a farewell, too."

"Oh?" Kit asked, confused.

"Yes." The cleric sighed. "There was a departure, you see, only a few moments ago. A very sad departure."

Mickley leaned over to Kit and whispered in his ear, "Must've been that coach what passed us on the way in."

"I see," Kit mumbled to Mr. Lutton, not knowing what else to say. It was obvious that the "departure" had been painful for the vicar, but Kit did not feel it proper to ask questions.

Sowell, the butler, intervened at that moment to remind Mr. Lutton that the staff was waiting. The vicar nodded, expressed the hope that he would see His Lordship at Sunday's service, and walked off. Meanwhile, Sowell led the two newcomers toward the front door, where, astonishingly, the crowd had assembled itself into two rows, one of women in starched, gleaming-white aprons and caps, and the other of smartly liveried men. Kit was startled not only by the efficiency with which they'd assembled, but by their number. "Good God," he exclaimed, looking down the rows, "I didn't *dream* there was a staff like this! My mother never had more than two in her employ."

"Indeed?" the butler murmured in disdain. "The late viscount's mother employed a staff of thirty, I recall. It was only when Lord Crittenden became ill and decided to cut out all social occasions that the staff was reduced to the present sixteen. But Miss Whitlow was an excellent manager, you see, so we were able to make do."

"Miss Whitlow?" Kit inquired.

"Miss Caroline Whitlow, His late Lordship's ward."

"I see," Kit said, but he did not see at all. He didn't know his uncle had had a ward. He'd never heard of a Caroline Whitlow, though he knew that his aunt Martha had married a Whitlow—Sir John Whitlow, if memory served. But there had been no offspring, he was almost certain of that. He would have liked to make some inquiries, but it did not seem the proper time, what with all the staff standing about staring at him.

He smiled at them awkwardly and said a few words about being glad to meet them. They bobbed and murmured their thank-yous, but Kit noticed that they would not meet his eyes when he looked directly at them and that not one of them smiled. After another awkward moment, the butler dismissed them.

When only Kit, Mickley, and Sowell remained, the butler took a deep breath. "I was told, Your Lordship, that you require only four in staff," he said with a kind of icy bravado, "but I was certain you would wish to reconsider after you'd inspected the property. The house has forty-four rooms, you see. The housekeeper informs me that, for a house this size, she doesn't see how she can manage with fewer than three chambermaids, even if no guests are present. Cook needs two assistants in the kitchen and one scullery minimum. And my two footmen are indispensable. With three men in the stables and two gardeners, we are at a total of sixteen. I have been told by both the cook and the housekeeper that they will hand in their notice if the staff is reduced further, as I intend to do myself in any case, as soon as Your Lordship is able to replace me. Meanwhile, my lord, what do you wish me to do about the staff?"

"I haven't the slightest idea," Kit replied in bewilderment. "Just tell them all that we'll make no changes for the time being. Meanwhile, why don't you show me around? Shall we start from the top and work our way down?"

The tour of the house lasted over an hour, and the stables and grounds took another. Kit became more amazed the more he saw. Though the furnishings and accoutrements of the household were very worn with years of use, they once had been luxurious—much more luxurious than he expected. Velvet window hangings, satin bedspreads, brocaded upholstery were everywhere, though some were patched and mended. Wonderful paintings hung over wallpaper that had once been elegant but that now was faded and in places even peeling. Everything was clean and well cared for, but much needed restoration or replacement.

The stables, too, were large and well cared for (relieving Kit's mind about the comfort of his four Spanish horses, all of whom were already happily established in their stalls), and the grounds were extensive and attractive. But some sort of drainage work had been started behind the main house and had evidently been abandoned, for a pile of stones lay alongside a huge, raw, open ditch. Money and labor were needed badly in many areas.

It slowly began to dawn on Kit that not only his legacy, but his responsibility for caring for it, were both greater than he'd imagined. The inheritance was not like winning a lottery, after all. There was a great deal more to it. "Damnation," he muttered to Mickley when Sowell went off see if their bedrooms were ready, "I should have stopped off in London after all, and met with that solicitor, Mr. Halford. I acted hastily. I shouldn't have come here without first making full inquiries."

"What inquiries?" Mickley asked.

"Inquiries of all sorts! I don't have any idea of what I own, what my income is, and how on earth all this is to be supported."

Mickley shook his head. "What's the rush? Ye wanted peace an' quiet, didn' ye? I don' see no reason why ye shouldn'a take yerself a few days' rest an' enjoy all this."

"But there are matters I ought to—"

"Nothin' that can't wait. Fer a few days whyn't ye play lord o' the manor—which ye are!—an' let these folks wait on ye 'and an' foot. Then, when ye've 'ad enough layin' about, we cin go t' the City an' see that Halford fellow."

Kit was tempted to follow his batman's advice. The prospect of spending a little time being waited on hand and foot was appealing. But something about the mood of the staff troubled him. In particular, the butler's demeanor, and his declaration of his intention to hand in his notice, made Kit uneasy. There was something disquieting in the air. How could he, in Mickley's words, "enjoy layin' about," when the atmosphere in the house was so tense?

By the time Sowell had shown Kit the room he'd selected for His Lordship's bedroom, Kit had made up his mind to find out what was amiss. "This is an excellent room, Sowell," he said to the frozen-faced fellow cheerfully. "Good size, fine view, wonderful bed. You've made a good choice."

"Thank you, my lord," was the cold reply.

"And I see that you've put Mickley right next door, just as I asked. You do like your room, don't you, Mick?"

"Aye, I do," Mickley said from the doorway that adjoined both rooms. "Best room I ever 'ad, an' that's the truth."

"I couldn't be more pleased," Kit told the butler. "Now all I need to feel perfectly comfortable is to find out why you feel it necessary to give notice."

This surprised the hitherto impassive Sowell. "Me, m'lord?"

"Yes, you. You did say, did you not, that you're giving me your notice no matter what I decide to do about the staff?"

"Yes, my lord, I did."

"Well, I'd like to know why."

The butler shifted on his feet, suddenly uncomfortable. "I don't think we should discuss this matter in front of your valet," he murmured, glancing at Mickley.

"Mickley isn't exactly my valet," Kit said. "He's special. I wouldn't be alive if not for Mr. Mickley. You must regard him as my friend, which he is."

"Yes, my lord," the butler said, unmoved.

"So, you see," Kit went on, "anything you wish to say to me may be said in front of him. He has my absolute trust. Now, tell us why you feel you must leave."

"Because, my lord, it will be impossible for me to run this house properly for you. Not anymore. Not without . . . without . . ." He paused and dropped his eyes.

"Without . . . ?" Kit prodded.

The butler looked up and met Kit's eyes, a look of angry accusation in his own. "Without Miss Whitlow."

"Miss Whitlow?" Kit's brows lifted. "Who is— Oh, yes. You mentioned her before. My uncle's ward, you said."

"Miss Caroline Whitlow, yes. She ran the household for your uncle during all the years he was ill."

"I see. But who the devil is she? She can't be my aunt Martha's daughter, can she? I didn't think Martha Whitlow had any children."

"No, my lord, she hasn't. Caroline was Sir John Whitlow's *brother's* daughter—your aunt Martha's niece by marriage."

"Then how is it she became my uncle Clement's ward? There was no blood relationship between them."

"That didn't matter to your uncle. When she was orphaned and in need, Lady Whitlow asked him to take her in. He grew very fond of her, His Lordship did. She was like a daughter to him." He paused and pursed his lips. "We are *all* very fond of Miss Caroline."

"Are you indeed?" Kit murmured, beginning to understand.

"Is she the one who left today? Was it her 'departure' the vicar spoke of?"

"Yes, my lord, it was," Sowell said, his tone a distinct reprimand. "Mr. Lutton will miss her. We'll all miss her. And her little brothers, too."

Kit, trying to understand the particulars of what had occurred, ignored the butler's insolent tone of voice. But Mickley, bristling, took a firm step into the room. "I'd cork up that clapper, man, if I was you," he barked, fixing the butler with a threatening glare. "I 'ave no likin' fer you implyin' that the lady's 'de-par-ture' was my cap'n's fault!"

"Hush, Mick," Kit said quietly. "Let me handle this."

The butler looked from one to the other. Then he squared his shoulders. "If you want the truth, my lord," he said belligerently, "it *is* your fault."

Kit's eyebrows rose. "But you're not making sense, Sowell. No sense at all. How can her departure be my fault when I didn't know the female existed?"

"But you wrote that you wanted peace and quiet. Sell their horses, you ordered. Cut down the staff. Take away her bedroom. What was she to think? She took all that to mean you didn't want her here, or her brothers either."

"Aha, so that's it," Kit murmured. "You and Lutton and everyone else in this place blame me for pushing some poor creature I never heard of out into the cold."

"Three poor creatures, my lord," the butler corrected. "Three."

"Blasted idiots," Mickley grunted under his breath.

Kit sank down upon the bed. "Where have they gone?" he asked after a long moment of silence.

"I couldn't say, my lord."

"Or won't say," Mickley put in.

Kit motioned his batman to silence. "Well, thank you, Sowell, for your frankness. You may go."

The butler nodded and bowed himself out. Kit rose tiredly from the bed, went to the window, and stared out. The afternoon had gone. The setting sun was casting long, depressing shadows across the south lawn. "Damn!" he muttered.

"Curse me for a bloody fool! I should have gone to see the deuced solicitor, as I was told to do."

"What diff'rence would that 'ave made?" Mickley asked.

"We would have had all this information and been prepared."

"Prepared to take the lady in, and her little brothers, too? Are ye daft?"

"Damnation, Mick, there *is* such a thing as familial responsibility!"

"She was yer *uncle's* ward, not yours."

Kit turned from the window and stared at Mickley through the gathering gloom. "Are you saying I should forget the matter?"

Mickley shrugged. "Fer the time bein' anyway. Take yersel' a bit of rest, like you been wishin' to do. Plenty o' time later to start facin' responsibilities."

"Perhaps. But do you know what I've been thinking for the last few minutes, Mick?"

"No. What?"

"That perhaps this inheritance of mine won't turn out to be quite so fortunate as I first thought."

6

Though Caroline and her brothers tried to put a good face on it, they were not very happy living in Letitia's little town house on Mortimer Street. They were grateful indeed for her many kindnesses, and fully aware of how much they owed her, but they could not prevent their feelings of misery from showing.

After a fortnight of watching their forced smiles across the dinner table, Letitia—who could be quite discerning despite her tendency to escape from reality into daydreams—admitted to herself that something had to be done. She put on her black bonnet, called for her coachman, and rode the short distance to Hanover Square. "Martha," she said urgently, as soon as she'd ensconced herself on the sofa in her sister's drawing room, "we must do something for poor Caroline."

Martha's eyebrows rose. "I thought we already had."

Letitia shook her head, causing the black rose on her bonnet to tremble. "We didn't think the matter through," she said, clenching her fingers in her lap. "They are all dreadfully unhappy with me."

"Nonsense," Martha declared firmly. "How could you possibly make them unhappy? You are the kindest, most good-natured female in the world."

Letitia was so startled by this unexpected praise from the sister who so regularly insulted her that she was rendered momentarily speechless. When she regained her voice, she launched into as full an explanation of the situation as she was capable of. But the difficulties Caro and her brothers faced were caused by circumstances that Letitia, with her limited experience, could not fully understand.

To begin with, there was the house itself. It had (as Caroline realized but Letitia could not) an atmosphere that was basically uncongenial to boys. Though they appreciated the good-natured affection with which "Aunt Letty" showered them, the boys found it difficult to live in a house that was pathetically tiny and overcrowded, especially when compared with the huge, uncluttered homestead they'd been accustomed to. They could find no space for games, for exploring, or for simply larking about. What was worse, the small space that *was* available was completely taken up with feminine accoutrements. Every room was full of small ornaments that could fall over and break if a boy merely breathed too hard. Every shelf, every table, every surface of every room held a profusion of knickknackery—porcelain figurines, china vases, crystal sculptures, framed miniatures, enameled flowers, and every other sort of delicate decoration. The house seemed to the boys like an overcrowded museum, its fragile contents poised for inevitable disaster.

It took only two days after their arrival for the first disaster to occur. Gilbert, having nothing better to do, decided to examine a Dresden shepherdess on the mantel of the downstairs sitting room. He lifted her up gingerly and turned her about in his hands. Somehow (though he never could explain how) she slipped from his fingers to the brick hearth, where she crashed to her doom. Caro, viewing the remains, was utterly devastated, but Letty, in her kind way, assured them that she had never liked the piece anyway. Both the culprit and his sister knew she lied. "I know they know I lied," Letty admitted to her sister after relating the incident.

Not two days later, during an insignificant, commonplace, brotherly scuffle, Arthur backed Gilbert into a chairside table in the drawing room. The table toppled with a horrifying crash, bringing to ruin a Chinese enameled bowl, two glazed-pottery cats, and an antique etched-glass vase that Aunt Letty, years ago, had carried all the way from Italy in her own two hands. Though she said not a word of blame, the pain in her eyes as she picked over the pieces of the remains was so obvious that, ever since, the boys tiptoed through the rooms with terrified restraint, their arms held tight to their sides and their elbows tucked in.

While life inside the house was difficult, life outside was not much better. Endlessly fascinating as London could be to most inhabitants and many visitors, it was a kind of prison to two lively young boys who'd been bred in the country. Arthur and Gilbert did not find living in London nearly as exciting as living at the Grange. Aunt Letty kept no horses other than the sturdy old pair that pulled her carriage, so the boys couldn't go riding. And although Hyde Park was not very far away, Caro would not let Gilbert go out without being accompanied by Arthur or one of the footmen. The footmen seemed to resent this extra chore, and Arthur, too, seemed unwilling to toss balls with his brother in the park. "Though you mustn't blame him," Letty was quick to explain to her sister. "Arthur is a dear, but he's fallen into a slough of despond."

Letty's diagnosis was quite correct. Before his uncle Clement died, he'd promised that Arthur would be sent to Eton before he turned fifteen. The boy was now well past his fifteenth birthday, yet not a word had been said about his going away to school. Well aware that his sister could not now afford to send him, he tried his best to give up yearning for it, but his spirit was depressed.

"And I believe," Letty went on, sighing sadly, "that Caro is depressed, too, though she makes a brave show of it. I suspect the poor girl cries herself to sleep at night."

It was quite true. Caro often wept herself to sleep, tormented by her inability to provide for her brothers the sort of life they'd hoped for. She wished she could supply Gilbert with a tutor, a few friends, and a place in which to run about freely. She wished she could furnish Arthur with a horse, a wardrobe, and complete tuition for Eton. But she had no money of her own, and her prospects for employment were poor. She had every intention of looking for work as a governess or a teacher in a girls' school—her only prospects. But such employment would not pay very much. She could never afford any of the things she wanted for her brothers.

Though her disappointment in the move to Mortimer Street differed from her brothers', Caro, too, was finding London a less than joyful place to be. Most young women who lived in the country yearned to come to London—to feel the excitement of the crowds, to shop at the Pantheon Bazaar, to drive a high-perch phaeton through Hyde Park, to dance at Almack's, to see a play at Covent Garden, to dress for a ball. But Caro could not take advantage of any of those delights. They all required money, proper clothes, and social connections. Caro had none. "I'd have been overjoyed to do something to cheer her," Letty told her sister tearfully. "I offered to escort her to Almack's. I begged her to go with me to the bazaar. I even tried to take the girl to my own modiste and buy her a gown, but Caro is too proud to accept anything but the bare necessities."

"Yes, I'm beginning to understand," Martha said. "We should indeed have thought this through more carefully."

The two sisters discussed the matter for a long time. They considered all sorts of possibilities. Letty was willing to incur the expense of hiring a tutor for Gilbert. Martha reckoned she might, with careful manipulation of her limited income, manage to pay Arthur's tuition at Eton. But that still left the problem of Caro. They knew the girl would refuse to accept their financial assistance. "She'd guess it would be a sacrifice," Letty said.

They sat in troubled silence for a long while. Then Martha, with a deep sigh, pulled herself to her feet. "There's nothing for it," she declared, "but to pay a call on our dastardly nephew, Christopher Meredith, the new Viscount of Crittenden. And that's exactly what I'll do."

"Martha!" Letty gasped, wide-eyed. "You can't mean you intend to go all the way to Shropshire!"

"That's just what I intend."

"But what good would come—"

"That man," Martha said in a tone that brooked no argument, "needs to be made aware of his obligations!"

Thus, two days later, with her traveling hat firmly pinned in place, her bags packed, and her carriage ready at the door,

Martha descended the stairs to embark on the trip to Shropshire, the longest trip she'd undertaken in over ten years. Her sister, who'd hovered over her all morning offering advice on how to deal with Kit Meredith ("Remember, now, Martha, don't let yourself become contentious, or you'll find yourself in a dreadful argument with the boy—"), followed her down the stairs. "Promise you'll not to lose your temper," she repeated worriedly as they were about to round the final turning of the stairway.

It was at just that moment they came face-to-face with the butler, who was making his way up. Martha frowned at the man in annoyance. "What is it, Kaynes? Must you bother me now? You know I'm determined to be on my way by noon!"

"I'm sorry, Your Ladyship," the butler said in a voice that barely hid his excitement, "but you have a visitor."

"Dash it, Kaynes, I have no time for callers now! You know I'm ready for departure. Why didn't you send whoever-it-is away?"

"But, ma'am, when you hear . . . you would not wish . . . that is, I believe the visitor is the very gentleman you're traveling to Shropshire to see!"

Both sisters gaped. "*Wh-what?*" Letty asked breathlessly.

"What *are* you babbling about?" Martha demanded in disbelief.

The butler looked nervously down over the banister before replying in a hissing whisper, "The gentleman—he's waiting downstairs in the drawing room—he said his name was . . ." He paused and gulped.

"*Who,* dash it!" Martha barked. "*Who?*"

"Meredith," the butler answered, goggle-eyed. "Christopher Meredith. The Viscount Crittenden himself!"

7

Kit had spent the day before in Mr. Halford's chambers in the City. It had been an edifying time. He'd learned that he had an income in excess of ten thousand a year from a long list of small properties and investments. Kit was overjoyed. Though from the point of view of some of Britain's peers it was not great wealth, to Kit it was a fortune, large enough to do all that was necessary to keep up—and even improve—his beloved Grange.

The solicitor, however, had kept him from flying into alt. "You must be aware, my lord," he'd warned, "that the income will decline if these properties are not supervised nor the investments watched."

"I'm ready to do whatever I should," Kit assured him. "I admit that I'm completely ignorant in business matters, but I'm eager to learn."

"Good," Mr. Halford said with an encouraging smile. "One should not postpone business decisions, as the late Lord Crittenden was wont to do his last years. I did my best during that time, but I shall be relieved to have your guidance on a number of matters."

They spent many hours going over papers, checking figures, making choices. Kit, completely inexperienced, let himself be guided by Mr. Halford's advice. But he found himself learning quickly and very much enjoying the process. And at the end of the day, when Mr. Halford said that "Your Lordship has shown a remarkable affinity for finance," he was not a little pleased with himself.

But pride ever goes before a fall. Kit enjoyed barely five minutes of self-satisfaction before Mr. Halford took him down with a harsh reprimand, scolding him at length for neglecting what he considered the most important matter of all—the problem of the late Lord Crittenden's wards.

"Why are they my problem?" Kit asked, instantly defensive. "They are no relation to me. In fact, I never even heard of their existence until my uncle's butler told me of them."

"But it is my conviction that the estate owes something to them. Your uncle often expressed the intention of making provision for them in his will, but—I hope you'll forgive my frankness, my lord—he was a dreadful procrastinator."

Kit felt the weight of responsibility fall upon him like a stone. He had no wish to be saddled with a pair of irksome little boys and a spinsterish female, but it seemed he'd inherited them along with the estate. He had to accept them with the rest. "What had my uncle intended to do for them?" he asked with a sigh.

"What any parent would do. See to it that the boys receive a proper education and that Miss Caroline is properly settled."

"Properly settled? Married off, you mean."

The solicitor shrugged. "Yes, if that should come to pass. I believe your uncle would have provided her with a generous dowry. Or an adequate competence if she should not wed."

Kit rubbed his chin thoughtfully. "The woman's an ape-leader, I suppose."

"Ape-leader?" Mr. Halford eyed his client suspiciously. "I'm afraid I have no familiarity with the jargon of the sporting set."

"It comes from Shakespeare, I believe. Something about old maids being doomed 'to lead apes into hell.'"

Mr. Halford frowned in disapproval. "I would hardly call Miss Caroline an old maid. Although she is twenty-four years of age—I suppose in your circles that would make her past her last prayers—I find her to be quite presentable."

Kit knew a set-down when he heard one. Though he didn't consider himself a member of what Mr. Halford called the "sporting set," he realized his words had been as thoughtless as if they'd been said by one of the Corinthians the solicitor so evidently scorned. "I beg your pardon," he said, shamefaced. "I'm sure the lady is very . . . er . . . deserving."

"Yes," said the lawyer in reproof. "Quite."

"I assure you, Halford, I would be perfectly willing—happy, in fact!—to do for the Whitlows whatever you think is right." Kit rose, hoping that this concession would be the end of the matter. "You have my permission to make them a bequest in as generous an amount as my uncle would have wished."

"That *is* good of you, my lord! Very good indeed." Mr. Halford rose also, his face beaming in relief. "You will, of course, see to it that Miss Caroline and her brothers are informed of your intention?"

Kit stiffened. "I? Why can't *you* inform them?"

The solicitor shook his head. "Miss Caroline is very proud. She knows that her guardian failed to provide for her. She will therefore realize that this is an act of generosity on your part. 'Charity' might even be a more accurate word. She will not accept charity. She must somehow be convinced she has a *right* to the bequest. I don't believe anyone but you will be able to convince her."

"Damnation!" Kit swore. "Isn't it enough that I'm willing to give it? Must I also beg her to take it?"

"I'm afraid so, my lord."

Kit sighed in surrender. "Very well, Halford, give me her direction."

"I don't know it. But I'm certain your aunt Lady Whitlow will know where she is." He jotted something down on a piece of notepaper and handed it to Kit. "Here, my lord—your aunt's direction. I'm sure she'll be a help to you."

And now that very aunt was standing in her library doorway, arms akimbo and hat askew, glaring at him. "So, Kit Meredith," she was saying in a loud, angry voice, "you have courage, I must say, to dare to show your face here!"

"You give me too much credit, ma'am," he said, bowing. "I didn't know it required courage to call on my aunt."

Letty brushed by her sister and, aided by her cane, hurried

into the room. "Kit, dearest boy!" she cried, throwing her free arm about him. "You're as handsome as ever . . . but so *thin*! Didn't they feed you in the dragoons?"

Kit laughed, relieved that *someone* in the world cared enough to greet him with enthusiasm. "Aunt Letty!" he said, returning her embrace. "How good to see you!"

"Letty, you idiot, let the fellow go!" her sister ordered. "I'll not permit you to make a hero of him, at least not in this house."

Kit released himself from Letty's grasp and, grinning, crossed the room to the other sister. "Why not, Aunt Martha? I *am* a hero, am I not?"

"I might have thought so once," she retorted, forcing herself not to notice the slight limp in his walk. A war wound, assuredly, she thought, but she would not let it affect her. She faced him sternly. "Since you dispossessed poor Caroline, you are no hero to me."

Kit winced. "That deuced accusation has been plaguing me for the past fortnight. Dash it, Aunt Martha, I did *not* dispossess poor Caroline! I did not know such a person as poor Caroline existed until the day I arrived at the Grange."

Aunt Martha stopped short. "What are you saying?" she asked, staring at the young man in disbelief. "Caro lived at the Grange for a dozen years. Do you think you can make me believe that Clement never mentioned her? Not even in his letters?"

"My uncle Clement never wrote me any letters."

"*Never?* I don't credit it for an instant!"

"It's quite true. I haven't had a word from him since the day he and my father quarreled."

Martha put a trembling hand to her forehead. "But . . . you were his *heir*!"

"And he *adored* you. Always!" Letty added.

"He might have, when I was a child. But his rage at Papa must have flowed over to me, for he never spoke to either one of us again. I wrote him once or twice from Spain, but he never responded. That I was his heir came as a complete surprise to me."

Martha sank into a chair. "Let me understand all this. Are you telling us that you *didn't* throw Caro out in the cold?"

"How could I? I'd never even heard her name."

"Good God!" Martha muttered. "This puts a whole new light on the matter."

"Not to me." Letty beamed, clapping her hands together joyfully. "I *knew* our Kit could never act in so dastardly a style."

"Thank you, Aunt Letty," Kit said, sitting down beside her and taking one of her bony hands in his. "You are the only one who did."

"Be that as it may," Martha cut in brusquely, "we are still left with the problem of what's to be done about poor Caro now. You will not believe it, Kit, but I was just about to depart for Shropshire to lay the matter squarely in your lap."

"Were you? Then my timing is most fortunate, for not only have I saved you from a long trip, but I'm here to relay the news that the problem is solved."

"Solved?" Martha eyed him dubiously. "How?"

"Just yesterday I arranged with Mr. Halford to supply to Miss Whitlow and her brothers the bequest that Uncle Clement intended them to have. The bequest is, I understand, large enough to provide for their present and future comfort."

"Oh, *Kit*!" Letty exclaimed, her eyes shining with tears.

Martha, too, was moved. "That was very good of you, my boy, I must say."

But Letty's joyful expression immediately faded. "She won't take it, you know," she murmured, half to herself. "Never."

"What?" Kit peered at her in dismay.

"She's quite right," Martha said, sagging back in her chair. "She won't. Not Caro."

"Why not?" Kit leaned forward, making an earnest plea. "It's not charity, you know. It's her due."

"You can say all you like about her due," Martha explained,

"but she won't accept it. The fact remains that Clement didn't mention her in the will."

"A mere oversight," Kit insisted. "She must know what his intentions were."

"Intentions are not facts," said Martha glumly.

Letty nodded. "That's so true. And Caro is very proud."

"Yes, so I've heard." Kit clenched his fists, wishing he could wring that blasted female's neck. How, he wondered, would he ever rid himself of this irksome responsibility? He lifted his head and, with a last vestige of hope, pleaded, "But surely you both, between you, can convince her—"

"No, she won't listen to us in this matter," Martha said with finality.

"But, Martha," Letty said, a note of optimism creeping into her quavery voice, "perhaps *Kit* himself could—"

"Yes," Martha agreed, her eyes lighting up eagerly. "You must do it yourself, Kit. If there's any hope at all of convincing the girl, it lies with you."

Kit looked from one sister to the other, reading in their faces their complete—and completely groundless—faith in him. "Somehow," he murmured, shaking his head in disgust, "I knew that's what you'd say."

8

Kit called at his aunt Letitia's house that very evening, asking to be permitted to speak to Miss Caroline Whitlow. "I'll see if she's in," said Letty's butler, Melton, a small fellow who, elderly and frail as Letty herself, nonetheless moved with youthful energy. He led the visitor to the drawing room, where he left him to his own devices. Then he carried Kit's card to the upstairs sitting room, where the family had retired after dinner.

Caroline was sitting at a round table in the corner, giving Gilbert a lesson on the division of fractions. On the other side of the room, near the fire, Letty was working at an embroidery frame, concentrating on keeping the pain in her gnarled fingers from altering the proper direction of her needle. Arthur sat deep in an armchair, ostensibly reading but in reality brooding over his dull existence.

Melton tapped on the open door to announce his presence and crossed the room to the table. "A caller, Miss Caroline," he announced, holding out the card tray.

"For me?" Caro asked in mild surprise. But when she read the name on the card, surprise deepened to shock. "Good God! It's *Crittenden*!"

Everyone looked up. "Then you must go down at once, my love," Letty said calmly.

"Go down?" Caro rose to her feet in magisterial fury. "I will most certainly *not* go down!" She tossed the card back on the tray. "Return to His Lordship, please, Melton, and tell him that I am not at home. Not now. Not ever. Not to him."

"Wait a minute, Melton," Letty said, sticking the needle into her work and rising nervously from her chair. "Caro, dearest, you mustn't send such a message. You don't know. . . ."

"What don't I know?"

Letty picked up her cane and hobbled across the room to the angry young woman. "I *told* Martha that I should be the one to prepare you, but she said Kit should tell you himself," she said softly, putting a soothing hand on Caro's arm. "You see, we've been quite wrong about him." And she launched into a detailed account of what had passed that morning at her sister's house.

Caro listened, but the way her lips were pressed together and her arms crossed over her chest as if to defend herself from an assault indicated to Arthur, who was watching the scene in fascination, that she was not impressed. Her next words proved him right. "I don't wish to offend you, Letty dear," she said tightly when Letty had finished, "but I've always felt that you are too fond of your 'Kit.' Naturally, since he's your nephew, the family connection gives you every right to your affectionate feelings toward him. But I have no such connection. I needn't accept his lame excuses, his belated attentions, or his charity. In short, I want nothing to do with the man."

"But, Caro, he merely wants to explain to you that it's *not* charity," Letty argued, taking a deep breath to prepare herself for the exertion she knew she would have to expend to change the stubborn girl's attitude.

Meanwhile, Arthur, quite unnoticed, slipped behind the butler's back to the doorway. Signaling his brother to follow, he stole out the door and down the hall to the stairs. When Gilbert caught up with him, he said in an excited whisper, "Hurry, Gil! Let's go down and get a glimpse of the dastardly Crittenden before Melton shows him the door!"

The two boys tiptoed down the stairs and made for the drawing-room doorway. The door, however, was closed. "You can't unlatch it," Gilbert hissed. "He'll hear."

"No, he won't, if I'm careful," Arthur mouthed, and he slowly turned the knob.

Inside, Kit did indeed hear the latch opening. He turned from the fire to discover two pairs of eyes peeping in at him through the small opening of the door. "Do come in," he said, smiling. "I promise not to bite."

The two boys entered sheepishly. The gentleman facing them was very tall and loose-limbed, with a manly face and kind gray eyes. Arthur liked him at once. "Sorry," he mumbled. "Didn't mean to . . . to . . . spy on you."

"That's quite all right," Kit assured him. "If *I'd* been dispossessed by a monster, I'd want to get a look at him, too."

"You don't look like a monster," Gilbert said, also responding to the kindness in the man's eyes.

"I hope not, indeed." Kit ruffled the boy's hair. "You must be Gilbert."

"And I'm Arthur," the older boy said, offering his hand.

Kit shook it solemnly. "I hope this is a peace offering. I never meant to dispossess you, you know."

"We know. Aunt Letty just told us."

"Good. Then all is forgiven?"

Gilbert and Arthur exchanged looks. "As far as *we're* concerned, I suppose it is," Arthur said.

Kit's brows knit. "But not as far as your sister's concerned?"

Arthur dropped his eyes, saying nothing.

Gilbert, however, was less guarded. "You're page one in Caro's black book," he said frankly. "She's *really* down on you."

"Dash it, is she? Even after Letty explained—"

"Your name's too black to erase, I'm afraid," Arthur admitted.

Kit's brows knit in frustration. "But surely she'll be willing, at the very least, to come down and *talk* to me?"

"No, she won't," Gilbert said.

Arthur nodded in glum agreement with his brother. "Not Caro."

Their prophecy was confirmed by the butler, who entered shortly thereafter with Caro's verbal message: she was not in to Lord Crittenden. Not now. Not ever.

9

Kit couldn't tell if he'd come by his strong sense of duty naturally or if it had been drilled into him during his years of military service, but however he'd acquired it, he couldn't rid himself of it. Though he longed to leave London and go home to Shropshire, that cursed sense of duty prevented him from leaving until he'd done what Mr. Halford, his aunts, and his conscience required him to do—to convince Caroline Whitlow to accept her bequest. Only then would he feel free to depart.

After a few days, however, his mission seemed hopeless. He'd called on the blasted Miss Whitlow every day, but whenever he sent up his card, the butler returned with the message that Miss Whitlow wasn't in. He tried varying the time of his arrival; sometimes he would call in the morning, sometimes during the afternoon, but it made no difference. Once, in desperation, he appeared on the doorstep after nine at night, an unheard-of hour for paying calls. It had all been in vain. The stubborn, irritating chit would not see him.

Her two brothers were quite another matter. Having taken a liking to him at their first meeting, they'd told the butler to inform them when he called. They never failed to keep him company during his hours of fruitless waiting in Letty's drawing room. The time was spent exchanging stories of their lives. The boys asked Kit about his part in the Peninsular campaign, and he asked them about their lives at the Grange. Their conversations were fascinating to all involved.

Kit was becoming very fond of the two boys. It did not take him long to discover that Gilbert's moodiness could easily be turned to liveliness when someone paid attention to him, and that Arthur's seriousness came from a thoughtful, intelligent mind. Now he had another reason for wishing that Caro would speak to him; he wanted to convince her to let him pay for proper schooling for the two of them.

One day, after giving up hope that Caro would come down, he invited the boys to go riding with him through the park in his phaeton. They had a rousing good time, and Kit won Arthur's undying affection by permitting the boy to hold the reins. Then, on another day, after another failure to make contact with Caro, he took the boys on a tour of the Elgin marbles, an awe-inspiring exhibit during which they learned more about ancient Grecian culture than they would have in hours of tutorials. The boys enjoyed the outing so much they could hardly wait for the next one.

How could Kit guess that these simple activities would make their sister even angrier at him? But they did. Caro, who continued to blame him for driving her from her beloved Grange, now blamed him for the additional crime of worming his way into her brothers' affections. "Every day since the Vexatious Viscount began to make his appearances on your doorstep, Aunt Letty, both Arthur and Gil have done nothing but sing his praises," she complained to Letty one evening after the boys had been excused from the dinner table.

"The *Vexatious Viscount*?" Letty echoed, horrified.

Caro had the grace to blush. "That's what I call him in my mind," she said, dropping her eyes to the wineglass she was turning in her fingers.

Letty threw her a look of disapproval. "My dear, you're quite wrong about Kit." She pushed back her chair and rose. "Quite wrong. And to be irked at the man for being kind to the boys is grossly unfair."

"It *would* be unfair, if his motives were *really* kind," Caro argued, "but he's only doing it to win me over." She, too, got to her feet. "I won't be won over, Aunt Letty, no matter what tricks the man uses."

Letty shook her head in discouragement. "You're a very stubborn creature, Caroline Whitlow," she said as the two women made their way to the stairs. "Your brothers have been more animated since Kit's arrival than I've ever seen them. Shouldn't you feel grateful for that, at least?"

"Grateful?" Caro stopped in her tracks. "I don't feel *at all* grateful! Did you *hear* the boys tonight? They babbled incessantly about nothing but Kit. Kit's horses, Kit's carriage, Kit's army tales, Kit's knowledge, Kit's jokes. If you want the truth, Aunt Letty, it made me want to *scream*!"

They proceeded up the stairs in silence, but at the top Caro paused. "Things can't go on this way, Aunt Letty," she said thoughtfully. "I am a trial to you, I know. And so are my brothers. I must find work."

Letty's face fell. "But, my dear, that's not true! I love having you all with me!" she cried.

"You are too good," Caro said, taking her hand and squeezing it affectionately, "but I can't continue to impose—"

"You are not imposing, I assure you. We've been getting on so well, haven't we? It's only on the subject of Kit Meredith that we disagree."

"I know. Of course we get on. You have the most congenial nature. You don't even get angry when we disagree. But I'm constantly aware of the sacrifices you must make in our behalf. At least, if I find work, I can help defray the expenses—"

"Nonsense," Letty said firmly. "I have more than enough income to manage. I don't even need Martha's help, though she would gladly offer it. Besides, my love, it is not seemly for a lady to work for wages. You will lose all your chances to make a proper marriage, and you mustn't do that. You mustn't!" Her eyes suddenly filled with tears, and she pulled a handkerchief from her sleeve and dabbed at them. "Oh, my dear Caro," she said in her trembling voice, "no one knows better than I how p-painful it is to be unmarried."

"Aunt Letty, don't!" Caro cried, taking the thin old woman into her arms. "I never meant to upset you. I am a beast."

"You are the dearest girl in the world!" Letty wept into her shoulder. "That's why I want you to have the h-happiness I never had."

"But, Aunt Letty, I don't understand." Caro tilted up the

wrinkled face and, taking the handkerchief from her, wiped up the wet cheeks. "Everyone says you turned down all your suitors. You never wished to marry, they say. Isn't that true?"

"No, it's not. I was very foolish. I lived in a world of dreams." She straightened up and, leaning on her cane, set off down the hall. "If I had it to do over, I'd wed one of those flawed fellows instead of waiting for perfection . . . for my dream to materialize. I'd be more . . . more of a realist."

Caro followed her. "But in looking for a post, isn't that what I'm trying to do?" she asked. "Trying to be a realist?"

"No, I don't believe you are," Letty said, looking back over her shoulder at the younger woman, her brows knit. "I think, in your way, you're as bad as I was. You expect people to live up to your dream of them."

Caro stiffened. "If you're referring to my view of the Vexatious Viscount again—"

"No, I wasn't referring to him only. I was also thinking of your decision to look for a position. I don't think that will be what you dream either."

"Perhaps not. But I'm convinced I should try."

Letty turned, hobbled back to her, and grasped her arm. "Please, Caro, don't be hasty. Think about it. Promise me you won't do anything to spoil your future."

Caro looked down into the watery, worried eyes that gazed up at her so beseechingly and could do nothing but make that promise. But in her heart she knew it was an impossible promise to keep. How could she guarantee that she would do nothing to spoil her future? Life had taught her enough to know (even if Letty didn't) that the future comes with no guarantees.

10

It soon began to seem to Caro that matters would go on forever in this dreadful fashion. Another week had gone by, yet the viscount was still making daily calls to which she refused to respond, the boys were still singing his praises, and Letty was still insisting that she should not try to find work. But nothing goes on forever, and the future, which she promised Letty she would try not to spoil, was about to burst upon her.

The significant event that was to change everything occurred, as significant events often do, on an inauspicious but rather lovely day. The sky was clear, the breeze fresh, and the weather just a trifle cool for April. Caro woke that morning determined not to put off any longer looking for a post. She could not, she felt, continue indefinitely to take advantage of Letty's kindness. Therefore, while she and Letty lingered over their breakfasts she surreptitiously studied the advertisements in the *Times*.

There was only one that offered promise: an advertisement for a governess in a household only a short distance from Letty's house on Mortimer Street. Caro said nothing aloud, but she memorized the address in the advertisement. She made up her mind to apply for the position at once . . . and in person. Excusing herself, she ran upstairs to dress.

She brushed her hair until the curls were restrained into a smooth line sweeping back from her face. Then she selected from her wardrobe a neat, workaday walking gown of yellow-and-blue striped muslin, but after she'd buttoned the high collar, she wondered if it was, perhaps, too severe. To counteract that impression, she put on a pretty, small-brimmed bonnet, the crown of which was trimmed with gold satin ribbon that had been twisted into charming little rosettes. Then she studied the effect in her mirror. Satisfied that she looked properly governess-ish, she stole down the stairs and slipped quietly from the house.

But the interview did not go well. It was so disappointing, in fact, that she wondered if Letty was not right about her—that she lived in a dreamworld. Certainly the reality of the experience was not at all what she'd dreamed. The lady of the house, a Mrs. Duckett, was a vulgar woman who asked foolish, irrelevant questions that Caro found embarrassing to answer, like, "Why ain't ye married?" or, "Where on earth did ye purchase yer bonnet? My milliner can't never seem to make the trimmin's on my bonnets as pretty as that." Caro, her cheeks burning, wished she'd worn something else.

Mrs. Duckett had four children, all of whom ran in and out of the room while their mother was conducting the interview, interrupting her rudely, demanding attention, and ignoring her snarled orders to be quiet. They all appeared to be monstrously spoiled and ill-behaved. Caro found them so disruptive that she barely knew how she managed to answer the rude queries at all.

Nevertheless, at the end of the interview, Mrs. Duckett surprised Caro by offering her the post. Then she enumerated the conditions of employment: for the meager sum of seventeen pounds per annum, Caro would be expected to be on duty every day (except for a three-hour period on Thursday afternoons when, if no emergency required her presence, she could go to visit her family), to give all four children their lessons, dine with them upstairs at the nursery table, see to all their needs (including their washing up and dressing), and to help serve dinners downstairs in the formal dining room when guests were present.

Caro could scarcely believe her ears. "Seventeen pounds a *year*?" she asked, stunned.

Mrs. Duckett, her eyebrows raised as if offended by the vulgarity of being forced to discuss money matters, defended the salary by declaring, "After all, Miss Whitlow, ye'll be livin' here, in your very own room, and ye'll have no expenses except yer clothes."

Caro, numb and disappointed, told Mrs. Duckett that she would have to think the matter over. But even through the fog of discouragement, she realized that she could not accept the post. If she took a position that required her to "live in," she would have to send the boys away to school, but at a salary of a mere seventeen pounds per annum, she could never afford it. The situation seemed hopeless.

She left the Duckett household so disheartened that she failed to notice that the weather had completely changed. The sky had darkened, and a steady rain had begun to fall. The pretty bonnet that had so entranced Mrs. Duckett wilted as she walked back toward Mortimer Street in an obvious daze, her steps slow and her thoughts muddled by a deep depression. Was a position like the one she'd just been offered all she could expect? *Is that to be my future?* she asked herself in despair as she stepped off the curb and started across the cobbles of Mortimer Street, ignoring the puddles that soaked her shoes.

A short distance away, on the other side of the street, Kit, his head lowered under a large black umbrella, was walking away from his aunt's residence, on his way back to his rooms at Fenton's Hotel. He'd just made one of his useless calls to try to speak to Caro, and, not having bothered to drive his phaeton on this occasion, was making his way back on foot. Irritated by having made another fruitless visit, he was remembering something he'd read in Latin during his college days: *A man who understands the disposition of women knows that when you will, they won't.* He couldn't help smiling at the recollection. It was strange how the sayings of the ancients came back to haunt one later with their truth. Who'd said it anyway? he asked himself. Cicero? Marcus Aurelius? Terence? Yes, that was it! Terence.

Just then, his musings were interrupted by a terrible noise, coming from a distance down the street. He looked up to see a cart, drawn by two cob horses, trundling toward him at breakneck speed, the driver shouting curses as he pulled back on the reins in a desperate but useless attempt to get the cobs in control. But what stopped Kit's pulse was the sight of a young woman who, engulfed in some sort of daze, was heedlessly crossing the street in their path. "Look out!" he shouted in terror.

The young woman, blinking out of her reverie with a start, looked up and saw the horses almost upon her. She froze in horror. Kit, without thinking, dropped his umbrella, leaped into the street, threw himself upon her, and rolled them both out of the way. The horses and cart raced by in a thunder of hooves and shouts, spraying the puddles of water in all directions, crushing Kit's hat under one of the cartwheels, but missing the two bodies by inches.

With the breath knocked out of them, neither of the fallen pair was able to make the effort to get up. Kit, to regain his breath, panted heavily. He soon realized that the woman beneath him was in a worse way. He could feel her breast heave as she gasped in deep, guttural terror. Still shaken, he got to his feet. "Are you hurt, ma'am?" he asked, leaning down to help her up.

She looked up at him, eyes still wide with terror. "I don't . . . think so," she managed.

His eyes met hers, and he blinked. The woman—much younger than he'd at first thought . . . a girl, really—was startlingly appealing. Not what he would ordinarily call pretty he thought, but something beyond prettiness. Even now, with her bonnet crushed, wet, and askew, her short curls tousled and falling over her forehead, and her lips and cheeks white with shock, she made him catch his breath. There was an exquisite sweetness in the slightly rounded face and trembling mouth, but the most striking features were her wonderful gold-flecked eyes. They seemed to say everything that she could not—terror and relief and gratitude all at once. They were the sort of eyes a man wouldn't easily forget . . . eyes that, if a man weren't careful, could capture him for life.

He helped her up, but her knees buckled under her. "You *are* hurt!" he said, alarmed.

She clung to his arm and steadied herself. "No, no," she assured him, her voice choked and still short of breath. "Just shaken."

"No wonder! That deuced drayman should be shot!"

Still keeping herself supported by his arm, she looked up at him, taking in his face for the first time. It was a likable face, lean, with lined, somewhat weathered skin, a square chin, and a full-lipped, generous mouth. But what she was instantly drawn to were the eyes, light gray and sharply keen, yet unmistakably kind. "I believe, sir," she said slowly, "that you saved my life."

"Not at all," he said. "I just prevented a few bruises."

She shut her eyes with a shudder and shook her head. "More than a few, I think. One of those horses . . . I saw him *rear*! I was almost *under* him. I truly believed, in that flashing moment, that I was done for."

"Well, you weren't," Kit said almost brusquely, to cover a flush of embarrassed modesty, "so let's make an end of it."

"How can I? You risked your life for me. Doesn't that put me in your debt?" She threw him a sudden smile that he found utterly charming. "Isn't there a rule somewhere—a principle of conduct of some kind—that specifies what one owes to another for saving a life?"

He laughed. "You mean that unwritten code of honor that says a life for a life? That you are now my slave or some such thing? I must say I rather like that idea. To have a beautiful young lady follow ten paces behind me everywhere I go, ready to fan me in the heat or hold an umbrella over me in the wet . . . a most appetizing vision. But in truth, ma'am, I can't accept the theory that you are indebted to me at all. You'd probably have jumped back from that rearing horse at the last minute without any help from me. I may very well have tackled you and knocked you to the ground for no good reason."

"Nonsense! Don't make light of what you did, not to me. I know quite well that I froze to the spot. I won't permit you to minimize your splendid act of courage."

"Splendid act of courage, indeed!" Kit snorted. Still embarrassed, he turned away from her admiring gaze and searched about for his hat and his discarded umbrella. The hat, a hopelessly crushed and sodden mess, he kicked aside. But the umbrella, when he found it, was unhurt. He shook it out and held it over her. "Please, ma'am, you mustn't exaggerate the incident. Since you are, fortunately, quite unscathed, it would be best to put it out of your mind."

"Very well, I'll try. But you have my everlasting gratitude."

"Thank you, ma'am. Now, do you think you can walk?"

"I think so." She took a couple of shaky steps. "There, you see? I'm fine." She looked down at her sodden skirts and added ruefully, "Except for my gown, of course. I must look dreadfully bedraggled."

"Well, your bonnet is a bit off-kilter," Kit teased, "but if you'll take the word of a connoisseur, you are otherwise a charming sight."

She righted her bonnet at once. "A connoisseur, are you?" she asked, her lovely eyes twinkling.

"A boastful one, I fear. And a selfish one, to keep you standing here in the rain. I shouldn't be surprised if you were wet through. Shall I find a hack to take you home?"

She shook her head. "Since I live only a little way down the street, I shall do very well on shanks' mare, thank you, sir."

"Then, please, ma'am, take my arm and let me see you home."

She gave him a small smile in acquiescence and took his arm. As they started down the street she noticed his slight limp. She stopped short. "Good heavens," she exclaimed, "all this while you've worried about me, and it's *you* who's been hurt!"

He shook his head. "No, no. My limp is from an old injury. Nothing to do with today."

"Oh, I see," she said. She would have liked to ask more about it, but it seemed in poor taste to inquire.

"You needn't look so concerned," Kit said, smiling down at her reassuringly. "I don't even notice it now. I quite enjoy walking, even in the rain."

"Nevertheless, I'm glad my house is but a step away," she said. "Over there. The second house from the corner."

He almost stumbled. "*Which* one?" he gulped. The second house from the corner was his aunt Letty's house!

"That one," she said, pointing.

It took an effort for him to keep walking. It can't be . . . ! he said to himself dazedly. She and the blasted Caroline . . . they can't be one and the same!

But obviously, they were one and the same, for no other young woman was living in Letty's house. This lovely creature had to be Caroline Whitlow! Good God! How different she was from the person he'd imagined. Why, he'd even called her an ape-leader! No wonder Mr. Halford had given him a set-down.

He glanced down at her, feeling a heady delight. So this was Caroline Whitlow, the stubbornly irritating female who'd caused him so much difficulty and had kept him cooling his heels for days. Well, he had the upper hand now. She couldn't refuse the bequest any longer. She was indebted to him, she'd said so herself. He almost chortled aloud.

But the feeling evaporated almost at once and gave way to misgivings. How would she react when she learned *his* identity? Would this sweet warmth in which he was presently basking give way to cold rejection? Would her smile die, her face fall, her soft mouth tighten, her wonderful eyes fill with utter dislike? Would the sound of his name snuff out the stirring of attraction that had sparked between them? Would the tiny flame be instantly doused? Extinguished forever? That dreadful prospect created an ache in his innards.

They had reached the wrought-iron fence that fronted Letty's neat little town house. Caro paused at the gate. "Let me thank you again, sir," she said softly, taking her hand from his arm and offering it to him. "Whether you like it or not, I am in your debt."

He lifted her hand to his lips. "Balderdash," he muttered. He had no idea what to say next. Now was the time for him to introduce himself, but he could not bring the words to his tongue. He had an urge to play the coward and run off, but he didn't do that either. He just stood there, stupidly immobile.

She waited for an awkward moment for him to go on, but when he did not, she did it for him. "I didn't introduce myself," she said shyly. "I'm Miss Caroline Whitlow. I should be happy if . . . that is, I should like to . . ." She blushed and dropped her eyes. "The least I can do to show my gratitude is to invite you to tea."

His heart swelled in his chest. What she'd just done was a brave act for a girl. Some might even call it brazen. *He* should have been the one to offer his name and ask to call. But since he'd said nothing, she'd swallowed her pride and invited him. Could it be that she, too, had felt the spark? That she actually wanted him to call on her? If she'd been anyone else in the world, he would have been the happiest of men. But since she was who she was, how could he accept her invitation without identifying himself?

This second hesitation, though only as brief as a blink, caused a shadow to darken her eyes. He couldn't bear to see it. It clearly told him that his hesitancy had hurt her. All he wanted now was to erase that shadow. "I would be delighted to come to tea," he said quickly, his voice so unsteady he hardly recognized it. "Shall we say tomorrow?"

Her eyes immediately brightened. "Tomorrow would be lovely. We serve tea at three."

He bowed, tipped his hat. "Tomorrow at three," he mumbled, and set off quickly down the street.

"But, sir," she called after him, "you haven't told me *your* name."

He turned back, his stomach knotting. He couldn't tell her his name now. He'd put it off too long. But he had to say something. Anything. Any other name. His mind raced about desperately. "Terence," he said, throwing out the first name that came into his head. "Marcus Terence."

She made a little bow. "Till tomorrow, then, Mr. Terence."

He tipped his hat and watched as she ran up the short path to the door and disappeared inside. Then he lifted his umbrella and turned away, wincing. The enormity of his lie made him feel ill. How was he ever to get himself out of this muddle that his cowardice had got him into?

With every step he took he felt worse. It did not help that the rain pelted him unmercifully despite the fact that he'd angled his umbrella like a shield against the spray. As he angrily sloshed through the ever-deepening puddles, heedlessly abusing his best boots, he thought about the ramifications of his lie. He'd made a very bad bargain. In order to keep alive for the moment the little spark that had ignited between them, he'd surely doomed it for the long run. That blasted lie would affect everything badly: his relationship with the boys and with his aunt; Caro's attitude toward the bequest; and, of course, her attitude toward him personally. Just thinking of the complexity of problem made him groan aloud. "Damnation," he swore in self-disgust, "*what* have I *done*?"

11

Just after ten the next morning, Kit set out for his aunt's abode. He strode along the rainwashed streets with a swing in his step, for his mood, like the weather, had changed overnight. For the weather, the morning had brought a bright blue sky and fresh breezes redolent of spring. And for Kit, a plan to deal with his lie.

He entered Letty's dark, tiny hallway fully aware that everyone in Letty's household would have finished breakfast by this time and dispersed to attend to their morning occupations. He handed his hat to Melton, the butler, as he always did, and asked to see Miss Whitlow. Melton led him to the drawing room, as he always did, took His Lordship's card, as he always did, and disappeared up the stairs. In a few moments he was back, as he always was, to inform His Lordship that Miss Whitlow was not at home.

So far, everything was proceeding just as Kit wished.

He'd come to the house on Mortimer Street with a plan. He'd concocted it the night before, when he hadn't been able to sleep. But the idea hadn't come easily. He'd prowled his room during all those long, rainy hours, trying to decide what to do about his lie. He kept wishing Mickley were there with him, for the batman was never short on sensible, practical advice, the sort of advice he desperately needed. But Kit had left Mickley behind to watch over things at the Grange. And that was another problem: Kit was not at all sure what difficulties the batman might be facing. Kit should have returned to the Grange more than a week ago. Mickley would surely be wondering why his business in London was taking so long.

Perhaps he never should have come to London. In the

protracted struggle with Caroline Whitlow, he was neglecting the Grange, where his attention was so badly needed. He could hardly wait to start work on the improvements. If it hadn't been for Caroline's stubbornness . . .

But he'd stopped himself from completing this habitual thought. Now that he'd met Caro, he felt quite differently about her. If he could only find a way to change her feelings toward *him,* he would not regret this London visit. But how was he to do it?

He'd struggled with the question all night. By morning he'd concocted the plan. He would play the role of Mr. Marcus Terence until he and the girl were better acquainted. Then, once he'd secured her approval of his character (*if* he'd secured her approval—he was not such a coxcomb that he believed it was a certainty), he would reveal his identity. If she grew to like him, there might be some hope, then, that the knowledge of his real identity would not disgust her.

But first he would have to convince Aunt Letty and Caro's brothers to go along with the temporary deception. That was why he'd come this morning, in his own identity. He knew Caro would not come down. For the first time, her refusal to see Viscount Crittenden suited his plans. "Well, then, Melton," he said to the butler with a smile, "will you please tell my aunt that her nephew would like to speak to her."

Letty came in shortly afterward, moving as briskly as her weak legs, with the aid of her omnipresent cane, could manage. "Kit, my dearest, good morning!" she said cheerfully, offering her cheek. "Melton tells me that Caro has refused you again. I must say, my love, that I'm touched by your persistence. A young fellow with less character would have given up by now."

"Thank you, Aunt," Kit said, helping her to the sofa, "but my call today was not really to see Caro. It was a ruse." And perching beside her, he launched into an account of the events of the day before.

He had barely begun to relate the details of the runaway horses when Letty interrupted with a gasp. "Good God!" she exclaimed. "It was *you*?"

"What?" Kit asked, taken aback.

"The fellow who saved her life? It was you?"

He gaped at her. "How did you know . . . ?"

"She's spoken of nothing else but the brave gentleman who dashed under the rearing horses to save her!" Letty exclaimed, beaming at him.

"I did no such thing," Kit declared. "She insists on making a hero of me. That is, of *him*." He stared ahead of him unhappily. "I wonder if he'd have been quite so heroic in her eyes if she'd known he was Kit Meredith."

Letty's face fell. "The Vexatious Viscount," she murmured. "Yes, I wonder."

"The Vexatious Viscount? Is *that* what she calls me?"

"I'm afraid so."

"Charming," Kit muttered in disgust.

"But do go on, Kit. How did you become Mister . . . Mister . . . ?"

"Mr. Terence. Marcus Aurelius Terence, if you please. Did you ever hear anything so ridiculous? It was all I could think of." He related the rest of the story without further interruption. At the conclusion, he looked at his aunt, shamefaced. "I don't expect you to approve," he said. "It was a cowardly thing to have done."

"Not at all," Letty said, a twinkle appearing in her eyes. "I think it was a very *good* thing to have done. By becoming Mr. Terence, you will soon make your way into her good graces—if you're not there already. I assure you that Mr. Terence has already made a noteworthy first impression."

"Then you don't think the lie was a stupid mistake?"

"No, I don't. I have a feeling it will all turn out very well."

"I wish I were half so sanguine." He got to his feet and began to pace. "Very well, then, we'll proceed with the deception. Do you think, Aunt Letty, that you can face me at tea and pretend I'm an absolute stranger?"

Letty smiled, drawing herself up proudly. "I played Portia at school. It was a stellar performance, if I do say so, as I shouldn't. One doesn't lose that sort of talent with the years, does one?"

Kit grinned back at her. "One certainly doesn't. I see I have no need to be concerned. Then the only other thing I'll ask of you is to instruct Melton not to give me away. I'll talk to the boys."

He found them in the back sitting room, desultorily playing a game of hearts. He let them play out the hand before telling them what had happened the day before. When they realized it was he who'd rescued their sister from the runaway horses, they were overjoyed. "You should've heard the great things she said about you!" Gilbert chuckled.

But Kit took no pleasure in their pride in him. He was shamefaced as he related how he'd deceived her about his identity. But they only laughed loudly. "Serves her right," Arthur said. "She should never have set her hackles against you in the first place."

"Perhaps it was all right in the first place, when she didn't properly understand why you sent us off," Gilbert pointed out, trying to be fair to his sister. "But we've been telling her every day what a good sort you are, so she should've come round by this time."

"Did you really tell her I was a good sort?" Kit asked, smiling at the boy fondly. "That was very kind of you."

Gilbert shrugged. "Well, you are."

"Will you still think me a good sort when I ask you to join me in deceiving her for a while?"

The boys looked at each other for a moment. Then Arthur, reading agreement in his brother's eyes, spoke for both of them. "Yes, we will. We love Caro, but we're on your side, Kit. There's nothing we want more than for Caro and you to be friends. Perhaps a small deception is the only way."

"Besides," Gilbert said, his whole face alight with eagerness, "it'll be a great lark watching you humbug her at tea today."

Kit's smile died. "Good God," he muttered, "I didn't think of that. Do you and Caro always take tea together?"

"Most always," Arthur said. "Why?"

Kit ran a nervous hand through his hair. "I don't think I'll be able to do it with the pair of you watching. I can't act a lie in front of you."

"Why not?" Gilbert demanded.

"I don't know." He smiled ruefully. "Perhaps it's because you think me such a good sort."

Arthur nodded with an instinctive understanding. "We won't go to tea, then. We'll make ourselves scarce."

But Kit shook his head, frowning. Despite the boys' quick acceptance of his planned deception, he didn't feel right about it. "Dash it," he muttered, disturbed, "this is all becoming too deucedly Machiavellian. Let's give it up. I'll tell her the truth and be damned."

"No, dash it, Kit, don't give up," Arthur begged. "There'll never be another opportunity like this one. Saving her life like that . . . it was a stroke of luck that won't happen again. You can't waste it."

"We don't have to be there at teatime," Gilbert offered generously. "We can say we have to go on an errand for Aunt Letty. To her milliner or something."

Kit was touched. "You're a good fellow, Gil, truly you are. But you know Letty would never send you boys to her milliner's. It's a footman's task."

"We sometimes do footmen's tasks," Gilbert insisted. "We went to Berry Brothers on St. James Street last week to pick up some bohea tea."

"Yes," Arthur seconded. "Aunt Letty knows we like the chance to walk about outdoors, so she often sends us on errands. Go ahead with your plan, Kit, please! Leave this detail to us."

Kit let himself be persuaded, but he remained worried long after he'd left the house.

The boys, too, were worried. They weren't sure what errand they could suggest that Letty would agree to. But they needn't have troubled themselves, because Caro solved the problem for them. At about two in the afternoon she herself came looking for them, followed closely by Letty. "Would you mind missing tea today?" she asked them, her cheeks pink. "Aunt Letty would like you to go on an errand for her."

Arthur and Gilbert exchanged glinting glances. "But, Caro," Arthur demanded with exaggeratedly wide-eyed innocence, "isn't this the day your savior, Mr. Terence, comes to tea? We want to meet him, don't we, Gil?"

"Sure as check we do!" Gil grinned.

"There may be other times to meet him," Aunt Letty said, throwing them a darkling look. "Today, he and Caro should spend the time becoming acquainted, not making conversation with inquisitive boys."

Caro's blush deepened. "Wouldn't you rather take a stroll to Gunther's and have some chocolates than stay to tea and listen to some dull conversation?"

"I'd rather hear the conversation," Arthur said, unable to resist the game.

"We *like* conversation," Gilbert added with mischievous enjoyment.

But Letty, afraid that this teasing might be pushed too far, elbowed Gilbert warningly in the ribs. "But you like going to Gunther's more, don't you?" she asked pointedly.

Gilbert nodded. "Yes, I suppose I do. Gunther's shop always smells of baking biscuits and apricot jam."

Arthur sighed in pretended surrender. "Very well, we'll go to Berkeley Square if you wish it."

"Get along, then," Letty ordered, pressing a half guinea into his palm and urging him toward the door. "But don't spend more than two shillings for chocolates or you'll make yourselves ill. Bring home some fruit tarts and a box of sugarplums. And don't lose the change."

"And Arthur," Caro added, her eyes lowered and her cheeks aflame with embarrassment, "you needn't hurry back."

12

"Mr. Terence" presented himself at the Mortimer Street house promptly at three. A blank-faced Melton announced him from the doorway of the drawing room. Caro, all smiles, rose to greet him. "Mr. Terence, good afternoon. Do come in."

Kit's eyes drank her in. If she was breathtaking yesterday, today she was bewitching. Her eyes shone with warmth, her short, thick curls bounced with youthful charm, and the flounce of her flowered cambric gown flipped with every step she took toward him, revealing a pair of shapely ankles. He hadn't realized how slim and supple her body was, and how a softly clinging gown could add a new dimension to an already glowing loveliness. Gulping down his admiration, he took the hand she held out and bowed over it, hoping that his manner did not betray how his heart was thumping in his chest.

Caro, for her part, also discovered that her heart was thumping. Mr. Terence appeared even more likable than he'd seemed yesterday, if that were possible. All night she'd tried to envision his face, convinced that it could not possibly be as appealing as she remembered it. She'd told herself that the emotion of the close escape had enhanced his appearance in her mind. She'd warned herself not to be disappointed if the second sight of him was less prepossessing than the first. But here he was, every bit as winning as she remembered. Nay, more so! "How good to see you again," she managed, albeit a bit breathlessly. "May I present my aunt, Miss Meredith. Letty, dear, this is Mr. Terence."

Kit turned and bowed. "How do you do?"

"Mr. Terence," Letty cooed, "I'm so very glad to make your acquaintance. I can't tell you how I appreciate having this opportunity to thank you. Your heroism has earned my undying gratitude."

"Dash it, Aunt Letty, don't overdo it," Kit muttered under his breath as he bent over her hand. Aloud he said, "Heroism is much too strong a word, ma'am. Your niece overestimates my action." He turned to Caro with a smile. "Didn't you promise me you'd put the incident out of your mind?"

"I promised to try. But it's an impossible task."

"But it's not, I hope, impossible to drop the subject from the conversation."

"Must we? I asked you to tea expressly for the purpose of thanking you."

"Really? Is that the only reason? If so, I'm sorry I came."

"No, please, you mustn't say that," Caro said.

"Of course you mustn't," Letty seconded. "There are certainly other reasons. You came to have tea, for one. Shall we sit down? I'll ring Melton to bring in the tray."

Over the teacups, Kit tried to keep the conversation safe by asking Caro all sorts of questions about herself. But she was determined to learn more about him. She quickly ascertained the most important information: that he was neither married nor betrothed. That information quickened her pulse, but there was a great deal more she wanted to know. "Do you live in London?" she asked at the next opportunity.

"I only visit," he replied, determined to keep as near to the truth as possible so that when the time came for confession, there would not be too much to correct.

"Oh?" There was a hint of disappointment in the word. "Do you stay long?"

"I fear not. I only came on a business matter, which I suspect will soon be settled."

Dashed, Caro stirred her tea in silence. Only when Letty coughed did she lift her head. Then, with a forced smile, she asked, "Where *is* your home, Mr. Terence?"

He wanted to say Shropshire, but he feared it would lead him into murky depths. She would undoubtedly respond that she, too, had lived in Shropshire, and she would then probably ask exactly where in Shropshire his home was. Replying to *that* question would lead too close to the truths he could not tell. To avoid that danger, he answered, "Yorkshire," and learned, as all liars soon learn, that one lie invariably begets more.

To keep the conversation safe, he turned the subject to politics. Napoleon's emergence from Elba a month ago was on everyone's lips. The trouble again brewing in Europe always made for lively conversation. When Mr. Terence expressed his disgust at the halfhearted support Russia and Austria were giving to the European alliance, he was pleased that Caro fully agreed. He was even more pleased when she said that she was sure Lord Wellington was more than capable of leading the allied troops. She sounded so sensible now that it was hard for him to understand why she'd seemed so unreasonable before.

When the subject turned to books, Caro, on her part, discovered that Mr. Terence took as much pleasure in the novels of Walter Scott and the poetry of Wordsworth as she did herself. It was a surprise to him and a delight to her to learn that they had so much in common.

Two hours flew by. It was with reluctance that he stood up to go. Caro accompanied him to the door. "I know you don't wish me to refer to the forbidden subject, Mr. Terence," she murmured as he took her hand. "You have the true hero's modesty. But, since you'll soon be returning to Yorkshire and I may never see you again, you must let me thank you one more time."

He looked down at her with a twinkle. "In the first place, ma'am," he scolded with mock severity, "I find being taken as a hero utterly embarrassing and quite undeserved. In the second place, there's been quite enough of thanking. And finally, Miss Whitlow, if you truly believe you'll not see me again, you have too little appreciation of your own charm or my resolve."

She found herself reddening again. "I don't think I understand . . . ?"

He met her eyes with brazen directness. "If you don't understand me now, ma'am, I promise you soon will."

13

Caro leaned her forehead against the door for a moment after Mr. Terence left and took a deep breath. Then she lifted her head, turned about, and flew across the floor to where Letty had just risen from the sofa. In a quick swoop, she gathered the frail woman up in her arms, swept her off her feet, and whirled her about the room, humming a waltz tune.

"*Caro,*" the elderly woman cried breathlessly, "have you gone mad? Let me down!"

Caro, her eyes sparkling and her cheeks pink, stopped her spinning and, laughing, set Letty gently on her feet. "I'm sorry, dearest," she said, kissing the withered cheek. "I just felt like dancing."

"Did you, indeed?" Letty muttered dryly as she tried to catch her breath. She dropped into a chair and fanned herself with her hand. "I wonder why."

"You know perfectly well why," Caro retorted, grinning. "You liked him, too, didn't you?"

"He seemed pleasant enough," Letty said blandly.

"Pleasant enough?" Caro regarded her suspiciously. "Is that all you can say about him? Pleasant enough? Didn't you find his eyes remarkable? His face manly? His hair dark and thick? His address assured? His comments witty? His smile delightful?"

Letty looked back at her with a noncommittal shrug.

Caro floated to the door. "Very well, say nothing. I understand. You think it's midsummer moon with me. I'm in alt. Smelling of April and May. And you're quite right, dearest Aunt, quite right. But I rather like being in the clouds. It's a rare feeling for me."

"Is it?" Letty asked, studying the girl from the corners of her eyes, her head cocked like a bright-eyed bird but her expression enigmatic.

"Oh, yes, very rare. A first, really. So, dearest, let me remain in the clouds for a little longer. Don't bring me down to earth just yet. If you're not going to sing his praises to me, I'll ask you to excuse me so that I can go up to my room and sing his praises to myself."

Letty shrugged again. "Very well, my love. Go along, if you must."

Only when the door closed on the girl did Letty permit herself to smile. It was, like that of the proverbial cat who'd swallowed the canary, a smile of utter satisfaction.

14

Mr. Terence waited only a day before inviting Caro to take a drive with him in his phaeton. Caro found it a most enjoyable outing, except that every time she asked him something about himself, Mr. Terence noticed something interesting in the view and quickly pointed it out. The man was, despite his charm and good looks, strangely evasive. Nevertheless, Caro later said to Letty, her eyes shining, that she'd never found London so much to her liking.

The next day, Kit, emboldened by the success of the previous day's outing, repeated the invitation, but this time he included the boys. He warned both of them in advance to be careful not to address him as Kit. "I've heard that bungling names is the most common mistake that actors make," he explained, "and in a sense we're actors in this affair."

His warning was not completely effective. There was one bad moment. It occurred when an ornate carriage passed them by. "Oh, look, Kit," Gilbert cried excitedly, "isn't that the prince?"

At Gilbert's spontaneous use of his real name, Kit felt himself flush in alarm. But no one, not even Caro, noticed it. Everyone had turned to look at the passing equipage. "Yes, it's Prinny himself!" Arthur declared, pointing to the crest at the side of the royal carriage. They all gasped when the royal personage within, who'd heard the boys' cries, actually turned, smiled, and waved at them. In the excitement of this encounter with royalty (and to Kit's intense relief), no one else noticed Gilbert's slip.

In the week that followed, there were three more outings, two with Caro alone and one with the entire household, including Letty. Letty also invited him twice to join them for dinner. These events were all exceedingly pleasurable. Kit was becoming convinced that Caro was finding him a likable companion. A few more occasions like these, he thought, and he'd feel secure enough of her approval to be able to tell her the truth.

He knew he'd have to tell her soon. For one thing, he was extending his London stay much too long. For another, it was clear that he couldn't maintain this false guise indefinitely. Already matters were growing awkward. She was beginning to notice that he was avoiding escorting her to public places. But how could he *not* try to avoid crowds? Although it had been many years since he'd made the social rounds in London, there were several people who might still recognize him—fellows from school, for example, or someone who'd been with him in the dragoons, or old friends of the family. Running into an old acquaintance could lead to disaster. He couldn't take such a risk.

His fear of that danger was responsible for one of his worst moments with Caro. It occurred after one of Letty's dinners. Caro escorted him to the door, a practice that he usually enjoyed, for in those private moments there was a feeling of comfortable intimacy between them. That evening, however, Caro remarked casually that she would like to find an escort to a ball being given by an old friend of Letty's. When he heard those words, Kit's spirit plummeted. As Mr. Terence, he couldn't escort her to a large, crowded ball: What if an old friend from his school days should come up to him when he was in her company and cheerfully greet him by his real name? That would surely spoil everything. Therefore, while Caro searched his face for a response, Kit pretended not to understand her hint and spoke of something else. However, the pretense—and the look of confusion in her eyes—made him miserable. He knew then and there that Mr. Terence's time on earth was growing short.

He couldn't take her to the ball, but, he thought, he could arrange another type of special evening that would please her . . . one that would be less dangerous. To that end, he called at Mortimer Street early the next day and extended an invitation to both Caro and Letty to accompany him to the opera at the King's Theatre in the Haymarket. "I've managed to procure a box," he said eagerly. "Catalini is singing. I've never heard her, but everyone says she's a wonder."

Caro seemed to hesitate before accepting, but Letty acquiesced with pleasure. When he left, Letty turned to Caro curiously. "Is something wrong between you and Mr. Terence?" she asked. "You seemed a bit reluctant to accept the invitation."

"I'm confused, Aunt Letty," Caro said worriedly, sinking down on the sofa. "I don't know what Mr. Terence wants of me."

"Wants of you?" Letty echoed, her smile fading.

"Yes. Is he courting me or is it merely companionship he's seeking while his business keeps him in London?"

Letty sat down beside the girl, not knowing how to answer this frank and troubling question. "What is it you want of *him,* my love?" she asked.

"Perhaps it's too early in our acquaintance to be certain. But it's beginning to appear that I'm more eager to be courted than Mr. Terence is to do the courting."

"What makes you think so? Has Mr. Terence done something out of the way?"

"Not exactly. But sometimes his behavior is strange. He's very eager for my company for riding in the park or for dinner here with the family, but he evades all personal questions and he seems reluctant to appear with me in public groups. When I hinted that I'd appreciate an escort to the Drummonds' ball, he changed the subject."

"But he's taking us to the King's Theater tomorrow," Letty pointed out in his defense. "That's as public as a place can be."

"Yes, that's true. But it's a theater, and for the most part dark." She sat for a moment in silence. "Perhaps I'm being missish," she said after a while. "We women can be overly sensitive at times. But it seems to me that . . ." Her voice died, and she looked down at her hands, the fingers tightly interlocked.

"What, dearest? Tell me."

The girl's lashes flickered against her cheek, signaling an inability to meet Letty's eyes. ". . . that . . . that he doesn't want anyone to believe he's . . . he's in any way *attached* to me."

Letty didn't know what to say. She knew Caro had formed an attachment to Mr. Terence. But Kit was not Mr. Terence. And though in his role as *Mr. Terence,* he appeared to feel an attachment to Caro, that did not necessarily mean that *Kit* felt it. Kit's expressed purpose for this whole charade was a desire to win Caro's good graces so that she would accept her legacy. Once he'd achieved that goal, he would be, in effect, rid of all responsibility for her. Would he then still want to see her? Letty did not know. He had not said anything about his feelings, and she hadn't asked. If there was anything of courtship in his behavior, she couldn't say . . . and didn't dare to guess. "Perhaps the wisest thing you can do, Caro dear," she advised, rising and reaching for her cane, "is to wait and see."

"Yes." Caro sighed. "That's all I can do."

15

The evening of the opera began with happy expectations. Caro and Letty dressed for it in their finest evening clothes. Letty wore her best black lace and a brocaded turban trimmed with peacock feathers. Caro wore a raisin-colored lustring gown which she'd brought with her from the Grange but had never before had the courage to wear. It had been a bit daring for country assemblies in Shropshire, with its bare shoulders and tight bodice. But she'd always loved the dark color with its glints of red, the wide velvet bow set just under the breast, and the way the skirt fell in soft, clinging folds from the high waist. It would not be too daring for the King's Theater in London, she told herself. Besides, she wanted Mr. Terence to take notice. The last time she'd dressed to please a man's eyes, it had been for Mr. Lutton. She'd carefully selected a sedate blue muslin with a high collar, and much good that had done her!

Later, after she'd put on the gown and placed among her curls a jeweled pin that Letty had insisted on lending her, she studied herself in the mirror dubiously. Had she overdone it? Were her shoulders too bare? Was the silky lustring too great a contrast with her pale skin? Was the jeweled pin too ostentatious? But it was too late. She could hear, downstairs, that Mr. Terence had arrived. She hurried to the stairs, pulling on a pair of long white gloves.

At the bottom of the stairway Mr. Terence, resplendent in a new black evening coat and satin breeches, stood gazing up at her. One glance at his face and all her doubts vanished. If ever a man's eyes showed admiration, they did now.

Letty came up beside him. "You are a vision, Caro, my love," she said with a pleased smile.

"What flummery," Caro said, blushing.

"No, not flummery at all," Mr. Terence assured her. "You will distract every man's eyes from the stage." Then, with a little bow to both ladies, he offered each one a charming nosegay. "To have two such beauties on my arms will make me the most envied man in the theater."

The flowers, the extravagant praise, and the atmosphere of celebration made for a merry beginning of the evening. They climbed into his carriage in high spirits.

For the first three hours, it was a lovely occasion. Madame Catalani was in fine voice, the music was magnificent, the surroundings sumptuous. At the intermission, Mr. Terence bought them champagne. During the second act and well into the third, Caro felt his arm on the back of her chair, warm and protective and affectionate. Her fears were groundless, she decided. She'd never felt so happy.

Kit, too, was happy. Seated between his favorite aunt and this lovely young woman, listening to Handel's lushly melodic music, he felt all his cares evaporate. At one point, when Catalani was particularly impassioned, Caro turned her head slightly, and he felt her rub her cheek against the back of his hand. That simple act caused a joyful constriction in his chest. She *must* like him, he thought. The little gesture was proof. Life was good. He would soon tell her the truth, and everything would be well.

The feeling lasted barely a moment. In the next moment, he recognized a man he'd served with in Spain seated just a few boxes away. It was Jack Higgins, an officer who'd sold out shortly before Salamanca. He was a hearty, backslapping sort, with whom Kit had spent many a raucous, drunken evening. If Jack spotted him, he would surely shout out his name. Kit could guess his very words: "Kit Meredith, you old blackguard! Is it you?" And everything would surely be lost.

Kit hastily turned in his seat. He spent the remaining two acts of *Semiramide* sitting awkwardly sideways, praying that the fellow would not recognize the back of his head.

Caro's attitude became more reserved after that, but so great was Kit's relief at not having been recognized that he dismissed it from his mind. When they returned to Mortimer Street, however, Caro's mood remained cold. What had he done? he wondered. Had she noticed his strange behavior?

Aunt Letty, sensing drama in the air, promptly excused herself and went up to bed. Kit suddenly felt uncomfortable and bowed his good night, but Caro held him back. "Can you spare me a moment or two, Mr. Terence?" she asked. "There's something of import I'd like to say to you."

"Of course," he replied, and followed her into the drawing room.

To his surprise she closed the door. "Please sit down," she said nervously.

He sat uneasily on the edge of a wing chair. "Is something amiss, ma'am?" he asked.

"I don't know." She sat down on the sofa opposite him and faced him squarely. "Don't you think it strange that, after all the hours we've spent in each other's company, you still call me ma'am?"

He blinked in surprise. "I didn't think . . . do you wish me to call you Caroline? You never suggested before that I should."

"How could I, when you seem to be content with *my* calling *you* Mr. Terence?"

"Oh, I see." He threw her a grin. "Is that what's made you so Friday-faced? It's just that I don't particularly like my given name. Marcus, ugh! It makes me sound a dreadful grind."

"Not at all," she said, not returning his grin. "I rather like it."

"Then use it, by all means. I should very much enjoy calling you Caroline."

"I'm Caro to my friends," she said, still frowning at him.

"If you mean by that that you number me among your friends, I'm honored."

The remark made her wince. It was not the response she wished for. It was too correct, too formal and distant; what she wanted was some sign of intimacy. He'd be honored to be her friend, bah! Dash it, she asked herself, doesn't he want more?

Evidently he didn't, for he was rising from his chair and looking down at her with a smile of relief. "If that was all that's troubling you, ma'am . . . I mean, Caro—"

"No," she snapped, "that's not all."

His expression changed to sincere surprise. "Then what is it?"

She took a deep breath. "You must promise that you will answer me honestly, no matter how difficult it may be. The one virtue that I prize above all is honesty."

His heart sank. Honesty was the one virtue he didn't have, at least not in his dealings with her. "I'll try," he said, discomfited.

She dropped her eyes awkwardly. "This . . . what I want to ask . . . is not easy. If I had a father, he would surely have had this conversation with you in my place."

Kit was utterly bewildered. "A father?"

"Yes. Don't fathers always ask a girl's suitors what their intentions are?"

The question struck him like a blow. *"Suitors?"*

"You *are* a suitor, are you not? You've been calling on me every day for more than a fortnight. Isn't that what suitors do?"

"I don't know. I've never . . . that is, I hadn't thought . . ."

She turned quite pale. "You hadn't thought of being a suitor? Are you saying that it never occurred to you . . . ?"

He sank down on the sofa beside her, his brain whirling in confusion. A suitor? Is that what she thought? The truth was that it hadn't occurred to him that she might interpret his attentions as a sign that he was seeking her hand in marriage. How could he be a suitor for her hand while he was playing the role of someone else? He couldn't ask her to wed Mr. Terence, who didn't even exist! All he'd thought about, until this moment, was that he wanted to break her resistance to his real self. When she'd forgiven him for being Kit Meredith—if that ever happened—there would be time, then, to think of other things. But not yet. First things had to come first.

He stared down at her whitened face, unable to speak. How could he have been so stupid? He'd led her to believe his purpose was something far from what it really was. She wanted honesty, and that's what he'd never given her. He should have told her the truth earlier. He'd made that mistake the first day he met her, and now he'd done it again. He'd waited too long to tell the truth. "Caro, I . . . never meant . . ."

Her eyes widened in shock. "You never intended to . . . to court me?"

"Please don't look at me that way," he muttered, agonized. "You don't understand!"

She swallowed. "There doesn't seem to be anything else to understand," she said slowly. She believed she understood it all. He'd enjoyed her companionship but obviously had not even *considered* anything more. She'd foolishly assumed that he felt as she did, but now that she realized it was not so, her female pride suffered a mortal blow. Humiliated, she rose from the seat. "You m-must excuse me, sir," she said, her voice shaking. She turned and, head lowered, made for the door. "You can let yourself out. You know the w-way."

"Caro, wait!" He was on his feet and at her side in three quick strides. He grasped her arms and forced her to face him. "You've got to let me . . ." he began. But the sight of her eyes looking up at him tightened his throat. Those wonderful, gold-flecked eyes that said so much, what were they saying now? They were wide with pain and mortification and . . . something else. But he could not let himself read what that something was, for it was meant for Marcus Terence, not for him.

She, waiting for words that did not come, tried to wrench her arms free. "Dash it all, Mr. Terence, let me go!"

She was very close to him, her breath rapid, her lips apart and trembling, her skin irresistibly smooth and pale against the dark of her low-cut gown. As his eyes roamed over her a flush suffused her breast and slowly rose up over her throat to her face. It seemed to him that she'd never been so utterly desirable as at this moment. The sight of her filled him with an ache so overwhelming that he committed his worst sin yet—he pulled her into his arms. He stared down for a moment at her astonished face and pressed his mouth to hers.

To kiss her had been the farthest thing from his mind. He knew it was a dreadful mistake. But now that he'd done it, he couldn't stop. He suddenly felt as if this, not her good opinion, was what he'd been seeking all along. Every part of his body responded to the sensation of holding her close. It was as if he'd been parched, and she was the water he needed. He tightened his hold and drank her in hungrily. He'd kissed a number of women in his time, but none of those experiences had prepared him for the urgency and deep desire he now felt.

She, too startled to resist, let herself respond. But even while her limbs turned to water, and her breast lifted itself to him, and her arms crept up over his shoulders, and her hands clasped themselves tightly at the back of his neck, and her lips softened against the steely pressure of his, her mind told her there was something wrong. This kiss made no sense; it didn't follow what had gone before. Where had it come from?

"Oh, God!" he muttered when he let her go. Shaken by the unexpected strength of his desire, he couldn't speak. He knew that everything he was doing was wrong. After his thoughtlessness in not anticipating her expectations, he'd now indulged himself in an act of unforgivable lust. How could he expect her to forgive him? And if she wouldn't forgive him for *this,* how could he expect her to forgive his other heinous crime—his lie about his very identity? What would she feel about what he'd just done when she realized that he was the man she disliked most in the world?

She was gazing up at him, her mouth swollen and her breath coming in short gasps. She didn't know what to make of his behavior. After all his evasiveness, after finally admitting that he had no intention of courting her, he'd taken her into an embrace that could only be described as shattering. "What did that *mean*?" she asked in bewilderment.

He ran his fingers through his hair in a gesture of desperation. "I don't know. I lost my head. I'm . . . sorry."

"Sorry?" The word brought a pain to her chest so sharp she had to press her hand against it.

"I've made a dreadful muddle—"

She put up a hand to stop him. "Please don't say anything more," she ordered. "Every word you utter only increases my mortification."

"Caro, I couldn't—"

"Please, Mr. Terence, just *go*!"

Perhaps that's what he ought to do, he thought. She was distraught, and so was he. The wisest thing to do might be to retreat. He would come back tomorrow and make a clean breast of everything. For now, it was probably best to let matters cool. He went to the door.

"Mr. Terence?"

He turned around. "Marcus," he reminded her.

"Mr. Terence." She was standing erect, her hands clenched at her sides. "I think it would be best if you did not call again."

He opened his mouth to protest, but shut it again. He'd made such a mull of everything tonight that he doubted he could succeed with any argument he might offer now. A good military officer knew when it was time to surrender. With a sigh of defeat, he made a silent bow and left the room.

Tomorrow, he promised himself as he closed the door behind him. I'll surely do better tomorrow. It's certain I couldn't do worse.

16

Kit spent all night in an agonizing review of the circumstances of his relationship with Caroline Whitlow. He could only conclude that everything was his own fault. The words she'd said last night rang in his ears: *The virtue I prize above all others is honesty*. Yet he'd been anything but honest.

By morning he'd decided what to do. He'd tell Caro the truth at once. It was his procrastination that had started this proliferation of blunders. If only he'd given her his true name on that day when he'd saved her from the runaway horses, he might not have found himself in his present predicament.

And it was a predicament—the worst one yet. Before, it had been only Kit Meredith she refused to see. Now it was Kit *and* the deuced Mr. Terence. How was he to set things straight if he couldn't get to see her?

There was only one way, and he took it. Promptly at three, when he knew the family would be gathered for tea, he appeared at the door, brushed by Melton, and burst in on them.

All four—Caro, Letty, and the two boys—were seated round a small tea table in various attitudes of gloom. But Kit's abrupt entrance caused every head to turn in his direction. "Good afternoon," he said pleasantly.

"Ki—Mr. Terence!" Letty cried, her eyes lighting up.

The two boys also brightened. "How do y' do, Mr. Terence," Gilbert greeted.

"Have you come for tea?" Arthur asked, jumping up to get him a chair.

"Sit down, Arthur," Caro ordered, rising like an angry goddess from the deep. "Mr. Terence has made a mistake and is about to leave. I think he's forgotten that he is not welcome."

"Not welcome?" Letty exclaimed. "Caro, what . . . ?"

"I haven't forgotten anything," Kit said, his eyes fixed on Caro's face. "I know I forced my way in, but I had no choice. There's something I must tell you."

Letty, who'd guessed from Caro's black mood that matters had not gone well after she'd retired last night, gave Kit a warning look. "Perhaps, my boy, this is not best time—"

"The best time, I'm afraid, is long past," he said bluntly.

Letty, alarmed, pushed back her chair and threw the two boys a pointed glance. "Then, my dear boys, perhaps we should leave your sister and Mr. Terence alone to—"

"You will not leave!" Caro declared furiously. "It's Mr. Terence who will leave."

Kit ignored her. "You needn't go," he said calmly to his aunt. "I won't be saying anything you and the boys can't be privy to. You may as well stay and hear my—"

"I shall call Melton and the footmen and have you thrown into the street!" Caro threatened between clenched teeth.

"You needn't bother," he retorted. "By the time they'd accomplish it, I'd have said my say."

But she would not listen. "Melton!" she shouted, stalking toward the doorway.

Melton, however, was already there. He was looking past her to the interloper. "Someone's here to see you, my lo—Mr. Terence," he said, coloring in confusion. "He wouldn't give me a moment to explain—"

A stocky fellow in army breeches and a soldier's cap loomed up in the doorway behind the butler and now burst into the room. "Praise be, Cap'n," he said, "*here* ye are! I've tracked ye down at last."

"Mickley!" Kit gasped. "What on earth . . . ?"

"I been searchin' fer ye everywhere. Damnation, Cap'n, ye should've left me yer direction. I had the devil of a time."

"Yes, but what's amiss?" Kit demanded worriedly.

"Bad news. There's been a terrible fire at the Grange. The stables're burned to the ground!"

Kit whitened. "Good God! The horses . . . ?"

"We got 'em out, don't ye take on about that."

Arthur, also pale, got to his feet. "All of them? Windracer, too?"

Mickley stared at the boy. "Aye, Windracer, too. But 'oo might you be t' know of Windracer?"

Caro had been listening with her brow puckered. "What do *you* know of Windracer?" she asked the batman curiously. "Are you speaking of the stables at *Crittenden* Grange?"

He pulled off his cap. "Well, yes, ma'am, a' course I am."

"But what has Mr. Terence to do with it?"

"Mr. Terence?" Mickley scratched his head in confusion. "'Oo might this Mr. Terence be?"

But the truth had already burst on Caro. "Oh, my *God*," she muttered, "it *can't* be!" She stood stock-still for a moment, trying to grasp the implications of this shocking new thought. Then she whirled on Kit furiously. "It's *you*, isn't it? *You're* the Vexatious Viscount!"

"Yes, I am. Kit Meredith of Crittenden."

She stared up at him in horror. "There is no Mr. Terence at all, is there? It was all a . . . a . . . *lie*?"

"Yes. I'm sorry."

"Sorry, *again*?" She clenched her trembling fingers. "I am growing weary of your sorrys, Mr. Ter . . . Your Lordship. Very weary."

Kit could not bear to see her so distraught. "Please, Caro, don't look at me so," he said softly. "I came here today to tell you the truth." He took a step closer to her and reached for her hand in a gesture he hoped would be soothing.

"To tell me the truth? Oh, yes, very likely!" She snatched her hand away and turned her back on him. "All this time . . ." she said, half to herself. ". . . to have lied to me all this time . . ."

Aunt Letty hobbled up to her. "Caro, my love, don't take on like this. He truly intended to tell you all."

"Wait a moment!" Caro stared at Letty as new implications burst on her. "You *knew*, didn't you? You knew all along!"

"Yes, of course I did," Letty admitted. "How could I not? He's my nephew, after all. I'd known him from birth."

Caro put a trembling hand to her forehead. "And the *boys*, too. They'd met him before." She peered at her brothers, white-lipped. "You've *all* been lying to me!"

Arthur sank down in his chair, shamed. But Gilbert, innocent of heart, met her horrified glare with stalwart courage. "It's your own fault, you know, Caro. You were too stubborn to meet with him, even after we told you what a good sort he was."

"Good sort? You can *still* call him a *good sort*?" Chest heaving, eyes distraught, and cheeks flushed with fury, she wheeled back to Kit. "I hope you're satisfied," she cried. "You've turned my brothers into liars, you've made it impossible for me to remain here with Aunt Letty, and you've made a . . . a complete fool of me. It's quite a d-day's w-work!" And bursting into tears, she fled from the room.

Letty, with a little sob, sank down at the table and dropped her head in her arms. The boys looked at each other miserably. Mickley, goggle-eyed, peered from them to the butler, who seemed to have frozen in place, and then to Kit's tight and tortured face. "Blimey," he muttered, blinking in confusion, "did I say somethin' wrong?"

17

Caro, red-eyed and weary after a sleepless night, came down to breakfast, but only after she was sure the others had finished. She had no wish to face her brothers or Letty just yet. They had lied to her; it was a breach of loyalty and honor that was hard for her to forgive so soon.

She sat down at her usual place at the table and discovered a letter propped up against her teacup. She lifted it with trembling fingers and broke the seal, fully expecting that it was an apology from the unspeakable person whose repellent behavior had replayed in her mind all night. But it was not. It was from her aunt Martha.

She was aware of a sting of disappointment, but she immediately pushed the feeling aside. She didn't really want to hear from Mr. Ter—Kit Meredith. She didn't! If she never heard another word from him as long as she lived, that would suit her very well. With a firm reprimand to herself for her momentary weakness, she turned her attention to the letter.

My dearest girl, Martha had written, *my sister has informed me of the troubles you've been enduring. You have my heartfelt sympathy. I understand that you are determined to change your situation, but before you do, I would like to offer some suggestions that may be of help. I would be greatly obliged, therefore, if you would call on me this afternoon at four. I remain, as always, your fond aunt, Martha Whitlow.*

Caro peered at the letter in astonishment. How could Martha have already learned of yesterday's contretemps? The clock had just a moment ago struck ten. Had Letty ordered her carriage at dawn? Or had she run to her sister yesterday, right after the scene had taken place, without even waiting for matters to cool a bit?

In any case, Caro could not see what suggestions Martha could make that would help her in this impossible situation. Martha would undoubtedly offer her a home, but she would not accept. She'd had enough of charity. This time she was determined that, somehow, she would find for herself and her brothers a place of their own. How could Martha possibly help her accomplish that? Nevertheless, she donned a bonnet and shawl and made her way to her aunt Martha's at the appointed time. It would have been rude and ungrateful to do otherwise.

Kaynes, the butler, admitted her. She entered the hallway to find Martha already standing there waiting for her. "My poor dear," Martha cooed as she kissed the girl's cheek, "you have been ill-used. I must apologize for my sister's part in your humiliation."

"I'm sure she didn't mean any harm," Caro said, instinctively rushing to Letty's defense. Letty was really a dear, and she'd always been very kind to Caro, too kind for Caro to listen to or to say anything detrimental about her. "It was her affection for her nephew that caused her to act as she did."

"Yes, that's true," Martha readily agreed. "Letty can never see a fault in Kit Meredith. But, my love, let's not speak of him. It's you I wish to speak of."

"That's very thoughtful of you, Aunt Martha, but I don't think—"

"Let's not discuss matters here in the hallway," Martha said, cutting her off. "Do go down the hall to the drawing room, my dear, and make yourself comfortable. I'll follow in a moment."

Caro did as she was bid. But as soon as she stepped over the threshold of the drawing room, she knew she'd made a mistake. She heard the door close behind her, and suddenly suspicious, she wheeled about to find Kit Meredith standing between her and the door.

For a moment she felt a surge of gladness, as she had in the morning when she discovered the letter. But the feeling was short-lived and immediately turned to absolute fury when she realized that he and Martha must have joined forces to trap her in this way. Her anger rendered her almost speechless. "You . . . you despicable *b-blackguard*!" she sputtered when she recovered her voice. "You've tricked me again!"

"I'm sorry," he said, nevertheless keeping his back against the door.

"Another of your sorrys! If that were true, if you were *truly* sorry, you wouldn't have done this."

"You're right. I'm not sorry." He seemed infuriatingly cheerful. "This was a necessary trick. You left me no alternative."

"If you don't let me out of this room," she said through clenched teeth, "I shall scream and make a dreadful scene."

"Scream away. Kaynes has orders not to hear."

She glared at him in frustration. "Hang it, have you no conscience? No ethics? No honor?"

"As a matter of fact, ma'am, I've been giving that question a great deal of thought," he said, "and I've decided that I have. I admit that my lying about my identity made me feel quite like a rotter, but—"

"There are no buts. You *are* a rotter."

"No, I'm not. After thinking over the matter dispassionately—something I should have done from the first—I realized that I am all but guiltless. Everything I've done has been with the best of intentions. My dishonesty and vacillation are more your fault than mine. Your own brother, Gil, put it best. He said that I'm a good sort, but that you are too stubborn to accept the truth of that."

"Hah! The judgment of a twelve-year-old!"

"A twelve-year-old with an open mind. A mind free of prejudice and . . . and infatuation."

She blinked. "Infatuation?"

"Yes, ma'am. *You* were blinded by prejudice and *I* by infatuation."

Caro felt her heart flutter. Was he saying he'd been infatuated with her? What did he mean by the word? That he cared for her? Or that he'd been only momentarily attracted and was now over it? It was most likely the latter. The term itself implied a temporary feeling. Suddenly she was overcome with shame. Why should she even *care* what the deuced fellow felt? Not only was he a liar, but his having kissed her so rudely the other night proved him to be a libertine. Why should she even be bothering her head about a liar and a libertine?

She wanted to stamp her foot in exasperation at herself, at him, and at everyone who'd been trying so hard to thrust him at her. To be forced to remain in this room alone with him was infuriating. She lifted her fists and began beating at his chest. "Dash it all, let me *out* of here!" she cried, her voice a strident rasp. "I won't be coerced—"

He caught her wrists and held them in a tight grasp. "Confound you, Caro, take a damper! Will-you, nill-you, you'll hear me out. I won't permit you to leave this room until you do."

She wrenched herself loose. Rubbing her wrists, she turned her back on him. "It seems I have no choice."

"I only want to discuss your legacy," he pointed out, "nothing more."

"I have no legacy," she retorted impatiently. "How many times do I have to hear that I do?"

"Just this last time. After you hear me out, I shall follow whatever instructions you give me, no matter how much I may dislike them. Does that meet with your approval?"

She shrugged. "I suppose so." She turned slowly and faced him. "Very well, then, say what you have to say. I'm listening."

"Thank you. Will you please sit down? I'd rather not present my case while standing here on guard duty."

She went to the sofa and sat down stiffly. He followed and took a chair facing her. "Now, then, ma'am, here is the situation. Mr. Halford, whom I believe you know and respect, has set aside a sum of money he believes my uncle intended for you to have. He and I and everyone else in the family believe the amount to be just. If you agree to accept it, my mission will have been accomplished, and this interview can end."

"My dear Lord Crittenden," she said with icy formality, "is

it not true that there is nothing written in the late Lord Crittenden's will to that effect?"

"Yes, but—"

"Then it was *you,* not Uncle Clement, who authorized the bequest?"

"That is only a technicality—"

"From your point of view, perhaps. From mine, it is an act of charity from you—someone who owes me nothing."

"Rubbish! Can't you be sensible, Caro? This is not charity on my part but a simple acknowledgment of what is fair!"

"Are we going to argue the point all day? It is my long-considered decision not to accept this so-called legacy. It was to avoid this very argument that I repeatedly refused to see you when you so repeatedly called at Mortimer Street."

"But—"

"Blast it, man, did you not say a moment ago that you'd follow my instructions? Well, I'm instructing you to accept my decision to refuse the money. Now have done."

Kit sighed. "Very well, ma'am. Now it seems *I* am the one who has no choice. I surrender. I have no more ammunition for this battle. Besides, I've spent too many weeks on this affair. It's time I got back to the Grange."

"Go, then. I certainly won't stop you."

"Not quite yet, ma'am, not quite yet. There's one more suggestion I must make. It concerns your brothers."

"My brothers?"

"They have legacies, too. Quite separate from yours."

"Separate legacies? I had not heard—"

"Frankly, it's a new strategy. I couldn't come here today without having one last ace up my sleeve."

"I don't see why you believe that 'ace' will make a difference."

"Don't you? Consider, ma'am, the full implication. It's one thing to refuse for yourself. But would it be fair to refuse for them? Why not let them decide for themselves whether or not to accept their own legacies?"

This was a poser. Caro blinked at him, arrested. "I don't

know. It was a clever ruse to divide the legacy. I hadn't thought . . ."

"Think about it, then. It would be a bit arrogant of you, wouldn't it, to decide for them?"

"Perhaps it would." She got up and began to pace. "They are not of age, you know," she suggested, throwing a glance at him.

"There is no stipulation that they be of age to accept a bequest."

"I thought that's what you'd say." She continued to pace for a moment before turning back to face him again. "You're assuming, my lord, that if you asked them directly, they would accept."

"I make no such assumption. They would certainly refuse if they thought you'd disapprove. They care too much for you to go against your wishes."

"But if it were not for me, they would take what you offered, is that what you believe?"

"Yes, I think they would. Arthur certainly would. He could then go away to school, something he very much desires. As for Gil . . ."

"What about Gil?"

"I'm not sure about Gil. He's too young to need or even to think about finances. He'd give it all to you, I suppose. So that you and he could have a home."

"But that's just it, don't you see?" She came back across the room, sat down, and leaned toward him. "I would then have the benefit of the legacy whether I wished it or not."

"And of course," he said with heavy sarcasm, "you can't allow that. It would be accepting charity, which is intolerable even from *Gil*."

"Mock me if you will, but charity, even when funneled through Gil, is abhorrent to me." There was a pause. "Of course, I *could* . . ." Her voice died away as she became lost in thought.

Watching her, his eyes lit with hope. She evidently was seriously considering a compromise. It would not be all that he wished—far from it!—but whatever it was, it was better than nothing. "You could . . . ?" he prodded.

"I could permit Gil to stay with Letty. He could pay his way, and I, since I would not be there, would not be beneficiary in any sense."

"But what about you? Where would you go?"

She lifted her chin. "That is no concern of yours."

"Don't be a fool," he snapped. "How could it *not* be a concern to me?"

She would not answer that question, tinged as it was with implications of emotions she would rather not probe. Instead she answered the earlier question. "If you must know, I shall be a governess. I've . . . I've already been offered a post."

"A post as governess. How splendid." He got up and crossed to her, grasping her shoulders angrily and pulling her up to her feet. "Damn you, Caro, do you really believe that's what Uncle Clement wanted for you?"

"We will never know, will we? If he'd wanted more for me, he should have seen to it properly. And as for you, Kit Meredith, you are neither family nor guardian to me, so your 'concern' is inappropriate. Furthermore, I'd appreciate your releasing your grip on me. You're hurting me."

He lifted his hands from her and held them high. "Very well, go. You've put me in my place. Since I'm not family or guardian or . . . or anything else, I hereby abolish all my concern."

"Thank you," she said, striding to the door.

"But before you go," he called after her, "let me be perfectly clear on what we've accomplished. Arthur may have his legacy and go off to Eton, is that right?"

"Yes, if he agrees."

"He will, if you will. And Gil may have his, too?"

She nodded.

Kit went to her at the door. "You realize, of course, that when you and Arthur are gone from Mortimer Street, Gil will be a very lonely child."

Caro's eyes fell. "Yes," she said, her voice breaking, "I

realize that better than you. But oh, dear God, what else can I do?"

"You can do what I've been asking all along. Take your bequest and make a home for the three of you."

She glared up at him. "I thought I'd made it clear that I can't do that."

"Then I have one last suggestion. You can give Gil to me."

She blinked. "What?"

"Let me take him with me to the Grange. It was his home, after all. He was happy there. And he does find me a good sort."

The idea was stunning. Gil, back at the Grange he loved so much! He could run about freely, outdoors and in, ride a horse, receive proper tutoring from Mr. Lutton and proper nurturing from a full household staff who already doted on him. What a blessing it could be!

She gazed up at the man, transfixed. He seemed so different today . . . different from the Kit Meredith she'd imagined . . . different from the Mr. Terence who never was. Could it be that he really was a "good sort"? Could a man be a liar, a dissembler, a trickster, and a libertine to one person and a good sort to another?

The fact was, though she was reluctant to accept it, that her brothers had taken to Kit Meredith from the first. And there were other things about him that seemed admirable—his instinctive courage when he'd dashed under the wild horses to save her life, for one. But how did one measure the good against the bad in a man's character? How could she tell if he'd make a proper guardian for Gil? Of course, if she *could* trust him with her brother, it would take a great load from her heart. It would be the answer to a prayer she didn't know she'd made.

"You are staring at me, ma'am," he said dryly.

She dropped her eyes from his face. "Sorry," she muttered.

"No need for sorrys. You were wondering if so dishonest a fellow as I would make a proper guardian for your brother."

"Yes, I was. How did you guess?"

"Your eyes give you away. Will it help you to feel more secure if I invite Letty to live at the Grange, too?"

Caro's eyes widened in astonishment. "Would you *do* that?"

"Yes, of course. It would give me a family . . . some much-needed life in that big, empty house."

She not only didn't know what to say but could barely speak. Her emotions had constricted her throat. She was finding it very difficult to think clearly about this man—a man who she'd made up her mind was a thoughtless, dishonest, selfish reprobate—who could also be kind and brave. "I must think. . . ." she murmured.

"By all means, think. And discuss the matter with Mr. Halford, or the aunts, or anyone else you wish. But most of all, talk it over with your brothers. Arthur has a great deal of sense, I think. And Gil is nothing if not honest. They will help you to come to a reasonable decision."

"Blast you, Kit Meredith, I'm quite capable of coming to reasonable decisions on my own!" She stalked off down the hall, head high, but after three steps she paused and turned back. "Nevertheless, my lord," she said with a touch of conciliation in her voice, "I shall discuss your suggestion with my brothers. And if it is what they wish, I shan't object to their accepting your offer."

Kit looked down at her with an unreadable expression. "Thank you, ma'am," he said softly.

Her throat constricted at the gentleness of his tone, but under no circumstances would she permit him to see that she was moved. "There's no need to thank me," she said coldly, putting up her chin. "I don't want and haven't earned your thanks. I'm not the same as my brothers, you know. Whatever they may think of you, I shall never be able to think of you as a good sort. Not till my dying day." And to keep from either saying or hearing another word, she ran off down the hall and did not stop until she'd shut the outside door behind her.

18

Matters concerning the bequest were settled very quickly. Once the boys understood that Caro would make no objections, they eagerly agreed to the arrangements Kit had made for them. Kit himself had departed for Shropshire, but his presence wasn't needed to make matters official. All that had to be done was for the boys to pay a visit to Mr. Halford's office, sign a number of documents, and shake the lawyer's hand. Less than a week later, an exhilarated Arthur, promising his tearful sister that he would write often, departed for Eton. Gilbert was due to leave for Crittenden a mere week after that. Everything was happening so quickly that there was no time for Caro even to entertain second thoughts.

Meanwhile, she paid a call on Mrs. Duckett to see if the post of governess had been filled. After all, two weeks had elapsed since her interview. Mrs. Duckett received her in her drawing room and, after hearing Caro explain that she was willing to accept the post, studied her through narrowed eyes. "The conditions're still the same," she said. "Seventeen pounds per annum, an' ye live in."

"Yes, I understand," Caro said bravely, swallowing her revulsion for the woman and her conditions.

Mrs. Duckett gave her a broad smile. "Then go home an' get yer things together, missy. Ye start on Monday."

What Caro could not know was that the position *had indeed* been filled. As Mrs. Duckett explained to her husband at dinner that night, "As soon as Miss Whitlow left, I ran upstairs an' gave Miss Fain three days' notice. An' a real pleasure it was to do it, let me tell ye." She chortled in glee as she added, "I exchanged 'er for a woman with a deal more style, an' I saved us five pounds o' salary in the bargain!"

Mr. Duckett, a successful manufacturer (he made brass Argand lamps, a very popular device for lighting the sitting rooms of the well-to-do), had little interest in his wife's miserly methods of household management. He merely grunted from behind his newspaper. It was not until he caught his first glimpse of the new governess, many days later, that his interest was captured. But, at this early stage, that dramatic moment was still far off.

Caro, ignorant of Mrs. Duckett's machinations or of the problems lying in wait for her in the Duckett household, returned to Letty's house. It was Friday. Gilbert would be leaving on Sunday. She had two days left of her familiar life—two days to pack up Gilbert's belongings and her own, two days to enjoy the company of what remained of her family, two days to accustom her mind to her dreary prospects. Major changes were occurring much too rapidly. How in this short time could she fully grasp their significance? But there was nothing she could do to slow things down.

Mickley came for Gil early on Sunday afternoon. Everyone in Letty's household, including Melton the butler, the cook, and both maids, came crowding out on the doorstep to see the boy off. Caro could not keep her tears from falling. Gilbert, giving Caro a last embrace, begged her not to cry. "I'll be fine, Caro, really I will," he assured his sister. "Aunt Letty will be moving up to Crittenden next month. And meanwhile, Kit will take the best care of me, I know he will. After all, he's really a very—"

"I know," Caro said, wiping her eyes. "A very good sort."

The next day there were more tears shed as Letty and Caro said their good-byes. "I wish you didn't find it necessary to do this, Caro," Letty sobbed, repeating the words for the hundredth time.

"But it *is* necessary," Caro said firmly. "For my pride, if nothing else."

And so, loaded down with a bulging portmanteau, a stuffed bandbox, and her pride, Caro waved a last good-bye to Letty and marched away from Mortimer Street to her new life.

19

Caro looked round the schoolroom with a small sigh of satisfaction. It had taken a month, but the Duckett children were at last beginning to show signs of acceptable behavior. Jackie, aged eleven, the eldest of the four Duckett children, was sitting at the schoolroom table struggling with his sums. Though his attitude was resentful, he was at least doing them. Florrie, ten, had read through half of *Dick Wittington and His Cat* with a semblance of enjoyment, although she was now standing at the window, pouting. Peter, seven, sat on the floor playing quietly with his toy soldiers, and Sally, the baby, not quite four, had fallen asleep in Caro's lap. It was a peaceful scene, out of the ordinary in the Ducketts' noisy household.

Caro had struggled hard, in the month of her employ, to achieve this sort of peace. She'd had to use all her firmness of character to make Jackie attend to his studies, to keep Florrie from throwing tantrums, and to prevent the younger children from following their bad examples. But she'd achieved some success. Every time they lapsed back into their unruly habits (which they did with discouraging frequency), she fixed them with a disapproving frown and warned them there would be no bedtime stories. Firmness, common sense, and control of her temper had helped, but the stories were her best device. No one had ever told them stories before, and they loved hearing them almost as much as they loved the candy treats their mother showered on them.

Florrie turned from the window. "I don't see why you have to go away this afternoon," she whined. "Jackie always teases me when you're not here, and pushes me about, and steals away my toys."

"Then why not take your reader to your own room and shut the door?" Caro suggested. "You know that I go to visit my aunt on Thursday afternoons."

"I wish you didn't have an aunt," the girl sulked.

I won't, after today, Caro thought with a stab of pain. This would be the last visit before Letty moved to the Grange. Caro could hardly bear the thought of being so alone. She'd had occasional letters from her brothers that cheered her—they both sounded quite happy in their new lives—but there was little else in her days in the Duckett household to nourish her soul. Her Thursday afternoons with Letty were the most pleasant hours of her week. Except for her brothers' letters, they were the only events she had to look forward to.

Florrie, however, was only concerned with her own wishes. "Mama says she didn't promise you that you could go away *every* Thursday," she said, beginning to sniffle.

"That is a matter best left to your mama and me," Caro replied, outwardly calm but inwardly irked that Mrs. Duckett had not only discussed such matters with the child but had also denied the terms she'd explicitly pledged. (*Three hours on Thursday afternoons,* she'd promised, *unless an emergency requires your presence.* Florrie's tantrums, being such commonplace occurrences, could scarcely be construed as emergencies.) Caro feared it would soon be necessary to confront Mrs. Duckett on this subject. Under no circumstances would she give up her free afternoons, even after Letty was gone. After spending every waking hour on the third floor of this disorderly household, shuttling between the schoolroom, the childrens' bedrooms, and her own tiny closet of a room, with no companionship but these selfish, loutish children and the dour upstairs maid, she needed time to herself. Desperately.

It had been soothing to Caro's soul to have a weekly visit with Letty, but after Letty was gone she would surely find other pleasurable activities to fill her Thursday afternoons. Even a walk in the park or a stroll through the Pantheon Bazaar would bring relief from the incredible strain of life with the Ducketts. Besides, there was still another aunt she could visit; Martha would still be living in London. She'd felt somewhat estranged from Martha since the day her aunt had helped Kit to trap her in her drawing room, but Martha had meant well. Perhaps it was time to forgive and forget.

But that was a plan for the future. Meanwhile, there was Florrie to deal with. Caro glanced over at the child framed in the window—a pretty little thing who could be almost lovely if she weren't so spoiled. "Now, Florrie," she said in gentle rebuke, "it will do you no good to sniffle. And use your handkerchief, please. You know very well that your sleeve is not meant for that purpose."

"I don't care," the girl whined, nevertheless taking out her handkerchief from her apron pocket. "I don't *have* to obey you, you know. You're only a servant."

"That's true," Caro said in unperturbed agreement, "but servant or not, the whole purpose of my position here is to see that you *do* obey me. Isn't that so?"

"I don't care. I don't *want* you going away all the time."

"Well, I'm not going away at this moment, so let us not waste this precious time together. Why don't you take up your book and read aloud to me the rest of the tale of Dick Whittington?"

Florrie allowed herself to be distracted, and the morning passed quietly enough. In the afternoon, despite Florrie's continued objection, Caro placed the children in the charge of the upstairs maid and, dressed in her prettiest straw bonnet, her most cheerful walking gown (a cornflower-blue figured muslin with a deep flounce that fluttered with every step), and a white shawl enlivened with silver threads, she started out on her few hours of freedom.

She flew down the stairway from the third floor, her spirit already dancing to the joyous music of freedom. But as she made the last turning she came face-to-face with a ruddy-faced gentleman who was making his way up. "Oh!" she said in surprise. But she deduced at once that this was Mr. Duckett, who'd evidently come home from his factory at an unusually early hour. Since he rarely came home before ten at night (by which time everyone on the third floor had retired), and since he'd not bothered to come up to see his children in the month since Caro had joined the household, she'd never met him before. Her one quick glance at him revealed a man who perfectly matched his wife—large, florid, and unabashedly self-assured.

"An' 'oo might ye be?" Mr. Duckett asked, stepping in her way.

"I'm Miss Whitlow," Caro said with a bob of a curtsy, "your children's governess."

"Ah, yes!" His bulging eyes lit, and he surveyed her from top to bottom with a measuring gaze so rude that Caro felt herself blush. "An' a right pretty poppet ye are, to be sure."

Caro did not like the words or the tone. "If you'll excuse me, sir," she said stiffly, "I'm just on my way out."

"Are ye? Without yer charges?"

"This is Thursday afternoon. My own time."

"Ah, I see. Then of course I won't keep ye." He stepped aside to let her pass. "But I'll see ye again, ye can be sure o' that," he murmured in her ear as she went by. The leer in his voice was upsetting enough, but then, to her utter astonishment, she felt a nip on her bottom. The dreadful man had *pinched* her! She wheeled about, instinctively ready to slap his face, but the fellow was marching away up the stairs, whistling with merry innocence.

She gaped after him, completely bemused. Never had she been so rudely used, but never before had she been a servant, either. Is this the way female servants were treated by their masters? It was certainly not so in any household she'd lived in before. Uncle Clement would never use a female in his employ so ill, she would swear to that.

She went slowly down the stairs, still thinking about the incident, and crossed to the small entryway. There she found Rudd, the butler, holding the front door for her. "Watch out for him, miss," Rudd said in an undertone. "Our Mr. Duckett can be more than a bother to a pretty poppet."

Caro nodded gratefully. "Thank you, Mr. Rudd," she murmured as she went past.

All the way to Letty's house, Caro mulled over the matter. Finally she decided that she would do or say nothing of the incident yet. She would stay out of the man's way (which, she surmised, would not be difficult, since she'd not encountered him once before in the entire month of her employ), but if any such incident recurred, she would take action. She didn't quite know what that action would be, but she *did* know that she'd not permit herself to be insulted a second time. Not she! Not even if it meant losing her post.

When she arrived at Letty's house, she found everything in a turmoil. The rooms were full of boxes and barrels and the paraphernalia of moving, and the servants bustled about from room to room seemingly without purpose or direction. Melton took her shawl with his customary impassivity, but the rest of the house teemed with confusion. "Oh, Caro, my love," Letty cried the moment Caro appeared in the sitting-room doorway, "you can have no *idea* of what a nightmare this packing up has been! My loveliest Chinese vase broke while Melton was wrapping it, we can't find the mate to the Chippendale corner cabinet, and the coachman says we shall have to hire two additional carts if we are to manage to move everything." She sank down upon a sofa that had already been draped with a Holland cover and wrung her hands. "And that's not the worst. What's really been keeping me awake nights is . . . is . . ."

Caro sat down beside her and took the trembling hands in hers. "What is it, my love? Tell me."

"I hate to complain, Caro. Kit has been the kindest—"

"Oh, pooh!" Caro interrupted, making a face. She had little sympathy for Letty's unwavering devotion to the Vexatious Viscount. "What has that rotter done now?"

"No, nothing," Letty assured her hastily. "Nothing at all. You mustn't call him that. He's done more for me than anyone can expect. That's why I shouldn't say a word."

"Dash it, Letty, speak up. You are making this move more

for my sake than your own. If something is amiss, you must *tell* me."

Letty shook her head. "I'm *not* moving for your sake, not a bit!"

"Very well, then, for Gil's."

"Not even for him. It's for me, truly it is. I have lived alone lo these many years, but I shall have a family in my dotage. You have no idea how happy that prospect makes me."

"Then what . . . ?"

Letty sighed. "It's just . . . well, you see, even though Kit has promised me an apartment of my very own, I know I shan't find space for all my things."

"Is *that* all that's troubling you?" Caro asked, not quite believing her.

"I know it sounds trivial, caring so much about glassware and chinoiserie and claw-footed tables and such. But you see, I've spent years collecting these things. I've grown accustomed to having them around me. If I must give them up—"

"Nonsense, my love," Caro reassured her, "you won't have to give up a thing. The Grange is positively *enormous*. You may take my word on it, for I spent years seeing to the upkeep. Just tell Lord Crittenden to give you the second floor of the west wing. There are nine rooms up there, all standing empty, in addition to a gallery and a large open space at the top of the stairs that I don't even know how to describe. It's a kind of reception room, with huge windows and a wonderful, beamed ceiling. Why, this sitting room, your drawing room, and your entryway could all be fitted into that one space! You'll not only have a place for everything, you'll have space for a great deal more."

"Oh, Caro, really?" Letty's watery eyes brightened. "How utterly delightful! But don't you think it would be presumptious of me to ask Kit for so much?"

"Not at all. The house has more than forty rooms. He'll probably be delighted to put a portion of them to such good use."

Letty, much relieved, threw her arms about the young

woman. "Caro, dearest, you have completely relieved my mind. You do seem to know the house so well. How I wish you were going with me!"

Caro dropped her eyes. "Yes, so do I," she admitted. "I do so love that place."

They sat in silence, each lost in her own thoughts, until Melton came in with the tea tray. Caro, now a servant herself, suddenly found herself wondering how he felt about Letty's move. Would he be able to find himself another post? she wondered. Was he worried about his future and that of the other members of the household staff? She studied his face curiously while he poured the tea, but his stolid expression told her nothing.

After he left, she couldn't help remarking to Letty that she felt sorry for him. "He must be quite heartbroken to be losing this excellent post after all these years."

Letty looked up from her teacup with raised brows. "Lost his post? Whatever gave you that idea? No, no, indeed he hasn't. Kit has hired everyone on my staff who wishes to come with me."

Caro gaped at her in astonishment. "Good Lord, why?"

"I'm sure I couldn't say, except that, as I've told you time and again, he's the very kindest of men."

But Caro would not accept the reasoning. "Really, Letty, no one is as kind as all that. And I have the clearest memory of His Lordship's first letter to Mr. Halford, in which he said he wanted only a staff of four."

"At that time he probably didn't know what sort of house he'd inherited," Letty said in Kit's defense.

Caro frowned at her. "Must you always make excuses for him?"

"I don't. But I will admit that his hiring my people was not a purely philanthropic act. I have the impression that he's having difficulty getting enough staff to work for him."

"Really?" Caro knit her brow in thought. "I wonder why. When I was running the Grange, I never had the least difficulty in finding people to work for me."

Letty had no answer, so the subject was dropped. But Caro couldn't help wondering if the baffling Kit Meredith was too hard a taskmaster or too tightfisted to his staff. What other reasons could there be for his having difficulty finding people to work for him? And if her reasoning was sound—if he really was hard-hearted and tightfisted—was she wise in leaving her little brother in his care?

She'd thought about the Vexatious Viscount often in the month since she'd last seen him. Her thoughts had been as confused as the atmosphere in this house. On the one hand, he had proven himself to be thoughtless and dishonest. On the other, he had sometimes shown surprising generosity and kindness. She did not know what to make of him. And to complicate the matter, she often dreamed of him in the guise of Mr. Terence. In those dreams she was still enamored of the fellow. When she woke up, she was always disgusted with herself.

But whatever she felt about him was unimportant. What was important was how her brother was faring in his care. She had to make it clear to Letty that she must be Gil's protector. Letty must observe the viscount's behavior with eyes unclouded with affection. Could she do it? Could Letty be counted on to be a fair judge?

The conversation between the two women, for the short time remaining, dwelt mostly on how they would miss each other and how often they would write. When the clock struck five, signaling the end of Caro's free time, they made their tearful good-byes and, arms about each other's waist, walked slowly to the door. "Letty, dearest," Caro asked before leaving, "will you keep a sharp eye on Gilbert and determine if he's truly content?"

"Of course I will," Letty answered promptly, but then her eyes became troubled. "Do you suspect he isn't?"

"No, no, I don't. His letters sound cheerful enough."

"Then why . . . ?"

"I'm not there to see for myself," Caro admitted frankly. "What if Gil is unhappy but reluctant to trouble me?"

"I scarcely think—"

"I don't think so either, not really. But let us suppose for a moment—I know you don't like even to consider the possibility—that Kit Meredith is not the paragon you think him."

"How can I suppose anything so unlikely?" Letty retorted, loyal to the end.

"But you *must* suppose it, if you are to judge Gil's situation with an open mind! Please, Letty, for my sake, do you think you can suspend your affection for Kit Meredith only long enough to make an objective judgment of what goes on at the Grange, and report back to me?"

"I can, my love," Letty responded, giving the younger woman a last, fervent embrace. "I can and I will."

Caro, returning the embrace, gave a silent, helpless sigh as she said to herself, The poor dear . . . she can't and she won't.

20

Rain fell steadily for three days after Letty's departure. People on the streets remarked that this was the most dreadful spring in memory. It certainly was dreadful for the Duckett children, for they were forced to remain indoors; the garden behind their house, where they usually played, was as soggy as marshland. Nevertheless, on the afternoon of the third day of rain, when the morning's downpour had subsided to a mild drizzle, Caro succumbed to Jackie's persistent pressure and let him go outside, though not before making certain that his head was covered with a wide-brimmed hat and his feet protected by a pair of sturdy galoe-shoes.

In the wet garden, near its overflowing pond, Jackie discovered a little frog. Since it was a delicate creature, and only three or four inches long, it could not jump far enough to escape capture. Jackie pounced on it with glee. He cupped it in his hand and studied with boyish interest its mottled green back and pale underside. But soon that interest waned, and he wondered what naughty use he could make of the creature.

The answer was not long in coming. He promptly hid the frog in the pocket of his trousers and came stealing up the stairs to the schoolroom. Hiding behind the doorjamb, he peered inside. Miss Whitlow was busy in the far corner, showing little Peter how to buckle his shoe. The baby was curled up on the window seat, napping. But his sister Florrie was just where he hoped she'd be. Jackie smiled wickedly. She was conveniently seated where he could get at her—at the worktable bent over a slate, struggling to copy a row of capital letters.

Jackie remained in the hallway until he'd removed his outer garments and heavy shoes. Then, with the frog in his hand, he stole into the room on tiptoe and crept up behind her. With two swift movements, he pulled back the neck of her dress and dropped the frog down her back.

Florrie's bloodcurdling screams reverberated through the entire house like a shrill alarm bell. Even the cook came running up from the belowground kitchen to discover what had happened. The first to arrive at the schoolroom doorway was Mrs. Duckett herself, her eyes popping and her breast heaving. Crowding behind her were the upstairs maids, Rudd, the butler, all four footmen, the cook, and even the girl from the scullery.

It was a mad, noisy, ludicrous scene that met their eyes. The baby, having been awakened so abruptly from her nap, was bawling in lusty, four-year-old panic; Florrie was jumping up and down, flailing her arms and shrieking like a banshee; the governess, with Peter clinging tightly to her leg, was vainly trying to calm Florrie's hysterics while attempting at the same time to reach down into the child's dress to recapture the tiny frog that was taking frightened little leaps deeper and deeper down her back; and Jackie was rolling on the floor, convulsed with guffaws, reveling in glee at the turmoil he'd caused.

It took Caro almost an hour to disperse the onlookers, unfasten Peter's grip on her leg, quiet the baby, banish Jackie to his room, settle Florrie on her bed with a cold cloth on her forehead, and restore a very frightened little frog to the pond in the garden. Only then did she permit herself to face the fuming Mrs. Duckett in the downstairs sitting room.

"Well, Miss Troublemaker, here you are at last," the woman said angrily, still fanning her overheated cheeks. "Is everything settled down?"

"Yes, ma'am," Caro assured her. "All's quiet now."

"And now, missy, what 'ave ye to say for yerself?"

"Say for myself?" Caro looked at her mistress with sincere surprise. "Why, nothing, ma'am. What is there to say? It was a little boy's prank that got out of hand, that's all."

"So *that's* how it seems to ye, eh? Well, missy, let me tell ye, it don't seem that way to me! Ye should never 'ave let Jackie out in the rain in the first place."

"It was only a drizzle. The boy had been cooped up indoors for days."

Mrs. Duckett threw down her fan in disgust. "I *don't* want to hear *excuses*, missy. I hold ye completely responsible for the entire foofaraw."

Caro shrugged. "I'm quite willing to accept responsibility, ma'am. I am Jackie's governess, after all. I fully intend to talk to the boy . . . to try to make him understand that all God's creatures, even frogs, should be treated kindly. But since no permanent harm was done, I don't think any other punishment is called for. I trust you will agree."

"Not by a long chalk I don't! It ain't Jackie but *you* who should be punished. Yer carelessness gave me a terrible jolt, and ye'll pay the price of it, missy, like it or not."

"Price?" Caro put up her chin. "What price?"

"Ye'll 'ave no Thursday afternoons fer a month. That's the price. An' it's a light punishment, considering the fright ye gave me."

Caro paled. "You must be joking!" she gasped.

"If that's what ye think, ye're fair and far off. I ain't a jokester when it concerns my children."

The governess's mouth tightened. "I'm sorry, ma'am, but I do not deserve—nor can I accept—such a punishment." Besides, I am promised to my aunt Lady Whitlow, on Thursday."

"Well, hoity-toity! Don't think ye can flummery me with yer la-di-da relations!"

"I don't mean to flummery you, Mrs. Duckett," Caro said firmly, "but I don't mean to lose my Thursday afternoons either. If you insist on this so-called punishment, I shall have to give my notice. The decision is yours. Meanwhile, if you'll excuse me, I shall go up and see how Florrie is doing." And she turned on her heel and stalked out.

Mrs. Duckett stared after her, nonplussed. She'd never had a servant talk back to her in that way, and her resentment lasted for several minutes. Then she remembered the governess's threat to give notice. Losing Miss Whitlow's services was something Mrs. Duckett did not want. It belatedly occurred to her that she might have gone too far. Had she painted herself into a corner? She didn't want to back down, but neither did she want to lose the best governess she'd ever had . . . and at such a bargain of an annual wage. She would have to do something to save the situation, but one thing she knew: she couldn't back down. Not Mrs. Amelia Duckett. She'd have to think of something else. But since Thursday was only two days off, she had to think quickly.

Later that evening, while finishing a late dinner, she posed the problem to her husband, who was, as usual, barricaded behind his newspaper. "It ain't that I'd mind 'er goin' off to Her precious Ladyship aunt," she explained after giving a detailed narration of the day's events, "but it'd bruise my pride to back down after all I said."

Mr. Duckett lowered his newspaper, his expression revealing a sudden interest. "This Thursday, ye say? It says here in the *Times* that there's to be a balloon ascent from St. George's Field on Thursday."

His wife glared at him. "An' what has that to say to the purpose?"

"Why don't ye take the little ones to see it? That way, you'd be taking the children off her hands, see? Then, with no one left at home, there'd be no reason yer little governess couldn't take herself off to this aunt o' hers."

Mrs. Duckett regarded her husband thoughtfully for a moment and then smiled at him with admiration. "What a good idea, Dan'l!" she exclaimed. "Damme if I don't do that very thing!"

"Good," he muttered, and retired behind the *Times* again.

"But who's to tell 'er? If I say she can go, it'll be just like backing down."

"Don't tell her," the man advised, not looking up. "Just leave the house. She'll take the hint."

"But what if she don't? What if she stays 'ere at 'ome? She'll give me 'er notice the very next day, if I'm any judge."

One of his hands reached out from behind the paper to pick up his brandy glass. "Do you want me to do it?"

Amelia Duckett peered across the table in surprise. "You?"

Mr. Duckett lowered his newspaper, carefully casual. "I can come home early, find her here without the children, and tell her she can go off."

"Would ye do that fer me, Dan'l? Come home early an' all?"

He shrugged and ducked back behind the paper. "Why not?"

She rose from her chair and went round to his. Leaning down, she planted a kiss on the top of his head. "Ye cin be a good man," she chortled in cheerful relief as she strolled from the room, "when ye've a mind to be."

When the door closed behind her, Mr. Daniel Duckett lowered the paper and reached again for his brandy glass. Instead of raising it to his lips, however, he turned it round in his thick fingers, gazing thoughtfully at the darkly colored liquid still left inside. A small smile turned up the corners of his mouth. With any luck, he thought, Thursday would turn out to be a fine day for a balloon ascension. And for some other activities he had in mind.

21

Thursday dawned with a darkly clouded sky. Mrs. Duckett kept peering out her window periodically all morning, checking the weather. If rain came, there would be no balloon ascension, and all her plans would go awry. By midmorning, however, the sky had lightened somewhat. It was just enough to give hope but not enough to give assurances.

Nevertheless, she went ahead with the plan. She'd avoided Caro all day Wednesday. Now, close to noon on Thursday, she sent her abigail up to the third floor with the request that the governess dress the children for an outing. "Ye mayn't b'lieve it, Miss Whitlow," the much-abused maidservant confided, "but the missus says she's gonna take all the children to see the balloon ascent, just by 'erself. She really thinks she can manage 'em without you along."

"Perhaps she can," Caro said, but without conviction.

"Huh!" The abigail sneered as she departed. "Very likely that is."

Caro sank down on a chair, wondering what this news signified. Mrs. Duckett had made no further reference to her "punishment," but the fact that "the missus" was taking the children away for the afternoon surely meant that she'd given in. The woman would not expect Caro to stay at home if the children were not there, would she?

The governess brought her four charges—their faces washed, their coats brushed, and their shoes shined—to the bottom of the stairs at the appointed time. Mrs. Duckett, dressed to the nines in a bright green walking gown, a velvet pelisse, and an elaborate bonnet trimmed along the brim with a whole row of plumes, ushered the children out the door without meeting

Caro's eye or exchanging a word with her. But she did speak to the butler in the governess's presence. "Rudd," she said loudly, "do not expect us before five."

Caro, more confused than ever by her mistress's peculiar behavior, nevertheless was determined to follow her usual Thursday schedule. She would take her three hours, as she always did, and let the chips fall where they may.

She clothed herself in her usual Thursday finery and hurried down the stairs just as the clock struck two. After making the second turning, she was startled to come face-to-face with Mr. Duckett again. This time, however, she had the distinct impression that he'd been lying in wait on the landing. "Mr. Duckett," she exclaimed, dropping an awkward curtsy, "good afternoon."

His answer was a leering smile.

His expression frightened her. She tried to brush by him and continue down, but he blocked her way. "Excuse me, sir," she said tightly, "but I must pass. I am late for—"

"It's my understanding that ye're not to have Thursday off, not for a while," he said, grinning.

She frowned at him. "I have no such understanding, sir. A period of three free hours on Thursdays is a condition of my employment."

"Is it indeed? Well, I've no objection, I assure ye. Such a pretty little poppet as you should have ye way. All I ask is a bit o' yer time."

"My *time*? Now?"

"Yes, m'dear, now. 'Tis an opportunity we shan't get very often." Without warning, he reached out, grasped her waist in his two thick-fingered hands, and pulled her to him. "A perfect opportunity."

"Mr. *Duckett*!" Gasping in shock, she tried to push away from him. "Let me *go*!"

"Come now, my girl, smile at me. I've never seen ye smile."

"Dash it, Mr. Duckett, release me *this moment*!"

But Mr. Duckett, pinioning her hands behind her with one of his own, took her chin in his free hand, lifted her head, and lowered his own. In horror, she realized that this repulsive man was about to kiss her! She wrenched her chin from his grasp and turned aside. "What are you *doing*?" she gasped, struggling to free herself.

"I been waitin' fer this chance, y'see, countin' the hours like a deuced boy," he murmured, tightening his hold on her.

She tilted her head back as far away from him as she could. "Do you want me to scream and cause a scene?"

"No one's here," he chortled. "I gave the staff the day."

This news alone was enough to turn her blood cold, but even more frightening was his hand, now grasping her bodice. Despite her obvious revulsion and the furious struggle she was putting up, he was reaching for her bosom. In desperation, she put all her strength into one last attempt to shove him away. It was an abrupt movement and took him by surprise. Keeping his grip on her bodice, he nevertheless tottered backward. Caro took that opportunity to wrench herself free. But he didn't completely let go, and she felt a rip of fabric at her bodice as she backed away. But he, close to the edge of the lower stairway, lost his footing in his backward movement. She saw him reach out with his hands, but there was now nothing he could grasp to stop himself. With a sharp cry of alarm he tumbled down, heels over head. It was a wide oak stairway with eighteen steps. She watched in horror as he bumped down four steps . . . five . . . six. She feared he would roll down all eighteen, but at six the rolling somehow stopped. He lay absolutely still, with his head lolling fearfully and his arms and legs spread wide over the entire width of three steps.

With her breath frozen in her chest, Caro cautiously crept down three stairs and stared at the prostrate form. At best, she thought in terror, he'd surely have broken some bones. At worst, he was dead.

She stood there staring down at him, aghast. She did not hear the knocking at the door, not its opening, nor the footsteps crossing the entryway. Stunned, her head throbbing and her knees shaking, she stood paralyzed, not knowing what to do next. It was only when she heard someone call her name that she was shaken from her stupor. She turned her head in the direction of the sound and found herself staring down into the shocked face of Kit Meredith. "Caro!" he exclaimed. "Good God!"

She could not believe her eyes. "Mr. *Terence*!" was the name that came to her lips, while her heart leaped up in her chest with a joyful feeling of relief, relief that here was someone to come to her aid.

"Kit," he reminded her as he came up the stairs two at a time. He looked from the body spread-eagled on the stairs to her ashen face and torn bodice. "Are you all right?"

"I don't know," she murmured, forcing herself to look down at the inert Mr. Duckett. "I . . . I . . . p-pushed him down the stairs. Is he d-dead?"

Kit knelt beside the body and felt for a pulse in his neck. "He's very much alive," he assured her, tapping Mr. Duckett's side with the toe of his boot. Mr. Duckett obligingly stirred and moaned.

Caro sighed in relief. "Thank goodness I didn't kill him."

"Yes," Kit agreed, getting to his feet, "for it gives *me* the chance to kill the fellow myself, when he comes to." He looked over at her with a worried frown. "He didn't hurt you, did he?"

"No, not really. The only damage seems to be to my gown." Flushing in embarrassment, she put a trembling hand to her torn bodice and tried to secure it. "What are you doing here, my lord? How did you manage to find me?"

"Aunt Letty gave me your direction. As for what I'm doing here, I came to—"

Another moan issued from the throat of the stricken Mr. Duckett. The fellow opened his eyes, groaned piteously, and struggled painfully to sit upright. Then he took notice of the two people who stood looking at him, one from the stair above and one below. At the sight of Kit Meredith, who was glaring at him in disgust, he flushed beet red. "An' who the devil might you be?" he asked in defensive belligerence.

"Never mind who I am," Kit said between clenched teeth. He

grasped the man by his neckerchief and hauled him to his feet. "Did you maul that lady?" he demanded.

"Wh-what business is it o' yourn?" Mr. Duckett countered nervously, backing up along the wall.

Kit tightened his hold. "I asked you a question."

"An' I asked you one." Duckett eyed the stranger sullenly as he tugged helplessly at his collar. "This is my house, blast ye. How'd ye get in here?"

"I knocked, but no one answered. Then I found the door unlocked. When you plan a seduction, you mawworm, you should be more careful about the door. That *is* what you were planning, wasn't it? To have your way with the governess?"

"Don't know as it's yer right to question me," the red-faced fellow muttered. In a spasm of fear, he wrenched himself loose and quickly scrambled up the stairs.

Kit sprang after him and caught him at the landing. He grasped the man by the lapels of his coat with his left hand and pulled him so close they were nose to nose. "You damned lecher," he hissed, "if you're well enough to make it up those stairs, you're well enough for a taste of my fives. Perhaps this will make you think twice before you try anything like that again." And with his right fist, he swung hard at Duckett's chin.

The blow knocked Mr. Duckett back against the wall with such force that he bounced off and fell forward on his face. He lay unmoving, legs spread out across the landing and one arm hanging pathetically down between the slats of the banister. Kit glared down at him for a moment and then, rubbing his knuckles, stepped over him and marched down to Caro. "Let's get out of here," he said, reaching for her arm.

"But Kit . . . Your Lordship . . ." she murmured dubiously, edging away from him up a stair. "I can't just leave like this. I have to give notice. There are the children to think about. And I'd have to pack my—"

At that moment they heard the front door fly open. "Rudd? Where the deuce are ye?" they heard Mrs. Duckett shout. Caro was startled. They were not to return before five, and it was now scarcely three. Something must have gone wrong. She threw Kit a pleading glance and went down to the entryway. Mrs. Duckett was just stepping over the threshold, surrounded by her four children. They all looked irritated and disheveled. Mrs. Duckett's fine bonnet was askew, her pelisse was dirty, and she looked a great deal less grand than she had when she'd started out. As for the children, Jackie's coat was torn, Florrie had spilled something on her dress, Peter had a scraped knee, and the four-year-old's nose was running. It had obviously not been a pleasant outing.

Mrs. Duckett, after giving the governess a quick glare, went directly to the mirror-topped table at the right of the doorway and proceeded to remove her bonnet. "I must say, missy," she said in disgust, "ye don't seem to have improved the conduct of these brats one whit! They were so wild I couldn't bear to stay another minute. We didn't even see the ascension. It seems to me that after a month under yer tutelage, they should be better beha—"

Florrie had wandered over to the stairway while her mother was scolding the governess and now saw fit to interrupt. "There's a strange man here, Mama," she said, staring up at Kit.

Jackie ran over to look. "And Papa's layin' on the landing," he added as he wriggled out of his torn coat.

Mrs. Duckett, puzzled, turned from the mirror and stalked to the foot of the stairs. She gaped for a moment at Kit and then turned to glare at Caro. "Miss Whitlow!" she exclaimed angrily. "Have ye been entertaining a *male guest* in my house without . . . ?" And then she caught sight of her husband, who'd just begun to stir and groan again. "Oh, my *God*!" she screeched. "What's been going *on* here?" She wheeled on Caro, her face reddening in alarmed hysteria. "Just what've ye been *doin'* . . . ?"

Caro bit her lip. "Perhaps, ma'am, you should ask Mr. Duckett. Peter, come here and let me see your knee."

But the hysterical woman would not be put off. "I demand to know what's *happened* here!" she shouted.

"And I demand," said Kit firmly, having seen quite enough,

"that Miss Whitlow *not* be the one to tell you. In fact, I demand that she have nothing more to do with you. Any of you. Even Peter with the bloody knee." And without waiting for Caro to say a word in reply, he lifted her up, slung her over his shoulder, marched past the openmouthed children and their flabbergasted mother, and stalked out the door.

22

Kit stood framed in Martha's drawing-room window, the dim evening glow silhouetting his form. Caro and Aunt Martha, from their places near the fire, could not see his face. Only by the intense fury in his voice could they determine the extent of his irritation. "Confound it, Caro, how can you possibly wish to go back there," he stormed, "after that blasted bag-pudding mauled you?"

"I *don't* wish to go back," Caro explained patiently, "but I haven't the luxury of indulging my wishes."

It was a few hours since he'd carried her from the Duckett household. ("Like a deuced sack of potatoes!" she'd snapped when he'd finally put her down.) They now sat in his aunt Martha's drawing room arguing bitterly about the day's events. Martha had insisted that they take tea and calm themselves, but even after she'd provided them with a sumptuous repast, they were not calm. "And to even *consider* returning to the employ of that vulgar woman is beyond my understanding," he went on. "She's too overbearing for words! And she hasn't the least appreciation of your merits—"

"Please, my lord, enough of your ranting. I've learned that there are many people—most, perhaps—who must endure putting up with overbearing employers if they want to eat."

"But *you* are not in such desperate circumstances," Martha put in. She'd promised herself not to interfere, but she could not contain herself. "You could live here with me and eat as much as you like. You know I'd be delighted to have you."

Caro merely shook her head. Her feelings about accepting charity had been expressed too often to bear repeating.

"But there are other posts," Kit said, coming forward and

taking a chair opposite her. "You could work for me. That, you know, is the reason I came to see you today."

"To offer me a post?" Caro asked suspiciously.

He raised his right hand. "The truth and nothing but."

"What sort of post, may I ask? As my brother's governess, perhaps?" she asked sardonically.

"Nothing so fine as a governess, I'm afraid," Kit answered in perfect seriousness.

Martha gaped. "Good heavens, Kit, you cannot insult the girl by asking her to take some menial post like a . . . a . . . housemaid!"

"I would not consider being a housemaid too menial," Caro said to her aunt, "except that I would never consider accepting His Lordship's employ. Whatever post he would offer me would be an act of charity . . . as much an act of charity as your offer to give me a home here."

"That, ma'am, is not true," Kit declared. "I truly *need* you to come to work for me. Sowell has left my employ because he believes I drove you from your rightful home. And he's convinced everyone else in Crittenden of it as well. No one will work for me unless he's truly desperate for employment. However, if you yourself came to manage the household, Sowell would be proved wrong. Then, perhaps, the locals would realize that I am not an ogre."

"Let me understand this." Caro leaned forward and peered at his face, her brow knit. "Are you offering me a post as your *housekeeper*?"

Kit dropped his eyes and shifted in his seat awkwardly. "I know you must find such an offer humiliating. . . ."

"Humiliating?" Martha jumped to her feet. "I should *say* it's humiliating! How can you insult—"

"No, Aunt Martha, wait," Caro said, putting up a hand to restrain her aunt. She remembered Letty's remark that Kit was having difficulty hiring a staff. Was it really because of her? If so, perhaps this offer was sincere. With her head cocked, she studied Kit closely. "Do you honestly believe you need *me* to organize your household?"

"Yes, I honestly do. To run it as you did for Uncle Clement."

There was a long moment of silence. Kit leaned forward, waiting. Finally Caro spoke. "What would my wages be?"

Kit's eyes lit with hope. "Whatever you think is fair."

"If I remember rightly, Uncle Clement paid his last housekeeper seventy-five pounds per annum."

"That would be agreeable to me."

"And to me, my lord," Caro said, throwing him a smile. She was coming up in the world, she thought, amused. She'd just made a great improvement over the seventeen pounds her last employer had offered her.

Kit grinned back at her, feeling a glow of triumph. "Do you think, ma'am, that now that we've come to an agreement, you could cease addressing me as my lord? My name, as you well know, is Kit."

"Oh, no, my lord. I must behave as any housekeeper would, and you must treat me as such. No proper housekeeper would call her master by his given name."

His grin died, and he jumped to his feet in irritation. "Damnation, Caro!"

She raised her head proudly. "You will be addressed as 'my lord' and I as 'Miss Whitlow.' Can you agree to that?"

Seeing the resolution in her expression, his shoulders sagged. The triumph had been short-lived. "If I must," he muttered.

"And of course I must have my own room in the servants' quarters."

Kit raised his eyes heavenward, striving for patience. "But, dash it, Caro, that won't be necessary. You could just as easily have an apartment in the west wing, near Letty."

She stiffened at once. "No! I must be a servant, like any other, or I will be forced to consider your offer charity."

"Now, Caro, *really*!" Martha objected.

Caro waved her to silence. "Well, my lord?"

He sank down in his chair and dropped his chin in his hands. "Very well, ma'am," he said, defeated, "the servants' quarters it will be."

"And I will eat downstairs with the other staff."

"Now, *that* is the outside of enough!" Kit slammed an angry hand on the arm of his chair before jumping to his feet again. He leaned over her until his face almost touched hers. "Ma'am, you go too far!"

"Yes, Caro, you do," Martha agreed.

Caro met his eyes, her own narrowed and unwavering. "Those are my conditions."

"Blast it, woman," Kit sputtered, pulling himself erect and stalking across the room away from her, "what will people *think* when they learn that you are not eating at the family table? What will *Gilbert* think? They will all assume it was I who banished you belowstairs. They will think me a *monster*!"

"Gilbert understands how I feel about charity. And as for everyone else . . ." She looked over at him, her lips twitching with a suppressed smile. "I don't care if they *do* think you a monster."

"Of course." Kit sneered. "How could I be so foolish as to expect you to care about anything so unimportant as my reputation?"

She ignored his ire. "Well? Have we a bargain?"

He hesitated, running his hand through his hair in a gesture of helplessness. Then he sighed deeply. "Very well, *Miss Whitlow,* we have a bargain. Though I feel in my bones I shall live to regret it. Aunt Martha, I'd be much obliged if you'd see to it that this impossible creature is ready for departure at noon tomorrow. Meanwhile, I bid both of you a good night."

"Good night, my lord," Caro threw after him, her tone sugary sweet.

He turned back to glare at her. "If I had a grain of sense, I'd throw you over my shoulder again, carry you back to the Ducketts, and drop you on their doorstep," he growled before slamming out of the room. "Then, at least, I'd *deserve* to be called a monster."

23

She was coming to the Grange at last, Kit thought with some satisfaction as he drove his open carriage along the rutted Shropshire road. He looked over at the seat beside him, where Caro sat with her hands primly folded in her lap. Given the girl's stubborn nature, he supposed that her presence was in itself a kind of triumph, but Kit could not feel as pleased about it as he would have liked. What she'd given with one hand, she'd taken away with the other. In her determination to take nothing in charity, she'd created a situation that made any friendly contact between them almost impossible. Even here in the carriage, before officially assuming her duties as housekeeper, she was keeping her distance, forcing them both into the roles of master and servant.

She'd even dressed herself like a housekeeper. Her lively curls were hidden away under a lace-edged widow's cap, on top of which she'd set a plain straw bonnet. Her dress was a dark blue muslin with only a white collar for trim. She looked very different from the glowing girl who'd sat beside him at the opera not so long ago. Not that she wasn't still beautiful. If she thought her severe clothing would change *that*, she was out in her reckoning.

She was out in her reckoning on many things, he thought. Too stubbornly proud, she interpreted every attempt he made to reach her as charity. Her determination to keep their relationship free of what she saw as charity was keeping them frustratingly distant from one another. How could he even get close enough to her to tell her that he loved her? And if he could manage it, how would the irritating chit react? If he offered her his name, his wealth, his heart, would she call it charity?

This trip to the Grange was a sign of what was to come. He'd looked forward to it, for they would be sitting side by side on the box for several hours. It was, he'd hoped, a chance for intimate conversation. But she was so determined to hold to her role that she'd hardly exchanged a word with him. She quelled every attempt at conversation by giving monosyllabic responses to every comment. An hour before, he'd stopped the coach at an inn and asked her to join him for a light luncheon. "Oh, no, thank you, my lord," she'd said. "It would not be seemly."

He'd eyed her in disgust. "Cut line, Caro! You are not yet my housekeeper. And even if you were, there's no one but my tiger to see you being unseemly."

"We should not slip into bad habits, my lord," she'd responded with firm formality.

He'd been so irked that he'd whipped up the horses and wheeled out of the inn's courtyard without another word. If she wanted to play this game, he would show her he could play it as well as she.

When the carriage rolled onto the curved drive in front of the Grange, Mickley was the first on hand to greet them. He was followed by Melton, Letty's butler, who, on his arrival at the Grange a few weeks earlier, had assumed the post that Sowell had vacated. Mickley stepped aside to give the butler the honor of greeting the lady, while he held a whispered conversation with Kit. "Convinced 'er to come, I see," the batman said, winking. "Well done."

"Not so well done," Kit grumbled. "I may have convinced her to come, but I've had my way in nothing else. That stiff-necked female doesn't bend even when you think she's bending."

Meanwhile, Melton handed Caro down. "Good afternoon, Miss Whitlow," he greeted with a smile of unbutlerish warmth. "Welcome back to the Grange. Everyone, belowstairs and above, will be so glad to see you."

No sooner had her foot touched the ground than Gil came

dashing out of the house. He flung himself upon her in an enthusiastic embrace. "Caro!" he cried joyfully. "You're here at last!"

To Caro's eager eyes the boy seemed to be almost a foot taller, brimming with health and good spirits, and brown as a berry. It was clear that her decision to send him off with Kit had been a good one. A better one, she was sure, than the decision to come here herself. All the previous night she'd vacillated between sticking to her decision and changing her mind. If only she could be sure she was really needed here . . . that it was not an act of kindness on the viscount's part to employ her. She could bear to be beholden to him for her brother's sake, but not for her own. If she should discover that he didn't really need her to run the house, she'd promptly take her leave.

At that moment she looked up to see Letty hurrying out the door. The two women embraced delightedly. Caro was relieved to see the elderly woman look so hale and well rested. She'd been afraid that Letty might not thrive away from the London she was so accustomed to, but that was obviously not the case. Letty's color was good, she barely leaned on her cane as she walked, and, Caro noticed, she was not quite as stooped as she'd seemed in London. "The country air has done you good, Aunt Letty," she exclaimed.

"Oh, yes, indeed it has!" Letty beamed, squeezing her hand. "It's been quite wonderful. I love it here. And wait until you see my rooms. They're even more spacious than you described!"

But seeing Letty's apartment had to be put off, for Gil was determined to show Caro all the changes that had been made on the grounds since she'd left. The boy grasped her hand and dragged her round the property, babbling excitedly as they talked about the two huge fish he'd caught when Kit had taken him fishing, about the times Kit had let him drive the curricle, and about the wonderful Spanish horse Kit had given him. "I call him Bellerophon," Gil said with eyes shining, "because when I gallop him, I feel like we're flying!"

This was obviously a happy boy, except when he had to answer questions about his studies. Mr. Lutton, Gil informed her, was his tutor, but he was evidently reluctant to go into any further details. Caro did not press him. There would be time to discover for herself what the problem was.

Gil showed her the site of the new stables, where work had already begun. The burned-out debris of the old stables was almost gone, and the foundations of the new already laid. So Kit *was* able to find people to work for him, Caro thought. Was that evidence that he didn't really need her after all?

There were other signs that work had been progressing on the grounds. The most outstanding progress had been made at the back of the house, where the drainage ditch that had remained gapingly open for years was now covered over. The ground was still raw, but Caro could see that, when it was properly landscaped, there would be a remarkable improvement in the appearance of the rear of the house and the back fields. She wondered if His Lordship would permit her to extend the kitchen gardens to this area. The thought pleased her, and she smiled to herself. Perhaps there were a few things she *could* do here.

As she and Gilbert turned to walk back to the house, Caro tried to prepare the boy for her changed position in the household. "Before I was almost mistress in this house," she explained, "but now I am only the housekeeper." Carefully, she described the conditions under which she'd agreed to come.

Gil seemed to take it all quite well until she told him that she'd not be taking meals with the family. "Oh, I *say*!" he cried, his face falling. "That's much too rare and thick! If you can't sit at table, then I won't either. We can *both* eat in the servants' hall."

"No, Gil, don't raise a dust. You're His Lordship's guest. I'm but a hireling. Lord Crittenden *did* invite me to join you all at table, but I didn't think it would be right. It would adversely affect my relations with the staff, you see."

Gil nodded glumly.

"Don't look so sad, Gil," she said, putting a comforting arm about the boy's shoulder. "We're lucky, really. This is a post I shall very much enjoy, especially when I compare it to being governess at the Duckett ménage. I'll be quite content to be eating downstairs. And, best of all, I'm *here*. You'll see me every day. I'll even come to your room at night to tuck you in."

"I'm too big to be tucked in," he said, brightening nevertheless, "but it'll be like old times when you come in to bid me good night. Kit's been doing it, you know, but now I'll have both of you."

"Kit comes in every night?" Caro asked, surprised.

"Oh, yes. And sometimes he tells me stories. He knows the most exciting tales, the kind boys like. You know the kind I mean . . . stories about pirates, or battles, or raging beasts with bloody fangs."

"Bloody fangs, eh? Just the sort of tale to lull a boy into peaceful sleep," she muttered dryly.

"Take a damper, Caro," the boy snorted. "The stories don't frighten me."

"*Take a damper?* That's not the sort of phrase to use to a sister, is it?"

"Yes, it is, if the sister's being silly. Kit's stories are the best I've ever heard!"

"Well, I suppose it *is* very kind of him," she said, wondering again if she were really needed here at all.

By the next day, however, she realized that Lord Crittenden had not exaggerated his problems. She *was* really needed. While His Lordship had managed to increase the grounds staff, the household staff was much diminished. There were signs of neglect everywhere, from the scullery to the upstairs bedrooms. The cook, who'd been on the verge of giving notice because of lack of kitchen help, greeted her with open arms. "I'm that glad t' see ye, ma'am!" she declared, tears in her eyes. "Now I know things'll be right."

And Gladys, the only upstairs maid left of the four Caro had employed, described how she'd had to skimp on the polishing and dusting and other necessary chores. "I just 'ave to skip the guest bedrooms an' the upstairs sitters, an' I never even *look* into the rooms in the east wing," she admitted. "There just ain't time."

That very afternoon, Caro asked Mickley to drive her into town, where she paid calls on some of the young women whom she knew or who had worked for the old viscount. By the time she returned to the Grange three hours later, she'd hired three more maids, a scullery, and two footmen. Mickley was impressed. "Ye do 'ave a way with ye, ma'am," he said admiringly. "That saucy baggage, Betty Rhys, wouldn't even talk to me when I tried to 'ire 'er."

"She was overly devoted to me, I'm afraid. That's why she left. When you tried to rehire her, she'd already started to work for the miller." Caro flicked a teasing glance at the batman. "Besides, Mr. Mickley, Betty told me that when you called on her you were more interested in flirting than hiring."

"Me, *flirtin'*?" Mickley drew himself up in offense. "I never did! I ain't the sort fer such bobbery. An' even if I was, I wouldn't choose Miss Betty Rhys."

"And why not, pray? Don't you want to settle down someday with a pretty lass?"

"Per'aps, but not with 'er sort. She's too sharp-tongued and too . . . too . . ." He searched about for a proper word that wouldn't offend his companion. "Too plump."

"Pish-tush, Mr. Mickley, you *are* a finicky fellow."

He grinned with self-satisfaction. "That I am, ma'am, that I am. Even the cap'n says so."

"Does he? You are referring, I take it, to the viscount. Do you always address him so?"

"Yes, ma'am. I called 'im Cap'n fer so many years, I can't custom meself to callin' 'im Yer Lordship."

"Doesn't he mind your informality?"

"Mind? *'Im?*" Mickley snorted. "The cap'n ain't in any manner, shape, nor form so 'igh in the instep as t' mind what I call 'im."

Caro studied the fellow thoughtfully. "It seems you stand on very good terms with him."

"I'd say so, yes."

"Good. Then you are the very best person to speak to him for me about plans for the house and changes I'd like to make."

"Yes, ma'am, but why can't you speak to 'im yerself?"

"Because I . . . well, you see, I'm not on such good terms with him as you are. You can serve as our go-between. And you can start, when we get home, by asking him if I may set up a kitchen garden on the fresh soil covering the ditch."

"I'd be 'appy t' do it, Miss Whitlow, but 'e's surely goin' to ask me why you don't ask 'im yerself."

"It isn't proper for the housekeeper to deal directly with His Lordship. You act as his steward, don't you?"

"We never put no name on what I do fer 'im. I'm 'is batman, that's all. Like a valet, I s'ppose."

"No matter," Caro insisted. "You can still bring him messages from me, can't you?"

Mickley eyed her worriedly, shaking his head in disapproval. "The cap'n won't like no go-betweens, ma'am. Take me word fer it. He won't like it at all."

24

Word spread rapidly through the neighborhood that Miss Caroline had come home to the Grange. Mr. Lutton was among the first to hear the news. Eager to lay eyes on her again, he took the opportunity, that very evening, to call at the Grange to extend a personal welcome. Melton admitted him. "If you'll wait in the library, Mr. Lutton," the butler said, "I will tell His Lordship you're here."

"No, Melton, not His Lordship," the vicar said cheerfully. "It's Miss Caroline I've come to see."

"Miss Whitlow?" Melton blinked at him for a moment, nonplussed. One didn't ask a housekeeper's caller to wait in the library. But of course, he reasoned, Miss Whitlow was different. Exceptions would have to be made for her. And, besides, no one was in the library at the moment. He gave a mental shrug and pointed the way to the library. "Very well, sir, if you'll wait there, I'll get her."

He hurried down the hall toward the back stairs, but as he passed His Lordship's study the door flew open. Mr. Mickley came stalking out, with the viscount close behind him. "Don't rip up at me, Cap'n," the batman was saying. "It ain't my fault she acts so brummish."

"I didn't say it was," His Lordship snapped. Then he noticed the butler. "Melton," he said, his voice angry and his words clipped, "find Miss Whitlow and send her here to me at once."

The butler blinked. "Miss Whitlow, Your Lordship?"

"That's what I said."

"But . . ." Melton made a gesture in the direction of the library. "But she's expected in—"

"Didn't you *hear* me, man?" the viscount shouted. "I said *at once*!" And he strode back into his study.

Melton and Mickley exchanged looks. "You'd better find 'er," Mickley said, walking off. "He's in a devil of a pucker. I knowed 'e would be."

Melton gaped at the study door, for he'd never heard His Lordship shout before. He wondered what Miss Whitlow had done to raise the viscount's ire. But since there was no one to tell him, and there was nothing he could do about it anyway, he hurried down belowstairs to find her.

The housekeeper was not in the servants' hall or in the little room beside it that she'd already made her office. He wandered about uselessly for several minutes until it occurred to him to look in the kitchen. There she was, helping Cook prepare the family dinner in the absence of the new kitchen maid (who was not to start work until the next day). "Ah, there you are, ma'am," Melton said, panting from his exertion. "You're wanted upstairs. You've a caller in the library—it's Mr. Lutton to see you—and a summons from His Lordship."

Caro frowned at him. "A *summons*?"

Melton nodded worriedly. "A definite summons. If I were you, I'd see His Lordship first. He sounded . . . er . . . chagrined."

"Did he, indeed?" She put her chin up in a way that boded no good. "Well, he can cool his impatience for a moment or two. Did you say you put Mr. Lutton in the library?"

"Yes. I didn't think it fitting to bring him down to the servants' hall."

"You were quite right," she said, taking off her apron. "It would be awkward for all concerned." She tossed her apron on a chair and started toward the stairs.

Melton trotted after her. "I think I should tell you, Miss Whitlow, that His Lordship said 'at once.'"

"Thank you, Melton. You've delivered the message. Leave the rest to me."

She went upstairs, determined to ignore Kit's "summons."

She was in his service, that was true, but she was not his slave. She didn't have to jump whenever he chose to snap his fingers.

On her way to the library, however, she had to pass by his study. She did not pause, nor did she deign to so much as glance at the door. But he must have heard her step, for she hadn't gone another half-dozen paces before the study door was flung open. "Miss Whitlow! In *here,* please," he ordered.

"Yes, Your Lordship, in a moment," she said, making a saucy little curtsy. "I am expected in the—"

"In *here,* I said!" he roared, holding the door open for her.

It was obvious that the order should not be ignored. With a sigh of resignation, she turned about, strode past him through the doorway, and went inside. He followed and shut the door with a slam.

Caro looked quickly about her. This was the first time she'd seen his study. It was a room that had been kept closed when the old viscount was alive, but she saw now that Kit was wise to have chosen it. It was a good-sized room, with one wall completely taken up with large windows offering a lovely view of the south lawn. The other walls were lined with bookshelves, all of which stood empty. The reddish rays of a setting sun shone slantwise across a massive desk covered with a disorderly array of books, ledgers, and papers. More books and ledgers overflowed the wooden boxes that were stacked willy-nilly about the room, obviously waiting to be shelved. "What a shambles," she said, running a finger over a dusty mantelpiece. "I shall send one of the maids in here tomorrow to straighten things up."

"If this were a task to be done by a housemaid," he retorted impatiently, "don't you think it would have been done by this time? This is the mess the late viscount left behind. Records, accounts, documents, bills, contracts, leases, and God only knows what else! I have to go through it all page by page. It will probably take me a year. But don't think, ma'am, you can throw me off the track. I didn't send for you to discuss this disarray."

"No, my lord, I didn't think you did."

"No, you probably know *exactly* why I did. How dare you, ma'am, suggest to Mickley that he be used as go-between? Am I such an ogre that you cannot speak to me directly?"

"You are now," she taunted.

"Confound you, Caro, be serious!"

"Not Caro, please. I am Miss Whitlow, remember. Your housekeeper. And to answer your question regarding my need for a go-between, let me point out that it is not seemly for me to be forever running to you with questions and problems."

"See here, *Miss Whitlow,* I did not hire you to teach me how to conduct myself with my servants. I *like* informal relations with my staff. Any one of them may speak to me freely. My door would be open to any woman who was my housekeeper, even if her name were *not* Whitlow. In fact, my door is open to anyone in my employ."

"Then, if I may speak honestly, my lord, I think you have much to learn about your position. If you kept your door open to the whole staff, you would find yourself with no time for anything else. You'd be inundated with complaints from morning to night. Of course, you must behave as you see fit. But then, so must I. I intend to conduct myself as a proper servant should. Just as the maids and the cook should bring their problems and complaints to me, I should bring mine to Mr. Melton and Mr. Mickley as your stewards. Such behavior is the only kind I can consider seemly."

Kit ground his teeth in fury. "If I hear that word *seemly* from your lips again, ma'am, I shall . . . I shall *box your ears*!"

Her lips twitched to suppress a laugh. "Now, that, if I may say so, my lord, would *truly* not be seemly."

He stared at her for a moment and then threw up his hands helplessly. "For a servant who claims her behavior is seemly," he muttered, turning to the window, "you certainly have managed to snatch the upper hand away from me."

"The upper hand? I don't know what you mean."

He gazed moodily out of the window. "I mean, ma'am, that you've found ways to thwart every order I've given you."

She blinked at his profile, lit in a golden light by the setting sun. His brow was knit in frustration, and the corners of his mouth turned down in an angry frown, but he was nevertheless wrenchingly handsome. Something in the way the light accented his features reminded her of how he'd appeared to her when she believed he was Mr. Terence. The memory of Mr. Terence made her breast clench in pain. If only Mr. Terence had been real, she thought, what a happy couple they might have been! But aloud she only said, "I'm sorry, my lord."

"So am I," he muttered. "Sorry that I was not born Marcus Terence, with no connection to Crittenden Grange . . . or to you." He turned and looked at her through the golden light. "But I'd hoped, when you agreed to come here, that we could at least be friends."

Her throat tightened. "I think it's too late for that," she murmured, finding it difficult to keep her voice steady. How strange it was that their thoughts had been so similar. She had better flee, she thought, or she might burst into tears. "May I be excused, my lord?"

He winced. "Yes, go." He made a dismissive motion of his hand and turned back to the window. "And use Mickley as your go-between, if you must. Talking to you face-to-face doesn't do me much good anyway."

25

Caro stood in the corridor outside Kit's office, trying to get hold of herself. She had to erase the image of Kit's sunlit profile from her mind. That image, and its impact on her emotions, was too troubling. When she'd accepted his offer of employment, she'd pushed from her mind the possibility that close proximity to him might bring painful reminders of Mr. Terence . . . reminders of the infatuation she'd felt for the man who never was. If she was to remain here as housekeeper, she would have to school herself to banish Mr. Terence from her thoughts . . . and even from her memory.

Determined to do just that, she squared her shoulders and marched down the hall to greet her visitor. She found Henry Lutton looking over the books on the library shelves, patiently awaiting her arrival. "Henry, my dear," she said with enforced heartiness, "how *good* of you to call."

He turned from the bookshelves, his long face brightening at the sight of her. "Caro! Back with us at last!"

They sat down side by side on one of the room's two window seats, smiling at each other like the old friends they were. "You are looking well," she told him.

"And you, my dear, are more beautiful than ever."

"Oh, yes, quite"—she laughed—"especially in my cap and bombazine. It's not like you, Henry, to offer me Spanish coin."

"You know me better than that." He tilted his head and studied her carefully. "I can't say I like the cap, but the face under it is as lovely as ever."

"What balderdash! But never mind. Tell me all the town gossip I've missed in these past months."

"*You* are the primary subject of gossip these days, Caro.

Everyone is agog to learn what brought you back to this house."

"Are they? It's not a story that will feed much gossip, I'm afraid. It is merely that I wasn't happy as a governess, and when Lord Crittenden offered me this post as his housekeeper—"

"Housekeeper?" Mr. Lutton's expression darkened, and he leaped to his feet. "Good heavens! I had no *idea* . . . ! You poor dear, how can you permit that arrogant fellow to humiliate you in this way?"

Caro stared at him in surprise. "Humiliate me?"

"It was bad enough when he drove you from your home. But for him to bring you back as a servant . . . !"

"Just a moment, Henry," she said, putting up a hand to stop him from jumping to conclusions. "As Gil likes to say, take a damper! Your interpretation of the events is not at all fair. Lord Crittenden is not in the least arrogant. Not only did he save me from a dreadful situation at my last post, but he's given me a position for which I'm well qualified and in which I shall be quite happy. I'm doing exactly what I used to do—but without the title and wages—for the old viscount. This time, however, I'm being given a very generous salary."

The vicar, not quite mollified, sank down beside her again. "I can't quite believe that you don't mind being a servant in the place where you were once the mistress."

"Mistress?" She blinked for a moment as a new thought struck her. "I was never the mistress here, Henry. Strange, but I didn't realize until this moment that I was as much a servant then as I am now. I was but a poor orphan Uncle Clement took in in kindness." Her eyes widened with shock. "A *charity* case!"

"No, no, child," the vicar cried, taking her hand in his. "Your uncle Clement never thought of you in that way."

Confused though she was by this new way of looking at her past, she didn't wish to dwell on it now. She passed a hand over her forehead to wipe the thought away. "Let's not speak of it anymore, Henry," she begged. "Let's speak of something that

I'm much more concerned about—Gil's studies. From what he's told me—although he's said very little—I surmise that he's not doing very well."

"No, I'm afraid he's not. He seems to have become a little wild."

Caro's brows rose in alarm. "Wild?"

"Perhaps that is not precisely the right word. Restless might be a better one. He prefers running about outdoors, throwing a ball about, or trotting off to the river to fish, or riding his horse posthaste over the hills. I told His Lordship that the boy was too young to have his own mount, but my advice was ignored. The result is that Gilbert sits over his books as if he were imprisoned, inattentive and bored, waiting only for the three schoolroom hours to end."

"Oh, dear," Caro murmured worriedly.

The vicar, having said the worst, now felt it time to give comfort. "I don't question the boy's ability to learn, Caro. He's quite bright enough. I've no doubt he could master it all if he'd only concentrate."

She nodded. "I'll speak to him. Perhaps—"

The library door opened at that moment. Lord Crittenden entered with an armload of books. At the sight of the vicar seated in the window and holding fast to Caro's hand, he stopped short. "Oh!" he said, reddening. "I'm sorry. I was not told . . ."

"Good afternoon, Your Lordship," the vicar said, rising. "I came to say hello to Miss Caroline. I've not seen her for several months, you know."

Caro rose as well, slipping her hand from his grasp as she did so.

"Please don't let me disturb you," Kit said awkwardly, backing to the door. "I'll come back later. . . ."

"No, please, my lord," Caro urged, "we've quite finished. I am needed downstairs, at any rate."

"And since I am about to be deserted by the lady, my lord," Mr. Lutton said, crossing the room to him, "let me help you with those books."

"Well, I . . ." Kit glanced from one to the other and then shrugged. "I'd be glad for your assistance, Mr. Lutton. I was going to find place for them on the shelves. They've been packed away in boxes, you see, but they'll be much more accessible if they're here in the open."

"Then, if you gentlemen will excuse me . . ." Caro said, starting toward the door.

"Just a moment, ma'am," Kit said. "Mr. Lutton, since it's already past six, and the sorting of these volumes will probably take a while, I'd be pleased to have you remain to dine with us."

"Why, thank you, my lord," the vicar said. "I'd be delighted."

Kit turned to Caro. "Will you please tell Cook we'll have a guest for dinner?"

"Yes, of course, Your Lordship," she said, and whisked herself out.

She had only gone a short distance down the hall when she heard the library door open and close. Then she heard Kit call her name. "Miss Whitlow?"

She turned. "Yes, my lord?"

He strode down the hallway toward her. "I don't suppose you'd agree to have dinner with us," he said, his eyes pleading. "Lutton came to see *you,* after all."

"You know the rules," she said. "Besides, I may have to help serve."

He made a face. "That's what I thought you'd say." He wheeled about and started back to the library, muttering angrily to himself.

"Did you say something, my lord?" she asked dryly.

"I'm only complaining to myself about my unsalvageable reputation," he threw at her over his shoulder. "When Mr. Lutton lets it be known in town that I made you serve dinner and that I then banished you belowstairs to eat, that will finish me. I'll become a monster by tomorrow. Sooner than I expected."

She eyed his retreating back speculatively. He was right

about his reputation, she thought. If even Mr. Lutton, the vicar of Kit's own parish, already thought of him as arrogant, what would the rest of the townsfolk think of him if they heard that she was not welcome at the family table? This was not what she'd intended when she'd refused to eat with him. She didn't mean to make people think him a monster. "My lord?" she called after him.

He'd just put his hand on the library doorknob. "Yes?"

"I've decided that I'll come to dinner after all."

His brows rose. "Will you, indeed?"

"Yes," she said, lifting her chin and striding off away from him. "This once."

26

"Admiral Swain smiled coldly as he watched the first mate leading the blindfolded pirate to the yardarm. 'You'll hang there dangling and kicking your legs for a good while before you die!' the mate mocked, laughing cruelly. Black Bart, head erect, walked toward the tip of the yardarm, while the first mate and the admiral exchanged looks of satisfaction. Then the admiral spoke. 'The high seas will never again be troubled with the likes of Black Bart!' "

Kit was telling Gil a sea story. Outside in the corridor, Caro stood listening. It was just the sort of story Gil had led her to expect, full of swashbuckling action and buckets of gore. Gil was obviously enraptured, for when Kit's voice ceased, the boy let out a cry of objection. "Oh, I *say,*" he groaned, "you're not going to stop now!"

"To be continued tomorrow." Kit laughed. "Good night, boy."

"But, Kit, will that really be the end of Black Bart?" Gil persisted anxiously.

"You don't think I'll answer that now, do you? I want you in suspense. Never mind, old fellow. You'll get the next part soon enough."

Outside Gil's bedroom door, Kit came face-to-face with Caro. "Were you waiting for me to finish?" he asked, greeting her with a warm smile. The dinner with Mr. Lutton, earlier that evening, had been a pleasant affair, and Kit was still feeling grateful for her relaxation of her rule about eating in the servants' hall. "I'd have cut the tale short if I'd known you were waiting out here."

"Gil would not have forgiven me," she said, smiling back at

him. "He certainly prefers the adventures of Black Bart to a scolding about his schoolwork."

"Is that your intention? To scold him about his studies?"

Her smile faded. "I'm told he doesn't concentrate on them. He's more eager to go running about outdoors than to pay attention to his books."

"Do you blame him? Mr. Lutton, not the most fascinating of lecturers even for his parishioners, is a dull tutor, I'm afraid, for an energetic twelve-year-old."

"Are you criticizing Mr. Lutton's teaching?" Caro demanded in immediate offense, having been the one who'd recommended Mr. Lutton as Gil's tutor.

Kit held up his hands as if in self-defense. "I'm sorry. I didn't know that Mr. Lutton's tutoring was above reproach."

"It is *not* above reproach. But a tutor is neither a jester nor a storyteller. Lectures in history and mathematics are not supposed to be diversions."

Kit shrugged. "Agreed. But a little less formality and a little more humor would not be amiss."

She glared up at him. "I suppose Mr. Lutton would meet with greater approval from you if instead of instructing the boy in long division, he told tales of Black Bart!"

The good feeling generated by the dinner was now completely dissipated. Kit was surprised that her defense of the vicar was so ardent, but he was *not* surprised that it was turning into an attack on *him*. Nothing he did *ever* pleased this woman. "Even long division could be made more interesting if Black Bart were involved in it," he pointed out in mild self-defense. "For instance, the arithmetic principle could be illustrated by having Gil work out how the pirate would divide his booty among his henchmen."

"Too bad you're not Gil's tutor, then," she said, her voice dripping sarcasm. "With your imagination you could make stories out of all the subjects . . . pirate stories for mathematics, knighthood stories for history, stories of the myths for Latin. The boy would never want to miss his hours of tutoring. The schoolroom would become a place of delightful frivolity."

"You're right, of course, as you always are," Kit retorted with equal sarcasm, irked beyond words that the exchanges between them, no matter how innocuously begun, always ended in war. "I'm much too frivolous to tutor a child. You are better off with a teacher of real depth, like Mr. Lutton. Forgive me, ma'am, for even *suggesting* otherwise." And he stalked off down the hall.

She, in her turn, stormed into Gil's room and delivered her scolding in a much angrier manner than she'd ever intended. But if she'd asked herself why she was suddenly so irate, she wouldn't have been able to answer.

27

After Gil's dreadful accident, Caro wondered if her unfair, too angry scolding had been, somehow, the cause of it. But it would never have occurred to Gil to blame his sister. She'd been quite right in her scold, he thought, and he'd tearfully promised her, that night, that he would try harder.

The chastened boy went to the schoolroom the next day determined to pay attention to his lessons. He sat through a long hour of arithmetic problems, and then a longer one of the history of the English kings of the thirteenth century, all without fidgeting. But the last hour—spent entirely on the conjugation of Latin verbs—became too much for him. He could scarcely sit still. The air was stifling, the subject utterly beyond him, and the tutor irritated and impatient. "I warn you, Gilbert, that unless you get a firm grip on these conjugations, you'll not make it to Eton next year," Mr. Lutton declared in disgust.

For poor Gil the hour was worse than imprisonment; he felt like a butterfly—a particularly stupid one—impaled on a pin. As soon as the time was up, he leaped from his chair and ran down the stairs and out across the field to the stables like a creature being chased by demons.

At the stables, Dolph, the head groom, tried to talk Master Gilbert out of taking the ride. There had been a brief shower that morning, and the grass was still wet. "It's slippery on those 'ills, me lad," he warned, "an' if ye push yer Bellerophon too fast, ye'll find yersel' in trouble."

But Gil had had his fill of warnings . . . from Caro, from his tutor, and now from Dolph. Besides, children are warned about one thing or another every day of their lives: *don't eat those sweets or you'll get sick; don't run so fast or you'll fall.* Most days, despite those warnings being completely disregarded, the dire predictions don't come to pass. Thus the children become convinced that either their elders are speaking nonsense or that their lives are charmed. Warnings become mere words that may safely be ignored. Gil therefore took little notice of the groom's warning. He merely nodded and galloped off at top speed. In a moment he was out of sight of the house.

Freed from the restrictions and tensions of the schoolroom, Gil let his imagination loose. He could feel the ripple of the powerful muscles of his horse under him and the whip of the wind blowing deliciously against his face, and his spirits began to rise. He began to experience an exhilarating sense of lightness. It seemed to him that *his* Bellerophon, like his namesake of myth, was truly flying. Horse and rider flew over the sodden ground, spraying small clods of wet earth behind them. Over the west field they flew, across a narrow road, round a row of outbuildings, through a shallow brook, and over a small hillock. It was thrilling . . . stirring . . . the pure joy of physical exertion taken at breakneck speed.

When they approached a low wall, one that they'd flown over dozens of times before, Gil felt not a twinge of concern. Today, however, because of the rain, the ground was not as firm under the animal's feet as was usual. During the headlong approach, as the horse tensed his hind legs for the jump, one leg slithered back, dislodging a piece of wet turf, and skidded off balance. The little skid upset the forward momentum and decreased the height of the lift. Bellerophon, not winged like his namesake, couldn't make it. His front leg struck the top of the wall as he tried to reach the far side. It all happened so quickly that Gil didn't realize it would have been better to let himself be thrown. Instead, he clung tightly to the horse's neck. The horse toppled forward with a horrifying whinny and tumbled to the ground. Gil felt his head hit the wet earth as the horse rolled over on his side, pinning one of Gil's legs under him. There they lay, Gil unconscious, and the horse shuddering in dreadful, heaving spasms, his eyes wild and one foreleg waving helplessly in the air.

Meanwhile, back at the stables, Dolph was feeling uneasy. He hadn't liked the hasty way in which the boy had ridden off, but it was beyond his authority to refuse to permit Master Gilbert to ride. After debating with himself on what course of action to take, he sent one of the stable boys to fetch Mr. Mickley.

The boy found Mickley in Kit's bedroom, trailing behind the new housemaid, Betty Rhys, as she did the dusting. The batman was annoyed at being interrupted, for he'd been engaged in what was, for him, a most unusual pastime—flirting. He'd been trying to convince the girl (who, he'd once told Miss Caroline, was too plump and too saucy by far) that he was a more desirable catch than the fellow in town with whom she was "walking out." "What do ye want with a slowtop like that?" he was asking. "The fellow owns an inn. 'E'll 'ave ye slavin' away every night in the taproom, fendin' off brutes 'oo itch to pinch yer bottom."

"It ain't a much worser prospect than fendin' off a brute what follows me round when I'm dustin'," the maid threw back at him with a toss of her pretty head.

It was just then that the stable boy burst breathlessly into the room. "Dolph wants ye in the stable, Mr. Mickley," the boy said. "Right away."

Mickley frowned. "Tell 'im I'm busy," he said curtly, but he immediately reconsidered. Dolph had never before sent for him. Something worrisome must have occurred at the stables to have caused the groom to make this unusual and urgent summons. Perhaps—dreaded prospect!—there was something wrong with one of the captain's Spanish horses. "Wait," he said to the stable boy, and, with a last, rueful glance at the indifferent, plump-and-saucy Betty, followed the boy out the door.

When he learned the substance of Dolph's fears, the batman immediately mounted one of the carriage horses and set out to search for Gil. It was more than an hour before he came upon the scene of the accident and discovered the boy, still unconscious, lying under a trembling, whimpering, doomed animal that, in his fall, had badly injured three legs, two of his own and one of the boy's.

Mickley carried Gil in his arms back to the house, pausing at the stables only long enough to instruct Dolph to have the suffering animal shot. Gil, now awake and white-lipped with pain, shuddered at those words. He had enough experience of horses to know that the shooting was necessary, but he couldn't keep back a flood of bitter tears. His own pain was nothing when compared with the agony of realizing that he'd caused the injury that would end the life of his beloved Bellerophon.

Betty Rhys, who was not as indifferent to Mr. Mickley's attentions as she'd pretended, had kept watch at the window for his return. She was the one who first saw Mickley approaching the house with the limp boy in his arms. By the time Mickley reached the front door, she'd alerted the entire household. Kit, Letty, Caro, and a number of the servants were already in the doorway, tense with alarm. They made way for Mickley, who brought the boy into the drawing room and laid him down on the sofa. Caro and Letty followed. Caro immediately gave Gil a small dose of laudanum for the pain, while Kit, at the doorway, ordered a footman to ride out for the doctor and sent the rest of the onlookers about their business.

The anguished child continued to sob. Caro cradled him in her arms, Letty wept, and Mickley went about the difficult business of cutting off the boy's boots. Kit shut the door and crossed the room. He sat down on the edge of the sofa and spoke to Gil softly but honestly about the necessity of ending Bellerophon's pain. Nevertheless, the boy was inconsolable. Caro had never heard him weep so bitterly. "It's all my fault," he wept. "All my fault. I should never have ridden him out today."

The doctor—an elderly, bewhiskered, kindly man who'd treated the Whitlow family for many years—soon arrived and made a swift examination of the wounds. He found, to everyone's relief, that the blow to the cranium was not serious.

But the boy had suffered a badly broken tibia. After assembling the needed splints and bandages, the doctor began, in a surprisingly gingerly manner, to feel the now bared leg. Kit wondered at the doctor's seeming hesitation. His movements, a moment ago so quick and assured, were now slow and awkward. Mickley and Kit, who'd had much experience with broken bones, exchanged troubled looks. "Have you set many fractures, doctor?" Kit asked, restraining the man's arm.

"In truth, Your Lordship, not many," the doctor admitted. "I usually bring in a bonesetter when I have a patient with a fracture, but the fellow has gone to visit his brother in Ashton. It will take three hours to bring him here, and 'tis best for the boy if I set the bone at once."

"Then, if you'll stand aside and supervise," Kit said, drawing Mickley to his side, "*we* can be your bonesetters."

The doctor looked dubious, but he could not countermand the orders of the viscount, no matter how politely given. "Have you done it before, my lord?" he asked as he stepped aside.

Caro, startled and terrified, cried out, "No, Kit, please!"

Letty, equally frightened, asked in a shaky voice, "Can't we wait for the man with experience?"

"Waiting can be more dangerous than any wrong these men can do," the doctor told her.

"Don' ye worry none, ma'am," Mickley assured Caro as Kit knelt down beside the boy and slid his hands up and down the leg. "The cap'n an' me's done this more'n once. An' I meself set the cap'n's leg back in Spain, an' anyone can see how good he's walkin' now. Hardly limps at all."

Caro, feeling helpless, said not another word. She merely covered her mouth with her hand to keep from crying out again. But her eyes were fixed on the scene before her. With Mickley holding down Gil's legs at the ankles and the doctor holding back the boy's arms, Kit quickly and confidently wrenched the bone into place. Poor Gil screamed and fainted, but they did not try to revive him until the splints and bandages were all in place.

Later, when Gil was propped up in his own bed upon a

massive pile of pillows, and all but Kit and Caro had been sent from the room, Caro tried to give him another dose of laudanum so that he might go to sleep. But the boy tearfully refused it. "Why won't you take it, dearest?" his sister asked. "It will ease your pain."

"I deserve this pain," Gil said bitterly. "I k-killed my horse. A wonderful horse Kit brought all the way from Spain. I deserve w-worse than this."

Caro opened her mouth to argue, but Kit stopped her. "Let the boy be, ma'am," he said, taking the glass from her hand. "And let him go ahead and blame himself for what's happened, if he must. He says those things because he's young. The young are always hard on themselves. It takes maturity to be able to forgive oneself for a mistake."

Caro looked at Kit questioningly. Why was he being so unkind to the poor boy?

Gil had stiffened in offense. "Are you s-saying I'm a b-baby?"

"No, of course he isn't," Caro quickly assured him.

But Gil wanted assurance from Kit. "I can be mature," he said, his bottom lip trembling. "It's just that this was a very b-big mistake."

"Yes, I know." Kit looked down at him kindly. "That's why you'd have to be *very* mature."

Caro now caught on to Kit's motive. "And you're only twelve," she added, playing along. "It's hard to be mature at twelve. Especially when you're hurt and aching so badly."

"I'm almost thirteen. I can *so* be mature. Don't you think I can?"

"It's not for me to say." Kit sat down on the edge of the bed and riffled the boy's hair. "Are you willing to forgive yourself, even for a very big mistake?"

"I g-guess so," Gil said, wiping his cheeks with the back of his hand.

"Good! Then let's see you drink this down."

Gil eyed the white liquid suspiciously. "How long will it take before I fall asleep?"

"About fifteen minutes, I should think," Caro said.

Gil took the glass. "Will you tell me the next adventure of Black Bart while we wait?" he asked Kit plaintively. "Just to take my mind off . . . off other things?"

Kit threw Caro a quick glance but said, "Of course," without waiting for her response. "Black Bart was last seen standing on the yardarm, isn't that right?"

"Yes," Gil said, almost eagerly, "tied and blindfolded and about to be hanged."

Kit nodded. "Black Bart, pirate of pirates, most daring of the daring, despite his blindfold, whirled about on the yardarm on one foot like a tightrope walker and swung the other at the nearest seaman, knocking him down onto the deck. Then, as the admiral and crew watched in astonishment, he broke from his wrist bonds, pulled off the blindfold, waved in farewell, and dived into the sea. . . ."

Five minutes later—Black Bart barely had time to swim back to the pirate ship—Gil was asleep. The laudanum had done its work. Kit covered the boy and stood up, looking round for Caro in the hope—nay, the expectation—that she would at least offer him a word of praise for his ingenuity as a storyteller, if not for his skill as a bonesetter. But he was to get no word of praise. She hadn't waited to hear what happened to Black Bart. She was gone.

28

He didn't go looking for her, not consciously. But as he walked down the corridor toward his own apartments, he heard a muffled sob. It was coming from a small, infrequently used sitting room only a few doors down from Gil's bedroom. The door was ajar, and he peered in. The room was in shadows, dimly lit by the fading evening light glimmering in from the windows, but there she was, huddled on the window seat, embracing her knees. Her forehead was lowered upon them, and she was sobbing softly. "Caro!" he exclaimed, striding across the room. He dropped down on the seat beside her and lifted her head to his shoulder. Her cap tumbled off and fell unheeded on the seat behind her. Purely by instinct, she burrowed her face into his neck and continued to weep.

"What is it, my dear?" he murmured, his fingers wandering fondly through the mass of her curls. "There's nothing to cry about. A boy's bones knit with remarkable ease. He'll be good as new in little more than a month, I promise you. And meanwhile, we'll fit him with a pair of crutches. In a matter of days you'll see him hopping about the place like a cricket."

"I know. But, you see, this is all m-my f-fault!" she cried into the hollow of his shoulder.

"Good God! You, too? What nonsense is this?"

"I upset him with my scold last night. I was m-much too severe. I know I was. I made a s-scene that s-set him on edge."

He grasped her shoulders and, holding her off from him, gave her an angry shake. "Dash it, woman, must I deliver to you the very same homilies I—" he began, but the sight of her face stilled his tongue. The evening light from the window illuminated not only her tousled curls (that had been hidden from his view for so long under that irritating mobcap that he'd almost forgotten how lovely they were), but her eyes, now wide with surprise, the wet curve of her cheek, and her beautiful mouth that was swollen by her brief indulgence in weeping. His breath caught in his throat, his blood seemed to bubble in his veins, and his eyes fixed themselves on that soft, trembling mouth. He was caught, helplessly caught, by an urge so overwhelming that no act of will could stop it. Slowly, like a sleepwalker directed by a force not his own, he pulled her into his arms and lowered his mouth to hers.

She, shocked, froze in midsob. For a moment she didn't quite realize what had happened. Again acting purely by instinct, she sagged against him, letting her lips go soft against his and her body bend to the pressure of his arms. It was a lovely feeling, soothing away the anxiety and distress she'd been experiencing for hours. There was warmth here in his arms, and a most unfamiliar sense of security. It was brought on, she supposed, by her gratitude for what he'd done for her today, setting Gil's bone, getting him to forgive himself, and even entertaining him with stories. She was more than grateful, she realized. She was in his debt. But all that could not explain this other feeling—an almost inexpressible delight. She might have remained basking in this silvery moment indefinitely, but suddenly his hold tightened, and the pressure of his mouth became more demanding. Warmth turned to heat, and heat brought fear . . . and dismay. What was she *doing*? she asked herself, and worse, what was *he* doing?

She wrenched herself from his hold and pulled herself back away from him until stopped by the window frame. She glared at him, ready to do battle. But the expression on his face stopped her. It was a look of surprise greater, if possible, than on hers. He was staring at her with eyes wide with wonder, as if he had been embraced by *her,* not the other way around. What was going on here? "Kit . . . ?" she asked, confused.

He blinked, shook his head as if coming out of a dream, and then, as if it were the most natural act in the world, took her back in his arms and kissed her again, a kiss as long, as lingering, as passionate as the first.

It was all too much. She struggled vainly in his grip, all the while quite aware of her body's shockingly warm response to this unwarranted embrace. This was exactly how she'd felt when Mr. Terence had kissed her. If only this man had really been Marcus Terence . . . ! If only he were not Kit Meredith . . . ! If her mind were not so firmly set against him, she might very well take delight in this embrace. But as it was, this act was deplorable! It would only make life in this house more difficult. She was a servant here. She had better remember that fact. She was in a situation that she herself, in her pride, had insisted upon, and she would not permit Kit Meredith to undermine it in any way, especially in so demeaning a manner as this! "Dash it," she cried, wrenching herself free again, "have you lost your *mind*?"

He took a deep breath and, his eyes glowing, smiled slowly. "It is entirely possible."

"I ought to box your ears!" She jumped to her feet and glared down at him. "I would have given odds that Kit Meredith, trickster and dissembler though he is, was not the sort to stoop to *manhandling* his *servants*! For shame!"

"*Servants?* Caro, for heaven's sake!" he groaned, the glow fading from his eyes.

"Yes, servants! I am a servant here. And if you ever again forget that fact, I shall be forced to conclude that *you* are even worse than *Mr. Duckett*!" And she stormed from the room.

He gaped at the door, stunned not only by his own reaction to the embrace but even more by hers. She would not admit by so much as a blink that she'd been as stirred as he. She was the most stubborn, most wrongheaded, most exasperating female it had ever been his misfortune to know. "Damn the woman!" he swore, and having no other way to assuage the fury that welled up in him, smashed his fist through the nearest windowpane.

29

"How could ye *do* such a fool thing?" Mickley scolded as he bound Kit's hand with a thick bandage. "Ye might've severed an art'ry!"

"But I didn't," Kit snapped, "so you can stow your gab."

"Don't comb *my* hair, ye looby," the batman retorted, unperturbed. "*I* ain't the one that's turned yer noddle to mush."

"Mush, is it?" Kit glared at him. "I can still best *you* in a game of chess."

"Not of late ye can't. Admit it, Cap'n. It's bellows to mend with ye, if I'm a judge."

Kit, painfully aware that his man was right, merely shrugged. Then he got to his feet and flexed the fingers of his wounded hand. "So you think I'm out of countenance, eh? Something more seriously amiss than a cut on my hand?"

"I think," Mickley said as he gathered up the remaining bandages and dropped the bloody swabs into a basin, "that *she* 'as ye trapped, toppled, an' trussed up like a piece of mutton."

"She?"

Mickley snorted at Kit's pretense at innocence. "Ye don't think to cut a wheedle with me, do ye, Cap'n? Ye've been at sixes and sevens ever since ye first laid yer peepers on Miss Caroline."

"Have I?" He let out a long breath and turned to the window. "Yes, I suppose I have. I just didn't know it was so obvious to everyone."

"I ain't everyone. No one in this 'ouse knows ye like I do."

"Thank goodness for that." Kit stared glumly out of the window at the thin band of twilight glow that was quickly disappearing from the western horizon. "I wouldn't want the rest of the world to know that a woman's turned my 'noddle' to mush."

"Nothin' to be ashamed of, Cap'n. There's 'ardly a man alive what didn't make a fool of 'isself over a petticoat sometime 'r other."

Kit turned from the window and cocked at eyebrow at him. "Even you, Mick?"

The batman blushed. "Even me."

"You don't say!" In his surprise, Kit forgot his own troubles and grinned broadly. "Who is she, man? Someone here at the Grange?"

Mickley shrugged. "One o' the maids. Betty Rhys."

"Ah, yes. The pretty one with the blond braids. I compliment you on your taste."

"She ain't so pretty as all that," Mickley muttered, dropping his eyes in embarrassment. "Too plump by far."

"Not at all," Kit insisted. "A pleasing armful, I'd say."

"It don't matter. She won't 'ave a thing to do with me. She's spoken for."

"Oh?" He eyed his man with sympathy. "Wed, is she?"

"Not yet."

"Then don't give up, Mick. You're a better man than most. All you need do is convince her of it."

Mickley shook his head. "What's the use? Once a chit makes up 'er mind, there's no changin' it. Ye're a good man, too, ain't ye? The best, if ye ask me. But yer Caroline don't see it, does she?" With his medical supplies gathered up in his arms, he trudged to the door. "Women!" he muttered in disgust. "Too silly an' stubborn to use the brains God gave 'em."

Kit turned back to the window and gazed out morosely at the rapidly darkening sky. "Yes," he said in a voice as dispirited as Mickley had ever heard it, "it seems we've *both* fallen into the dismals. Confound it, Mick, nothing about this deuced inheritance is turning out as I expected. Sometimes I think it might have been better all around if we'd remained in Spain."

30

Caro needed her sleep badly, but she lay tossing on her bed, wide-awake. Despite her utter weariness and the fact that she would have to rise at first light, she couldn't make sleep come. Her mind was in too great a turmoil. She tried to force her thoughts into safe channels—planning tomorrow's menus, for example, or envisioning a proper rearrangement for the storing of the linens. She even tried counting sheep. But her mind would not obey. It kept reliving the emotionally disturbing moments of the day . . . her brother being carried in . . . Kit's setting of the bone . . . and, not least, the scene in the little sitting room when Kit had taken her into his arms.

Kit was the basic cause of her discomfiture, as he'd been from the first. She'd known from the moment she'd learned his name that he would cause her heartache. And that was what was keeping her awake now—heartache. She tossed about restlessly on her bed in a vain attempt to ease that all-enveloping pain, but it would not go away.

The problems was that Kit, in her eyes, had two conflicting sides—the Mr. Terence side that was kind and generous and brave, and the Vexatious Viscount side that was selfish and domineering and dishonest. And the terrible truth—a truth that was slowly beginning to break into her consciousness—was that she loved them both.

She'd known, of course, that she loved Mr. Terence. But when she'd discovered that he was nothing but a fabrication created by Kit Meredith, she'd buried her feeling for him deep inside herself and replaced it with fury—a fury directed toward the man who'd tricked her. Every time she looked at Kit's face, however, she saw Mr. Terence there, too. It was a face she loved and hated both at once.

Those mixed feelings were troublesome enough, but what made matters even more confusing was the fact that Kit had, time after time, saved her from a difficult situation. He'd sent Arthur to school, taken Gil under his wing, and saved her from the Ducketts. Today, too, he'd managed to put her in his debt by his competent setting of her brother's broken bone. It did not help her state of mind to be so constantly beholden to the man who made her furious!

Her pride could hardly bear it! The only way she'd been able to assuage that wounded pride was to come here to the Grange as housekeeper rather than as guest. And she'd been living with this compromise fairly well . . . that is, until tonight. Tonight he'd kissed her. Twice.

Tonight's caresses had been very reminiscent of the embrace Mr. Terence had given her that last night of his existence. Marcus Terence's kiss was one she didn't want to remember, for he'd followed it with an embarrassed admission that he was not a suitor for her hand. It had been, for her, a most painful scene, and she had no wish to relive it even in memory. But tonight Kit had brought it back most forcibly to her mind.

That they'd both been stirred by tonight's embraces was obvious, but what he'd meant by them was not. He'd never, in either of his guises, indicated that he loved her. Was he merely playing with her—a master taking advantage of a woman in his employ? That was what she'd accused him of, but she didn't really believe it. The act had not been a calculated one. He'd been as surprised and shaken by the kisses as she'd been. But then, why had he never, that last time or this, indicated that he cared for her in a serious way?

She would never forget how shocked Mr. Terence had been by her suggestion that he might be a suitor for her hand. Of all the painful memories of that episode, that rejection was the worst. She'd been more hurt that evening than ever before in her life. It was beyond mere bruised pride; she'd been cut to the quick.

But if Kit Meredith, like his fictitious creation Marcus Terence, did not care for her as a prospective wife, what *did* he intend by that shattering embrace? He could not be asking for a carte blanche, for he was not a fool. He surely knew that neither he nor she was the sort to engage in an illicit arrangement. What, then, did it all mean?

She could find no answer. If her own feelings were so confused and so difficult for her to analyze, how could she possibly analyze his, which were an even greater mystery to her?

These thoughts went round and round in her head until, suddenly, she realized that the gray light of dawn was seeping in through the gaps of the draperies. The night had passed, having given her nothing but a jumble of confused emotions, a myriad of unanswerable questions, and no sleep.

31

Gil was trying out his new crutches. Caro, Letty, and Mickley were gathered in Gil's bedroom watching Kit give instructions to the boy. Caro and Letty noticed Kit's bandaged hand at the same moment. "Goodness me, Kit," Letty gasped, "what happened to you?"

Kit, who'd managed to hide his fist in his pocket during the past three days, flicked Mickley a warning look. "Nothing much," he murmured. "A cut across the back is all." And he hastily turned to the boy. "Now, Gil, come to me. Don't be afraid. Put your weight on the left as you swing."

Caro had seen the warning look and was also aware that Kit had turned the subject. "What happened to his hand?" she asked Mickley quietly. "Tell me!"

"Nothin' to tell," Mickley whispered back. "An accident with a pane of glass. Not worth speakin' of."

"A pane of—"

But Gil had made his first two hops, and everyone broke into applause. Caro let the subject of His Lordship's accident drop.

Gil was pleased with himself. "I can do it!" he exclaimed happily. "Watch me cross the room."

He swung himself over to the window without mishap, but to turn himself around for the return required extra care. As he hesitated he saw something outside the window. "I say! There's a carriage pulling up."

Both women hurried to the window to see. "My goodness, it's Martha!" Letty cried. "I'd recognize that dreadful old barouche anywhere."

It was indeed Martha. The intrepid old woman stepped out of

her ancient black coach and announced to Melton, who'd hurried out to help her down, that she'd come for a visit. From the large number of bandboxes and portmanteaux that the footmen were already carrying inside, the visit was apparently going to be a long one.

Martha was eagerly greeted, and a festive welcoming tea was immediately arranged. Everyone gathered in the large downstairs sitting room for the occasion, including Gil, who, still too unsure of himself on the crutches to manage the stairs, was carried down by Mickley. Even Caro permitted herself to attend. But when Kit took her aside to request that, under the circumstances, it was only proper that she join the family for dinner, she refused. "Martha is fully aware of my position here, my lord. There is no need to break the rules on her account."

The presence of an unexpected guest lent a holiday aura to the household. Caro helped the cook prepare a special dinner, the highlight of which would be roast grouse with truffles. The number of diners at the dinner table was expanded not only by Martha but by Mr. Lutton, who'd dropped by to see his pupil and was coaxed by Kit to remain for the evening. It was a cheerful meal, for although everyone present was conscious of Caro's absence, Kit kept a lively conversation going. It was only when Caro herself came in, dressed in proper housekeeper fashion in black bombazine and white apron—and carrying a large apricot soufflé as the pièce de résistance of the meal—that an awkward silence fell.

When the festivities were over and everyone had retired, Martha invited Caro to her bedroom for a private chat. "Tell me, my girl," the elderly woman demanded bluntly as soon as Caro had shut the door, "how long do you expect to continue this charade?"

"Charade?" Caro stared at her aunt, startled.

Martha, already in her nightshift, was sitting at her dressing table, plaiting her wiry gray locks. She looked over at Caro with a frown. "You know what I mean. Playing at being a servant here."

"Why do you call it *playing,* ma'am?" Caro asked, surprised. "I work very hard."

"Yes, I'm sure you do. But you must realize you are playing a role. And if you ask me, it's a role that doesn't suit you."

"Why not?" Caro, offended, put up her chin. "Are you implying that I'm not capable of handling the work?"

"Don't speak nonsense. You are capable of anything you set your mind to. What I'm saying is that your insistence on holding a menial position in this household is making everyone else uncomfortable. Not only the servants, but Letty, Kit, and even Gil."

Caro blinked at her aunt for a moment, those harsh words striking little blows at her heart. "Good God! It's true! I *do* make everyone uncomfortable."

Martha, seeing the girl's stricken look, felt a tinge of regret for having been so blunt. But, she told herself, she'd done what she had to do. "I hope I haven't hurt you, my dear, but it had to be said. I know that Letty is too mealymouthed to speak frankly to you of the situation, but I am not."

Caro sank down on the edge of the bed, the color gone from her cheeks. "I'm glad you said it, Aunt. I never thought of it quite that way."

"Then think of it now."

The poor girl, much disturbed, twisted her fingers in her lap. "I only took the post because I thought I was needed here. That Kit . . . His Lordship . . . needed me."

"I'm sure he does. But in the position you held when you lived here with Clement. Not as a housekeeper who takes her meals belowstairs."

"But . . ." She peered at her aunt in troubled urgency. "Can't you see my position? I had no choice but to live as a servant here. The new viscount is not the same as the old. I can't live here on his . . . his *charity.*"

"Why not? You lived here on Clement's charity, didn't you?"

Caro winced. "Yes, I suppose I did. But I was much younger then. And Uncle Clement was . . . was . . ."

"Much older?"

Her cheeks grew hot, and she threw her aunt a guilty glance. "Yes, I suppose the fact that Kit . . . His Lordship . . . is so much closer to my age has something to do with it."

"You needn't blush, girl," Martha said, not unkindly. "Do you think me so naive that I don't know how unseemly it would be for you to live here as the 'guest' of a virile young man? Why do you suppose Letty moved here?"

Caro's eyes widened with shock. "Good God! Is *that* why she came? To ensure that the *proprieties* are observed? I don't believe it!"

"You may *well* believe it, for it's true. She and I discussed the matter thoroughly before she made her decision."

"I thought she came for Gil's sake."

"So she did. And for her own sake, too. *All* those reasons entered into her decision. But top of the list was what you call the 'proprieties.' Moreover, if you don't believe that those proprieties were in *Kit's* mind, too, when he invited her, you're fair and far off."

"That's . . . that's ridiculous!" Caro sputtered. "I hadn't even decided to come here then."

"He knew you would, someday. If only to visit your brother."

"Yes, of course. You must be right." She bit her lip thoughtfully for a moment, overwhelmed by the sudden awareness of how much her welfare had been of concern to others. But then she stiffened. "Aunt Martha, I'm afraid that none of that matters. Even with Letty living here, I can't remain here as a guest. I can't live on Kit Meredith's charity. I just can't!"

Martha put down her hairbrush and turned to face the younger woman. "That's *it,* you know," she declared. "That's the *real* difficulty, my girl."

"What is?"

"Your pride. Your blasted pride."

"I suppose so," the girl admitted in a tearful voice. "But I can't help it. My pride is all I have."

"I know." Martha sighed in discouragement and turned her face away. "It's a flaw from which I suffer myself," she murmured in a low voice.

Caro leaned her forehead against the bedpost. "Then what on earth am I to do?" she asked brokenly.

Martha rose from the dressing table and crossed the room to the bed. "I've been thinking about something all evening," she said, suddenly brisk. She sat down beside the stricken girl and patted her shoulder. "Do you realize that the vicar—what is his name . . . Layton? Langston?"

"Lutton. Henry Lutton."

"Yes. Lutton. Do you realize he's quite taken with you?"

Caro regarded her aunt curiously. "Well, yes. I . . . we . . . Why do you ask?"

"He may be the solution to this problem. He seems quite an acceptable young man."

"Acceptable?" Caro echoed, her eyebrows raised.

"Yes. He has polish and presence. He seems well informed. And evidently the parish provides a comfortable living. If he were to come up to scratch, and you accepted him, you would have a respectable place in society, a decent life, and a residence here in surroundings where you and your brothers feel so much at home."

"Yes," Caro said dubiously, "but, Aunt Martha, it would not be a . . . a love match. You and my uncle Whitlow were such a loving pair. How is it that you are recommending something quite different for me?"

"You're not a green girl, Caro. If you've not yet fallen in love at your age, perhaps it's time to compromise."

"Compromise?" Caro's eyes fell. "What an unromantic word."

"The results of compromise are not necessarily unromantic, my dear." Martha took one of Caro's hands in hers and squeezed it sympathetically. "There are many cases, you know, where love comes later, after the wedding has been consummated."

Caro lifted her head and stared out into the middle distance, her eyes pained and unseeing. "I'll think about it, Aunt," she said in a small voice. "If I'm making everyone uncomfortable going on in this way, I shall have to make a change. So I'll think about your suggestion. I'll think very hard."

32

After searching for Caro through the nether regions, an area of the house with which Kit was completely unfamiliar (and which he determined needed as much improvement as the upper part of the house), Kit found her at her desk in her little office adjoining the servants' hall, bent over an account book. "Excuse me, ma'am," he said politely, tapping on the door, "do I disturb you?"

She looked up, blushed, and jumped to her feet. "N-no, of course not," she stammered, taken by surprise. "I'm just working on the kitchen accounts."

"I won't keep you long. I only wish to ask if you'll join me tomorrow on my visit to the cottages."

"Tomorrow? Yes, of course. But you didn't have to come all this way down to find me. You could have sent for me."

"Could I indeed?" He raised a scornful eyebrow. "I've permitted you to bully me in many ways, my dear," he warned, "but don't go too far."

"I don't see how you can call it bullying, my lord. Any man in your position has a right to expect his housekeeper—"

"I've gone along with most of your ridiculous demands, Miss Whitlow," he cut her off icily, "but you know quite well that you are no 'housekeeper' to me. To expect me to order you to come running at my beck and call is the outside of enough."

Caro, remembering Martha's words of a week before, dropped her eyes from his face. She *had* gone too far. "I beg your pardon," she said, her high color deepening.

"Very well, ma'am. Let's say no more on the subject."

"On the matter of the visit to the cottages," she said,

hurriedly returning to a safer subject, "shall I prepare some baskets of food for you to give to the cottagers?"

"Why, yes! That's a fine idea. Thank you. I hadn't thought of that."

"It's not always done, but it should be. The cottagers will be grateful."

"Good," he said, starting away. "The bailiff will join us, and I'll take Mr. Mickley, too." He took a few strides away from her and then abruptly turned back. "I hope to make Mickley my land agent one day soon," he said in a confiding tone, his eyes suddenly taking on a gleam of amusement.

"Indeed?" Caro had no idea why he was giving her that information. "How fortunate for him."

"Yes, for a very good income will go along with the position." He paused for a moment and then grinned. "You might mention it to that upstairs maid with the blond braids."

"What?" Caro gaped up at him blankly. "Are you speaking of Betty? Betty Rhys?"

"Yes, that's the one. I think a land agent might easily compete with an innkeeper in a girl's eyes, don't you?"

Caro, after a moment of complete incomprehension, suddenly had a burst of understanding. She gave a gurgling laugh. "Yes, I suppose he might very well compete. I'll be sure to mention it."

"Thank you," Kit said, walking off.

"Mickley told *me* he found her too plump and saucy," she called after him. "Honestly! Men!"

Kit's only answer was a snort of laughter.

The next morning, when the group going to the cottages assembled, Caro studied Mickley's face to see if her hint to Betty had done him any good, but though the fellow seemed cheerful enough, she could not be sure. This was not the time to make inquiries, however, for the men all had other matters on their minds. They set off without ado, Kit taking Caro and her food baskets up in the curricle, and Mickley and the bailiff riding alongside on horseback.

At each cottage door, the women welcomed Caro in, while the men walked about outside, observing the condition of the buildings and taking notes of needed repairs. Caro noticed that the viscount was usually greeted with polite coolness, as if the cottagers were still suspicious of his nature and intentions. "See, Miss Caroline," one old woman explained to Caro, "the ol' viscount was a real good sort, but even 'e never did get round t' fixin' the roof. So why should we think this'n will?"

"But he will," Caro assured her. "The viscount is young, you know, and much more energetic than the old Lord Crittenden. What's more, if he promises to do a thing, he'll do it. I've never known him to break his word."

The woman, Mrs. Jemima Griggs, who'd lived on the property for more than four decades and knew all the gossip, cocked her head and peered at Caro like a curious bird. "Treatin' *ye* pretty well, is 'e?" she asked. "I 'eard he keeps ye belowstairs like a slavey."

"That's not at all true, Mrs. Griggs," Caro replied earnestly. "You know how wrong these gossips can be. I'm treated with more respect than ever in my life. I couldn't be happier. I hope you'll tell everyone what I said."

Mrs. Griggs evidently did her work well, for by late afternoon the viscount was being greeted with eager friendliness. "I don't know how you accomplished it, ma'am," Kit told Caro when they were riding back home, "but your being with me evidently dispelled their animosity. I don't know how to thank you."

"There's no need for thanks," she said absently. "I only did what I was hired to do." Her mind was not on the cottagers anymore, for she had something important to tell His Lordship, and she wasn't sure how to go about it. But since Mickley and the bailiff had ridden on ahead, this moment of privacy was a good time to do it.

She'd been thinking about the matter for days, ever since she'd taken Martha's advice about Henry Lutton. Once she'd made the decision that Martha's advice was sound, Caro had not waited long to speak to the vicar. Only two days after her conversation with Martha, she'd waited for him outside the schoolroom after Gil's lessons and, without roundaboutation, told him that she'd reconsidered . . . that she was now ready to wed him, if he was still of a mind.

The conversation had not been easy. At first both she and Henry had been quite awkward with each other, but by the time she'd finished explaining that she now believed she could be content with the "arrangement" they'd discussed before, the tension had eased.

"Do you *mean* it, my dear?" Henry Lutton had asked, his eyes alight. "You said, when you refused me the last time, that you didn't think a marriage of convenience would be, in your word, honest."

"I've thought about that, Henry," she'd replied, "and I've come to the conclusion that what matters is that we are honest with each other. The rest of the world may believe what they choose about us."

"And do you now believe, as I do, that so long as we are honest with each other, we are honest with God?"

"Yes," she'd said softly, but in her heart she wasn't sure that her answer was true. Would God forgive her for the small deceit of saying "I will" when directed to "cleave unto him"? There would be no "cleave" in their marriage. There would be companionship, tenderness, respect, good works—much that was honorable and good. Life with Henry Lutton might turn out to be both pleasant and worthwhile. One could, she supposed, learn to live with the inner ache caused by the "compromise" of one's dreams. She was giving up all prospect of love, of passion, of the joy of bearing children, but these were all selfish wishes. Surely she would be forgiven for solving her problem by self-sacrifice.

But Henry Lutton had no such qualms. He'd taken her hand and kissed it. "You've made me more happy than I can say," he'd murmured, and the look on his face showed that he was utterly sincere.

So the matter was concluded, and she was betrothed. Now she had to tell Kit. She glanced over at him. He was looking straight ahead at the road, his face calm, the reins held lightly in his hands. He had the look of a man satisfied with his day's work, content with his life. She wondered if her news would disturb that look. *Will he care at all?* she asked herself. *Or will he merely be relieved that he no longer has to feel responsibility for me?*

She couldn't help wondering what marriage might have been like with him. There would have been many quarrels, she was sure, but beside the conflict there would have been laughter, passion, and perhaps the lively noise of children. Kit would have made a wonderful father, she thought. Despite what she'd said to him outside Gil's bedroom that night, she'd really preferred his Black Bart way of teaching arithmetic to the humorless way that Henry had. That thought was disloyal to her betrothed, however, and she tried to stifle it. Her throat tightened with the effort, however, and a little gurgle of pain escaped her.

Kit swung about at the sound and peered down at her. "Is something wrong?" he asked.

She gulped. "No. It's just . . . I have something to tell you." She took a deep breath. "I must . . . give you notice."

"Notice?" He gave her a look of bewilderment. "What . . . ?"

"Isn't that what one does when one leaves a post? Gives notice? I'm giving you a month."

He stiffened. "Are you trying to tell me that you plan to *leave* the *Grange*?"

She lowered her head so that her bonnet hid her face. "Yes. You see, I'm to be married. To Mr. Lutton."

There was a long, long silence. After a while it was more than she could bear. She turned her head so that she could take a look at him. He was staring down at her, his mouth set, his eyes glittering but unreadable. The only sign that he'd received a blow was the pallor of his cheeks. "You needn't be upset, you know," she said, babbling foolishly to cover the uncomfortable silence. "We will surely find you a competent housekeeper in that time."

"Thank you," he said in a voice so cold she didn't recognize it. "Finding a new housekeeper was *exactly* my concern."

"What other concern . . . ?"

One corner of his mouth turned up in a sneer. "None. None at all. Why should I be concerned? You know what you're doing. You're always so confident, so certain of the rightness of your decisions, that it would be foolish of me to feel any concern at all."

"You needn't take that tone, my lord. It *is* a right decision."

"You and *Lutton*? Oh, yes, of course. A perfect match."

She hadn't expected this icy sarcasm. It threw her off balance. "It is!" she cried, feeling a need to defend herself but not knowing how. "We've been, Henry and I . . . for a long time . . . before I knew you . . . he asked me . . ."

"You needn't go on with that wonderfully coherent explanation, ma'am. You don't owe me one. And even if you did, I don't want to hear it." He whipped the horses to a gallop, and before she recovered her breath, they were at the door. He leaped down, waved back the footmen who'd come running out to take the reins, and came round to help Caro down. He put his hands on her waist and lifted her from the carriage step. But he didn't set her down. He held her against his chest, her head just above his. She could feel his hands trembling. "I suppose you think I should wish you happy," he muttered, glaring up at her.

"It would be the gentlemanly thing to do," she said, trying to ignore the pounding of her heart.

"I'll be damned if I will," he spat out, lowering her until they were face-to-face. Then he kissed her, a kiss that was hard and angry and meant to hurt.

When he let her go, she stood there trembling, unable to say a word. He glared at her in silent antagonism before turning on his heel and striding to the door. Suddenly he whirled around.

"You will take Gil away," he declared thickly, "over my dead body."

"I never *intended—*"

He didn't pay any heed to her. "Go ahead and ruin your own life if you must," he snarled as he threw open the door, "but hell will freeze before I let you ruin his."

33

Late in the afternoon of a lovely, somnolent June day, the pounding hoofbeats of a wildly racing horse rent the quiet air. Mickley was riding him. He'd galloped up from town waving the *London Times* aloft. At the door of the Grange, he leaped from the horse's back, threw the reins to a footman, raced into the house, and dashed up the stairs two at a time. He burst into Kit's study, chest heaving with excitement. "'E . . . did it!" he shouted, gasping for breath. "The . . . Iron Duke . . . *did it!*"

Kit, whose desk chair had been turned to face the window, looked round with no real interest. "What?" he asked, still as deep in the doldrums as he'd been these past two days.

"The *battle*!" the ex-batman shouted, wanting to shake his captain out of his lethargy. "Nappy's been trounced! For *good* this time. Old Wellington finally *finished* 'im!" He tossed the newspaper on the desk in front of Kit.

Kit, his interest piqued at last, read the news with an ex-soldier's eagerness. On June 18, a battle had been held at the Belgian town of Waterloo, and Napoleon had been defeated again. Roundly defeated. This time it was unmistakably the end of him. Kit, deeply depressed as he was, nevertheless could not fail to be elated at this news of his old commander's triumph. "Good for you, Sir Arthur," he muttered to the drawing of the triumphant commander in the paper. "Good for you!"

"Wellington ain't been Sir Arthur since Talavera," Mickley reminded him. "You were with 'im the night 'e learned they made 'im a duke, remember?"

"I remember," Kit said ruefully. "I wish I'd been with him this time."

Mickley fixed him with an accusing eye. "Is this all you're goin' to do to celebrate, just sit 'ere dreamin'? For shame, Cap'n. It says there in the paper that they're dancin' in the streets in London."

"I hope you don't expect me to get up and dance," Kit retorted, "but we can do something." He rose and started for the door. "I've a bottle of twenty-year-old cognac waiting for just such an occasion. Come with me, man. Let's get ourselves flummoxed."

They settled themselves in the library with two large glasses and the brandy bottle. By the time they'd drunk toasts to the Duke of Wellington, his staff, his line officers and troops collectively, and every man they could remember in their regiment individually, they were indeed flummoxed. "Le's drink t' women," Mickley suggested when no other male names came to mind.

"Not all women," Kit growled, refilling his glass. "Some of 'em don't deserve t' be toasted."

"Right. Won't drink to the underservin' ones. Like Miss Betty Rhys, blast 'er 'ide."

"Why not Betty Rhys? Very pretty creature, 's I recall."

"No. Too plump. An' 'er tongue's too saucy. An' she's set 'er silly mind on weddin' a fat ol' innkeeper, the silly chit."

"Then we won't drink to her. Silly chit. Doesn't have the leas' idea of what she's doing." He leaned forward and refilled Mickley's glass with an unsteady hand. "Le's drink to the females who don't marry, like my aunt Letty."

"Right. To Aunt Letty," Mickley declared, downing a stiff gulp.

"And t' those who marry f'r love, like m' aunt Martha," Kit said, his tongue feeling strange in his mouth.

"To Aunt Martha," Mickley agreed. After taking another drink, he stared into his glass glumly. "Wish Betty wuz like ol' Aunt Martha."

Kit focused his eyes and his thoughts on Mickley with difficulty. "Why? Doesn't she . . . don't you think she loves her innkeeper?"

Mickley grimaced. "If she did, why would she 'low me t' kiss 'er in the linen closet?"

"You dog!" Kit chortled drunkenly. "Did y' really do that?"

"More 'n once. An' she liked it, too. A fellow c'n tell."

"I don' know 'bout that," Kit said slowly. "I thought I could tell 'bout Caro, but then she . . . she . . ." His voice faded out, his head dropped, and his glass slipped from his fingers to the carpet, spilling what little was left of his brandy.

Mickley peered at him curiously. "She . . . ?"

"Nev' mind," Kit muttered. "Silly chit."

"I think . . . we're lushy," Mickley stated with surprise.

"Cupshotten," Kit agreed.

There was a long silence while Mickley drained his glass, lifted the bottle to refill it, and discovered it was empty. He stared at it in bewildered disbelief. "Can't be!" he cried.

Kit lifted his head, shook it, and glared at Mickley sternly. "Ask her!" he ordered.

Mickley blinked. "Whut'd ye say?"

"Ask her. If she's so enamored of her innkeeper, why'd she kiss you like that? Ask 'er, boint-plank."

"Boint-plank?"

Kit guffawed. "I mean point-blank. I think m' tongue's thick."

"I think yer brain's thick. You want me t' ask 'er why she kissed me?"

"Why not?"

Mickley considered the question. "Aye, Cap'n, why not?" He got clumsily to his feet. "I'll do it. Right now."

Kit nodded. "Good man."

Mickley staggered to the door. "Whew!" he exhaled, leaning on the doorframe. "I'm really webottled . . . bewottled."

"Tha's wha's made y' strong." Kit smiled at him woozily, waving him on in drunken encouragement. "Cup-valiant. Brav'ry in brandy. Onward, man!"

"Right. Onward I go!" And he stumbled out the door.

Mickley weaved unsteadily up and down the corridors until he came upon his quarry in the dining room. She and another maid were setting the table for dinner. He stood at the door for a moment, watching her move with supple grace round the table. Her neat striped dress and large, enveloping apron couldn't hide the voluptuousness of her full bosom and slim waist. Her beautiful blond braids were tied up round her head and hidden under her starched white mobcap, but he remembered—with amazing clarity, considering the fuddled state of his mind—how lovely her hair had looked in the linen closet when he'd taken it down and loosed it from its bonds. God, how I love that saucy chit, he thought as he staggered up behind her, grasped her arm, and pulled her round to face him. "Why'd ye kiss me?" he demanded bluntly, completely ignoring the fact that they were not alone.

The pretty housemaid gaped at him. "Mr. *Mickley*!" she gasped, throwing an embarrassed glance at the girl on the opposite side of the table.

"Mr. Mickley, am I?" The drunken batman sneered. "I was jus' plain Mick in the linen closet."

"Hush, for goodness' sake!" Betty hissed, coloring and making a gesture toward the other girl.

"Don't mind me," the other maid laughed.

"See? She don't mind," Mickley said. "So wha' my answer?"

"Yer answer, ye lout, is that I want ye t' let go o' me," Betty said under her breath. "Ye're crocked."

He snorted. "Drunk 's a lord. But tha's neither 'ere nor there. I mus' know, girl. If ye care so much fer yer innkeeper, why'd ye kiss me like that?"

"Hush, drat ye!" Betty threw another embarrassed look at her colleague before pulling Mick to the far corner of the room. "Why do ye *think* I kissed ye, ye looby?" she whispered. "Because I 'ad nothin' better t' do? There was a half-dozen beds t' change that day!"

"What're ye sayin', Miss Saucy-tongue?" he asked, not certain of her meaning, but his eyes lighting up with hope nevertheless.

"I'm sayin' I never kissed no man that way but you. So there!"

He peered at her, trying through the cloud of drunkenness to understand. "Damnation, I wish I wuz sober! Do ye mean ye *care* fer me? *Truly?*"

"Yes, truly! So now take yerself out and put yer head under the pump! And when y'r sober, I'll tell ye again." With another quick glance at the other maid—who was watching the scene with grinning delight—she cupped Mickley's face in her hands and kissed his mouth. "There, ye whoozy chubb! Now go, quick, before Mr. Melton sees me malingerin'!"

Meanwhile, in the library, Kit remained sunk in his easy chair, his brain spinning dizzily on too-quickly-imbibed brandy. It was good advice he'd given to Mickley, he was thinking. A man ought to know, when a girl kisses him, exactly where he stands. He himself had been fooled in that regard, not once but three times. He'd kissed Caro on three separate occasions—he was not so drunk that he didn't know how to count to three—and each time he'd been sure that she'd responded with as much feeling as he. But afterward, her behavior had completely upset his expectations. If he was any kind of man—even half the man Mickley was—he would do what he'd urged Mickley to do—ask her.

Yes, why not? he asked himself, heaving himself up from the chair. He wobbled unsteadily to the door and down the hall to the backstairs. He'd find her in that damned little office she'd made for herself near the servants' hall, he supposed, and that was where he was headed. He had to hold tightly to the banister to make it down the stairs. He hoped the effort of walking would clear his head, but by the time he got down—having stumbled dangerously down the last three stairs—his brain seemed more muddled than ever.

What was the question he was going to ask her? he wondered. He couldn't seem to remember it. Oh, yes, he thought, forcing his mind to concentrate, the kissing business. He'd rehearsed it with Mickley; he'd remember it well enough.

There was a short corridor at the bottom of the stairs. At the end of it was a sharp right turn into the servants' hall. To Kit's bleary eyes the corridor looked endless. The floor lurched crazily beneath his feet, and he had to cling to the wall to keep from falling. He was almost at the end of it when Caro herself came hurrying round the corner, carrying a tray of silver flatware for the dining table. He stumbled into her, causing the tray and all its contents to go clattering noisily to the floor. "Kit!" she gasped, caught unprepared.

He winced. "Sorry," he muttered.

She blinked at him. He didn't seem quite himself. "My lord, are you quite well?" she asked.

"Fine," he said with exaggerated clarity.

Unconvinced, she nevertheless knelt down to gather up the silverware.

"Came t' find you. Have t' know." He grasped her arms, pulled her up, and peered with woozy intensity into her eyes. "If you care s' much fer the blasted innkeeper, why'd ye kiss me in the linen closet?"

"What?" She stared at him in complete incomprehension for a moment. Then she gave a hiccuping laugh. "Good God! I do believe you're foxed!"

"Completely cast away," he said with a foolishly proud grin. "Makes one cup-valiant, y' know."

"Does it indeed?" She stared at him with amusement.

"So tell me, ma'am . . . why'd ye kiss me . . . ?"

"In the linen closet? I don't believe I ever did. Are you perhaps remembering a tête-à-tête with some other maid?"

He drew himself up in wobbly offense. "I take brummage . . . er . . . ummage . . . umbrage . . . at that remark, ma'am. I find it off . . . off . . . quite offensive." He put a hand to his forehead and shut his eyes. His other dropped from her arm, and he swayed on his feet. "I think . . . I must . . . sit down," he managed as his knees gave way.

She tried to hold him up by gripping him under his arms, but his weight was too much for her. The best she could do was slow down his fall, lowering him to a sitting position by going down with him. "Oh, Kit, really! How could you do such a childish thing!" she scolded, releasing her grip on him. "Letting yourself get knee-walking drunk!"

"Special occasion," he muttered, his head falling against her shoulder. "Nappy's trounced. Sir Arthur . . . trounced 'im."

"Well, that *is* good news! Nevertheless, it's no excuse for such excess. I never thought it of you." She pushed him off and tried to prop him against the wall, but his head lolled, and before she could prevent it, he'd slid down heavily upon her, his face half-buried in her lap. From the sudden relaxation of his body and the heavy sound of his breathing, she could tell that he'd slipped into blissful oblivion.

For a moment she glared down at him, wondering what to do next. He was too heavy to lift without help, especially in this comatose state. She could wriggle out from beneath him, she supposed, but that would leave him lying facedown on the cold stone floor. Finally she decided to stay where she was. Someone would surely come along shortly who could be sent for help. Meanwhile, she would make herself comfortable. She leaned back against the wall and straightened out a leg that was bent under her. Then she looked down at him, studying what she could see of his half-obscured face. He looked strangely boyish, his lashes making a dark shadow on his flushed cheek, and a slight smile turning up the corner of his mouth. She wanted, suddenly, to smooth the lines from his forehead, touch his cheek, brush back his fallen locks of hair. She felt unexpectedly content, and giving way to the compulsion, she let her fingers make their way, slowly, tenderly, through his damp, tousled hair. It was suddenly quite pleasant to be sitting there with Kit snuggled in her lap in this dank hallway amid the scattered pieces of silverware. To her utter astonishment, she realized she was wishing that time might stand still for a while . . . or, since that was not possible, that she might have a good long wait before anyone found them.

34

Kit's head, the next morning, felt huge and hollow and filled with little men with hammers. He got up and dressed with great effort, but he had no stomach for breakfast. Although his memory of the events after he and Mickley had started drinking was not at all clear, he was quite sure he'd somehow made a fool of himself with Caro. It was a blessing, he decided, that he had no memory of the particulars. Not wishing to face anyone this morning, he hid himself away in his study, where he drew the drapes, sat down at his desk, dropped his head on his arms, and prayed for death.

A knock at the door sent a shudder through him. "Come in if you must," he muttered.

His two aunts entered the room. "Goodness, Kit," Martha declared in her stentorian voice, "why is it so dark in here?" She immediately crossed to the windows and threw open the draperies.

Letty studied him closely. "Aren't you well, my love?" she asked gently. "Perhaps we should come back another time."

"No, no," he said, forcing a smile, although the light from the windows seemed to have set fire to his retinas. "I'm perfectly fine." He struggled to his feet. "Is there something I can do for you ladies?"

"Yes, there is," Martha said, pulling a chair up to his desk. "We have a plan we wish to propose."

He crossed the room, carefully holding his heavy head erect (for he fully expected it to roll off his neck if he turned too abruptly), and drew another chair to the desk for Letty. After assisting her into it, he returned to his seat and dropped down on it with an inner sigh of relief. "A plan?" he asked.

"Yes, my dear. A very exciting plan," Letty said eagerly.

"We wish you to hold a ball," Martha explained.

"A *ball*?" If he had a list of a thousand things he had no wish to do today, planning a ball would probably go to the top. "Good God, why?"

"To celebrate," Letty said with an excited gleam.

"To celebrate what?"

"Several things," Martha said. "Wellington's victory for one. And Arthur's coming home from school for summer vacation tomorrow for another. And your arrival in the neighborhood, for a third. After all, Kit, you've been here a few months, yet you've never entertained the neighboring gentry."

"I didn't know it was necessary."

"Of course it's necessary."

"You should give them a chance to meet you, Kit," Letty said. "You don't want them to think you toplofty."

"Right," Martha said with a vigorous nod. "And then there's Caro."

He lifted a brow. "Caro?"

"You've heard, of course, of her betrothal?"

Something in his chest clenched. "I've heard."

"Then don't you think that it should be announced to the public? And that there should be some sort of celebration?" Martha asked.

"I don't see why it requires a ball," he said grumpily.

"Because Caro deserves it, that's why." Martha crossed her arms over her large bosom, the epitome of matronly purposefulness. "A betrothal is a very significant event in a girl's life, you know."

"Perhaps the most significant," Letty said in support.

"I see." Kit glanced at his aunts in growing dismay. They wanted a ball, and they would have it no matter what he thought. He was, he realized, mere putty in their hands. "If we *did* give a ball, how many people do you think we would have to invite?"

"I've made a tentative list," Letty said. "It came to thirty-two. Quite a satisfactory number, don't you think? More than a sprinkle but less than a crush."

He groaned inwardly. "When would you wish it to take place?" he asked, feeling defeated.

"Within a week," Martha said promptly.

The answer surprised him. He thought that balls took a great deal of planning. "Why so soon?"

"Because I would very much like to attend," Martha said, "but I'll be leaving after that."

Letty turned to her in surprise. "You're only staying another week?"

"A fortnight is time enough for a guest to stay," Martha replied, looking suddenly uneasy.

"I don't hold with any such rule," Kit assured her. "You are welcome to stay as long as you like. But of course, since you love Town so much, I won't dissuade you."

"Good," she said shortly, as if impatient to drop the subject. "Then you agree to a ball?" Both ladies looked at him expectantly, eager for his answer.

He hesitated. "I don't know. I've never . . . I have no idea of what I must do to prepare—"

"You won't have to do a thing," Letty chirped. "We'll do everything."

"Shall we say next Thursday?" Martha pressed.

Kit wanted nothing but to be left alone. "Yes, yes," he said with a dismissive wave, "do whatever you think best."

He stared at the door after they were gone. "A ball for Caro's nuptials!" he muttered. "Just what I needed!" And he let his hammering head fall down on the desk with a thud.

35

Arthur's welcome, when he arrived from school, was not unlike that of a soldier returning from battle. The women of the household surrounded and embraced him as soon as he stepped from the carriage. "You're a head taller!" Caro gasped at her first sight of him. The boy *was* taller, and he seemed to Kit to be a great deal more mature than when he left. He'd quite enjoyed school, he told the family over tea, but he was delighted to be home at the Grange, free of schedules, free of books, and free of scholarly discipline. In answer to Caro's questions, he said he'd done passably well in all his subjects but Latin. Later, when he went out walking with Kit (with Gil swinging alongside easily on his crutches), he revealed that his greatest triumph at school had been his winning of the hundred-yard dash. He had a medal to prove it.

Meanwhile, preparations for the ball were proceeding apace. Kit was only dimly aware of them. He knew that extra help had been hired from the village, that the large, hitherto unused ballroom in the east wing had been opened, that there was a great bustle of cleaning and polishing, and that several crates and boxes had been arriving daily, some even from London. But none of the increased activity centered on him. Letty and Martha, true to their word, were seeing to everything themselves. Later, he supposed, when it was all over, he would be handed the bills.

On the afternoon of the day of the ball, when the preparations were at fever pitch and what seemed to Kit a veritable army of footmen, housemaids, and kitchen help was running madly about, he spirited himself into his study to be out of the way. He'd spent the morning riding with Arthur, with Gil tucked safely in front of him on his saddle. But now the boys were occupied, Gil with lessons and Arthur pressed into service to help hang festoons on the ballroom windows. He himself did not want to hang festoons. His study, he thought, was the perfect hideaway, providing an island of peace in the midst of chaos. He was surprised, therefore, when Melton appeared at his door announcing that Mr. Halford had arrived from London and was wishing to see him. "Send him up," Kit said, puzzled.

The solicitor entered the room with a nervous step, his portfolio tucked under his arm, his pince-nez perched precariously on his nose, and his entire appearance showing the strain of a hurried, uncomfortable ride. What was worse, Kit noticed a frown, so troubled that its cause was probably more serious than merely the discomfort of the trip from London, creasing his forehead. It was plain that the solicitor was bringing him an enormous problem. "I don't know what you've come to tell me, Halford," he greeted, rising and gripping the solicitor's hand, "but if I've lost my fortune on the 'Change, you've picked the worst day in the world to inform me of it. This ball my aunts have insisted on giving will undoubtedly cost me a thousand quid."

Mr. Halford barely smiled. "Your fortune is quite safe, my lord. The ball will not even make a dent."

"That's a relief. But you haven't the look of a man who carries good news."

"My news is not good. But it doesn't relate to your own fortune. It has to do with your aunt, Lady Whitlow."

Kit threw him a surprised glance before motioning him to a chair beside the desk. Mr. Halford flipped up his coattails and took the seat. "My aunt?" Kit prodded impatiently.

"Yes. Her man of business, a Mr. Quentin Fleer, sold her out of the funds more than two years ago, and then disappeared with the capital. I've been trying to find him, but I fear it is hopeless. Meanwhile, your aunt, not knowing her capital was gone, kept piling up debts. In April, it all came to pieces. Your aunt lost every penny. I had to sell her house to keep her from bankruptcy."

"Good God!" Kit could hardly believe his ears. "Her house?"

"I'm afraid so. The sale will be final at the end of the month."

"Dash it, man, this will be a dreadful blow to her. At her age, it might even affect her health." He thought for a moment and then looked up. "How great a debt is it? Do you think we can cover it and keep her going? That way, she needn't ever know."

Mr. Halford removed his glasses and stared at him. "I don't think you understand, my lord. She *already* knows."

Kit gaped. "She *knows*? That's not possible! She hasn't said a word!"

"I was afraid that would be the case. That's why I came. She absolutely forbade me to tell anyone, but I thought that you, as titular head of the family, ought to know."

"Of course I ought to know! What can she be thinking of? If her house is gone, why did she say she plans to leave here after the ball? Where will she go?"

"I have no idea, my lord."

Kit ran an impatient hand through his hair. "Why on earth didn't she come to me?"

The solicitor shrugged. "I suggested that she turn to you for help, but she refused. She has a great deal of pride, I'm afraid."

Kit made a face. "It seems to be a family trait."

Mr. Halford nodded understandingly. "You are thinking of Miss Caroline."

"Yes. My nemesis. I hope I'm more successful with my aunt."

"You intend to offer to help her, then?"

"Of course. I'll simply have to convince her to accept a gift. Can you keep from concluding the sale of the house until you hear from me?"

"I can certainly try." He rose and put out his hand. "You've much relieved my mind, Lord Crittenden. I had no idea, when we first met, what a very good family man you are."

Kit was surprised at the compliment. "Am I?"

"Indeed you are. With a very difficult family. You have my most sincere admiration."

The solicitor refused to remain for the ball for fear of facing an irate Martha Whitlow. "She would know, the moment she laid eyes on me, the purpose of my visit," he explained as he took his leave. After he left, Kit remained at his desk, reviewing the situation in his mind. Would he have as much difficulty with Martha, he asked himself, as he'd had with Caro? And if so, what could he do? The woman had no assets. Where did she think she would go? Did she intend, at her age, to follow Caro's example and go into service? It was madness!

The more he thought about it, the angrier he became. This was all Caro's fault. If she hadn't been so adamantly stubborn about the inheritance, Martha would probably not have had her example in mind and might not have been so resistant to being helped. It was infuriating to think of all the ways that stubborn, irritating, curly-headed chit had made his life a hell almost from his first day on English soil.

He stalked about the room, his temper rising with each step. Suddenly he threw open the door and shouted for Melton. The butler appeared in the doorway in short order, breathless with surprise at the shouted summons. "Send my so-called house-keeper to me," Kit ordered, snapping out his words. "Tell her I want to see her at once!"

He was seated at his desk when Caro arrived. Her surprise at being sent for was obvious, though she tried not to show it. "Did you send for me, my lord?" she asked from the doorway.

He did not rise. "Come in and shut the door," he said through clenched teeth, his voice ominously low.

She felt the tension and came in with real trepidation. She stood before him at the desk, waiting for him to ask her to be seated, but though there was a chair at her right, he did not invite her to sit. Instead he thrust a paper at her. "Do you know what this is?" he demanded.

She glanced at it quickly. It was some sort of legal document, the terminology of which was too difficult to grasp in one glance. She gave it back to him and shook her head. "I have no idea," she said.

"It's a notice of foreclosure," he said icily, "on your aunt's house."

"What?" She peered at him in confusion. "Which aunt? Martha? Her London house? I don't understand."

"She didn't confide in you, then?"

"Confide what?"

"That she is penniless. That she's lost even her house."

Caro could only gape at him. When the full meaning of his words burst on her, her knees gave way. "It's can't be," she gasped, sinking down upon the chair. "She's going home tomorrow, is she not?"

"She intends to go, but not to her home. She has no home to go to."

"Then . . . where?"

"I haven't the slightest idea."

"Didn't you ask her?"

"How could I? She didn't confide in *me*, either. If Mr. Halford hadn't called this afternoon and informed me of her situation, she would have left tomorrow without anyone being aware that she had a problem."

"Are you saying she doesn't intend to discuss this with you at all?"

"She evidently doesn't want me to know anything about it!" He stood up and leaned over the desk toward her. "And you know who's to blame for that, don't you?"

She stood and backed away, blinking in alarm. "I? Are you implying that all this is my fault?"

"Who else can be blamed? Who's spent the past four months trying to make the world think I'm some sort of monster?"

Caro put up a hand to ward off his attack. "What nonsense is this? I've never spoken against you except to your face."

"But your behavior has given her a fine example. *You* could not accept Lord Crittenden's despicable charity, so how can she?"

"Kit! You *can't* believe that I—"

"That you find my charity despicable? What else can I believe? You've gone to some desperate lengths to make the case, haven't you? First taking the post with the Ducketts, then this one as housekeeper, and finally your blasted—" He cut himself short and turned his back on her.

"My blasted what?"

He shook his head. "Nothing," he said, his anger suddenly exhausted. "I've made my point. I needn't go further."

She rose slowly from her chair. "Have I your permission, my lord, to speak to Martha on this matter?"

He wheeled about. "Why is it 'my lord' again? You called me Kit a moment ago."

"Have I your permission?" she insisted, ignoring his irrelevant remark.

"Do you think you can persuade her to seek my help?"

"I don't know. But I can try."

"Very well." He sighed, turning away again. "See what you can do."

She left without another word and ran up to Martha's room. Her aunt was already preparing for the ball. She was seated at the dressing table removing a row of curlpapers from the hair that fringed her face. Her purple gown lay spread out on the bed, and her turban and plumes sat imposingly beside it on a pillow. On a table near the window was an open portmanteau, partially packed. "Already preparing to depart, I see," Caro remarked without preamble.

Martha looked up at her in surprise. "Why are you not dressing? This ball is in your honor, you know. You must look your very best."

"There's plenty of time. I asked you if you're preparing to leave us."

"You know I am. I told you I shall be gone by tomorrow noon."

"To where?"

Martha stiffened. Then she turned slowly from the mirror. "Home, of course. Why do you ask?"

"You have no home. So where are you planning to go?"

Martha's wrinkled lips trembled. "How did you find out?" she asked in a small voice.

"Never mind how. I want an answer."

Martha peered at her for a moment, wringing her hands. "I w-wanted everything to be p-perfect tonight," she said as she lowered her head until her chin rested on her heaving bosom. But she could not hide the pair of tears that ran down her cheeks.

"Dash it all, Martha, don't cry," Caro said in quick self-reproach, crossing the room and kneeling down beside her. "I didn't mean to be cruel, even though I *would* like to wring your neck." She drew a handkerchief from her sleeve and mopped the elderly woman's cheek. "Tonight will be just fine. It's tomorrow that worries me. Where did you intend to go?"

"To D-Dorset," Martha blubbered. "I h-have an old s-school friend th-there. She wrote that I m-might be able to rent a little c-cottage near her."

"And how would you pay for it?"

Martha lifted her head proudly and sniffed back her sobs. "I have a few jewels I can sell."

"Oh, Martha!" She put her arms about her aunt's shoulders and cradled her affectionately. "How can you be so foolish? Dorset? A cottage? A few jewels? It's preposterous!"

"I know," Martha wailed.

"Why didn't you go to Kit? You know he'd be happy to help you."

Martha pulled herself from Caro's embrace and drew herself up. "How can you ask? You, of all people. You know I could not take charity, any more than you could!"

"But, my dear, it is not at all the same. You are his family. His blood! It's his *duty* to take care of you."

"You're speaking nonsense. I'm not his mother. He has no obligations toward an elderly aunt he hardly knew until he'd inherited his title. And even if he thinks it is his duty, I cannot bear the thought of being beholden—"

Caro winced at those words . . . her words. "There it is,

you see," she said. "Just as you said to me. The besetting sin that flaws us both—pride."

"Yes." Martha sighed.

"But you showed me, only a week ago, how my pride had blinded me to the discomfort I was causing everyone here by playing at being the housekeeper. Well, my love, your pride is doing something worse. You're giving Kit more than mere discomfort. You're hurting him deeply."

"What makes you say—"

"Can't you see what it would do to Kit every day of his life if he knew you were eking out a meager existence in Dorset while he had the means to make your last years comfortable and happy? Do you care so little for his feelings?"

Martha blinked at this new thought. "Do you really think he'd care so much?"

"How can you ask? Surely you've learned by this time what sort of man he is."

"Caro! Is this you speaking?" She rose slowly from her bench, her eyes wide in amazement. "If you, of all people, can say that about him, I suppose I should reconsider. . . ."

"Of course you should. If you act on your pride, you will make everyone here utterly miserable, while a little humility on your part will make all of us happy."

Martha began to tremble. The terrifying prospect of an impoverished old age had been a fearful weight on her chest for many weeks, but Caro was suggesting a way out. Weak with relief, she swayed on her feet. Caro took an alarmed step toward her. "Martha, you're not going to swoon, are you?" she asked.

Martha lifted her chin. "Of course not. I never swoon." After taking a deep breath, she beamed at the younger woman in overwhelming gratitude. "Oh, Caro," she cried, throwing her arms about the girl's neck, "I think you're right. A little humility. You can have no idea what you've done for me . . . how your words have relieved my mind! Honestly, my love, they are ringing in my ears like church bells!"

But Caro's words were ringing in her own ears in quite another way. How could I not have seen it? she asked herself in agonizing self-reproach. It was really so simple. A little humility. If she'd had any, she, too, could have spared many people a great deal of pain, her own pain most of all.

36

Caro gave herself a last glance in the pier mirror before going down to the ball. The young woman looking back at her did not look happy. She made herself smile. She was wearing the raisin-colored lustring gown with the bare shoulders that she'd last worn on the night of the opera, when Mr. Terence—or rather, Kit—had first kissed her. As she tightened the velvet bow just beneath her breast, she warned herself not to think about that night. It was tonight that should occupy her mind, the night her betrothal was to be announced—her betrothal to Mr. Henry Lutton. It was no time to remember the kisses of other men.

As she started down the stairs it suddenly occurred to her that Henry had never kissed her. He'd kissed her hand, of course, but those kisses did not mean anything. Tonight, perhaps, he would give her a true kiss. She wondered if it would stir her blood as Kit's had. It was unlikely, but if it did, she might find herself a little less blue-deviled about her prospective nuptials.

At the bottom of the stairs, she discovered that the first guests were arriving. The aunts had arranged for the whole family, Arthur and Gil included, to form a receiving line to greet them as they arrived. The family was already aligned when Caro came to take her place. Kit made room for her between himself and Arthur. She noticed that his eyes took on a look of burning admiration as they raked over her. Was he, too, remembering the last night she'd worn this dress?

Letty was wearing her old black lace and the peacock-feathered headdress. Martha, full of smiles, was regal in dark purple. Kit was, of course, top-of-the-trees in his black evening coat and satin breeches. But her brothers' appearance gave Caro the greatest delight. Arthur looked positively manly in his first evening coat. And Gil, despite the crutches, was adorable in his Sunday coat, with his neckcloth tied in the same fold as Kit's, his face scrubbed clean and his hair pomaded into tidy perfection.

Fifty guests were expected, for as Kit could have foretold, Letty's list of thirty-two was bound to grow. As the guests arrived Caro—the only in the line who knew every guest personally—introduced them to His Lordship and his aunts, after which they were led by a footman to the ballroom, where the musicians were already playing. As they passed down the line Caro could see that they were impressed with the new viscount and his surroundings. Kit greeted them all with friendly warmth until Sir Edward Braithwaite and his lady made their entrance. Sir Edward, a florid-faced, loud-voiced baronet who thought himself the jolliest of mortals, poked Kit in the ribs after they'd been introduced and chortled loudly, "Told m' lady you were no demon. She kept saying you'd turned our dear Miss Caroline into a servant and kept 'er locked away belowstairs, but anyone can see she's as much mistress of the Grange tonight as she ever was when the old viscount was alive."

"Oh, yes"—Lady Braithwaite giggled—"I did think you a demon. But I see now, with Caroline looking so perfectly ravishing tonight, that I was just foolish. I don't know how these silly rumors are circulated, but you may be sure, my lord, that I shall do everything in my power to restore your good name."

Kit murmured a polite thank you and hastily turned to the next arrivals, but Caro (who would have liked to shrivel away in shame and embarrassment for what she'd done to him) could see he was chagrined.

By the time the last guest had been greeted, the dancing was in full swing. Six musicians, stationed on a little platform in the far corner of the ballroom, were playing a country dance when the host party entered the ballroom. They were immediately absorbed into the merrymaking. Mr. Lutton detached himself from the group with whom he'd been chatting and came to claim Caro's hand for the next dance. Arthur, surprising everyone in his family, walked up to a pretty young lady at least two years older than he (the daughter of Squire Gundry, who lived two miles down the road), bowed, said a few words to her, and led her out to the floor, all with remarkable aplomb. Gilbert swung himself on his crutches along the edge of the dance floor to the musicians' platform, where he sat down to watch them perform. The aunts began to mingle with the other befeathered dowagers. And Kit was quickly surrounded by several of the local landowners who were full of questions about his plans for the renovation and improvement of the estate. He tried to concentrate on the conversation, but his eyes often flicked to the dance floor, where Lutton and Caro, looking decidedly well matched, were executing the figures of the Roger de Coverly. The sight so disturbed him that, despite his promise to himself after his last drinking debacle never to take another drink, he whisked a glass of champagne from the tray of a passing footman and downed it at a gulp.

He downed another glass the next time Lutton and Caro stood up together. He couldn't bear Lutton's unctuous manner or the self-satisfied smile on his face when he looked at Caro. It was a relief to him when the musicians struck up a waltz and the betrothed pair left the floor. Evidently Lutton did not feel that dancing the waltz was appropriate behavior for a vicar. For Kit, however, waltzing was almost second nature; if there was a single social grace an officer of the dragoons learned early in his career, it was the waltz. He decided, therefore, to take this opportunity and dance with her himself.

Caro accepted his invitation with a blush, and they walked out onto the floor. She'd never danced with him before and, what was worse, had never waltzed before at all . . . ever . . . except by herself in the privacy of her bedroom. Filled with abject terror—quite like a schoolgirl at her first dance—her heart pounded and her knees trembled. She would be tongue-tied and awkward, she thought miserably as he put his arm round her waist.

But as soon as he'd spun her into the first turn, her self-consciousness vanished. She found herself carried away on a whirlwind of motion, spinning and swirling like a leaf in a storm, her feet barely touching the ground, the flounce of her gown floating about her ankles, her curls bouncing on her forehead, her whole being borne on the air, nothing anchored, nothing secure but his hold on her waist and her desperate clasp on his shoulder. After a few moments, she seemed to lose herself in sheer motion, to become one with it, as she was drawn into the graceful pattern of light leaps and sweeping turns, his arm guiding her, bending her, moving her to the lilting rhythm of the music. This was no country dance where one could pause between figures, catch one's breath, and exchange pleasantries with one's partner. A country dance was restrained, polite, civilized. This was something else entirely. Restraint, conversation, even breathing had nothing to do with it. In the waltz, one could only surrender oneself . . . and dance.

When it was over, she looked up at him, wide-eyed with awe. "Oh, *Kit*!" she gasped with the last, tiny spasm of breath she had left.

He stared at her, wincing as if in pain. "Damn you, Caro," he swore in a hissing whisper, "don't look at me like that! Here, give me your arm. I'll take you back to your betrothed."

She did not dance again that evening. She couldn't. When Henry asked her to stand up with him for a quadrille, she pleaded fatigue. To ensure that she would not be asked again, she went to the dowagers' row and sat down beside Martha. "I knew the moment I saw your face this evening," she said when Martha turned to greet her, "that you'd had your talk with Kit."

"Yes, I did"—Martha beamed—"and it was not a bit embarrassing. He was very understanding. Can you believe, Caro, that he made my meal of humble pie almost pleasant?"

"Yes, I can. I'm afraid I've greatly misjudged him. But what did you decide to do?"

"He offered to buy back my house for me, but I declined."

"But *why,* dash it?" Caro glared at her in frustration. "I thought you'd decided to accept his help."

"I did. But I told him I no longer wish to live in London. That if he could bear to have another old lady taking residence here at the Grange, that is what I would like above anything."

This took Caro by surprise. "Oh, Martha, did you mean it? Don't you wish to go home to London, to your old friends, to your accustomed life?"

"Not anymore. At my age I have very few friends left, you know. Everyone I care for is here. And Kit—he is such a darling!—says he'd be happy to expand his family. He's going to give me rooms quite like Letty's. So now we shall all be together. Isn't that lovely?"

"Oh, yes!" Caro agreed, embracing her. "As lovely as can be!"

At that moment, Melton appeared in the ballroom doorway, striking a gong to announce that a late supper was about to be served. Fifty guests swarmed toward the large dining room, where a generous buffet awaited them. Caro stopped Gil at the door. "Isn't it time you went up to bed, young man?" she asked him pointedly.

"Ah, Caro, that isn't fair," the boy objected. "You let me stay for the dancing, which is the greatest bore, but you won't let me stay for the food! The buffet is the best part of the party!"

It was hard for her to find a counterargument, so, with a warning to him not to make a pig of himself, she let him stay.

There were many who would have agreed with Gil that the buffet was the best part. The long buffet table was heaped with treats: lobster cakes, rolled veal *à la royale*, smoked salmon fillets, mutton pâtés, piles of cheese buns, orange biscuits, and rolls *à la duchesse,* an assortment of aspics and gelatin molds, and all sorts of jellies, creams, soufflés, trifles, and cakes. When the guests had heaped their plates, they took seats at one of the five tables placed round the room, each of which was served by two footmen who filled their glasses with wine. When most of the eating was done, Kit tapped on his glass with his knife and rose from his chair. "My aunts have both insisted that I, as host, must be the one to announce the various reasons we have come together in celebration," he said, raising his voice so that he could be heard throughout the room. "I must admit that I'm not in the best condition to do this, being already very well to live. In addition, I am about to propose a number of toasts, so many that by the end of this speech you all will be as diddly as I am now, and I, I fear, will be completely cast away."

He paused to let the ripple of laughter die down and to be sure the footmen had filled all the glasses.

"First, let us raise our glasses to Arthur Wellesley, the heroic Duke of Wellington, who last week at Waterloo put Napoleon at last and finally to rout."

Again he paused. The guests rose to their feet and drank, several gentlemen shouting, "Hear, hear!"

"Next," Kit went on when they'd resumed their seats, "I'd like to toast all of you who've graced my tables this evening, with a special welcome to my nephew Arthur, who's just returned from school with a medal in the hundred-yard dash. To Arthur, and to you all."

Applause filled the room, the second toast was drunk, and the footmen again circulated, refilling the glasses.

"Now, may I ask that you all drink with special enthusiasm to my friend Mick Mickley and Miss Betty Rhys, whose banns were read in church this very week. May I offer my warmest congratulations on your coming nuptials. Stand up, you two, and let everyone see your radiant faces."

There was a buzz of voices that greeted this announcement as Betty, looking very ladylike in a blue muslin gown that Caro had given her, and with her hair (without a cap for once) done up magnificently in the fashion called *à la Grecque,* got awkwardly to her feet, with Mickley beside her, grinning in besotted pride. "Isn't she a housemaid?" one woman was heard to ask. But Kit began to applaud enthusiastically, and his example was soon followed by everyone else. If the viscount was eccentric enough to invite a housemaid to his table, they thought, it was his own business, and certainly not a matter to cast shadows on this generously opulent party. Mickley, in a burst of courage, kissed his betrothed on the cheek, bringing on another—and more spontaneous—round of applause as they both sat down.

"And finally," Kit went on, his smile fading. "I've been assigned to make the most important announcement of the evening, the principal reason for this gathering. . . ." He paused, reached for his glass and took a good, if unorthodox, swig. ". . . the principal reason for this gathering . . ." He looked at Caro, who was staring at him with an expression that hovered somewhere between smiling politeness and bone-chilling dread. ". . . the principal reason . . ." He could see from the corner of his eye that Henry Lutton was leaning forward in his chair as if ready to leap to his feet at a moment's notice. "I am honored to—no, hang it, I'm not honored! I'm *expected* to . . . to announce the upcoming nuptials of yet another happy couple. . . ."

He felt ill, desperate. If I don't get out of here, he thought, I shall lose my mind! He turned to Letty, who was seated at his right. "Confound it, Letty," he muttered, leaning down and speaking into her ear, "I can't do this. *You* do it!" He thrust the glass into her hand and strode out of the room.

Letty looked after him, her eyes moist with sympathy. Then, leaning heavily on her cane, she got to her feet and faced the now silent audience. "It gives me great pleasure," she said, her voice pitched achingly high, "to announce the betrothal of our beloved Caroline Whitlow to the eminent, respected vicar of our church, Mr. Henry Lutton."

There was a gasp of surprise, but before the listeners could raise their glasses, a youthful voice cried out, "No!" Gil, his underlip trembling, lifted himself from his chair, picked up his crutches, threw Caro a look of heartrending reproach, and hobbled from the room.

"Gil!" Caro cried, starting after him.

"Caro, my dear, you can't go now!" Martha hissed, grasping her arm.

Arthur jumped up. "It's all right," he said quietly to his sister, "I'll see to him." And he followed his brother out.

Caro reluctantly resumed her seat. With Martha prodding her, Letty raised her glass again. "To Henry and Caroline!" she said, trying her best to sound cheerful. "May they have the happiest of futures."

The guests, fully enjoying being privy to this private drama (and the prospect it gave them for delicious gossip later), rose and raised their glasses. "To Henry and Caroline!"

37

The guests were gone. Henry and Caro stood outside the front door, waving off the last carriage. When it was out of sight, Caro dropped her face in her hands. "What a fiasco!" she muttered.

"Only a small part of it," the vicar said, taking one of her hands. "Most of the guests had a fine time."

She shook her head. "We've provided them with enough scandal to keep them gossiping for months. Whatever made Gil behave that way?"

"I suppose he doesn't wish his stern tutor to become his equally stern brother-in-law. I am less disturbed by his outburst than I am by His Lordship's." He squinted intently at Caro's face, trying to read her expression in the dim glow emanating from the still-lit windows. "What do you make of his strange behavior?"

"I don't know what to make of it," she said.

He shook his head and gave her a chiding smile. "I thought we agreed to be truthful with each other."

Her eyes flew to his face. "Do you think I *lie*? Kit Meredith's behavior has *always* been confusing to me."

He drew her arm through his. "Let's take a stroll down the drive," he suggested. "It's a lovely night."

They walked along in silence. Caro braced herself for a sermon, which she supposed she deserved, but she wasn't certain why. "You and His Lordship danced the waltz as if you'd practiced together for years," he remarked after a while.

"Did it seem so? I've never waltzed before in my life."

"Indeed? Then it was an amazing performance. You seemed to enjoy it a great deal."

"I did." She stopped and looked over at him. "Was that wrong of me?"

"No, not wrong. It only makes me wonder how you will feel when you may no longer indulge in the waltz when we go to parties."

"Why may I not? I know you don't like it, but may I not dance it with other partners after we're wed?"

"I don't think it appropriate for the vicar's wife to dance the waltz with a man not her husband."

"Oh, I see." She walked on for a few steps, wondering in what other unexpected ways her life would be restricted after she married. Suddenly she swung about and faced him. "Henry, will you do a favor for me? Kiss me!"

That startled him. "Now? Here?"

"Yes, right now and right here. We are betrothed, are we not? And we're quite alone. In these circumstances, it *must* be permissible."

"Very well, my dear," he said. He took a step closer to her, cupped her face in his hands, and softly kissed her lips. "Is that what you wanted?" he asked when he'd done.

"I . . . suppose so," she said. She turned away, unable to meet his eyes.

"That's not the way Lord Crittenden kissed you, is it?"

Her eyes flew to his. "No," she whispered guiltily.

"I did tell you, remember, that I am not much interested in the physicality of wedlock."

"Yes, I remember."

"That may prove . . . er . . . difficult for you?"

"I don't know. It may."

There was a long pause. She could not read his face in the darkness. But suddenly his voice came to her in sharp, perfect clarity. "He loves you, you know. The viscount."

She threw him a look of amazement. "Don't be ridiculous," she said.

"I think you know he does. The question is, how do you feel about him?"

She clenched her fists. "I despise him."

"Do you, indeed? Why? Is it because he hired you as his housekeeper?"

"No, that was my doing, not his. He wanted me to live here in the same manner as I did with Uncle Clement."

"That was certainly good of him. Then what is it about him that bothers you so?"

"He is . . . there is a part of him . . . a selfish part, a dishonest part. . . ."

"Is that so? I've not seen that side of him. What makes you think so?"

"Well, you know how he made us leave the Grange that had been our home for so long. . . . "

"But he didn't do it on purpose. Your aunt Letty explained to me that he didn't know you existed."

"That's true, I suppose. But then he lied to me . . . pretended to be someone else . . . masqueraded with a false identity for . . . for weeks."

"That was certainly a dastardly thing to do. I wonder why he did it."

"Well, you see, it was after he'd saved my life, and when he realized who I was, he . . . he . . ." She made an impatient, helpless gesture with her hand. "Oh, it's much too convoluted to explain."

"Saved your life, did he?"

"Yes, but then, when he tried to force a legacy upon me . . ."

"Tried to force a legacy on you? Is *that* his crime?"

She heard, with a wave of annoyance, the lack of sympathy in his voice. "Dash it all, Henry, I didn't *want* his charity. And he did force it on my brothers, in spite of . . . of . . ."

"Let me get this clear in my mind, Caro. You despise the man because he saved your life, tried to give you a legacy, took your brothers under his wing, gave them a home, and offered a home to you as well. Yes, I quite see what you mean. He certainly sounds like a despicable fellow to me."

Tears stung her eyelids. "You d-don't *understand*! It's just too c-complicated to explain."

"Perhaps it is," he said gently, taking her hand and starting back toward the house, "but I think one thing is clear. He will be a better husband for you than I could ever be."

38

The little men with hammers were back in Kit's head. After he'd left the party, he'd thrown himself into bed and fallen into a stertorous sleep. But he'd wakened early, his mouth sour, his head thick and aching, and his spirits at their lowest depths. It was not yet dawn, but he'd gotten up and staggered down the hall to find Mickley, hoping that the ingenious batman could concoct a brew that might ease his suffering.

On the way, he heard sobbing coming from Gil's room, sobbing that seemed to express in pure sound what Kit himself felt in his soul. He knocked at the door and let himself in. Gil lifted his head from his pillow, took one look at the intruder, and fell into his arms. "I don't want Caro to marry Mr. Lutton," he wept. "I didn't even want her to do it last time, when I hardly knew him."

"Last time?"

"Yes, before we moved to London. Arthur said she'd do it, because we didn't have anyplace to go, but when it came to the point, she didn't. Why is she doing it now?"

"I don't know, Gil. Perhaps she loves him."

"She *can't* love him! He's so . . . so put-offish. And he's deucedly strict about silly things like shirts being properly tucked in. And he never laughs. When we go to live with him, Arthur says we won't even be able to say damn."

"But you aren't going to live with him, my boy. You're going to stay right here."

Gil lifted his head and gaped. "Really? Really, truly? How do you know?"

"Caro said so. Really, truly."

The boy sighed a long, shuddering, relieved sigh as a heavy

weight rolled off his heart. "Oh, *thank* you!" he whispered, raising his eyes to heaven. Then he threw his arms around Kit's chest and hugged him tight.

Kit lifted the boy's chin. "It's all right, then? For her to wed him, I mean."

The boy's face clouded. "I don't know, Kit. If she goes through with it this time, do you suppose I'll ever get used to it?"

Kit didn't answer. He tucked the boy in and ordered him to get some sleep. But as he made his unsteady way toward Mickley's room, the boy's words echoed in his aching head. *Do I suppose I'll ever get used to it?* he asked himself. Gil might get used to it someday, he thought glumly, but he never would.

Mickley made him a tisane of barley water, lemon juice, and cloves, but it did no good. Kit tottered to his study, sank down behind his desk, dropped his head in his hands, and groaned. The clock struck eight. The whole long day stretched before him without prospect of any ease of the pain in either his head or his spirit. He actually considered getting drunk again. He wondered if this disappointment in love would do to him what it did to so many men—drive him to drink. Was he doomed to end his days a pathetic old souse?

There was a sharp rap at the door. The sound set off a gong that vibrated in his brain. "Go away," he snarled in a voice that brooked no argument.

Caro put her head in the door. She'd covered her hair with her housekeeper's cap again, but she somehow managed, he thought in annoyance, to look as lovely as she had when he'd waltzed with her. "It's only me, my lord," she said with a repellent cheerfulness. "Can you spare me a moment?"

"If you've come to berate me for my performance last night," he growled, "you may save your breath. I'm being punished for it quite adequately."

"No, it's not about that. It's about my notice."

"Your *notice*?" He felt his innards clench. "You wish to cut it short? Don't tell me that you and your so decorous betrothed have decided that you cannot wait even one little month to take your vows."

"I didn't come to tell you that at all. Quite the opposite."

Something in that answer caught his attention. The little men inside him eased their hammering, as if they, too, were curious. "Come in and sit down, ma'am," he said, lifting his aching head.

She came in, shut the door, and took the chair at his desk. "I would like to *withdraw* my notice, my lord. It seems I shall not be getting married after all."

Kit gulped. This was news indeed! A bubble of excitement stirred in his blood. The little men stopped their hammering altogether. But, he warned himself, it was entirely possible that he didn't hear aright. Or that he'd misunderstood her meaning. It was even possible that he was only dreaming. "*Not* getting married?" he asked carefully.

"No, my lord. Mr. Lutton changed his mind."

He eyed her in utter disbelief. "Don't flummery me, girl. Mr. Lutton would be insane to change his mind."

"Not at all. Any man would change his mind if he believed his betrothed loved another."

"Are you trying to tell me that Mr. Lutton believes you love *someone else*?"

"Yes, he does. He believes I'm in love with . . . with you."

It was remarkable how a few words could relieve a blinding headache. And set a man to trembling. Kit had to clench his fists to steady himself. "Is that what he believes? The man must be an idiot." He peered at her intently. "Did you *tell* him that he's an idiot?"

She dropped her eyes. "No, I didn't."

"Why not?"

"Because, you see, he's . . . right."

A shudder went through him. An actual shudder. Had she said what he thought she'd said? He put a hand to his forehead. He was still too thickheaded to trust what he thought he'd heard. "Please, Caro," he muttered, shutting his eyes, "try to speak plain. I'm not sure I understand what you're getting at. What is it you want of me?"

"I want to stay here . . . to have my position back."

He opened one eye. "You want to be my *housekeeper* again?" he asked in disgust.

"Yes, if . . . if no better post is offered me."

"Better post? What better post?"

"If you can't think what that might be, then I can't help you," she said primly. "It wouldn't be seemly."

There was something about her—not only her words but her very tone of voice—that was puzzling. She was *flirting* with him, he realized with a shock. And today of all days, after all he'd been through, he had not the patience for it. "Dash it all, woman," he said, rising and stumbling round the desk, "I'm in no condition to play games." He grasped her arms and lifted her from the chair. "Did you or did you not say you loved me?"

"Well, I . . ." Her mouth seemed to be stifling a laugh, but her eyes were a little frightened. ". . . I said that Henry said it."

"You said he was *right*!"

"Yes, I did. He also said that *you* loved *me*. Was he right about that, too?"

He expelled a long breath and pulled her close. "Damnation, Caro, are you blind? How can you not have seen it? I've loved you since the moment I pulled you from under those horses!"

"Oh, *Kit*!" She gazed up at him, misty-eyed but not quite convinced.

He looked down at her glowing face, also afraid to believe this was real. How was it possible for the world to change so radically in only a few minutes? Could he be dreaming? But no, he told himself, he couldn't be. If this were a dream, she wouldn't be wearing that dreadful cap. He lifted his hand and pulled it off before tightening his hold on her. His happiness was now almost complete. All it needed was to feel his mouth on hers.

But when he bent his head to kiss her, she put her fingers on his lips to hold him off. "That's not true, you know," she murmured, her fingers caressing his mouth. "You haven't loved me as long as that."

"I think I should know that better than you." It was an offhand reply, made absently, for he was intent on grasping those moving fingers and kissing them.

She slipped them from his grasp. "But when you were Mr. Terence," she said, lowering her eyes, "you made it very clear that you didn't want to be a suitor for my hand."

"Good God! Has *that* been troubling you all this time?"

"Yes, it has," she admitted in a tiny voice. "More than anything."

"But how *could* I have been a suitor? I was living a cursed masquerade!" He gave a rueful laugh. "If you'd known my real identity that night, our whole history would have been different. I'd have been on my *knees*!"

That was all she needed to hear. The wound that had festered for so long was instantly healed. She slipped her arms round his neck and joyfully surrendered to his hungry embrace.

He kissed her for a long, long time. Then, without taking his mouth from hers, he lifted her in his arms and carried her to his chair. There, with the morning sun haloing their heads, they sat with arms entwined, enjoying to the full the blissful satisfaction of love requited after long postponement.

She was nuzzling his neck, and his lips were pressed against the curls on her forehead, when the door flew open and Letty wandered in. Caro, embarrassed at being caught in this position of intimacy, tried to jump from his lap, but he held her fast. Letty, however, had that abstracted, inward look in her eyes; she didn't really see them. "Kit, I've been thinking," she said, absently taking a chair opposite them, "that you ought somehow to make up to Caro for your rudeness last night. . . ."

"It doesn't matter, Aunt Letty," Caro said, giggling. "Not anymore."

Letty blinked. "Caro? Are *you* here?" She peered into the brightness, glimpsed the still-embracing couple, and gasped. "Good heavens, my dear, what are you *doing*? You're going to be *married*!"

"I *know*. Isn't it wonderful?"

"But surely you're not going to pretend it's proper to be sitting that way—" Then she gasped again. "Caro! No! *Truly?* You and *Kit*?"

"Yes." Kit laughed. "My housekeeper here insisted on a promotion to a better post, and the only way I could satisfy her demand was to promise to wed her and make her, once and for all, the mistress of this place."

"Oh, Kit!" Letty's face seemed to collapse, and she burst into tears. "I'm so h-happy! It's what I always p-prayed would happen!" She clasped her hands to her bosom and beamed as tears flowed down her cheeks. It took a while before she could get hold of herself. Then, after blowing her nose in her handkerchief, she got to her feet. "Please go back to what you were doing," she said excitedly. "I must go at once and tell everyone the news."

"Very well, Letty. Go on and shout the news to everyone in the world," Kit said, grinning at her. "Except the boys. You must let Caro tell Arthur. And I want to be the one to tell Gil."

"Of course, my dears, of course," Letty said, hobbling hastily to the door. "But you must let *me* tell Martha." She opened the door and threw them a smile that was almost as mischievous as it was euphoric. "She always boasts about never swooning, but when she hears this, she will faint dead away!"

Matched Pairs

Every couple is not a pair.
—Old English adage

1

TRIS DID NOT ANTICIPATE A QUARREL WITH JULIE about his plans to wed another girl. If there was one thing about which he and Julie were in complete agreement, it was that they would never wed each other. Nevertheless, he felt uneasy as he paced round the summerhouse, the capes of his greatcoat flapping in the chilly March wind. *Not that there's any reason for unease,* he told himself. *We've always sworn that we would never marry, no matter what our mothers said.*

This interview would not have been necessary at all if, nineteen years ago when Juliet Branscombe was born and he, Tristram Enders, was merely three years old, their mothers had not officially betrothed them. But they had. The two mothers, with wicked premeditation, had had the banns read at church and had even sent an announcement to the *Times.* Later, when the two victims were old enough to understand what their mothers had done, they had quite understandably rebelled. Since they were more like squabbling siblings than lovers, marriage between them was out of the question. "We don't have to comply with a compact in which we had no part," Tris would often declare.

"Just because our mothers arranged it," Julie would agree, "it doesn't have to follow that we must accept it."

Tris truly believed that arranging a betrothal between children was ridiculous. "No one makes birth-matches anymore," he'd said more than once.

"Royalty, perhaps," Julie would add, "but no one else."

"It's been out of fashion for centuries."

"Leg-shackling children at birth! Medieval, that's what it is!"

Thus they'd made a pact that, when the time was right, they would join forces and reject their mothers' plan. That was the one matter on which they'd been in agreement for years. So there was no reason for Tris to feel so deucedly uncomfortable now. No reason at all.

He turned and peered out past the hedges that separated Enders Hall's north field from Larchwood, the Branscombes' property. A stile that provided an opening between the hedges gave him a view of the grounds leading to the rear lawns of Larchwood, but there was no sign of human movement anywhere. What was keeping the girl?

He'd sent her a note asking her to meet him at the Enders' summerhouse, but he hadn't told her why. He'd chosen the summerhouse for the meeting because it was a place he knew would be safe from prying eyes. It stood at the far corner of the Enders' northernmost field, where the slope of the land kept it from being seen from either house. In summer the structure was beautiful; graceful and delicate, it was a cool retreat, with its open sides shaded by flowering vines that covered its latticed balustrades and its carved posts holding up a sloping hexagonal roof. But in other seasons it looked bare, as it did now. Today—on a day so chill and gray it was more like February than March—the place was depressing. The ornamental trees and shrubs that shaded it in summer were still bare of leaves, and there was not yet a sign of flowering on the vines. There was not a touch of color anywhere. Tris shivered as the winds, still wintry-sharp, blew a swarm of dead leaves about his legs.

Expelling an impatient breath, he leaned against a post and looked about him. The rolling lawns of his family home were just beginning to shed their winter dullness. Bits of green sprouts could be faintly seen pushing up beneath the frost-dimmed grass and glimmering along the edges of the shubbery. *I shall be in London when spring comes,* he thought with a momentary twinge of sadness. *I'll miss seeing the colors burst forth.*

The thought brought his primary problem right back to his consciousness. Why was he so reluctant to tell Julie what was on his mind? There was no reason to believe that she would not be in complete sympathy with his intentions. She'd always felt as he did on the subject of their mothers' oddities.

Tris recalled a conversation he'd had with Julie after his mother had ordered him to give the girl a heart-shaped locket on her seventeenth birthday. Julie accepted the gift without comment, but she'd known perfectly well that the gesture had been forced on him. Later, when they were alone, they laughed about it. "How dreadfully sentimental our mothers are," Julie said, carelessly swinging the silver bauble by its chain. "Did they really believe I'd be so moved by a trinket that I'd fall in love with you?"

"They're sentimental fools," he said, "both swooning over courtly love and chivalric behavior. I can't convince them that I'm not a white knight."

"Nor am I Elaine of Astolat. As if a heart-shaped bauble could inspire love! I sometimes think they actually *believe* in nonsense like charms and amulets and talismans. The trouble is that they're both too fond of literary romance."

"Fond? They're positively looney!" Tris declared. "One can see it in the names they gave us. Tristram, indeed. What sensible mother would name a son Tristram? I'm surprised your mother didn't name you Isolde."

"Heaven forbid!" Julie gasped. "Juliet is bad enough. What would you have done if your mama had named you Romeo!"

Tris shuddered at the very thought. "Romeo! I'd have been laughed out of school!"

Conversations like those did not mean that Juliet Branscombe and Tristram Enders were close friends. In truth, they often wondered if they really liked each other. Having been brought up together on adjoining estates and encouraged to do everything together—play together, study together, attend church services together, celebrate birthdays and holidays together—each claimed the other was often not only uninteresting but positively irritating. The one matter on which they agreed was that they could never have been, were not now, and could never be, lovers.

"We know each other too well," Tris would often remark.

"Much too well," Julie would second. "There's no excitment."

"No suspense."

"No mystery. Not the slightest tinge of mystery."

Thus they were in complete agreement that a match between them was not to be thought of. So there was no reason for him to feel like a scoundrel for having fallen in love with someone else. Julie would not care. She didn't want him anyway. He was quite certain of th—

"Tris?"

He turned in time to see Julie climbing over the top of the stile. The girl was her usual disheveled self. Her yellow bonnet had blown from her head and was hanging against her back by its green ribbons, thus allowing long strands of hair to blow wildly about her face. Her cheeks were ruddy from the cold wind, and the shabby old dull-green shawl, which she was clutching to her throat with one gloved hand, blended perfectly with the dead grass of the lawn behind her.

Julie jumped down from the stile with a clumsy thump of her muddy boots and waved his note at him. "What's amiss?" she asked as she hurried toward the wide wooden steps of the summerhouse. "I had to tell Mama a fib about where I was going."

"Nothing's amiss." Tris frowned down at her uplifted face in disapproval. She was a pretty little thing, with that silky auburn hair and those light hazel eyes that always seemed to be seeing something in another world. Any man would find her lovely if she had the least idea of how to show herself off. But he would not say that aloud; he rarely said anything kind to her. "Put that bonnet back on your head," he growled in disgust. "You've let the wind make a fair hodgepodge of your hair. We may have to disentangle the strands from your eyelashes."

"Thank you, sir, you flatter me as usual," she responded dryly. "You, on the other hand, look very fine. You haven't dressed that way just for me, I'd wager."

"You'd win that wager. But never mind my clothes. What dreadful fib did you tell your mother?"

"I said I was going to call at the vicarage. Mrs. Weekes is, fortunately for us, ailing."

"Mrs. Weekes is always ailing. Call on her before you go home, and then you'll not have fibbed."

"That, Tris Enders, is a liar's reasoning," she retorted. "A fib's a fib." Then she looked up at him inquiringly. "If nothing's amiss, why did you send me this cryptic note?"

"I wanted to speak to you before I left."

She blinked. "Oh? Are you going away?"

"I'm going back to London this afternoon."

"Again?"

He nodded. The uneasy feeling, suddenly returning, caused him to look down at his boots.

"To see *her,* I suppose," Julie said, peering at him suspiciously.

"Her?" His eyes shot up to hers, his brows lifted in amazement.

"Your Miss Smallwood."

"Good God! You *guessed?"*

Julie shrugged. "Well, your one and only letter from town was so full of her . . ."

"Oh."

The girl studied him with interest. She'd known him all her life but she'd never known him to care for a girl. Had he actually fallen in love at last? "Since you've been home less than a fortnight," she ventured carefully, not wishing to sound as if she were prying, "I must assume you are so impatient to return to town because you have a real *tendre* for your Miss Smallwood."

"I wish I *could* call her mine," Tris said ruefully. "Cleo has yet to accept me."

Julie's eyes widened. "You've already *asked* her?" The matter must have progressed farther than she thought!

"No, not yet. That's what I intend to do, however, when I get back to town. Ask her."

"Oh. I see."

Though this response was given in one brief, quiet exhalation of breath, Julie was finding Tris's news staggering. Tris was truly in love! And intending to wed! Astounding!

Julie hadn't ever given thought to what such a development might mean to *her.* She'd always found Tris irritatingly high-handed, argumentative and critical, but though they were longtime adversaries, she had no good reason not to wish him happy. *Good-bye, good luck and God bless,* she ought to say to him. Why not?

But of course it was not that simple. There would be consequences that were certain to be unpleasant, not the least of which would be to face their mothers at last about the birth-betrothal. Facing their mothers would be far from easy. Tris's mother, Lady Phyllis, was soft-voiced and sweet, but she wore an iron determination inside her velvet glove. And her own mother, loud and overbearing, would surely make a scene. Julie hated scenes. The prospect of this one was so dreadful to contemplate that it tightened her chest.

Trying to catch her breath, she sat back against the balustrade and studied Tris with a furrowed brow. He was changing right before her eyes. He seemed to have suddenly become older than his twenty-two years. His face seemed leaner and less irritatingly mischievous than it had been just yesterday, when they'd been forced to dine with their mothers at the Branscombes' table. She couldn't even detect that annoying dimple that always appeared in his left cheek when he smiled. Today he looked . . . well, different. He was only of average height, but today he looked almost tall. It wasn't merely that he'd dressed for town, his usually tousled dark hair brushed into a modish Brutus and his new beaver hat with its stylishly curled brim set on his head at an especially rakish angle. Nor was it that that his shoulders looked broader than usual in the caped greatcoat he'd thrown over them. It was just that he seemed, all at once, more knowing, more purposeful, and more . . . more manly. Was it love that had done it? she wondered. Did love have the power to make one more mature?

"It's too cold to stand about," Tris was saying. "Let's walk."

He offered his arm, but she shook her head. In silence, they set off together along the gravel path that edged the woods shared by the two estates. Julie gathered her thick wool shawl more closely about her shoulders but let the wind blow her long auburn tresses freely about her face. "Tell me about her," she requested suddenly, feeling both fascinated and repelled.

"About Cleo?" He gave a careless shrug. "Not much to tell. Cleo's beautiful, of course, but in a different sort of way from the usual beauties."

"In what way different?"

Tris considered the question with a furrowed brow. "Her hair, for one thing. She cuts it short, little curls close to her head."

"Like Caro Lamb," Julie offered with a knowing nod.

"Yes. I find it charming. And she moves with the most enchanting swing of her limbs." His eyes shone with a reminiscent glow. "Her gestures are all like that, sort of . . . loose and . . . and wide. They're all of a piece with her character."

"Her *character* is loose and wide?" Julie asked, amused.

He threw her a quick glare, the kind he habitually tossed at her. "Of course not, you goose. What I meant was that her gestures are, in a manner of speaking, spontaneous."

"Spontaneous?"

"Yes. You might call them uninhibited. And . . . and self-assured. They seem to reveal her inner nature. She thinks well of herself, you see."

"Does she really?" Julie could not help being impressed by his description.

"Oh, yes. She's very sure of herself. Not simpering and missish like other girls."

Julie's step slowed. "That's a swipe at me, isn't it?" she asked ruefully. "I suppose you think that *I'm* simpering and missish."

"You?" He looked down at her in sincere surprise. "No, I didn't mean that at all. You're not missish. Not with me, at any rate. However," he added, reconsidering, "you may be so with other fellows. They all say you're too shy."

"Shy? *Me?"*

"I don't know why you're surprised. You know how you are when you're in your mother's shadow."

Julie winced. "Yes, I know."

"It's your own fault. You shouldn't let her overwhelm you as she does. I don't believe shyness to be an asset to a girl, Julie. Even being missish and simpering would probably be an improvement. At least you'd giggle and flicker your lashes at a fellow, instead of just . . . just hiding."

She stiffened. "Hiding?"

"Yes, hiding." Tris, ignoring her obvious dismay, barged on. "That's what you do in society, you know. You hide. Behind your dowdy shawls, behind your mother, behind your fan."

"Really, Tris," she said, her voice rich with sarcasm, "you shouldn't flatter me so."

"If you want flattery, my girl, ask someone else. You should be grateful for the truth."

"You're quite right. I'll write you a note of thanks as soon as I get home."

He laughed. "That's the spirit. That was saucy. Don't you see, Julie? That's how you *should* behave in society."

"You want me to be *saucy?* I could never—"

Disgusted, he shrugged and walked on. She followed, not speaking. But after a while, she caught up with him. "I'm not surprised that you love your Miss Smallwood," she remarked thoughtfully. "Someone who thinks well of herself . . . that must be rare."

"She is rare," Tris said. "I think you'd like her."

"I only hope— *Oooh!"* The gasp came from deep in her chest, and her whole body froze in horror. There in the path ahead of them lay a small, furry little animal, quite dead.

"Dash it, Julie, you needn't carry on so," Tris scolded. "It's only a dead rabbit." He stepped over it and put out his hand to help her follow.

But Julie hung back, staring down at the lifeless bit of fur. "Shouldn't we do something? Bury it or something?"

"Bury it? Good God, girl, one would think it was your pet! Must you always be so deuced squeamish? We'll leave it where it is. The groundskeeper or some passerby will find it and think himself lucky for coming upon a good dinner without having to waste a bullet."

Julie swallowed her distaste at the thought of the poor creature being turned into rarebit and surrendered to Tris's good sense. She took his hand, stepped over the body and proceeded down the path.

Tris, dismissing the incident from his mind, returned to the subject of their meeting. "So you see, I wanted to warn you. The next time you see me, when I've won Cleo's hand, we're going to have to face our mothers."

"We?" This time it was Julie who looked scornful. "In the first place, I don't see why this is any concern of mine. In the second place, what makes you so sure your Miss Smallwood'll have you?"

He stopped in his tracks. "Well, she seemed to encourage . . ." His eyes narrowed, and he peered at Julie through knit brows. "Do you think she won't?"

"I'm sure I couldn't say. I don't know the lady. But if it were me, I wouldn't."

"You only say that because you know I won't ever ask you. I'll have you know that Cleo hinted she considers me a catch."

"A *catch?"* Julie gave a disdainful little laugh. "Really, Tris, you can't be serious."

"Why not? I've a title, haven't I? And an estate that's not inconsiderable. And a certain confidence in address.

And I'm told that my appearance is pleasing. So why am I not a catch?"

"Because you're a peacocky, bumptious *ass* is why!" She stalked off down the path, tossing some of her long tresses over her shoulder contemptuously.

"Ass?" he echoed angrily, striding quickly after her, grasping her shoulders and pulling her round. "How dare you call me an ass?"

"I dare because you *are* one. Do you think you're *worth* your wealth just because you *have* it? Anyone who believes that a title and an income will win him a lady's heart *has* to be an ass. If the lady in question is half the creature you described, she'll be looking for more than mere superficialities in the man she weds."

"So that's what you think of me, eh? Merely superficial?"

"It doesn't matter what I think, does it?"

"No," he snapped back, "it doesn't matter one bit."

"Then why ask me?"

"I don't know why I did." He loosed his grip on her and threw up his hands. "It was a moment of weakness."

Julie relented. "You needn't look so murderous. Your lady may not find you as superficial as I do."

"Thank you, ma'am, for that encouragement. You are saying, therefore, that in order to succeed, I need only hope that my lady remains ignorant of the shallow nature of my character."

"Don't let my words worry you," Julie assured him with a sudden, unexpected smile. "She'll probably have you. Most girls would."

"Good God, ma'am, have I heard you alright? Did you actually say something kind?"

She laughed. "It was a moment of weakness." But then her eyes abruptly clouded. "*You'll* have to tell our mamas."

"Yes, soon or late." Tris, his expression darkening also, kicked at the pebbles in the path. "But not quite yet."

Julie threw a quick glance up at him. "Why not yet?"

"I haven't even made Cleo an offer. It's best to wait until the matter is a fait accompli, isn't it?"

"Is it? Or are you just being cowardly?"

Tris glowered at her. "Is that what you think? That I lack courage? That I'm a deuced muckworm?"

"My, my, you are quick to take offense today. I don't look on you as a muckworm, you gudgeon. I just don't see why you can't tell them now. Straightaway."

"Would you, if you were in my place?"

"Of course I would," she answered promptly.

"Ha! What a hum! You of all people."

She lifted her chin in offense. "Why not me?"

"You shudder at the sight of a dead rabbit!"

Her eyes fell. "I'm not saying it would be easy . . ."

"Easy!" He gave a mirthless laugh. "*Impossible* is more like it. I can just imagine the scene—my mother weeping copious tears, and your mother shouting the roof down."

Julie sighed in agreement. "I know, Tris. But you'll have to face it, as you said, soon or late."

"Better late. When I'm already wed, their tears and shouts won't have any effect."

"Tris! You're *not*—!" She stared at him in horror. "You can't mean you're planning to wed before telling your mother!"

"I'm not planning anything," Tris responded tersely, striding off angrily down the path away from her. "I told you before. Cleo hasn't even accepted me yet."

"Well, you needn't snap at me," she called after him. "It isn't my fault that she hasn't."

He paused and turned slowly back. "I'm sorry. I tend to lose my temper when I think of the fix our mothers put us in." He grinned sheepishly, the dimple in his left cheek making an appearance. "In a way, all this *is* your fault, you know. If you hadn't been born, our mothers couldn't have leg-shackled us."

"Yes," she said with a sneer, "that would have been nice for you."

"Nice? It would have been bliss."

"You wouldn't have had me to contend with."

"True. No discord. No wrangles. No bickering. Oh, the peace and quiet!"

"No two-family dinners. No shared birthdays. No being pushed to go to the assembly together . . ."

"A veritable heaven on earth!"

"Yes, heaven," she agreed, "but may I point out that it would have been just as heavenly if it were *you* who hadn't been born?"

"You have me there." He sighed in mock surrender. "I suppose we'll have to accept what is."

"Yes." She too expelled a sigh, but hers was real.

He studied her face with sudden, unexpected compassion. He was on the verge of escaping this life, but she was still mired in it. "Don't look so glum, Julie," he said cheerfully. "My betrothal to Cleo will change everything. Our mothers will have to admit defeat."

Heads lowered in thought, they slowly returned to the summerhouse. There they said their good-byes. "As soon as Cleo says she'll have me, I'll come back and deal with our mothers," he promised. "And after they accept the fact that they've lost this battle, things will change. Life is suddenly full of interesting possibilities."

"Yes, for you," she muttered glumly.

"For you too. Just wait. You'll see." He tipped his hat and started toward home, adding, "As soon as I'm betrothed, you'll be perfectly free to find yourself a fellow of your own."

"That *is* an interesting possibility," Julie said, throwing him a last wave.

She climbed the stile, but before dropping down on the other side, she looked back at his retreating figure. He looked almost tall in his fine beaver, with the capes of his greatcoat flapping in the wind. As the distance grew between them, she reviewed the one hopeful note that had been sounded in all that had been exchanged between them this afternoon. *You'll be perfectly free to find a fellow of your own,* her mind echoed as she watched him walk away. *A fellow of my own. Yes!*

But . . . who?

2

WITH HER CHAIR PUSHED BEHIND HER MOTHER'S, A mere six inches back from the line of seats placed along the edge of the dance floor, Julie sat quite literally in her mother's shadow. *But there's nothing remarkable about that,* she told herself ruefully as she watched the dancers swirling round the dance floor in a lively "Horatio's Fancy." Everyone at this small Derbyshire Biweekly Assembly knew she was always in her mother's shadow, figuratively as well as literally. Even Tris had said so.

Julie cast a glance over at her mother. It was no wonder she was overshadowed by the woman. The dowager Lady Branscombe was a formidable presence. In her stockinged feet Mama would have towered over all the other women in the room, but tonight she seemed even taller because her imposing head of carefully coiffed hair was topped by a jeweled turban with plumes. And she was not only noble in height but in breadth. With wide hips and an ample bosom, Julie's mother did indeed make an impressive picture.

The tall feathers of Lady Branscombe's turban were bobbing gently as she chatted with her best friend, Lady Phyllis Enders, who was seated on her other side. But after a moment, as if she felt Julie's eyes on her, Lady Branscombe turned and cast her daughter a look of disapproval. "Hiding yourself again, I see," she scolded. "Juliet Branscombe, you promised me when we set out this evening that you would try to have a pleasurable time. I would have no objection to your circulating about the room. Or even if you danced one or two of the country dances."

"Yes, Mama," Julie mumbled, coloring, "but—"

"You know very well why our dear girl is not dancing," Lady Phyllis intervened gently. "All the young men in the neighborhood are aware that you disapprove of them. She'd be dancing often enough if my Tris were here."

"Under duress on both our parts," Julie muttered under her breath.

"What did you say?" her mother asked suspiciously.

"Nothing, Mama."

"Hummmph!" was Lady Branscombe's only reply. She knew that Lady Phyllis had spoken nothing but the truth: all the young men who attended this weekly assembly (which drew its constituency from the fewer than fifty families comprising the entire society of the town of Amberford and its environs) were well aware of Lady Branscombe's intentions for her daughter. They knew there was no point in dancing with the girl, for as soon as they showed her the least interest, the mother would not permit them any further association—not even a second dance. Everyone understood the rules: Juliet Branscombe was spoken for.

Meanwhile, Lady Phyllis's underlip was quivering. "I'll never understand why Tris had to run off to town so suddenly."

"No need to shed tears," Lady Branscombe said brusquely. "What's done is done."

Lady Phyllis shrugged in defeat, and all three ladies turned their faces toward the dancers and watched in silence.

Tris, again! Julie said to herself in disgust as she settled back into her chair. It was always Tris. Since childhood, her mother had thrown Lady Phyllis's son at her head. How her mother and Lady Phyllis could have decided, the moment she was born, that she and Tristram Enders were meant for each other was more than she or Tris would ever understand. That deuced birth-alliance! In all the years since, the two mothers had never troubled themselves to wonder what the *subjects* of the agreement, Julie and Tris themselves, felt about the matter. Nor did the mothers acknowledge what their offspring repeatedly tried to tell them: that the whole idea was positively *medieval*!

Someone who did not know them would surmise that the ladies had made the arrangement for financial reasons. If Tris and Julie should wed, the estates would be unified, and the Branscombe lands would not be lost to the distant cousin who was the next male in the line. But Julie and Tris knew better. Julie's mother had a quite sufficient competence of her own, so holding on to Larchwood was not essential to her happiness. And as for Lady Enders, there was no need ever for her to be concerned about finances; the Enders family could only be described as wealthy.

The real reason for the ladies' stubborn insistance on the betrothal was more sentimental than financial. Lady Phyllis and Lady Branscombe had been best friends since childhood and, in their affection for each other, had decided that their offspring should marry and cement the friendship for all eternity. It was a silly conceit, but they had fancied it for so long they could no longer be made to see the foolishness of it. Neither mother could admit—or even *see*—that Juliet and Tristram were being made to suffer for their mothers' mawkishness.

Julie, her eyes fixed on the back of her mother's head, felt with renewed force the astonishment she always experienced when she thought about the close friendship of these two very different women. Lady Phyllis, Tris's mother, was small of stature, so delicate of feature that she still retained a youthful beauty despite her thick gray hair, and as gentle and soft-spoken in manner as she'd been as a girl; while Juliet's mother had grown in strength and size over the years until she'd become not only a large, imposing figure physically but strong and purposeful in character as well. *Too strong and too purposeful,* Julie thought with a sigh.

It was her mother's fault that she sat hiding in the

shadow. She was no longer asked to dance, even by the bumpkins attending this dowdy provincial assembly. Knowing they would never get Lady Branscombe's permission to court her, they'd all given up trying. Juliet Branscombe was always a wallflower these days. Even if a miracle should occur, and a stranger should happen to attend this modest country gathering, and *if* he should happen to notice a shy but passably pretty girl sitting in the shadows, and *if* he should happen to ask her to dance, and *if* she should have the courage to accept him, and *if* she should show the least enjoyment in the encounter (a great many *ifs* to have to become *whens),* her mother would frown at him so coldly and drag her daughter away so abruptly that he would never have the courage to approach her again.

Of course these suppositions were nothing but foolish imaginings. Tris's last words to her before he left had inspired these ludicrous fancies. In the first place, what stranger would possibly find his way to this backwater assembly?

At that moment, there was a stir at the doorway, and she looked up to see that the plump, officious Sir William Kenting, who always acted as master of ceremonies at these assemblies, was ushering in a tall gentleman Juliet had never laid eyes on. A stranger had *indeed* found his way to this backwater assembly!

And what a stranger! The mere sight of him caused Juliet's breath to catch in her throat. He seemed a creature who'd materialized from her dream of masculine perfection. His height and the breadth of his shoulders filled the doorway; his hair was dark except for one streak of gray highlighting a center lock that fell over a high forehead; his eyes were light and piercing, his nose as perfect as a Grecian statue's, and his lips full and curved into a thrillingly sardonic smile. And his clothes! No Derbyshire tailor could have fashioned that marvelously fitting evening coat, nor had any provincial valet tied that pristine neckcloth into such intricate folds. *Heavens!* she thought, a clench of excitement tightening her chest. *Have my silly imaginings become real?*

Her pulse seemed to stop beating as she watched the man's eyes roam over the room. Wouldn't it be wonderful, she asked herself, if this dazzling creature noticed her? And—absurd thought!—what if he actually asked her to dance?

Meanwhile, everyone else in the room was staring at him too. "Who *is* that?" Lady Branscombe asked, raising her pince-nez.

Lady Phyllis blinked at the gentleman in the doorway for a moment. "It must be the fellow who bought Wycklands. Canfield's the name, I believe. Lord Canfield."

"Oh, yes." Lady Branscombe nodded knowingly. "Canfield. I've heard of him. The eldest of the Granard brood. They say he's a toplofty libertine. Not a welcome addition to our assemblies, I fear. Well, we needn't take any notice of him." And she lowered her spectacles, dismissing him from her sight and her mind.

But her daughter continued to watch him with racing pulse. The fellow's gaze was encompassing the entire room, but he did not seem to take particular note of anyone, much less an inconspicuous young woman in the shadows. After a moment, in response to a request from Sir William, the stranger looked about once more, shrugged his beautifully clad shoulders in obvious dismissal of the entire company and followed his host into the card room.

Julie spent the next hour keeping watch on the card room door for his reappearance, but there was no sign of him. By that time Lady Branscombe had had enough of watching the dancing. She turned from her friend to her daughter. "Let us get our cloaks, my love," she said. "I think it's time we took our leave."

Julie, who for the first time in months was finding the assembly interesting, suppressed a sigh, obediently rose and followed her mother and Phyllis out of the ballroom. As they waited in the hallway while a footman ran to the cloakroom for their apparel, they saw Sir William leading the stranger toward the cloakroom. "Ladies," he chortled heartily as he came abreast of them, "how fortunate to have met you here. You must let me make you known to our new arrival. Lady Phyllis Enders, Lady Branscombe and Miss Juliet Branscombe, may I present Peter Granard, Lord Canfield, newly of Wycklands?"

They all murmured how-de-dos and made their bows. Then Lord Canfield took his host aside and whispered something in his ear. Just as the footman reappeared with their cloaks, Sir William, his plump cheeks quivering, hurried back to them. "Lady Branscombe, I beg you not to run off so early. Lord Canfield is interested in asking your Juliet to stand up with him." Lowering his voice and beaming, he added, "Let me assure you that he's truly interested. He says your daughter is the prettiest creature here."

Her ladyship frowned at the fellow coldly. "It's much too late, I'm afraid," she responded, so loudly that Lord Canfield had no choice but to overhear. "We already have our cloaks. Furthermore, Sir William, please inform his lordship that my daughter does not need to have butter-sauce poured over her."

Sir William colored to the ears. "Buttersauce, ma'am? Let me assure you he never meant to—"

Lady Branscombe, noting that the footman had draped all three ladies with their cloaks, cut the master of ceremonies short with wave of her hand. She then bid him a brusque good night and pushed her daughter toward the stairs, Lady Phyllis scurrying behind.

Julie, humiliated beyond words, threw a glance over her shoulder to see how his lordship had taken the slight. But Lord Canfield had already turned away; she could not see his face. If she *could* have seen it, she was certain that his expression would have revealed either utter disgust or, at best, nothing more than cool indifference.

She felt her heart sink. *I suppose,* she said to herself glumly, *that that's the last I'll ever see of him.* After her mother's foolish snub, who could blame the man if he never attended another of these dowdy, dull assemblies?

But later, as she climbed into the carriage after her mother and Lady Phyllis, it occurred to her that she might very well see the gentleman again. He had purchased Wycklands, which made him a permanent resident. In so narrow a society, they were bound to be invited to the same dinner party someday. Or she might, when making an afternoon call, find herself in the same drawing room as he. Or they might even attend one of Mr. Weekes's Sunday services at the same time. Unless the man was a recluse (and obviously he was not, for hadn't her mother called him a libertine?), they were bound to meet one day. Tris had said that life was full of promising possibilities. She'd doubted him at first, but at this moment she was quite eager to believe him.

3

Lord Canfield, who'd been on the verge of leaving the assembly before he'd succumbed to the temptation to ask the shy little chit in the hallway to dance with him, turned at once toward the cloakroom again.

Sir William followed at his heels. "I hope you've taken no personal offense, my lord," the master of ceremonies muttered worriedly. "Lady Branscombe is brusque to everyone, let me assure you. She is quite the dragon."

"Is she indeed?" Lord Canfield smiled down comfortingly at the red-faced fellow. "But I'm not in the least offended. In fact I rather admired her brusqueness. The lady didn't like me and indicated her dislike quite honestly. I much prefer brusque honesty to hypocritical politeness."

"But no, my lord, it wasn't dislike, let me assure you. She puts off anyone who tries to pursue her daughter."

"Oh?" Canfield threw the plump little fellow an inquiring look as he threw his evening cloak over his shoulders. "Is there something wrong with her pretty, dreamy-eyed daughter?"

"Oh, no, nothing at all. Juliet's a fine young woman, let me assure you, very fine. But her ladyship has planned for the girl to wed her friend's son—Lady Phyllis's boy, you know—and she becomes . . . er . . . uneasy if any other fellow shows the girl attention."

"Ah, I see." Lord Canfield, who was already moving purposefully toward the stairs, paused in his rapid progress along the hall and peered down at the master of ceremonies with brows raised in mild disapproval. "But, Sir William, if the girl is betrothed, do you think it was proper of you to encourage me to request her hand for the dance? In London, a young lady who is betrothed dances only with her intended or with friends who know her situation. She is not encouraged to dance with strangers."

"Let me assure you that is our way also. We are not such a backwater that we don't know how things are done in town. But in this case the matter is rather muddled. You see, the girl in question is *not* betrothed. At least not as yet." The master of ceremonies shook his head and sighed unhappily. "Her mother escorts her to these assemblies just as any mother of a marriagable daughter would do, seemingly expecting the girl to dance. Yet as soon as a young man shows the slightest interest, the mother snatches the girl away."

"How very curious," his lordship murmured.

"Curious it is," Sir William agreed glumly. "It certainly puts *me* in a strange position, let me assure you. I am enjoined to present partners to all the unmarried young ladies who attend our assemblies, but when I try to do so in this case, you see how I am abused."

"You certainly have my sympathy," Canfield said with a kindly smile, "but I feel even more for the girl."

"For the girl?" Sir William echoed in surprise.

"Yes, of course. She's in a more difficult situation than you are if she's forced to attend and then must sit out all the dances. How very awkward for her, pretty as she is, to be always a wallflower."

"Yes, it must be. Julie Branscombe, a wallflower! That, let me assure you, is a most ridiculous epithet for that sweet young girl."

"So it seems to me too," his lordship agreed. "She has the most amazing eyes. As if she were gazing at us from some other world." Then, realizing he was thinking aloud, he blinked and shook his head. A bit embarrassed, he quickly waved his good-bye to his host and started down the stairs. "If I ever come face-to-face with that pair again in similar circumstances," he said over his shoulder with a laugh, "I shan't let the dragon put me off so easily. I'll get that young lady on the dance floor yet. Let me assure you."

4

As the Branscombe carriage rocked over the unpaved road from Amberford to Enders Hall, Lady Phyllis gazed at the dozing Juliet with a look of such fond affection it could only be called doting. "Madge, my dear, you're much too hard on the girl," she whispered to her friend.

"I can't help it," Lady Branscombe muttered in an undervoice. "I am irked beyond words that she did so little to keep Tris from dashing back to London."

"It is more Tris's fault than hers," Tris's mother said in the girl's defense. "He'd set his mind quite firmly on going back to town. I don't believe *anyone* could have changed his mind. I very much fear . . ." Here her soft voice faltered.

Madge Branscome fixed a wary eye on her friend's face. "Fear what?"

Lady Phyllis's eyelids flickered nervously as she pulled a large, lacy handkerchief from the bosom of her dress. "I very much fear the boy has set his heart on some female in London."

"'Twould serve Julie right if he has!" Madge Branscombe's full bosom heaved in distress. "During Tris's entire visit, did she once wear any of the new gowns I had made for her? No! Did she do up her hair, blacken her lashes or behave in any way like a girl trying to attract a man? Of course not! All she did during the entire fortnight was bicker with him. Honestly, their perpetual wrangling makes me wild. Sometimes I want to wring the girl's neck!"

"I know. They do seem to be always squabbling." Phyllis's eyes filled with tears. "Do you think," she asked with a pitiful tremor, "that they will not marry after all?"

Lady Branscombe winced. "If he's given his heart to another, I suppose not."

"I know he seems to be behaving like a deuced coxcomb," Phyllis admitted, "but he can't actually have come to love someone else! He just *can't*! Perhaps he's only gone off to . . . to keep an assignation with a . . . a . . ."

"If you're trying to say the word *paramour*, Phyllis Enders, then just say it! This is no time to be mealy-mouthed."

"Well, I don't like to believe my son has a paramour, but I suppose that would be preferable to his falling in love with someone suitable. If he affianced himself to a proper sort of female, what could we do then?"

Madge dropped her head in her hand. "I have no idea," she mumbled in discouragement.

Lady Phyllis dabbed at her eyes with one corner of her huge handkerchief. "You don't think, do you, that it's time to admit that the matter is hopeless?"

Madge Branscombe threw her friend an angry glare. "I refuse to give up. We must not admit defeat. So long as the boy remains unmarried, there's still a chance—"

The smaller woman shook her head sadly while unwittingly twisting the handkerchief into a tight coil. "But, my dear, it may already be too late. During this past fortnight, I too looked in vain to discern a sign of a romantic spark between them, but there was never anything remotely affectionate. It's our fault, you know. We raised them too closely. They've become utterly uninteresting to each other."

"It *is* our fault." That was a difficult admission for Lady Branscombe to make; her whole body seemed to sag. "We should have kept them apart. If we'd forbidden them to associate, they would *then* have been delighted to defy us."

"Yes. I should have played Montague to your Capulet.

But that chance is quite lost. By this time, Tris is so accustomed to the sight of your beautiful Juliet that he doesn't even notice how lovely she is."

They both sighed together with the same hopelessness and fell silent with the same rapt concentration. The two women often showed this sort of similar reaction to the circumstances of life. Though their looks were very different, their tastes were very much alike. They'd become friends in girlhood, when they'd attended the same school. Phyllis, though she was the daughter of an earl, had from the first fallen under the spell of Madge Selwin, who, though her family had no titles, was the most clever and strong-willed girl in the school. Phyllis's delicate reticence was a perfect match for Madge's robust decisiveness.

The friendship grew even stronger with time. One month after Phyllis married Sir Charles Enders, Madge wed his cousin, Edward Lord Branscombe. (It was often remarked by people who knew them well that Madge Branscombe had chosen for her husband a man whose character was very like her friend's: a reticent, wistful fellow who permitted himself to be led round by the nose by his overbearing wife.) After their wedding, Madge convinced her husband to purchase Larchwood, an estate within walking distance of Enders Hall. From that time onward, there was rarely a day during which they did not spend some time together.

Each woman had one child, Lady Phyllis first with Tris, and three years later Lady Branscome with Juliet. Both ladies were widowed a few years later. Each declared with perfect sincerity that she could not have borne her loss without the support of the other. Through all the vicissitudes of their lives, they had remained fast friends. They could not have been closer if they'd been sisters.

But having similar tastes does not imply having similar characters. Not at all. Phyllis was as different from Madge as sugar from pepper. In the rains of life, one would dissolve in tears and the other explode in temper. This evening's conversation was a perfect example. In the matter of the betrothal between Tris and Julie, Phyllis was quite ready to surrender to fate, but Madge Branscombe was made of sterner stuff. "I shall never say die. I'll not give up," she said loudly.

"Shush!" Phyllis hissed. "You'll wake the girl."

"What if I do? Honestly, Phyllis, you mollycoddle her too much. Not that I blame you. Delicate flower that she is, she sometimes seems more your daughter than mine."

Phyllis sighed. "I hoped she *would* be my daughter. What did you mean when you said you won't give up? I don't wish to give up either, but I don't see what we can do."

"We can go to London," Madge declared with sudden decision. "We can take Julie and go down for the season. We didn't believe a come-out was necessary for a girl who was already betrothed, but since matters are not proceeding as planned, we'll give her one."

Phyllis blinked her misted eyes. "But, Madge, I don't quite see—"

"Don't you? It's simple. Giving her a season in town will make it possible to thrust the girl in Tris's path. Just leave it to me. He'll find her in his line of vision everywhere he goes."

"Yes! Oh, yes!" Phyllis clasped her hands to her breast, causing her handkerchief to flutter through the air like a pennant. Hope, that beam of sunshine, dissipated the clouds that had shrouded her eyes. "Madge, you're a genius! What a positively wonderful idea! When Tris comes upon her in those surroundings—in those London ballrooms, dressed in the most beautiful town finery we can contrive, prettier than any of those London chits and being pursued by hordes of swains—why, he'll see our Julie in a whole new light!"

Madge threw her a look of scorn. "I wouldn't count on hordes of swains, my dear. Julie hasn't any of that flirtatiousness necessary to attract hordes. But I certainly hope the rest of what you envisioned will come to pass."

The words had scarcely passed her lips when the carriage drew up at Enders Hall. Lady Phyllis glanced at the sleeping girl. "Tell her good night for me," she whispered to her friend before climbing down. "I'll see you tomorrow, and we shall make our plans."

But Julie was not asleep. She'd heard every word. She knew that eavesdropping was a wicked misdeed, but since she herself had been the subject of the conversation, she hadn't been able to resist listening. She soon discovered that the maxim *eavesdroppers never hear good of themselves* was quite true. Everything she'd heard during the endless ride had filled her with disgust.

The most troubling part was her mother's plan to take her off to London. She'd never wished to have a London come-out. She had no love for the whirlwind that constituted the "season" in town. Too shy to enjoy the noisy routs and fetes and balls of London's social life, she knew that the experience of a London debut would be nothing but torture to her. Furthermore, her mother's timing could not have been worse. When an interesting gentleman had finally moved into the Amberford environs and offered the promise of some excitement, that was the time when her mother decided on London! What an irony!

As if all this was not bad enough, there was Tris to consider. He was in love! How would he feel if both mamas descended on him in town? He didn't need meddlesome mothers interfering with his courtship.

As the carriage continued to rattle its way toward home, Julie's mind raced about trying to concoct schemes to avoid the horrid future her mother was devising for her. There had to be a way to prevent the interfering pair from dragging her to town. There had to be.

But she could think of only one thing to do. That night, before going to bed, she sat down at her writing desk, cut herself a fresh nib, and dashed off a note. *Dear Tris,* she wrote. *Something very dreadful is occurring. This matter is most urgent. Come, if only for your own sake. Please do not fail me, or we shall both be in dire straits. Hurry! Julie.*

5

THE NEXT MORNING, DESPITE A HEAVY SKY AND A light rain, Julie took out her horse. She loved her morning rides. She often rode with Tris, but she was just as content to ride alone. With Tris, she had to keep up a flow of conversation or worry about the condition of her hair. He always teased her about looking unruly. Alone, she could think her own thoughts, go at her own pace, and allow her hair to blow about as it willed, or, as now, to hang about her face in flat, dripping strands. This was just the sort of ride she liked, for she could go wherever she wished without a care for how she looked. Today she hadn't even bothered to put on her riding habit. She'd worn an old, dark skirt of heavy broadcloth, cut so full she could ride astride instead of sidesaddle, and she'd thrown her faded green wool shawl over her shoulders to keep off the rain. And of course she hadn't bothered to wear a hat. It didn't matter. No one would see her; no one else in town would be out riding on a day like this.

This morning she let her horse meander along the bank of what the Amberford natives called their river. It was, in reality, nothing but a stream that flowed from the north highlands down past the property line of Wycklands, through the town itself and on to the south, past the western boundary of Enders Hall. In a dry summer it dwindled to a mere trickle, revealing the rocks and rubble that made its bed, but in spring, when the winter runoff swelled its flow, it became a gurgling, rushing torrent, overspreading its banks and rampaging down the spills, as it did now. She loved to watch the water come bubbling over the stones, splashing and burbling along in a kind of happy hysteria. It was a sight to bring one joy, despite the rain.

In many places the water's overflow covered the banks, and she had to ride unusually close to the tree line. Occasionally a low-hanging branch grazed her face and had to be brushed aside. One such branch, much larger than the others, had to be bent and held firmly down to permit her to pass. When she passed and let it go, however, it caught the hem of her skirt on its tip and sprang up with vigor, pulling the garment up with it and revealing Julie's legs, bare except for a pair of brief pantaloons and her boots. The horse, feeling a tug, stopped. Julie pulled at the skirt, but it would not come loose. She lifted herself to a standing position on the stirrups but couldn't reach the skirt's hem. Even when she bent the branch, the tip remained out of her reach.

At that moment, to her horror, she heard the sound of hoofbeats squelching on wet ground. "Good morning, ma'am," came a pleasant male voice. "You seem to be in difficulty. May I be of assistance?"

She looked round to discover that the rider was the very man who'd taken her breath away the night before. Of all the men in the world, Lord Canfield was the last one she wanted to encounter at this moment. He looked, of course, as marvelous as he'd seemed last night. He was wearing chamois breeches, a tweed riding coat and a tall beaver which he was tipping politely. She wanted to die! She knew she looked a sight, with her dripping hair, her skirt lifted up above her knees, and her legs—bare!—hanging from the horse *astride!*

"Let me help you," he said, urging his horse between hers and the tree.

"No, please," she said, choked, turning away her head. "Just . . . go away!"

He laughed, stood on his stirrups, reached up and released the skirt. "There," he said, tipping his hat again. "No trouble at all."

She pulled down the offending garment, swung a leg

over the horse so that she sat sidesaddle and lowered her head. "Th-thank you, my lord," she mumbled miserably.

"Why, it's Miss . . . Miss Branscombe, is it not?" he asked, peering at her through the raindrops and the strands of hair that fell over her face. "We met last night, I believe."

"Yes, I believe we d-did," she managed.

"This is good luck," he said cheerfully. "I'd hoped to encounter you again."

"That is k-kind of you to say," she said, pushing tendrils of hair back from her eyes and throwing a quick glance at his face, "but I would have preferred a less humiliating encounter."

"Why humiliating? Anyone might have gotten caught in these deuced brambles."

"Perhaps," she said ruefully, "but not many would have revealed such . . . such bare legs."

"True," he agreed with a chuckle, "but not many would have such pretty legs to reveal."

Though she knew he'd meant the remark as a compliment, she couldn't take it so. It was too intimate for so brief an acquaintance. "I would have preferred," she said as proudly as her overwhelming embarrassment permitted, "that you hadn't seen them at all, even if they'd been covered with stockings and petticoats. Which, to my everlasting shame, they weren't."

He held up a gloved hand. "Were they not? I swear I never noticed."

A laugh hiccoughed out of her. "You lie, my lord, but like a gentleman."

"What makes you think I lie?"

"Because you say you didn't notice the legs were bare but noticed they were pretty."

"I'm a gentleman, my dear, but also a man. As a gentleman, I do not take notice of ladies' undergarments . . . or the lack of them. But as a man, how can I be expected not to notice such pretty legs as yours?"

She blushed. "Then, as a lady, I hope you will permit

me to thank you for your gentlemanly discretion and to ignore the . . . the rest."

"Done," he said, and offered his hand.

She took it. "Thank you." She smiled up at him timidly for a moment before removing her hand and picking up the reins. "And now I think it time we went our separate ways. You are becoming soaked."

"And so are you. May I not see you home?"

"No, thank you, my lord," she said, turning her mount about and starting off at a gallop. "You've seen quite enough of me for one day."

6

LORD SMALLWOOD PEERED OVER THE TOP OF HIS newspaper with a frown of disapproval. His daughter, who was sitting opposite him at the breakfast table nonchalantly buttering a hot raisin muffin, was, as usual, raising his hackles. Everything about her this morning, from her posture to her dress, was not what he liked. Although Lord Smallwood truly adored his daughter, he didn't quite approve of her. Widowed when the girl was only thirteen, he was responsible for her upbringing, but he'd often secretly admitted to himself that it was *she* who'd raised *him.*

Smallwood was a small-boned, short, soft-spoken man of sixty-two years who'd won the respect of his peers merely by the dignity of his bearing. He had fine features, a head of white hair, a retiring nature that made him avoid confrontation, and a somewhat pedantic, precise habit of mind. Yet his daughter, the twenty-one-year old beauty Miss Cleo Smallwood, had inherited none of his ways. That was the trouble.

He shook his head at her hopelessly. She was casually leaning one elbow on the table as she attended her buttering. *That girl,* he said to himself, *has no sense of decorum.* Not only was her posture rude and her hair unkempt, but her clothes were inappropriate. There she sat, brazenly swathed in a frilly morning robe meant only for the bedroom, with, undoubtedly, nothing underneath but her nightclothes. "Isn't it time you were dressed?" he asked plaintively.

"I'm in no hurry," the girl responded without a trace of

embarrassment. "I don't expect my caller until two this afternoon."

"Hummmph" was her father's only comment as he barricaded himself behind the *Times.* He knew the identity of his daughter's "caller," and he had no intention of entering into another argument over the fellow. If Cleo wanted to attach herself to a country bumpkin, it was her own affair. He was not the sort of father to lay down the law. And even if he were, it would do him no good. Cleo had a very decided mind of her own.

He rattled the newspaper, trying to concentrate on the news of the opening of a new bridge across the Thames, which was named Waterloo in honor of Wellington's triumph. But he could not concentrate on it; thoughts of his obstinate daughter kept intruding themselves on his consciousness. The girl was a charmer, that much was true. Any gentleman of the ton would agree. Tall and lithe, she had her mother's laughing eyes, a taunting smile, dimples that would come and go at unexpected times and a head of short, curly hair that set her apart from all the other girls with their loose curls or thick chignons. Her hand had been sought by at least three of the most desirable men in society, one a duke. Several others with lesser qualifications would have liked to ask, but they knew they would be refused. Why this most desirable creature should show a preference for the undistinguished newcomer Sir Tristram Enders was more than her father could see. "I don't understand you, Cleo," he muttered, unable to prevent himself. "Your mother, if she were alive to say it, would call you a fool."

"No, she wouldn't," Cleo declared firmly. "Mama understood a woman's nature. She knew what love is."

Lord Smallwood sighed. "Yes, she did, bless her soul. She would have known as well as I that what you feel is mere puppy love."

Cleo, completely unperturbed, continued to smooth the butter on her muffin. "If it *is* mere puppy love, my dear," she said complacently, "then it will fade in time. So why don't we just wait and see?"

"But if you go ahead and wed him and *then* learn it was only puppy love, it will be too late."

"I'm not marrying the fellow tomorrow, you know," his daughter laughed. "Besides, he hasn't asked me yet."

"But he will," Lord Smallwood muttered. "They all do, as soon as you give them the least encouragement."

Cleo smiled with only her green eyes, like a cat in the cream. "Yes, they do, don't they?"

Lord Smallwood was accustomed to her immodesty and took no note of it. "If you must be infatuated with someone, why did you choose Enders? The fellow is nothing more than a baron. You could have a duke for the asking."

Cleo nibbled at the edge of her well-buttered muffin. "The duke did not have Tris's charm. Nor his dimple. Nor his thick black hair. Nor his interesting blue eyes that show everything he feels. Nor his—"

"Enough!" Lord Smallwood retreated behind his paper. "Dimples, indeed. A good reason *that* is for choosing a mate."

"It's as good as any other," Cleo murmured absently, her mind already dwelling on the ride through the park she would soon be taking in Tris's ancient phaeton. Her father, taking another glance at her from above his newspaper, noted that she'd already left her muffin discarded and forgotton. After liberally covering it with butter, she was leaving it uneaten. It was typical of her. She would cover a vegetable with hollandaise or a cutlet with sauce and then push it aside after only a bite. He would never understand her.

But Cleo, if she'd been asked, would have explained that she could not keep her mind on food when life was so full of more interesting experiences. Who cared about something so mundane as breakfast? It was a lovely day—warm and pleasant, with a light wind from the south—and she would be spending it with the only suitor who'd ever truly captured her heart. Tristram Enders. Even the name was lovely. She smiled to herself in joyful anticipation.

Today, she was certain, would be the day he offered for her.

As her father watched her abstracted face, trying to read her thoughts, she sat staring with unseeing eyes at the discarded muffin on her plate. *For this special day,* she was thinking, *I must choose my costume carefully.* After long and serious consideration, she decided on her new rose-and-gold walking dress; it had a full skirt that would flutter enticingly in the breeze. With her wide-brimmed straw bonnet, yellow slippers and pale yellow gloves, she'd be top-of-the-trees. And she'd carry her ruffled parasol. From beneath it, she would gaze at Tris coquettishly from the corner of her eyes, eyes that many men had told her were spellbinding. Tris would not be able to resist. The circumstances were ideal. He would surely declare himself this afternoon. She could hardly wait.

Her father, of course, could not read her thoughts. But the cat-in-the-cream look in her green eyes told him as much as he wanted to know. *Poor Tris Enders,* he thought with a mixture of alarm and amusement, *your goose is cooked.*

7

Later that afternoon, when Cleo returned from that eagerly anticipated ride and strode in, alone, to the drawing room, her red-and-gold skirts swished and her mouth was tight with anger. Her father deduced at once that things had not gone as planned. "Aha," he chortled, looking up from the chessboard on which he was engaged in playing a game against himself, "so the fellow did not come up to snuff after all, did he?"

"No, he did not," Cleo said, handing her parasol to the butler who'd hurried into the room behind her.

"Good for him. Perhaps he's not such a bumpkin as I thought."

"Of course he's not a bumpkin," she said in disgust, dismissing the butler with a wave of her hand and dropping down upon the sofa. "But I can't imagine what's tying his tongue."

"Good sense, perhaps," her father ventured mildly.

She threw him a scornful look but let the quip pass. Instead, she began to review the details of the afternoon in her mind. But she could think of nothing that had gone awry. It was a mystery. She knew the fellow cared for her; she'd had too many admirers in the past not to know the symptoms. But something had kept him from making an offer. Perhaps there was a simple detail . . . some small thing that had gone askew . . . that would explain his default. "Is there something wrong with how I look?" she asked, rising and posing for her father. "Is my hat brim too wide? My lash-blacking smudged? My gown too gaudy?"

"You are perfect," Lord Smallwood assured her. "Absolutely lovely."

"That's what I thought. Then where can I have gone amiss?"

"Perhaps you overwhelmed the fellow. He's just a country bumpkin, after all."

"I wish you'd stop calling him that, Papa. He's as self-confident as any London native. And he was not the least shy during our ride. He joked and teased and was in every way perfectly comfortable with me."

"Then I see no reason for you to be in such a taking." He returned his attention to the chessboard and moved a pawn. "He probably merely decided to make his offer at another time and place," he added absently.

Cleo blinked at her father in sudden apprehension. "*Yes,*" she breathed, "I think you may be right! When he set me down, he did ask if I would be at home tonight. I was tempted to tell the idiot my evenings were engaged for the rest of the month, but . . ."

"But—?" her father asked, looking round at her curiously.

She smiled ruefully. "But his eyes looked so hopeful, I couldn't hurt him. I told him to call at nine." She sank back against the sofa cushions, her mood having swung from irritation to eager anticipation. "Do you suppose he plans to do it *tonight?*"

Lord Smallwood did not look up from his game. "I haven't the slightest idea."

But she didn't need her father's agreement. "Of *course* he does. How foolish of me not to have seen it! A shabby old phaeton in broad daylight would not seem a romantic setting to a man like Tris. He means to ask me tonight! Here in a proper drawing room. In candlelight!"

Her father turned about on his chair. "But you don't intend to accept him, do you?" he asked, suddenly worried. "You said this morning that you would wait and see."

"That was this morning. Now I'm absolutely certain of

my feelings. I love him, Papa. I truly do. When he asks me, I shall leap into his arms."

"Good God!" Lord Smallwood winced and put a hand to his forehead in a gesture of helplessness.

Cleo saw it, and her smile faded. She knew she often behaved with callous selfishness, but she truly loved her father. She hated to see him so upset. Rising again from the sofa, she crossed the room and propped herself on the arm of his chair. "Don't look so alarmed, Papa," she said gently. "You'll learn to love him, just as I did." She leaned down, brushed back a wisp of her father's white hair and kissed his forehead. "He's not as shallow and foolish as my usual swains, you know. He cares a great deal about politics and the state of the world. He spoke to me about the plight of the poor Derbyshire workers, just as you did. He's as sympathetic to their riots as you are. And you mustn't think he's a mere country squire. He has a lovely, large estate in Derbyshire and is delightfully plump in the pocket even though he does drive about in that aged phaeton. After we're wed, you shall spend months at a time in the country with us and dandle your grandchildren on your knee."

"Grandchildren!" Lord Smallwood shuddered. She was moving much too fast for him.

"Yes, grandchildren. You'll come to bless this day, really you will!" With that, she took hold of his chin and made him look up at her. "You *will* make yourself scarce tonight, after he comes, won't you, dearest Papa? To give us some time alone?"

The poor old fellow was, as always, putty in her hands. "You are a shocking minx," he muttered in a last-ditch struggle. "Do you think I can permit you to visit with a man without chaperonage?"

"Don't be so medieval. We've a houseful of servants at my beck and call should I need them. And I assure you, I won't need them. Tris is every inch the gentleman."

The white-haired man sighed in surrender. "Very well. I'll spend the evening at my club."

She threw her arms about him and planted another kiss

on the top of his head. Then she ran to the door. "I think I'll wear the ivory satin tonight," she said over her shoulder as she flew down the hall. "It has a shocking décolletage. I was saving it for the Harrington's ball, but tonight is more important. Yes, the ivory satin. It will drive him wild!"

A few hours later, when Tris was admitted to the candle-lit drawing room, he was indeed driven wild by the sight of her in the ivory satin. He actually gaped when he caught his first glimpse of her. She was standing before the fireplace, her slim body profiled in the firelight, her elbow resting on the mantel and her head turned toward him over her shoulder, her chin high. The firelight gave the room, her hair, the side of her face and the curves of her breast a golden glow. "You are a *vision,*" he whispered in a kind of breathless agony. "I never want to take my eyes from you."

She smiled. "Well, then, you needn't. Not for a while, anyway." This was the sort of greeting she'd hoped for. The evening was getting off to a very promising start. "You are free to gaze at me all evening long," she murmured, her voice a purr.

The young man's eyes dropped. "No, my dear, I'm afraid I can't."

"What?" She felt herself stiffen, as if something inside her—a basic female instinct—were warning her, before she actually knew why, that things were not going to proceed as she'd expected. "What on earth do you mean?"

"I've just had a message from home. An urgent message. I must leave."

She stared at him in disbelief. "Leave? Surely you don't mean . . . *now?*"

"I'm afraid so. My carriage is waiting. I just stopped in to explain . . ."

"Explain?" Her arm slipped from the mantel, and as a wave of fury swept over her, her fingers clenched into fists. "Yes, *do* explain. What is so dreadfully urgent that you must go dashing off tonight?"

"I don't know the details. She didn't say. But it's urgent,

right enough. It must be. Julie has never sent for me this way before."

"Julie?"

"Yes. Julie Branscombe. My . . . my closest neighbor. Her mother and mine are bosom bows, you see, and Julie and I were brought up together. Like brother and sister."

"Indeed." Cleo's voice was like ice. "Like brother and sister. How interesting."

"I wouldn't call it interesting," Tris said with boyish innocence, having no inkling of the storm to come. "Troublesome would be a better word. But something dreadful must be brewing or she wouldn't have written the way she did. Please forgive me, Cleo, for this abrupt departure, but I must go." With a quick bow and a rueful grin, he started toward the door.

"Just one moment, my good sir!" Cleo strode angrily across the room and blocked the door. "Let me be certain that I understand all this. You are breaking off an appointment with *me*—an appointment which you yourself requested and to which I *generously* agreed, despite having to cancel *several* others—to dash off to Derbyshire on the *whim* of a young woman named *Julie?*"

Tris blinked, suddenly recognizing the anger in her tone. "Yes," he said, puzzled and defensive, "but I don't think it's a whim—"

"A young woman who is *no* relation—not even a *sister?*"

"Yes, that's right, but—"

"And for an emergency the details of which you do not even *know?*"

Tris felt not only helpless but decidedly foolish. "Yes," he admitted. "That's more or less the gist of it."

"You don't know the details, but you deem the matter *more important* than an evening with *me?*"

"Well, I wouldn't put it that way, exactly . . ."

"No? Then how would you put it?"

"It isn't a matter of relative importance. Damnation, Cleo, don't look at it that way. You must know how important you are to me." He took a step toward her and grinned at her sheepishly, hoping she'd find it charmingly reassuring. "I'll return as soon as I possibly can, I promise. And then we can pick up right where we left off tonight."

"Is *that* what you think?" She stared at him for a moment in furious disbelief. Then, brushing by him, she swept across to the fireplace, her back to him. "No, my dear sir, you will *not* return," she said with ominous distinctness, "not to this house. Once you cross that threshold, you will never cross it again, not as long as I can take a breath."

"Cleo!" He stared at her, aghast. "You can't mean—!"

"I *do* mean it!" She turned her head to him, her eyes glittering with rage. "Take a *good* look, Tris Enders, for once you leave this house, this is the last you'll see of me."

"B-But—" he stammered, completely nonplussed.

"If you are going, then go!"

"You don't understand," he said desperately. "It isn't that I *want* to go. It's just something I must do."

"Then go and *do* it! No one's holding you."

He hesitated for a moment, wondering if he should forget Julie's note and stay where he was. Cleo was heartbreakingly beautiful at this moment, and she evidently wanted him to remain, while on the other hand, Julie's summons was vague. Couldn't he at least wait for tomorrow? He was torn, like a classic hero, between love and duty. But, like a hero, he chose the harder road. He turned away from temptation and threw open the door. "I *shall* go," he declared as firmly as his choked throat permitted, "but I'll be back. I'll be back, will you or nill you!" With that, he stalked out to the corridor, ran past the astonished butler and flung himself out of the house.

When Lord Smallwood returned home an hour later, he found his daughter lying prone on the sofa in complete disregard of the condition of her new gown, sobbing as if her heart would break. "Cleo!" he cried in alarm, kneeling down beside her. "What on earth has happened here?"

"Oh, Papa!" She raised herself up and flung herself into

his arms. "He doesn't l-love me! He doesn't care for m-me one whit!"

"Who? The bumpkin?"

Cleo could only nod.

"There, there," her astonished father murmured, patting her back helplessly. "You mustn't let yourself become upset over him. The fellow is a fool. A country bumpkin. What can he know of quality?"

But even as he said those words, Lord Smallwood's respect for Tristram Enders grew by leaps and bounds. Not one other suitor for his daughter's hand, not even the most sophisticated of city dwellers, had ever shown himself remotely capable of reducing his remarkable daughter to such bitter tears. He shook his head in grudging admiration. That deuced bumpkin must have depths of character . . . depths that he, Smallwood, had never suspected.

8

All through the long night's ride home, Tris relived the scene in the Smallwood drawing room. Over and over he questioned his own sanity. Had he made a foolish choice? Had he ruined his chances with the magnificent Cleo Smallwood? Had he sacrificed the one great love of his life (for he would surely never again find a woman as lovely, as charming, as perfect as Cleo) for what she'd called a whim? What on earth had made him feel so obligated to answer Julie's summons? Why had he taken her note so seriously? And why had she written to him in the first place? If it turned out that it *was* a whim, he would wring Julie's neck!

It was almost dawn when he arrived at Larchwood. He stopped his carriage at the foot of the Branscombes' drive, tethered the horses and stole on foot up the drive and round to the south side of the house. A gray light was beginning to pierce the darkness of the sky in the east. Placing himself in the shadow of a clump of shrubs, he threw a handful of dirt up to a curtained window on the second story. It took three more careful tosses before he saw the curtain being drawn. The window opened and Julie leaned out. "Is it you, Tris?" she called in a hissing whisper.

He stepped out into the faint predawn light. "Who did you think it was? Hurry and let me in before the whole household wakes."

"Yes. Go round to the veranda. I'll come down and open the door."

She came to the door wrapped in an old wool robe and

worn slippers, her hair in two plaits, like a child. It was strange, he couldn't help thinking, how careless she was about her appearance. Cleo would never permit herself to be seen looking so pathetically dowdy.

Julie, not at all conscious of how she looked, led him up the stairs to an unused room that had once been her schoolroom, and carefully closed the door. "There!" she sighed in relief. "No one will discover us here."

He perched on the child-sized table that still occupied the center of the room, while she blew out the candle she carried. They could talk in the darkness; she didn't want any servants discovering candlelight seeping out through the crevices of the door frame. Besides, it would soon be light.

"Well, what's amiss?" Tris demanded, his arms crossed over his chest. "This had better be serious . . . at least serious enough to warrant my traveling all night without sleep."

"It's serious enough. Our mamas have decided to give me a London come-out."

"What?" He gaped in astonishment at her shadowed shape looming over him. That she could have such a ridiculous reason for summoning him had never occurred to him. He wanted to murder her! "A *come-out?"* he ranted. "You summoned me here about a come-out? Are you *mad?* I thought that someone was deathly ill! Or that one of our houses had burned to the ground! Or—at the very least—that one of our mothers had lost a fortune on the 'change."

"Hush, will you?" Julie hissed. "Someone will hear you!" She sat down on the table beside him. "You don't realize how serious—"

"Serious? You call that serious?" He grasped her by the shoulders and gave her an angry shake. "Dash it all, Julie, do you realize what you've done? You made me lose my chance to win the most magnificent woman in London just so that you could tell me you're having a come-out. I ought to wring your blasted neck!"

She flung his hands from her arms. "What do you mean? How could I have affected your suit?"

"Never mind how! The fact is you did." He got up and strode over to the window, where he stood glowering at the slowly brightening landscape, feeling very sorry for himself.

She stared for a moment at his form silhouetted in the light seeping in from the reddening sky. Then she rose, came up behind him and put a hand on his arm. "I'm sorry, Tris. I never meant to cause you harm. I thought I was helping you."

"I know," he said softly, his anger melting away at her gentle touch. "I'm sorry I shook you. But how on earth did you think you'd be helping me by sending for me to talk about your damnable come-out?"

"It's not the come-out that's the problem. It's the ramifications. They are dreadful."

"Ramifications? What ramifications?"

"You'll be expected to play a part in the affair, don't you see?"

"No, I don't see. What has your come-out to do with me?"

"Everything. You see, the trip to London is intended to affect *you,* not me. Our mamas mean to make you escort me everywhere. To every ball, every dinner party, every gala and rout for which I'll require a partner. And furthermore, they'll see that I'm thrust in your way wherever you go. They're determined to make you see me in a new light . . . a London light."

"Good God!" he swore, gaping at her with sudden comprehension.

"Good God, indeed."

"It'd be worse than being betrothed!"

"Yes, just so! That's why I sent for you. It's the very situation we've been trying to avoid all these years."

They eyed each other in silence, each trying to envision being perpetually yoked to the other.

"You were right," Tris admitted at last, crossing back to

the table and sinking down upon it. "Something must be done."

"Yes," Julie agreed. "But what?"

"I don't know." Tris stared down at the floor glumly.

"You know, Tris, I've been giving the matter a great deal of thought ever since I heard them making their blasted plans, and I think the best solution is for you to wed your Miss Smallwood as soon as possible. Once you're wed, as you yourself pointed out to me, our mothers will be forced to give up."

"Yes, that *would* have been a possible solution yesterday," Tris said in disgust, "but didn't you hear what I said a few moments ago? I can't wed Miss Smallwood. I've lost her."

"Oh, Tris, no! Are you absolutely sure?"

"As sure as one can be in such matters. I fully intend to try my luck with her again, but at best I've set my chances back by weeks, or even months. It will take time to win her again. And my cause will not be helped if, while I'm courting her, they drag you to London, and I'm obliged to squire *you* about right under Cleo's nose."

"Yes," Julie sighed, despairing, sitting down beside him, "I see what you mean."

Tris turned to her. The light was now bright enough for him to see her plainly. Despite her plaited hair and shabby robe, she was undoubtedly a lovely girl. "It's *you* who must be wed, Julie," he said, taking her hands. "And quickly too."

She snorted. "Now you're grasping at straws. Who is there to wed me?"

"I don't know. Isn't there anyone in all of Derbyshire who's caught your eye?"

"You know perfectly well there isn't. Except of course . . ." A picture of Lord Canfield astride his horse, with rain pouring from the brim of his beaver, flew into her mind. "No, no," she muttered, shaking her head vigorously, "he wouldn't . . . he couldn't—No . . . it's impossible."

Tris's eyebrows lifted in immediate interest. "There *is* someone? Who?"

"No one. Nobody. Never mind. I was just jabbering. There's no one."

But he could see her cheeks redden. "Come now, my dear, this is no time to be coy. *Tell* me!"

"I'm *not* being coy," she declared, wrenching her hands from his hold and turning away. "It was very silly of me to even *think* of him."

He forced her to face him. "Think of *whom?*" he insisted angrily. "If I agree that it's really a silly thought, I'll drop the subject forever. I won't tease you, I promise."

She lowered her eyes. "A gentleman has bought Wycklands," she murmured. "His name is Canfield. Peter Granard, Viscount Canfield."

"Ah!" Tris grinned a wide, eager grin. "Canfield, eh? And you *like* him, do you?"

"How can I say? I've scarcely met him."

"Then why did you think of him in this connection?"

"Because he's a new face in the neighborhood. And because he asked me to dance. And because he's . . . he's . . ."

"What?" Tris prodded. "Because he's what?"

"Because," she burst out, "he's absolutely the most glorious man I've ever laid eyes on, that's what!"

"Well, well!" Tris chortled. "Will wonders never cease! A glorious man, eh? And he danced with you?"

Julie lowered her head. "He only asked. Mama didn't let him."

"Of course she didn't," Tris muttered. "I should have known."

"So you see, it's all quite hopeless," Julie said.

He lifted her chin and smiled down at her. "No, it isn't. I'm home now. I shall make it my task to meet this fellow and arrange some social events. Then I'll fix you over, dress you properly and teach you to flirt. And then, my shy Miss Branscombe, we shall see what we shall see."

"Oh, Tris, don't be such a fool. You can't mean . . . I couldn't possibly—"

"Yes, you can." He beamed down at her, his eyes shining in eagerness to meet the challenge he'd set himself. "What do you wager I'll make you Lady Canfield? I tell you, Julie, we'll have you wed to him before the month is out."

9

With a head full of plans, Tris left Larchwood and went home to Enders Hall to inform his mother that he was back. Though he intended to return to London sooner or later, he told her, he would remain at home for an indefinite—in fact an extended—stay. Then, despite the fact that it was seven in the morning, he kissed her cheek and went off to bed.

Lady Phyllis was beside herself with delight. She scurried across the fields to Larchwood as soon as she'd breakfasted. "Perhaps we won't have to subject Julie to a London come-out after all," she chortled to Madge Branscombe.

Lady Branscombe was skeptical. "Perhaps. But let's see how the two of them get on this time before we become too hopeful. What I'd like to know is why the boy has returned from London so soon. And why he's here for an 'extended' stay."

"Yes," Lady Phyllis agreed, her joyous mood somewhat dampened, "now that you mention it, so would I."

Tris spent the next six hours catching up on his sleep. But when he woke later that afternoon, the first thing he thought of was Julie's revelation. Never before had he heard her speak about a man in just that way, as if she were truly enamored of the fellow. If Tris could accomplish what he'd promised—actually get her wedded to this paragon who'd caught her eye!—all his troubles would be over. But perhaps he shouldn't have *sworn* he could do it. After all, he didn't know the man. Perhaps he would have been wiser to wait and see just what sort of person he'd be up against. He'd made a too hasty promise.

There was, therefore, only one thing to do: he had to get a glimpse of the fellow—and at once!

He dressed quickly, mounted his favorite horse, cantered through Amberford and over the two hills that separated the town from Wycklands and, in less than an hour from the moment he'd made the decision, was presenting himself at the viscount's door. "I'm Tris Enders of Enders Hall," he said to the butler, "here to welcome Lord Canfield to the neighborhood."

The butler kept him cooling his heels in the entry hall for what seemed a long while. When he returned, he led the visitor down a long corridor, past a portrait gallery and a series of impressively dignified rooms, until they reached what was obviously a library. But the condition of the room differed markedly from the other rooms Tris had glimpsed along the way. Those others had all been models of shining, well-kept elegance, but this room was a shambles. The long table and chairs which normally would have been placed at the center of the room had been pushed back against the window wall, and the rugs had been rolled up and also shoved aside, all to make room for a great number of wooden boxes which were scattered round the room. Some of them were open, their contents—a great multitude of books—spilling out and piled round them on the floor. And in addition to the disarray of the furnishings and the boxes, there was a general atmosphere of must and dust. A cloud of dust motes danced in the golden rays of the sun that shone in from the huge windows. The entire scene seemed to Tris to be incongruous in this well-appointed mansion.

The glare of the light from those tall, uncurtained windows blinded Tris for a moment. Not until his eyes accustomed themselves to the light did he see, standing among the wooden boxes, a tall, broad-shouldered fellow in his shirtsleeves. His hands were filthy, and his face streaked with dust. He'd evidently been caught in the act of shelving books. "Oh! I'm dreadfully sorry," Tris said awkwardly, trying to back out of the room. But the butler had already withdrawn and shut the door. "I seem to be intruding," he mumbled in embarrassment.

"Not all all," said the viscount, smiling and coming toward him, "not if you don't mind meeting me in all my dirt." He put out his hand. "I'm Canfield," he said.

Tris, noting that beneath the dirt the fellow was as imposing and handsome as Julie had led him to expect, grasped the extended hand. "I've never been afraid of a little dirt," he grinned. "Or a lot of it, for that matter."

Lord Canfield grinned back, his white teeth gleaming in his streaked face. "There's a lot of it here, I admit. It's these blasted books. They do seem to bring an amazing amount of dust with them. I'm trying to organize them, you see, but it's taking long hours of labor."

"I'm surprised you aren't leaving this labor to your servants," Tris remarked frankly.

Some might have found the remark rude, but the viscount did not take offense. "If I did, I'd only have to rearrange them later," he explained. "But let me not keep you standing. Come over here, where the dust is not so thick. I think that chair near the hearth is fairly clean. Shall I send for some tea? Or would you prefer a glass of port?"

Tris sat down. "Nothing, thanks. My mother expects me back for tea in a little while."

Canfield perched on the hearth before him, stretched out his long legs comfortably and peered closely at Tris's face. "So you're Enders," he remarked. "It's very good of you to put yourself out just to come and bid me welcome."

"Not at all. To be frank, I wanted to get a glimpse of you, having heard a great deal about you."

"From your mother? I met her, I believe. Last week at the assembly."

"Yes, I did hear about you from her. And from . . . others."

"Did you indeed?" Canfield's eyes glinted in amusement. "Am I the subject of gossip already?"

"You must realize, your lordship, that you are famous

here. Everyone in Amberford is talking about our new inhabitant, the viscount who bought Wycklands."

"I'm not surprised," Canfield said pleasantly. "That's to be expected in a town as small as this. No one's business is completely his own. I'd already heard about you too. But I was led to believe you were in London."

"Yes, but I've come back for a bit." He turned and looked about the room. Even with the confusion of boxes and the motes of dust revealed by the rays of sunlight, he could see it was a room of impressive grandeur. The ceiling was at least twenty feet high; wood panels, beautifully carved, covered three of the four walls and held dozens of shelves; the windows occupied all of the fourth wall in both breadth and height; and—the most magnificent touch of all—a shallow gallery, reached by carved circular stairways, circled the three unwindowed sides of the room. They contained more bookshelves, but these were already filled with leather-bound, gold-imprinted volumes. "My word, your lordship, you certainly have a great many books!" Tris murmured in awe.

"I've been collecting books all my life," Canfield said.

"And reading them all?"

"As many as possible."

Tris shook his head in disbelief. "How can you be a sportsman and a libertine and still find time—?" Realizing what he'd said, his face paled, then reddened in chagrin. "I'm sorry . . . I didn't mean . . ."

Canfield laughed. "Of course you did. You needn't look so stricken. I've heard myself described that way many times. And there's some truth to it, I suppose. I've spent more years than I care to remember in racing my horses and betting on boxing matches. And I've had more than my share of affairs of the heart. The town gossips blame me for at least three broken troths, for two of which I'm at least partially at fault. I'm not proud of those facts. That's why I moved here to Derbyshire."

"To escape from the gossip?"

"No, I don't think there's any escape from that. To change the way I live my life, I suppose. Since I left school,

I've spent too much time in dissipation, without truly enjoying it. I'm past thirty now, you see, and have become very bored with town life. I want to live quietly, here with my books."

Tris studied the man with some alarm. This did not sound like a fellow who would easily let himself be tempted into wedlock. "Are you saying you've become scholarly? That you're intending to become a . . . a recluse?" he asked, horrified.

"No, no, not at all. I'm not a scholar. Merely a country gentleman, with an estate to manage, a stable of horses to breed, a library to organize, books to read . . . a sort of life that I think will be more agreeable to me than the one I lived in town."

"Then you're not giving up social life entirely?" Tris asked, hope springing up in him again. "Or sporting activities either?"

"Of course I'm not. I have no intention of burying myself away. You seem to be a lively, healthy young fellow, so I assume you ride. If you do, why don't we go riding together one day soon, so that I can prove to you I don't intend to spend all my time dusting off books?"

"I'd be delighted, your lordship," Tris quickly agreed. "Shall we say tomorrow?"

"Yes indeed, if you're willing to ride early. And on the condition that you skip the your-lordships and call me Peter."

They made arrangements for the time and place, and Tris rose to leave. Canfield walked him to the door. "I was almost forgetting why I came," Tris said before departing. "My mother is giving a small dinner party on Saturday. Very informal, with no more than a dozen guests . . . her friend Lady Branscombe and her daughter Juliet, Sir William Kenting and his lady, and a few others from town. We thought it might be a good way for you to meet some of your neighbors in a rather more intimate setting than at one of those deuced assemblies." He looked at his host with an expression that combined hope and doubt. "After what you've told me, I suppose a small country dinner party like that—completely informal, as I said—will seem to you as dull as ditchwater, but if you think you could bear it for one evening, we'd very much like you to come."

"Of course I'll come," Canfield said, his bright smile reappearing. "I'm sure it won't be dull at all. And you have my promise that, even though it's informal, I *will* wash this dirt away before making my appearance."

10

LADY PHYLLIS DID NOT HAVE ANY DIFFICULTY IN persuading her son to escort her to the Branscombes for dinner that evening. To her astonishment, he seemed almost eager to join her. Was it possible, she wondered, that the situation between her son and Julie was about to change? Did the dream that she and Madge had shared so fruitlessly for so long suddenly have a hope of coming true?

However, she tried not to let herself climb too high into alt. The shreds of evidence that a *tendre* was developing between her son and Julie were too thin to count on. There were only two: Tris's unexpected return from London, and his willingness to endure an evening meal at the Branscombes'. Hardly enough reason to rejoice. Nevertheless, she could barely restrain her smiles as they set out in their carriage for Larchwood.

Tris could see that his mother was in high spirits. He decided, therefore, that this was a good time to inform her that he'd invited Lord Canfield to a dinner party for the coming Saturday night. When she heard his request, she stared at him blankly. "A dinner party? In less than a week?"

He shrugged. "I hope you won't find it too difficult to arrange the affair at such short notice."

"But you've never done such a thing before . . . invited someone for a party that hasn't even been arranged!"

"Don't look so flabbergasted," Tris laughed, patting her hand soothingly. "You arrange dinner parties so well that

I knew you'd not be overwhelmed by this last-minute request."

Lady Phyllis was indeed flabbergasted, for Tris had never before invited anyone to the house without giving her appropriate warning. But since she did not wish to spoil the good spirits of the evening by giving him a scold, she muttered an assent. Besides, arranging a dinner party in four days was *not* an overwhelming task for her. She had a large staff, after all, and would not have to do more than give them orders. "I'll send out invitations tomorrow," she said, merely throwing her son a look of mild annoyance.

The dinner at Larchwood was a pleasant affair, with Julie and Tris apparently on very good terms. Phyllis and Madge couldn't help exchanging gleeful smiles when, after dinner, Tris asked that he and Julie be excused to play a game of billiards. "Go right ahead," Lady Branscombe said, barely able to conceal her delight. "Don't worry about us. Phyllis and I always have plenty to talk about."

Once in the billiard room, Tris reported to Julie the details of his meeting with Canfield that afternoon. "I liked him," he concluded, "though I don't think snaring him will be easy."

"I told you that," Julie said sourly.

"Yes, but it's too soon to despair. I've arranged two social events already, so we may as well be optimistic."

"Two events?"

"Yes. One to go riding tomorrow and another for a dinner party at Enders Hall on Saturday." He smiled at her in triumph. "And you'll be present at both!"

Julie shook her head dubiously. "I shall attend the party, of course," she said, aware of a growing feeling of absolute terror, "but I don't see how your riding appointment can possibly include me."

"It's quite simple. You'll go out riding by yourself in the morning—something you've often done anyway—and you'll 'accidentally' come upon us."

Julie found the suggestion so revolting that it took Tris almost an hour of firm persuasion before she would agree.

When finally she did, he would not let well enough alone. "One more thing," he ordered, reaching for a billiard cue, "you are *not* to wear your old shabby riding habit. Didn't you say your mother had had a new one made for you?"

"Yes, but it's much too elegant for riding in the country," Julie said, her forehead still creased with worry about the scheme she'd so reluctantly agreed to. "It's fit for a princess to wear when riding about on the grounds of Windsor Castle, not for a country girl to sport when frisking about on the south fields of Larchwood. I'm embarrassed to tell you, Tris, that it actually has *satin lapels!* And sleeves puffed out to *here.* And Mama insisted on buying me one of those silly cocked hats to wear with it, the kind the London ladies wear tilted over one eye when they ride in Hyde Park."

"It sounds just the thing," Tris said, chalking his cue.

"Tris! You can't possibly expect me to bedeck myself in such a ridiculous rig. I won't do it!"

He leaned on the cue, eyeing her in exasperation. "Yes, you will!"

"See here, Tris," she snapped back, equally exasperated, "I've already let you ride roughshod over me by agreeing, despite my best instincts, to take my horse out for this 'accidental' meeting tomorrow. But ordering me to wear that ostentastious, immoderate, silly creation is pushing me too far."

"No, my dear child, *you* see here! If we're to succeed at this enterprise, you must put yourself completely in my hands. Completely. And that means following my orders on *everything!* I refer to such matters as clothes and hairstyles and conversation and flirtation and anything else I deem necessary. And unless you're willing to agree to that *one ruling principle* here and now, I shall drop the entire matter, take myself back to London and leave you to face a London come-out without any assistance from me."

She frowned at him in revulsion. "Indeed! I believe an ultimatum of that sort is called blackmail."

"Call it what you like. But choose now. Yes, or no."

She glared at him a moment more, considering the matter. This scheme of his would never work, she was sure of it. She could never win a man like Viscount Canfield, no matter how Tris dressed her up. He might try to bully her into acting like a flirt of the haute ton, but she was at bottom nothing but a mousy little country girl, and that was all she could ever be. No matter how she was disguised, her real nature would reveal itself before long and thus doom the whole enterprise. But there was one huge advantage in going along with Tris and his ridiculous scheme: it would cancel—or at least postpone—the dreadful prospect of a London come-out. That alone would make giving in to his demands worthwhile. "Oh, very well," she murmured, her shoulders sagging in defeat, "have it your way. There isn't much one can do against blackmail."

"Good. Then be sure to come riding along the south bank of the river tomorrow morning at eight-thirty precisely. Wearing the new habit *and* that hat!" He glanced over to where she was standing, her head lowered and her body drooping, and he felt a momentary twinge of conscience. But he ignored it. He'd been hard on her, he knew, but it was for a greater good. So he merely turned his back on her and said gruffly, "Now, let's stop this bickering and play some billiards."

11

DTRIS AND LORD CANFIELD MET A LITTLE AFTER eight the next morning. They'd not been riding long when Tris heard the bells in the Amberford clock tower strike the half hour. "Come this way," he said to his companion. "There's a fine bridle path along the river." And without waiting for an answer, he guided him over a rise toward the riverbank. There, precisely as he'd directed her, he saw Julie, a lone horsewoman silhouetted against the glowing morning sky, riding toward them. He smiled in self-satisfaction, for everything was going exactly as he'd planned. His clever machinations were apparently going to succeed.

But his pleasure was short-lived, immediately changing to anger when he saw that Julie was wearing neither her new riding habit nor the cocked hat. His teeth clenched in fury. *Damnation* he swore to himself, *I ought to wash my hands of her!*

But as they drew closer, he saw with a twinge of relief that she was not wearing her shabby old habit either. She'd chosen a walking dress of dark blue kerseymere with a full skirt. It covered an underdress of some sort of gauzy white material, with long sleeves and a soft collar that he had to admit was very becoming. She'd also pinned back her hair in a tight, neat bun so that it couldn't fly about her face as it usually did when she rode. Of course she was wearing her time-ravaged riding gloves (he'd not thought of ordering her to find herself a decent pair), but by and large, he concluded in relief, she looked passably presentable. "Look, Peter," he said aloud, "there's my friend Miss Branscombe. Do you mind if we ride over and greet her?"

"Not at all," Lord Canfield assured him, having already recognized the lone rider as the young woman whose eyes —and legs—he'd so admired.

Tris shouted a loud hello and rode quickly ahead of Canfield to exchange a word with Julie alone. "This makes *once* that you've disobeyed my orders," he muttered sternly, reining in his horse close to hers. "I'll say no more this time, but the next time you do it, I shall consider our bond broken."

She bit her underlip guiltily. "I'm sorry, Tris. I tried, really I did. That habit was just too dreadful . . ."

"All right, never mind it now," he whispered, scarcely moving his lips as he glanced over his shoulder. "You look fine. He's coming, so smile!"

The three horses pulled up together on the riverbank. Tris made the introductions. Julie gave his lordship a shy how-de-do, but, for some reason she could not explain, neither she nor Canfield indicated that they'd met before. Tris, to cover the ensuing silence, asked with sham innocence what she was doing out so early.

Julie, not liking the sense of subterfuge that seemed to permeate his every utterance, threw him a look of reproach. "I often ride before breakfast, as you well know," she said.

"Without escort?" Lord Canfield asked, throwing her a surreptitious glance.

"There's no real need for an escort," Tris explained. "We're only moments from the Larchwood lands. Besides, a young lady can ride safely in these environs. It's very quiet here."

"I see," his lordship said with his slow half smile. "I seem to be habitually thinking like a Londoner. In town, you know, it would not be permitted."

Another long silence followed, during which Tris studied Canfield's face, Canfield studied Julie's, Julie studied her hands, and the horses pawed the ground. "Why don't we follow the river to the Larchwood south fields?" Tris suggested at last. "We can have a good gallop there and then ride over to Enders Hall for refreshment."

The others agreed, and they turned their horses toward the south. As they rode, Tris managed to pull up close enough to Julie to whisper, "Now, listen carefully. I've a plan. Whatever I say this morning, be sure to agree with me."

She had no opportunity to ask what he meant, for his lordship, who'd ridden a bit ahead, was looking at them over his shoulder, his eyebrows raised curiously.

They caught up with him and cantered along the river in silence. When they came to the line of shrubs that bordered Larchwood, they all took the leap over the hedges with ease. As they started across the field at an easy trot, Tris pulled his horse to a sudden stop. "I say, was that your gardener I just saw?" he asked Julie abruptly.

She blinked, startled. "Jenkins? Why, no, I don't think it could've been—"

Tris cut her off with a furious glare. "I want to ask him something," he said, abruptly turning his horse toward the east. "Go on ahead, you two. I'll catch you up." And before either of the others could say a word, he'd spurred his horse and ridden off.

"Well, *he's* getting a good gallop, at any rate," Canfield observed dryly, looking after the rapidly disappearing horse and rider.

"Yes," Julie said awkwardly. "I must apologize for him. That was very rude."

"Not at all. I'm rather glad he's gone, actually."

"Really?" She lifted her eyes to his for the first time in their encounter. "Why?"

"It gives me the chance to talk to you. After all, I was not given that opportunity the last time we met. You rode off so abruptly."

Her eyes fell, and her cheeks reddened. "Yes, I remember. But I wish you would forget all about that encounter."

"It's not very likely. It was a memorable meeting. But I won't speak of it if you prefer that I don't."

"I do prefer it," she said.

"Very well, ma'am. Then let's speak of the *first* time we met. I was not given the opportunity to get acquainted with you that time either."

"I know. I was sorry about that. I would have very much liked . . . er, that is, I'd have enjoyed dancing with you. I'm afraid my mother is . . . is . . ."

"A bit of a dragon?"

His directness caused a laugh to gurgle up from her chest. "Yes, exactly! Did someone describe her that way to you, my lord, or did you come to that conclusion on your own?"

"Both, I think. She did seem to eat me alive that night. But must you call me my lord? Your friend Tris calls me Peter quite easily."

He blush deepened. "I don't think I can be expected to do it quite so easily as he does."

"Why not?"

"Because you two apparently have become . . . acquainted."

"But so have you and I."

"Yes, I suppose . . ." She threw him a quick, shy little glance. "But not very *well* acquainted."

"Ah, I see. And you won't call me Peter until we're well acquainted, is that it?"

She answered only with a small movement of her shoulder that didn't say yes or no. He studied her with interest, wondering how he could penetrate her shyness. It was like a wall she'd erected to keep her safe from the rest of the world, although even in the short time he'd known her, he'd caught glimpses of the charm she kept hidden behind it. "Is there something I might do or say to make us well acquainted?" he asked earnestly.

She did not have the courage to meet his eyes. "I don't think one can rush such things, do you?"

"You're probably right," he said in good-natured agreement. "Close acquaintance is akin to intimacy, is it not?

And in matters of intimacy, one must let nature take its course."

His understanding words were rewarded by a quick glance of approval from her dream-drenched eyes. "Yes," she said softly, "just so."

He gave her a rueful smile. "Though I can't help wishing I could push matters just a bit. At least enough to . . ." Here he had to pause to steady his horse, who was not accustomed to standing about. ". . . to permit you to use my given name."

"Your mount is growing impatient with our chatter," Julie said, thankful to have found a way to change the subject. "He wishes to run. Why don't we take a quick gallop right now? Since Tris was rude enough to leave us so abruptly, I feel no obligation to wait for him, do you?"

"Not in the least. Shall we race to that line of trees?"

She nodded, and they spurred their horses.

A few moments later, windblown and breathless, they reached their destination. Canfield grinned at her admiringly. "I think, ma'am, that you are the best horsewoman I've ridden with in many years."

"Thank you. It's because I'm a country girl. I have more opportunities for riding than the young ladies you ride with in town."

"Perhaps. But whatever the reason, I'd like another race." He looked over the terrain to suggest a destination, but at that moment caught a glimpse of Tris just riding over the horizon toward them. "Dash it," he swore under his breath, "I'd hoped we'd have a little more time."

He hadn't meant to say the words aloud, but she heard him. "Time?" she asked.

"Yes," he said, deciding to be frank. "Time to ourselves. To improve this acquaintance. That little bit of a race didn't deepen the acquaintance enough to make you ready to use my given name, did it?"

"Perhaps not quite enough," she said, softening the words with a small smile, "but the prospect seems less frightening than before."

His half smile reappeared. "That, at least, gives me

hope." His horse shied, and he bent to stroke the animal's neck. When he straightened up again, his eyes swept over her with an appreciative gleam. "The race has loosed your hair," he informed her. "It's blowing about in delighted liberation. This sight of you looking so unceremoniously windblown certainly increases my feeling of close acquaintance."

Her smile faded at once. "Oh, dear!" she murmured, trying desperately to gather the strands together. "Tris will be so annoyed with me."

"Will he?" His lordship peered at her curiously. "Why? What on earth has he to say about it?"

She shook her head. "I don't . . . I . . ." Her voice died away and her eyes fell.

"You have my word that you look quite lovely this way. Does it matter so much what Tris thinks?"

She bit her underlip and held up a hand as if to restrain him from further comment.

He immediately regretted what he'd said. "I'm sorry. It's not my affair. I shouldn't have asked."

"No, please," she murmured in a low voice, "you didn't . . . It's not important."

"I should have remembered what Sir William told me."

Her eyes flew to his. "What was that?"

"That you and Tris are betrothed. Or almost betrothed."

"No, we're not," she said. Her tone was decisive, more decisive than he'd yet heard it.

"Not even almost?"

"Not even that."

Tris was coming close. Whatever else Canfield wanted to say to her would have to be brief. "In that case, Miss Branscombe," he said quickly, "I shall feel free to repeat my request for a dance with you at my very next opportunity."

She paused in the act of pinning back her hair and looked up at him, a smile lighting her eyes. "Despite the dragon?"

He smiled back at her. "Dragons don't frighten me. I'm

quite capable of fighting them. I'm determined to dance with you one day, no matter how carefully you're protected by dragons. Or by not-quite-betrotheds, for that matter. So be warned."

12

DCLEO SMALLWOOD HAD SPENT THE DAY AFTER Tris's departure closeted in her bedroom, not even emerging for meals. Her father, listening at the door at intervals during the day, heard either sobs, agitated footsteps or fearsome silences. By evening he was becoming distraught. Such behavior was utterly unwarranted, he believed, and utterly self-indulgent. From time to time he pleaded through the shut door for her to be sensible. "Now, listen here," he declared when his patience became exhausted, "if you don't come out at once, I shall . . . I shall do something drastic!"

Her response was to ignore this dire threat and remain in seclusion for the next two days.

The following day, however, she emerged from the room in a completely different mood. Her movements were quick and lively, and her eyes glittered with determined animation. She informed her father that she was going out, and out she went, dashing about madly in a whirl of visiting, riding and shopping (each activity requiring a complete change of clothing), and then topping off the day by attending three routs in one evening. When she returned home at four in the morning—an hour at which no properly reared girl would still be awake—her father, who'd been pacing the floor anxiously, attempted a mild admonishment. "I am forced to have to tell you, my girl," he said as firmly as his mild nature permitted, "that this behavior will not do at all."

She glared him, ready to do battle. "I am not a child," she began belligerently, "a mere child who must be scolded for staying out la—" But all at once her face fell, and she burst into a flood of tears. "Oh, Papa," she wept, falling upon him, "I'm so m-m-miserable!"

"Good God!" he exclaimed, shocked at the vehemence of her emotions. "Cleo, my love, all this rodomontade *can't* be about that bumpkin Enders, can it?"

"Yes, it can," she sobbed, "and it is. He's broken my heart!"

"You poor child, I can see that he has, and I'm very sorry for you," he said, patting her shoulder, "but hearts can be mended, you know."

"Yes, b-but how?"

"I don't know. Time, I suppose. Time will make you forget him. That's what they say. What I *do* know is that you'll do yourself no good by indulging in this sort of emotional display."

"I know. I've been very foolish." She shuddered, gulped down what remained of her tears and sank down on the nearest chair. "But the truth is I don't wish to forget him. I want him back."

"If you wanted him so much," her father pointed out in the foolish way that parents have, "you shouldn't have thrown him out."

"No, I shouldn't have," she agreed glumly. "But what's done can't be undone."

"Quite. So let's end this useless discussion and go up to bed. We'll both feel a good deal better after a proper night's sleep."

"Perhaps you will, but I won't." She stood up and followed slowly after her father, who'd headed to the stairway. "Papa, would you be willing to help me win him back?" she asked from the bottom of the stairs.

He'd reached the first turning, but he paused and looked down at her curiously. "I? What could *I* do?"

"Something difficult. Important but difficult. Would you do it?"

"You know I don't think much of the fellow . . ."

"I know. But you'll change your mind once you know

him better." She climbed a stair and gazed up at him. "So, what do you say?"

"I don't know what to say. What is it you wish me to do?"

She twisted her fingers together uneasily. "I want you to accompany me to Derbyshire," she said in a small voice.

"To *Derbyshire?*" His voice was a loud squeal. "Are you considering *chasing* the fellow? To the *country?* Have you gone *mad?*"

"I think I have, rather. But the idea is not as mad as you make it sound. He did invite me, once."

"What sort of invitation? Did it have a specific date?"

"Well . . . no, but—"

"Then it wasn't a true invitation at all. Besides, even if it were, your quarrel would nullify it."

"I don't care," the girl said with a shrug. "Once we arrive on his doorstep, he'll have to welcome us. He *is* a gentleman, after all."

"Balderdash!" Lord Smallwood was a mild man, but even he could be pushed too far. He drew himself up to his full height and glared down at her. "I've never heard of such a thing! Are you actually suggesting that you wish to engage in a pursuit of a man who is quite beneath you? And that I accompany you all the way to Derbyshire to drop in on someone who isn't even expecting us? You *are* mad! You sound like an immodest, manipulative virago! I won't even discuss such a brazen idea!" And he turned on his heel and marched up out of her sight.

Cleo sank down on the step and leaned her forehead on the bannister, her mind in a whirl. It *was* a brazen idea, she thought, just as her father said it was. But it was also a good one. There was much she could accomplish in a visit to Tris's home. For one thing, he would, as her host, be forced by simple good manners to reconcile with her. She would meet his mother, for another. And she would get a glimpse of the mysterious Julie, the "neighbor" who had such power over him that one crook of her little finger had lifted him from her own arms and sent him rushing home. Cleo wanted more than anything else to get a look at that female.

Yes, it was in Derbyshire, rather than in London, that she, Miss Cleo Smallwood, could learn what she needed to know of the real Tris. And if in the process she appeared to her father—and to the rest of the world—to be a manipulative, immodest virago, so be it. It would be worth it.

Of course, she couldn't make the trip without escort; she wasn't such a virago as all that. But there was no one other than her father who could escort her. He'd refused to do it, and in terms that seemed to brook no argument. But she could change his mind; his refusal did not worry her. Papa would succumb to her blandishments sooner or later, she was sure of that. By the time she was ready to leave, she'd surely have won him over. She could always twist him round her little finger. When Tris had stormed from the house, she'd worried that she'd lost some of her power to charm men. But not her power over Papa. Good God, no! She couldn't have lost as much as *that.*

13

AN HOUR BEFORE THE GUESTS WERE DUE TO ARRIVE for the dinner party, Tris decided to look into the dining room to check on the preparations. What he saw struck him like a blow. This was not the small informal dinner he'd envisioned. The table had been expanded to its fullest length—seating twenty-four!—and was set with the finest china and plate. At least five goblets were lined up at each place, and two footmen were busily setting up floral centerpieces at three-foot intervals on the table, having already adorned the sideboards with an alarming number of decanters, silver servers, chafing dishes, candelabra, epergnes and trays. The room glowed as if in preparation for the regent himself.

Turning quite pale in chagrin, Tris immediately turned about and stormed up to his mother's bedroom. "Mama!" he shouted, bursting in on her with no more warning than an angry knock. "What have you done?"

She was sitting at her dressing table in an enormous dressing gown, her abigail doing up her hair. "Done about what?" she asked calmly, turning about in her chair to face her son.

"About tonight's dinner! It was supposed to be *small.* And *informal!*

"Smaller than twenty-four was not possible," Lady Phyllis explained, signaling the abigail to leave them. "If, for example, I'd invited the Frobishers without asking the Severns, the Severns would have been dreadfully offended. And the Kentings have two houseguests who had to be included. And the Harroway daughters are back from London, which of course I didn't know, for if I did I'd never have sent the Harroways a card. Those Harroway girls, you know, are the two most irritating chatterboxes in the world, and why they're called girls I never will understand, for they are thirty-five if they're a day! And I couldn't omit Lady Stythe and her sister—"

"Enough!" Tris said, holding his ears. "I see your point; you needn't go over the entire guest list. But didn't you hear me say it was to be informal?"

"Of course I did. The cards all said it would be informal. 'An informal dinner and musicale' are the very words I used."

"Then why are there five glasses at each place, for heaven's sake?"

Lady Phyllis raised her eyebrows. "Of course there are five glasses. Good heavens, Tris, it *is* a dinner party, after all. You don't expect the table to be set as for a picnic, do you?"

Tris groaned. "So anything less than five goblets makes a picnic setting, does it? And I suppose everyone will appear in all their formal finery too. Satins and jewels and such?"

"They will be dressed for a dinner party, which is exactly as they should. And if you don't stop berating me and take yourself off, I shall not be ready to greet the first guests."

Tris shook his head helplessly. "This is *not* the sort of evening I wished for. I thought it would be like an ordinary family dinner. That was how I described it to our guest of honor—a small, intimate affair, I said. What if he makes his appearance in his riding coat? How will you feel then?"

"He will do no such thing. He is a gentleman, is he not? He knows enough, I'm sure, to dress for dinner." She turned back to her dressing table, picked up a little bell and rang for her abigail to return. "Now, stop all this nonsense and go along and dress yourself."

Despite his mother's serene dismissal of his concerns, Tris remained worried all the while he dressed. He'd given

Julie complete instructions on how to behave toward Canfield this evening ("Let yourself be saucy instead of shy," he'd advised her, "and laugh at anything he says that smacks even remotely of wit."), but he'd been counting on a small group. Now that the group had become a crowd, there would probably be little chance for the guest of honor to converse with Julie with any degree of intimacy. And if Canfield should clothe himself in too informal a manner, the fellow would be embarrassed into awkward silence and would probably cut out as soon as politely possible. All Tris's efforts to set up this affair would have been for naught. The evening was bound to be a complete failure.

But Tris soon learned that he needn't have worried. Just as his mother had predicted, Canfield did indeed know enough to dress for dinner. In fact, when Tris went down to welcome him at the door, he found him quite resplendent in a superbly cut dinner coat and elegantly tied neckerchief. "Peter, you coxcomb," Tris greeted him as he led him up to the already crowded drawing room, "how did you know to wear such finery when I said we'd be informal?"

"I did tell you, didn't I, that I intended to wash before I came?" his lordship laughed. "Did you think I'd show up in shirtsleeves and breeches?"

"Well, I didn't think you'd come looking fit to meet Prinny. Though everyone else has dressed to the nines to meet *you.*"

"I thought they might, but not because of me. It's because of the cards your mother sent."

"The cards?"

"I'm not such a greenhead that I don't know what a hostess means when she cordially invites one to an 'informal dinner party and *musicale.*' That word *musicale* is a clear signal that one had better wear the proper evening clothes."

"Ah, so that's it!" Tris exclaimed, chuckling at his own ignorance. "I see I have much to learn of social conventions, even in my own circle."

Tris led his honored guest into the drawing room and introduced him to all the assembled crowd. His lordship seemed not at all discomfited by their large number and put everyone at ease by exchanging pleasantries with admirable unaffectedness. Meanwhile, Tris's eyes roamed the room, searching for Julie.

He discovered that she was seated, as was her wont, unobtrusively in a far corner. *I should have warned her against that,* he thought in annoyance. The girl was never able to think for herself about how to put herself forward. However, all was not lost, for Sir William's son, Ronny Kenting, was leaning over her shoulder, trying as always to make some headway with her. Tris usually found his persistent attentions to Julie as annoying as Julie did herself, but today he was pleased. It would be good for Peter to see other young men hanging about her. "I say, Peter, there's Miss Branscombe," he said to his guest. "Let me take you over to her. You remember her, don't you? We rode together a few days ago."

"Of course I remember her, you gudgeon," his lordship said, bluntly, "so there's not the least need for you to escort me. With your permission, I'll make my how-de-dos to her on my own." With that he gave his host a quick nod and crossed the room to Julie's chair.

Tris watched intently as the viscount approached her. He saw with real satisfaction that Julie smiled up at the fellow with what seemed to be real pleasure. Furthermore, she responded with a gurgling laugh to whatever it was that Peter said to her. It was such a warm, sincere laugh that Ronny Kenting withdrew with a glower. Could it be that Julie was actually doing what he, Tris, had told her to do? Not only that, but she'd managed for once to look just as she ought. Her hair was neatly but softly drawn back into a bun at the nape of her neck, her eyes had a most becoming glow, and her gown—a full-skirted, rose-colored silk concoction—seemed to radiate its color to her cheeks. *Good girl!* he chortled to himself. *Perhaps I can allow myself to believe that this evening might not turn out to be such a disaster after all.*

He could not know, however, that disaster was rapidly approaching—that a carriage bearing the Smallwood crest had pulled into the courtyard of the Peacock Inn in Amberford, and that, at that very moment, the coachman was jumping off the box to inquire of the ostler the direction to Enders Hall.

14

WHAT PETER HAD SAID TO MAKE JULIE LAUGH WAS "I've lived the last few days in the hope that tonight's 'musicale' will include dancing, Miss Branscombe. I've come prepared either to fight the dragon and stand up with you, or to perish on my sword."

Julie's gurgling laugh in response had nothing to do with Tris's orders to "laugh at anything he says that smacks even remotely of wit." She was truly charmed. But she had to tell him that his hope would be dashed. "Your encounter with the dragon will not occur tonight, my lord," she said, holding out her hand in greeting, "for the musicale will *not* include dancing, I'm afraid."

He took the proffered hand and held it for a long moment before making his bow over it. "And I see that my other hope—that you will call me Peter—is also to be dashed," he said as he made the requisite genuflection. "I am crushed."

"Oh, dear," she said with a mock sigh, "we mustn't have our guest of honor crushed. What if I promise to *try* to bring your given name to my tongue at some time during this evening? Will that possibility revive your second hope?"

"Oh, more than that," he assured her, his appealing half smile reappearing. "You've completely reanimated my spirits!"

At this point she laughed again, causing the disheartened Ronny Kenting to stalk away in chagrin and Tris, across the room, to beam in triumph.

Someone else heard Julie's laugh, but the sound

brought no sense of pleasure to that listener. It brought dismay. Lady Branscombe did not approve of Lord Canfield's flirting with her daughter. Worse, she could not bear the sight of her daughter flirting with Lord Canfield. Any man who received a favorable gleam from Julie's eye caused her mother to have palpitations of the heart, and this time her dismay was greater than ever before, because Lord Canfield was a more formidable threat than most. She stiffened at once, ready to do battle. She had not planned all these years for her daughter to wed her best friend's son only to have the girl snatched away by the first truly attractive man to come along.

As soon as Lord Canfield's tête-à-tête with Julie was interrupted (as it was bound to be in such a crowded room, in which everyone present wanted a word with the guest of honor), Lady Branscombe inched her way toward him, watching for an opportunity to catch his eye. It did not take long. "I've been wishing most eagerly to speak to you, Lord Canfield," she said when she was near enough to grasp his arm.

"And I to you, ma'am," Canfield said smoothly. "I have wanted to speak to you ever since the night at the assembly when you expressed some disapproval of me."

If Lady Branscombe was surprised at his frankness, she did not show it. "Did I express disapproval? I *do* regret having given that impression. I promise that it was unintentional."

"I'm glad to hear it, ma'am, for I understand that your approval will serve me in good stead in this neighborhood."

"You overestimate my importance, my lord. Nevertheless, the reason I wish to communicate with you *is* in the hope of doing you some good here." She used her tight grasp on his arm to propel him to a secluded corner. "You are a bachelor, I understand."

"Yes, I am."

"And I suspect that your mother is deceased, is that not so?"

His eyebrows rose curiously. "Yes, for more than a decade now. Why do you ask?"

"Because if she were alive, she would not have permitted you remain a bachelor for so long. You are, what, thirty? Thirty-two? She would have advised you that bachelorhood is not a desirable state, and that it is time for you to settle down."

"I suppose she would have felt so," he murmured, somewhat at a loss. "And I would completely agree."

"Good. Then you won't object to my acting in a motherly role and pointing out to you all the very desirable, marriageable young ladies who are here tonight?"

"No, I won't object at all." He suddenly guessed what her purpose was, and he realized with some amusement that his first joust with the dragon was about to begin.

"Then, first," she began, her tone seductively sincere, "there is Elinor Severn, over there at the window. She is a charming girl, barely twenty-one, with a fine education in all the arts. She paints very well—one of her canvases is hanging in this very house, in the hallway near the door—and she has a lovely voice. You will hear her sing later tonight."

"How very enchanting. I look forward to it."

"And over there, standing with Tris Enders, is Sally Halloway. She is past her first bloom, I admit, but her appearance is very youthful, is it not? And her conversation is so lively one never has to strain to find something to say to her. And just there, to your left, the girl in the pink brocaded gown, is Emmaline Frob—"

"Yes, I've met her," Canfield interrupted. Fully aware of the approaching dangers, he decided to waste no more time but throw himself into the fray. "But surely your ladyship realizes that the loveliest girl in the room is your own daughter."

He could feel her arm stiffen. "Thank you, your lordship," she said coldly, "but that is quite beside the point. We are speaking of eligible girls, those who are suitable for you to pursue. I must inform you that my daughter is not eligible."

"Oh, is she not? Why?"

"She is promised to another."

Canfield looked down at her with eyebrows raised. In this first tilt with the dragon, it was time to make a jab. "Is she indeed? I take it you are referring to Tris Enders. But Miss Branscombe told me quite explicitly that she was *not* betrothed."

The dragon barely flinched. "It has not been announced, but the betrothal has been in effect for years."

He kept jabbing. "If that is so, then why hasn't it been announced?"

"When the agreement was reached, they were too young to make an official announcement," Lady Branscombe explained, excusing the lie by telling herself that it was, in a sense, true. An agreement *had* been made, if not between Tris and Julie, at least between their mothers. "But it will be announced one day soon."

"I see. But until it is, surely another suitor may try to court her, may he not? Isn't that what society agrees is perfectly permissible?" She couldn't argue the truth of that, he told himself. She *had* to say that he was free to try his hand. Believing that he'd struck a wounding, if not mortal, blow, he waited for her capitulation.

But this dragon was not so easily slain. "Whatever society may say, my dear boy," she said so complacently that he realized he'd not even wounded her, "is quite beside the point. Anyone with motherly feelings toward you, as I have, would warn you not to try. Julie *loves* Tris. I, her mother, know this well. I tell this to you in confidence, for your own good. I don't wish to see you waste your efforts on a hopeless venture that would, in the end, only bring you pain. Now, as I was saying, Miss Frobisher there—"

"Yes, ma'am, I do thank you for your advice. But the butler has just announced dinner, and I'm ordered by our host—Tris himself—to escort your daughter to the table. So, if you'll excuse me . . ."

He bowed and walked off, but not before he caught a

glimpse of chagrin in her eyes. Yes, he'd had the last word and made the last point. But he hadn't defeated her. In his first fight with the dragon, he wasn't even sure he'd achieved a tie.

15

THE SEATING ARRANGEMENT AT THE DINNER TABLE was as formal as the setting. Lord Canfield, the guest of honor, was placed at his hostess's right. And Tris had made sure that the seat at Peter's other side was occupied by Julie. But not being content to let matters take their natural course, Tris had seen fit to take her aside, just before the viscount had come to claim her arm, to remind her of the instructions he'd given at least twice before: be saucy, and keep laughing.

Julie took her place feeling sick to her stomach. Tris's whispered instructions had completely overset her. She had believed that she and Lord Canfield were getting on very well, but Tris must have disagreed. Otherwise, he wouldn't have found it necessary to remind her of how she should comport herself. She wished he hadn't spoken to her; his deuced reminder did no good at all. She didn't know how to be saucy or how to laugh on cue. All he'd done was destroy her confidence and cause her to become instantly self-conscious and tongue-tied.

Julie glanced over at his lordship, who'd just settled in on her right. He seemed completely at ease. He complimented Lady Phyllis on her table, exchanged pleasantries with the vicar, Mr. Weekes, who sat opposite him and attacked his pickled salmon with cucumber dressing with gusto. Julie, barely able to eat a bite, was occupied with trying, without any success, to think of something saucy to say to him. In desperation, she glanced down to the foot of the table where Tris sat, only to find him watching her.

When their eyes met, he made a motion with his hand urging her on. To do what, though, she had no idea.

Lord Canfield, noticing that she was not eating, looked at her curiously. "Can it be you don't like the salmon? I find it delectable. Had I a poetic bent, I'd write an ode to it."

Julie wondered if Tris would consider the remark witty enough to qualify for a laugh. To be on the safe side, she tried to force one out. The sound that came from her throat rang out more like a high-pitched hiccough than a laugh. Canfield was taken aback by it. "I'm not joking, my dear," he said earnestly. "You really should try it."

Again she had the sensation of wishing she could die to avoid this feeling of humiliation. The smile on her face was so forced, she was sure it looked like a grimace. Her reaction to what was merely an innocuous comment on the food had been ridiculously inappropriate, and the realization made her feel so foolish that she couldn't utter a word. She could only lower her head and play with the fish with her fork.

When she sensed that Lord Canfield had returned his attention to his food, she glanced down the table toward Tris to see if he'd noticed her blunder. He was frowning at her as if he had.

Canfield, meanwhile, was puzzled at Miss Branscombe's sudden awkwardness and withdrawal. A few minutes before, out in the drawing room, she'd been warm and delightful. What had happened to transform a charming girl into this shy, distant creature?

It was then that he noticed Tris and Julie exchanging looks. It struck him that the glances were familiar and significant, the exchanges of two people who were intimately connected. The quality of those looks surprised him. *Did the dragon really tell the truth?* he asked himself. *Does the girl truly love Tris?*

The answer to the question interested him greatly, though he didn't quite know why. After all, it was not really a matter of concern to him. Although he'd permitted Julie's mother to believe he was interested in courting the girl, it was very far from the truth. He'd only said it as a weapon in the battle of wills between himself and Lady Branscombe. True, he'd found her daughter a lovely, taking young woman, and he was sincere in his determination to dance with her at the next opportunity, but that was as far as he intended to go. If and when he should decide to take a wife (and despite what he'd said to the dragon, he was not at all ready for such a change in his life), there were a number of young ladies in London who had prior —and stronger—claims on his attentions. He had not the least interest in courting Miss Juliet Branscombe.

Nevertheless, he had to admit there was something fascinating about the girl. Her character was quirky, unexpected, unique. He couldn't quite fit all the pieces together. She was a riddle he was drawn to solve. That was why he found himself watching her and Tris surreptitiously during the remainder of the meal. By the time the ladies rose from the table, he'd decided that Julie was indeed in love with her childhood companion. The way her eyes kept seeking his, with an expression that seemed to be asking for his approval, put the matter beyond any doubt.

By the time the gentlemen had finished their brandies and joined the ladies in the drawing room, the chairs had been set up in rows facing a long, narrow pianoforte that had been rolled or dragged to the center of the room. Sir William, who was evidently born to act the role of master of the revels, stepped forward, cleared his throat and announced the first selection: the ballad "She Wore a Wreath of Roses," to be snug by Miss Elinor Severn, accompanied on the pianoforte by Miss Juliet Branscombe. The conversation stilled, the two young ladies took their places, Miss Branscombe played a brief introduction, and Miss Severn began to sing. She had a very sweet voice only slightly marred by a tremulous vibrato, but the vibrations gave her performance an emotional quality that perfectly suited the sentimental lyrics. When she finished, she was so loudly applauded that she was obliged to agree to an encore. After a quick consultation with her accompanist, she sang a throbbing rendition of "Cherry Ripe." This too was very well received. Her cheeks glowed pink as the applause accompanied her all the way back to her seat. Miss Branscombe, meanwhile, slipped back into her own seat quite unnoticed—except by Peter, who thought she'd played very well (and incidentally had looked extraordinarily lovely perched on the piano stool with her rose-colored silk skirt spread out about her like flower petals, and the light from the chandelier haloing her hair) and who was irked that her performance had not been properly appreciated.

Sir William next announced that his own son, Ronald Kenting, would sing—a cappella—a sea chanty called " 'Twas in the Good Ship Rover." Ronny clumped to the front, took a deep breath and burst forth with a rousing rendition of the song in a deep baritone that actually rattled the crystal drops in the chandelier. When he took his bow to tumultuous applause (even louder than the ovation that had greeted Miss Severn), he cast a proud glance in Julie's direction, as if to say that if she were now sorry she'd neglected him, she had only herself to blame.

Next on the program of the musicale was a harp solo to be performed by Miss Eugenia Halloway. Two footmen came forward, rolled the long pianoforte to the side and carried in a harp. Miss Halloway, so tall and gaunt that she'd developed a severe stoop, rose from her chair and came modestly forward, her shoulders hunched as if to protect her face from being seen. Just as she took her seat, however, there was a sound from the back of the room. It was Livesey, the butler, clearing his throat. "Edward Lord Smallwood and the Honorable Cleopatra Smallwood," he announced awkwardly.

In swept Cleo Smallwood, head high, bonnet feathers bobbing and a stylish velvet cape fluttering behind her. She was followed by her tight-lipped, red-faced father. But when they saw the room filled with guests, they both stopped in their tracks, eyes widening in amazement. "Oh!" Cleo gasped. "I didn't expect—"

"Cleo!" Tris cried, leaping to his feet.

Her outstretched hand flew to her breast, and she took two steps backward. "Good heavens, I didn't know . . . ! Oh, dear! Please . . . excuse us!" She swung about, grasped her father's arm and headed for the door. "Dash it, man," she muttered to the butler as she went by him, "why didn't you tell us a party was in progress?"

Livesey, the butler, stiffened in offense. Not only was he unaccustomed to being spoken to in that tone, but he'd tried his best to tell the visitors that there was a party going on. The girl had demanded to be announced, and when he'd tried to object, she'd ordered him to hold his tongue and do as he was told. Angry as he was by her unjustified scold, however, he was trained not to show his feelings. His furious sense of offense showed itself only in an almost imperceptible spark in his eyes. "Sorry, madam" was all he said.

But Lord Smallwood didn't like his daughter's scold either. "The fellow didn't tell you," he muttered as soon as they'd crossed the threshold, "because you never gave him a chance. I *told* you not to insist on being shown in—"

But at that moment Tris came hurrying out. "Cleo, wait! It's all right. It's only an informal musicale. Do come back."

"No, no, I wouldn't dream of intruding," she said. "It was dreadful of us to barge in on you without warning."

"Yes," her father muttered dryly, "it's about time you realized that."

"No, please!" Tris motioned for Livesey to take her cape. "You're not barging in. I'm delighted to see you . . . both."

"That is kind of you to say, Tris," Cleo said, beginning to regain her equilibrium. "You are a true gentleman, and I am a . . . a virago."

Tris gave a snort of laughter. "Now, Cleo, really—!"

"I suppose I ought to explain," she went on. "Papa and I are on our way to . . . er . . . Scotland, and we stopped at the inn in Amberford—what was the name of it, Papa? The Pheasant, wasn't it?"

"The Peacock?" Tris offered.

She treated him to a brilliant smile. "Yes, of course, the Peacock. It was there we learned that Enders Hall was so very close by, and I remembered that you'd once said that if ever I should be in the neighborhood—"

"Of *course* you should have called on us!" came a new voice. It was Lady Phyllis crossing the threshold. Just then the rippling sounds of the harp commenced from within, and she quickly closed the door behind her. Then she crossed to the newcomers and put out her hand. "Any friends of Tris are always welcome here."

Tris threw her a grateful glance before making the introductions. "Lord Smallwood, Cleo, this is my mother."

Lord Smallwood stepped forward and bowed over her hand. "How do you do, ma'am. You are most kind to welcome us, but it is unforgivable for us to have intruded at such a time."

"Not at all," Lady Phyllis assured him. "I'm delighted to meet Tris's London friends. I hope you intended to spend some time here with us."

"We wouldn't dream of putting you out," the embarrassed gentleman murmured.

"You aren't putting us out at all," Tris said earnestly. "In fact I insist that you spend some time here with us before you proceed on your travels. We both insist, don't we, Mama?"

If Phyllis had any qualms, she hid them well. "Of course we insist. I shall have Livesey go down for your bags and establish you in adjoining guest bedrooms."

"That is most generous of you, my lady," Cleo said, bestowing her dazzling smile on her hostess. "We accept with pleasure, don't we, Papa?"

The white-haired fellow gave a helpless shrug and surrendered his hat and greatcoat to the butler. Lady Phyllis, sensing his reluctance and shrewdly guessing that he'd been coerced into this escapade, felt an immediate rush of sympathy for him. "Please give no further thought to the manner of your arrival," she assured him. "The only matter for concern is to see to your needs. Do you wish to rest after your journey? Or shall I arrange for you to have dinner? Or, if you'd prefer, you can join us for the rest of the musicale. There will be a light supper served afterwards."

"The musicale, of course," Cleo said at once, and then, in an afterthought, added, "if Papa agrees."

The dignified gentleman shrugged his agreement. Lady Phyllis took his arm. "You will stay, I hope," she said warmly as she opened the door. She urged him into the drawing room, where Miss Halloway, her head bent and her tightly curled forelock plastered against her forehead, which was wet from her exertions, was still plucking the strings of the harp with impressive enthusiasm. Tris and Cleo followed his mother in. Tris settled Cleo onto his chair, and Phyllis resumed her own. Two footmen appeared almost at once with chairs for the two men. All this was done so silently that Miss Halloway was not distracted. A few heads did turn to take another peep at the new arrivals, but the musicale continued without further interruption.

After two encores by Miss Halloway, and another sea chanty by Ronny Kenting, Sir William announced that the musicale was over. The guests rose and began to mill about. Lady Phyllis led the two late arrivals round the room and introduced them. Lord Smallwood responded to each greeting with monosyllables, but Cleo was soon completely at home, exchanging banter, laughing, and charming every gentleman in the room.

As the entire party drifted in pairs or groups to the morning room, where a buffet of light delicacies had been set up, the young lady from London was being observed with interest by several pairs of eyes. One of the observers was Julie Branscombe, who—after studying Cleo's carriage, her curly coiffure and the easy way she spoke to everyone she met—found her to be just as Tris had described: graceful, spontaneous and self-assured. *Good for you, Tris,* she thought.

Lord Canfield was another observer. He not only closely examined the new arrival, but he watched Julie watching her. He concluded that Miss Branscombe was in trouble. Cleo Smallwood was a beautiful, glib sophisticate, talented at flirtation. He'd seen the type before. If she wanted Tris Enders for herself, she would ride over the shy Branscombe chit like a trained racehorse over a kitten. He felt quite sorry for the unobtrusively lovely Juliet.

But the keenest observer of the new arrival was Lady Branscombe. As soon as she could, she pulled Phyllis aside. "Is that young woman Tris's London paramour?" she asked bluntly.

"Don't be silly," Phyllis whispered. "She's a very proper sort of girl. Her father's a baron."

"Hummmph!" grunted Madge, frowning. "That makes matters worse."

"Why do you say that?" Phyllis asked, feeling a sudden clench in her chest.

"Why do you think?" Madge snapped. "She's a beauty, and she's very sure of herself. Tris is evidently besotted. If she's of good family, we can have nothing at all to object to, should he decide to offer for her."

Phyllis's optimistic nature vied in her chest with a growing feeling of panic. "Yes, she *is* a beauty, I won't deny that," she said, her voice quavering, "but it's too soon to conclude that Tris is besotted, isn't it?"

"Is it? Take a look at him. He's been at her elbow ever since she arrived, positively slavering over her. If he paid that sort of attention to Julie, I'd be in alt."

"Oh, dear," murmured Phyllis miserably, "whatever shall we do?"

"Get rid of her," Madge answered without a moment's hesitation. "Get rid of her at once."

16

Getting rid of Cleo Smallwood proved to be no easy task. For one thing, Tris made the girl promise (without much difficulty) to stay at least a week. For another, Lady Phyllis could not think of a way to hasten her departure without causing the sensitive, quiet Lord Smallwood to be humiliated, for he would surely sense—no matter how subtle her hints—that she was trying to push them on their way. "Besides," she said to Madge as she walked with her to the property line after a brief visit, "if Tris is truly besotted, getting rid of the girl will only cause him to follow her to London. We'd then be in a worse case than we are now."

By this time, the Smallwoods were in their third day of what Madge now realized would be an extended stay. "I don't see how matters can possibly be worse," she said glumly.

"I still have hope, as long as Tris is here near Julie," Phyllis said optimistically. "Perhaps, if Miss Smallwood stays long enough, he'll tire of her and discover for himself how superior our Julie is."

"If *I* haven't discovered that Julie is in any way superior to the Smallwood creature," Madge muttered as she took herself off through a much used gap in the hedge, "I don't see how Tris will."

"You are an unnatural mother," Phyllis called after her. "I can think of a dozen ways."

"Then tell them to Tris," Madge flung over her shoulder. "It won't do any good for *me* to hear them."

While the mothers were bandying words, Tris was out

riding with Cleo. At his mother's insistence, he'd invited Julie too. Julie'd accepted the invitation at *her* mother's insistence, but she kept her horse well behind, knowing that she was intruding.

Tris was very grateful for Julie's tact. In the social flurry of the past two days, he hadn't had any opportunity to speak to Cleo in private. He guessed that she'd gone to great lengths of scheming and maneuvering to be here (the trip to Scotland was, he knew, nothing but a ruse), but this was his first chance to ask her why she'd come. "I don't understand you, Cleo," he said when he saw that Julie was too far back to overhear. "After what happened that last night in London, I thought you never wanted to see me again."

"You should've known that I never meant it," she said, throwing him a glinting look from under the brim of her rakish riding cap. "I was jealous, that's all."

"Jealous? Of whom?"

"Of Julie, of course."

"Julie! Good God, woman, how could you have been so foolish? I told you she was like a sister to me."

"You were leaving me to run home to her. A man does not run off from the woman he claims to love at the beck and call of a sister."

"This man does. She needed me. Now that you've met her, I hope you understand."

Cleo glanced back at the girl riding several yards behind. What she saw—a modest creature in a worn habit, shabby gloves and a head of hair that was blowing in dishevelment about a very pretty face that somehow turned no heads—confirmed what she'd felt from the moment of their first meeting: Miss Juliet Branscombe was not serious competition. "Yes, I do understand," she said, her renewed self-confidence making her generous. "I'm sorry for my outburst that night, Tris. Do you forgive me?"

"Forgive you?" He reached out and grasped her horse's reins, drawing the horses so close that he could whisper in her ear. "There is no question of forgiveness, Cleo. I love you and only you."

The horses shied apart. "We should speak of other things," Cleo said, her manner coy but her eyes sparkling happily. "Julie will see us."

But they needn't have worried. All the while they'd been trotting along the path near the river's edge, laughing and flirting and making up their differences, Julie had quite contentedly kept her distance, absorbed in her own thoughts.

The very person she'd been thinking of—Lord Canfield—was at that very moment out for his daily ride. As he came to the rise leading down to the river, he caught a glimpse of the scene. He could see that Tris and Cleo had their heads together, and that Julie was following at a distance. To him she seemed so forlorn that he found himself gritting his teeth. *Damnation,* he thought, *Miss Cleo Smallwood is moving right in, just as I suspected. And Julie is not even putting up a struggle.*

He spurred his horse and galloped down to the river's edge. He returned Tris's warm greeting, tipped his hat to Cleo and rode up to Julie. "Good morning, ma'am," he said, pulling his horse up alongside hers, "may I ride along with you?"

"I wish you would," she answered cheerfully. "Those two have given me no company at all."

"More fools they," he said.

Julie smiled at the compliment but shook her head. "I believe they have more interesting matters to engage them than to spend their time entertaining me."

"Have they, indeed?" He studied her face for a sign of jealousy, but he saw none. "Are you implying that there is an attachment developing between them?"

"It is not my place to say."

"You are very discreet. Though such discretion makes conversation difficult, I must admit it is an admirable quality in a woman."

"I know you mean that as a compliment. But it suggests that you believe most women are *in*discreet. For shame, my lord! If you were fair, you'd admit that indiscretion is a fault in both sexes."

He held his hands up against her attack. "Yes, indeed, you're quite right. Your point, ma'am."

They rode on in silence for a while, both of them watching the couple trotting so closely together in front of them. "I know that what you see there ahead of us must give you pain," Canfield said at last, unable to resist the urge to offer her his sympathy.

She blinked in surprise. "Pain?"

"Forgive me. It's none of my affair. I have no right to interfere. But I pride myself on being a shrewd observer, and it's plain to me that you care a great deal for Tris."

Julie gaped at him in confusion. "*Care* for him?" she echoed, not quite knowing what to say. "Yes, of course I do. I've known him since childhood. But I wouldn't say—"

"No, Miss Discretion, of course you won't say. But I have no qualms about speaking frankly. And frankly, ma'am, you can easily win him for yourself if you would but try."

Julie was so astounded she could only gasp. "Win him for *myself? Tris?*"

"Miss Smallwood is a beauty, I admit. But you, Miss Branscombe, are just as lovely in your own way. In a more subtle, deeper way."

Those lovely words drove everything else from Julie's mind. Her heart began to pound, and a flush of warmth swept up from her throat to her cheeks. "I . . . I . . . don't know what you mean to . . . ," she babbled, ". . . what you wish me to . . . say . . ."

"I've no wish for you to say anything. I didn't intend to embarrass you, my dear. But, you see, I'm very well versed in the ways of London flirts. Miss Smallwood is one of the most talented, but there's nothing in her packet of tricks that you couldn't learn."

"Tricks?"

"Oh, yes. Truly, ma'am, I could teach you everything you need to know."

Julie, suddenly grasping what he was getting at, stared

at him in utter disbelief. "Are you suggesting, my lord, that you want to help me to . . . to . . . ?"

"To win Tris back from Miss Smallwood, yes. With my help, you'll have him at your feet in a fortnight."

Her heart sank in her chest like a stone. She didn't want to believe that she'd understood him properly. He *couldn't* mean what she thought he meant! "At my f-feet?" she managed to mutter.

"Yes. If you're willing to try. There's nothing at all difficult about it. Just a few little strategems, like—"

"I know," she muttered dryly. "Like being saucy and laughing at all his jokes."

This brought a surprised guffaw from him. "Yes, just so," he said, grinning at her admiringly. "I can see already that you're a quick study."

She shook her head, keeping her eyes from meeting his. "No, I'm not. I have no talent for such . . . such games."

"Yes, you do, I'm certain of it. It needs only firmness of purpose. If you tell me you are firm in your resolve, we can start at once."

"At once?" she echoed, hardly hearing him, so deep were her spirits sunk in disappointment and confusion.

"Right now. The first thing we'll do is leave them. We'll ride off without a word, over to the field where we once raced. If they come looking for us—and I hope they will—they'll see us having a delightful time together. Are you game?"

Unable to speak, she merely nodded. He threw her a broad smile, spurred his horse and started off. She followed absently, her mind in a whirl. The situation was just too absurd. First Tris swore he'd have Canfield at her feet, and now Canfield was swearing he'd have Tris at her feet. Each man was dedicating himself to *passing her off to the other!* It was a most ridiculous situation. She would have laughed out loud if she didn't feel so much like weeping.

17

The note from Tris instructed Julie to meet him at the summerhouse at five. She knew why he'd selected the hour—it was the time of day when the ladies rested before dressing for dinner—but she had no idea why he wanted the meeting. Nevertheless, she was there at the appointed hour.

Tris was already waiting. He'd come early enough to observe how the two brief weeks since he'd last come here had brought about a change in the appearance of the place. A patina of spring green shimmered over every living thing. The grass was beginning to show new life, the shrubs glimmered at their edges with new growth, and little shoots of fresh green buds were appearing on the climbing vines. Everything surrounding him had a look of hopeful anticipation, as if in reflection of his own optimistic mood.

He was very happy with himself and the world. Even Julie's careless appearance, as she came into view, did not upset him. If Peter did not mind her tousled hair, her faded skirts and worn dull green shawl, then why should he? He jumped down from the platform of the summerhouse and ran to meet her. He greeted her with a shout of triumph. "I *told* you it would all work out. Isn't it splendid?"

She paused in the act of climbing the stile. "I don't know what you mean," she said, puzzled. "What's splendid?"

"Come now, Julie, it's not like you to be coy. I realized yesterday that Peter is taken with you. He's smitten, surely as I breathe. He'll come up to scratch before you know it, and then our troubles will be over!"

Julie gaped at him in astonishment. "You're speaking utter nonsense," she said. "He's not in the least taken with me."

"You are too modest, as usual. Take my word for it, my girl, your Peter is entranced. I watched him all during the party for signs, and I swear he never took his eyes from you. When you played for Elinor, the fellow had eyes only for the pianist, not the singer. And it was you he applauded when you took your seat."

"Good heavens, Tris," she objected, "a little thing like that doesn't mean—"

"And what about yesterday? Did he or did he not ride off with you with never a second thought for Cleo and me?"

"Yes, but—"

"But me no buts. I saw how you two were laughing and joking with each other when we came riding up to find you. Why, the very manner in which he lifted you from your horse was sufficient proof of—"

"But he was only acting that way because . . . because . . ." She paused, wondering suddenly if it would be wise to tell Tris what his lordship's real intentions were. Tris would surely find the information upsetting. And he would only redouble his efforts to make her saucy and flirtatious, all to no purpose. On the other hand, if he kept believing—for a while, anyway—that Lord Canfield was in love with her, he would cease his attempts to change her. That would be a relief!

Besides, if she *had* to be taught to flirt, she much preferred Canfield's tutelage to Tris's. Lord Canfield made her feel less awkward, less artificial. And he himself had undertaken a great part in the scheme: he was pretending to pursue her. Even if his attentions to her were not sincere but only a sham to make an impression on Tris, she nevertheless enjoyed them. It was a lovely pretense, and she wished the game would never have to end. Certainly telling Tris the truth would bring the end much too soon. No, she decided firmly, she would say no more.

"Well?" Tris was prodding curiously. "He was only acting that way because—?"

"Because . . . because . . . Oh, I don't know what I meant to say. But I will tell you, Tris, that if you put too much stock in your foolish theories, you are letting yourself in for a huge disappointment."

Tris glared at her in disgust. "I'm losing all patience with you, Julie! You push modesty too far. Such humility is not an appealing quality in you." He stalked off angrily, looking back over his shoulder only once, to add, "I hope, when you wed him, you will be generous enough *then* to acknowledge how right I was."

Julie sat on the stile, gazing after him with troubled eyes. Tris was still a boy, she realized. One of these days, when it was finally clear that his lordship had no intention of wedding her, Tris would have to admit how wrong he was. And then he'd see that there was no easy solution to his troubles. If he wanted to wed the girl of his dreams, he'd have to face his mama with the truth. *Tris,* she addressed him in her mind, *the only way for you to win is to become a man.*

18

A MORNING RIDE BECAME ROUTINE FOR TRIS, CLEO and Julie, and they were invariably joined by Lord Canfield. Even the frequent April showers that dampened their clothing during the ride did not deter them from this enjoyable exercise. One morning, however, after a week of passable weather, the riders suddenly found themselves deluged by a torrential rain. Riding through a shower was fun, but through a deluge was not.

Since they were at that moment closer to Wycklands than the Enders' estate, they spurred their horses to Canfield's stables. Once the horses were comfortably sheltered, the riders ran for the house. Dripping wet, yet laughing good-naturedly at their condition, they gathered round the drawing room fire to dry and warm themselves. His lordship, assuming that the rain would not let up very soon, requested his butler to do what he could to arrange an extemporaneous luncheon for his unexpected guests. The staff rose to the occasion by providing, with this minimal notice, a hot, two-course luncheon of York ham with poivrade sauce, quail stew, river trout, poached eggs, potatoes au gratin, an assortment of greens, gooseberry tarts and a most delectable Highland cream, all served with gracious ease in the smaller of the mansion's two dining rooms.

After the cheerful and leisurely meal, the diners discovered to their chagrin that the rain still poured down too heavily to permit them to resume their ride. But Lord Canfield would not allow his guests to languish in boredom. "There is a fine billiard room upstairs," he suggested. "Shall we go up and play for a while?"

"Oh, what a splendid idea!" Cleo said eagerly.

"Yes, splendid for you," Tris laughed. He turned to explain to Peter that Cleo had a real talent for wielding a cue and would promptly put the men to shame. "But Julie doesn't care much for billiards," he added with a sigh.

Julie recognized a look of slyness in his eyes. He was plotting something, she was certain of it. "I'll be happy to play, if that's what you all wish to do," she assured them.

But that was not what Tris had in mind. He didn't wish for her to play at all. "No need to sacrifice yourself on our account," he said with bland innocence while giving Julie a surreptitious wink. "Perhaps Peter will show you about the house while Cleo and I play."

"That's an excellent suggestion," Peter said at once, his voice so eager that Julie could have no doubt of its sincerity. "Ever since the night of the musicale, I've been most eager to show Miss Branscombe my pianoforte." He turned to her with a smile. "It was made by Zumpe, you see, and it has—"

"Pedals!" Julie cried, clapping her hands excitedly. "Oh, Peter, how wonderful! I've never actually tried a pianoforte with pedals."

"There, then, that's settled," Tris declared, throwing Julie a look of triumph before taking Cleo's arm and steering her toward the stairs. "You two go along to see the pianoforte, and we'll go up to the billiard room. Don't bother showing us up, Peter. I know the way."

Peter and Julie watched them disappear up the stairs. Then Julie glanced at Peter in embarrassment. "Tris maneuvered that on purpose, you know," she said. "To force you to be alone with me."

"I'm glad he did," his lordship said, taking her arm. "I've truly wanted you to try my piano, for one thing. And for another, Tris's machinations actually caused you to call me by my given name."

Julie reddened. "Did I?"

"Yes, you did. 'Oh, Peter, how wonderful.' Those were your very words. Music to my ears, I might add."

"What humbug," she said as they started down the hall toward the music room. "You needn't flirt with me when Tris is out of earshot, you know."

"I'm not flirting at all, you goose. Don't you know the difference between mere cajolery and sincere compliments?"

"Perhaps I don't. Tris says I don't tolerate compliments very well."

"He's apparently right. From now on, Miss Branscombe, please believe that any compliment I give you is utterly honest. Despite your mother's remark when we first met, I'm not the sort to pour buttersauce over a girl. Promise me you'll take my word."

"Very well, I'll promise. But in return you must stop calling me Miss Branscombe. If I've begun to call you Peter, surely you can call me Julie."

They'd arrived at the music room. Julie gasped at the sight of the magnificent instrument they'd come to see. It was longer than the pianos she'd seen before, made of highly polished rosewood, with curved sides inlaid with brass figures of Greek dancers and musicians. Six gracefully carved legs held up the L-shaped body. Julie immediately noted the lute-like appendage that hung down below the keyboard, bearing three brass pedals. Although she'd heard about this thirty-year-old innovation to the pianoforte, which deepened and enriched the tone, she'd never before seen an instrument that actually *had* pedals. The few pianos in Amberford were too old to benefit from the improvement. She took a step into the room and stared, awestruck.

"Go on, Julie, sit down and try it," Peter urged.

"Oh, no, I . . . I couldn't!" she muttered, backing off.

"Nonsense. No one here is capable of playing it, and it needs to be played."

"Don't you play?"

"I?" He shook his head, amused at the thought. "Men of my ilk are taught riding, hunting and fisticuffs, not music, I'm afraid. Please, Julie, do sit down and play something."

"Very well, if you wish it."

She sat down gingerly on the lavishly upholstered seat, turned the wheel at its side to adjust the height and began to play a simple étude. Her first attempts at pedaling made her jump—their effect on the sound was startling. But she soon accustomed herself to the change and, almost forgetting where she was, lost herself for a few moments in the sheer joy of the quality of the sound she could create on this wonderful instrument. It was only when she heard a distant clock chime the hour that she came back to herself. More than a few moments must have gone by, she realized. She must have been playing for more than twenty minutes! She looked round, embarrassed, and opened her mouth to apologize, but she found him gazing at her with such undisguised admiration that words failed her.

"That was lovely," he said softly. "Please go on."

She shook her head and jumped to her feet. "Thank you, but no. I didn't mean to bore you so long. Please forgive me."

"It was anything but boring. I could sit here and listen to you all day."

"Come now, Peter, you swore you'd give me no butter-sauce."

"And you promised to accept—and believe—my compliments."

She felt her throat tighten with grateful tears. No one had ever said such kind things to her before. "I think you should show me some more of the house," she suggested hastily, to hide her emotions.

He did not argue but offered his arm. As they strolled along the hallway, looking into the various rooms, he pointed out—as befitted a polite host—some of the noteworthy accoutrements he'd brought with him from his London house: a pair of magnificent Irish crystal chandeliers in the large dining room, an elaborately designed Persian rug in the drawing room and a number of family portraits they passed on the way. His manner was so pleasant and his remarks about his treasures so modestly humorous that she lost all feeling of self-consciousness and timidity. She felt deliciously comfortable and at home.

This sense of ease emboldened her. When they strolled by a pair of closed doors, and he made no mention of what they led to, she, barely hesitating, brazenly asked what was behind them.

"You don't want to see it," he answered. "It's not fit for guests."

"Aha! A Bluebeard!" she taunted saucily. "I knew you were too good to be true. Is that where you keep the heads of your murdered wives?"

He laughed. "Now that you've guessed my secret," he retorted with a mocking, menacing leer, twirling the ends of an imaginary mustachio, "you will soon find yourself among them. Come! I dare you to step over the threshold." He threw open the doors, his leer changing to a rather embarrassed grin. "It's my library, but as you see, hardly in condition for company."

But Julie, stepping over a pile of wrapping litter, looked about her, entranced. Though the state of the room had not much improved from the time Tris had last seen it, with boxes and packing cases still scattered over the floor, books still spilling out of them and dust still covering everything, she could see, nevertheless, what an impressive room it was. She gazed in wide-eyed admiration at the tall windows, the paneled walls and the lovely gallery. "What a wonderful room!" she breathed, clasping her hands to her chest. "Why have you left it in such neglect?"

"I want to arrange my books myself," he explained, "but I've had no time of late to attend to it, having become involved in the affairs of a silly chit who claims to need lessons in flirtation."

Her eyes fell from his face. "That is most selfish of her," she murmured. "You should tell her at once that you have more important things to do with your time."

He came up to her and lifted her chin, forcing her to meet his gaze. "Even if I find time spent with her more enjoyable than sorting through books?"

"M-more enjoyable? Really?"

"Infinitely more enjoyable."

She felt her heart swell up again. "If I had the choice," she admitted in her soft voice, "I would find sorting books more enjoyable than lessons in flirtation." Her eyes looked pleadingly into his. "We have time this afternoon. Tris and Cleo will play for hours. May I not help you with the sorting now?"

"Now? Impossible."

"But why?"

"Because it's filthy work, for one thing. Your clothes would become so grimy they would be beyond recovery. Take my word for it. My valet has already had to discard three of my shirts."

"I don't care a fig for these old riding clothes. Please, Peter. I'd love to see some of your books."

He could not resist. He took off his coat, tossed it over an unopened crate and led her to a packing case resting in the far corner. "I've just started on this batch—my poetry books," he said. "I plan to shelve them here, near the window."

She nodded eagerly. "How shall we proceed? I can sit on the floor, dust off the books one at a time, read off each title and hand the book to you for shelving. Does that sound efficient?"

"Oh, yes, quite. But I can't permit you to sit on the floor with a dustcloth like a housemaid."

"You have not the right to 'permit' me anything," she declared firmly, picking up a cloth and sitting down on the floor before he could say another word. "I may behave as I wish. Besides, I'm not above dusting. I've wielded a dustcloth many a time." She pulled a volume from the box, dusted it and read the words on the spine: "Edmund Spencer, *The Faerie Queen.*"

He hesitated a moment, unwilling to take advantage of her good nature. But after another glance at her determined expression, he shrugged and took the book from her hand. They proceeded with the labor in that way for a long while, going through half the packing case without deviation from the system she'd devised. When she handed him Herrick's *Hesperides,* however, she chanced to remark that it was a favorite of hers. "Of mine too," Peter said with a pleased smile, and he sat down beside her to read his favorite passages. This led to a reading of selections from Dryden's *The Hind and the Panther,* Thomson's *Seasons* and Milton's *Samson Agonistes.* So engrossed were they in the discovery of each other's poetic tastes that they did not notice that two hours had passed, that the rain had stopped and that the late afternoon sun was slanting through the windows and illuminating their bent heads. Peter, reading aloud Andrew Marvell's "A Definition of Love," had arrived at the penultimate stanza:

As lines, so loves oblique, may well
Themselves in every angle greet;
But ours, so truly parallel,
Though infinite, can never meet.

After reading those words, he looked up and saw that she had tears in her eyes. "Julie!" he exclaimed. "Why—?"

"Is that the definition of love?" she asked, embarrassedly wiping away the tears with her fingers, causing smudges to appear under both her eyes. "Two parallel lines that can never meet?"

"Not necessarily," he said with a smile, taking note not of the smudges but how the sun was haloing her hair. "Marvell is adopting Plato's definition—love as a longing that is never fulfilled. But one needn't accept—"

"I think there may be much truth in it," she said, sighing sadly and lowering her head.

"Come now, my dear," he said gently, "the verse has more poetic charm than truth. You are too lovely to believe that your life will be spent in unfulfilled longing." He reached out and lifted her chin again. "The parallel lines will bend for you, I promise."

Her mouth trembled. "You don't know—! You can't promise . . ."

Something about her—the liquid eyes, the parted lips, the smudged cheeks, the sun-tipped hair . . . he would never know what—aroused in him an irresistible impulse. Almost without thought, he leaned toward her and kissed her mouth. It was a gentle kiss, so soft she did not jump or pull away; she merely made a little sound in her throat, and her hand come up to his cheek. The touch roused him even more. Before he quite realized what he was doing, there in the mote-filled sunshine, he lifted himself up on his knees and pulled her into a tight embrace, his mouth never leaving hers.

It was at that moment that Tris came in search of them. He opened the door of the library and saw them. In the dusty light they appeared to be frozen into immortality, like the figures in a painting by an Italian master, their faces shadowed, their bodies outlined in gold. The sight was almost heavenly, so eloquently did the scene speak of rapture. To interrupt them would have been like interrupting a benediction. His throat constricted, and he silently backed out and closed the door.

But both Peter and Julie heard the sound; they broke apart at the instant of the door's closing. Peter's eyes flew to the door. "It must have been Tris, looking for us," he said.

She, however, was not able to turn her eyes from him. The embrace had been shattering for her. Never had she felt so overwhelmed with emotion. Every drop of blood in her body seemed to be dancing, every cell trembling with a kind of ecstatic agony. "Oh, Peter!" she gasped.

He gazed at her guiltily. "I'm sorry," he muttered. "I don't know what possessed me. The poetry, I suppose. Please, Julie, blame Andrew Marvell if you must place blame."

Her eyes clouded. These words were not what she wanted to hear. "I don't wish to blame—"

"I know," he muttered with a troubled frown. "You are concerned about what Tris must think. But you mustn't be. It will be all to the good. I can almost guarantee that at this moment he is writhing with jealousy."

Julie felt her heart sink in her breast. Peter had completely misunderstood her feelings. She could not care about what Tris was feeling, not after what she'd just experienced. The sad part was that Peter had not had a similar experience. For Peter, the embrace had apparently been nothing more than a careless impulse. For her, however, it had been all-encompassing, a whirlwind that had lifted her heart right out of her. After their lovely compatability during the poetry reading, when their feelings seemed so similar, how could they each react so differently to the kiss? They were indeed a pair of parallel lines that would never meet!

And as for Tris, she thought in despair, he was far from writhing with jealousy. If she knew anything of the matter, he was standing out in the hallway dancing with joy.

But out in the hallway, Tris was leaning against the wall, breathing hard. His mind was in turmoil. He should have felt happy as a lark, for his mission to get Julie wed seemed to be succeeding beyond his most optimistic expectations. Why, then, did he have this peculiar but unmistakable urge to take Peter by the throat and choke the life out of him?

19

ALTHOUGH LORD SMALLWOOD'S EYES WERE FIXED on the *Times* in his lap, he was not really reading. He was trying to find the courage to ask his hostess, who'd joined him in the downstairs sitting room and was placidly knitting, a very personal question. He needed to know the answer, but he was reluctant to broach so private a matter with a woman who was, to all intents and purposes, a stranger.

He knew that Lady Phyllis would have been offended to hear herself described as a stranger, for she'd been very companionable toward him since his arrival. She'd accompanied him on daily strolls, joined him for breakfast, engaged him in comfortable conversation in the late afternoons after they'd both napped, and done many other kindly acts to keep him from feeling deserted. But he thought of her as a stranger nevertheless, especially when it came to dealing with intimate matters like this.

Lord Smallwood had come to Amerford with the utmost reluctance, but after a fortnight at Enders Hall, he had to admit that the time was passing very pleasantly. It was not only the companionship of his hostess. It was also that the country air made him feel fit; that the meals Lady Phyllis laid before him were more delectable than any London cook could ever devise; that her ladyship never objected to his napping in an easy chair during the long, quiet afternoons; that the London newspapers were placed at his elbow daily; that his daughter was happily engaged in the rituals of courtship; and that the days were languidly peaceful. He would have been content to remain indefinitely, if he did not feel like a blasted interloper. After all, he and his daughter had imposed themselves on Lady Phyllis without so much as a by-your-leave, and he could not feel completely comfortable in taking continued advantage of her kind hospitality. Every morning, when he managed to see his daughter alone, he asked her to set a date for departure, and every morning she responded, "As soon as Tris makes an offer."

"But when is that to be?" he'd ask querulously.

"Any moment now. I'm sure of it."

But Lord Smallwood could no longer take the answer seriously. A fortnight of moments had come and gone, and Tris had not come up to scratch.

He looked across the room to where Lady Phyllis sat and cleared his throat. She looked up from her work, her eyebrows raised. "Did you say something, Smallwood?"

"I wish to ask you a question, ma'am," he said, hiding his unease by speaking too loudly.

"Yes?" she urged, thrusting the knitting needles into a ball of yarn to give him her full attention. "Go on, I can hear you."

"It is a . . . a rather personal question," he mumbled in a lower voice, "so if you decline to answer, I shall understand."

"Very well," she agreed.

He took a deep breath. "Does your son have any intention of wedding my Cleo?" *There!* he said to himself in triumph. *I've asked it, and I'm glad I did, no matter how she responds.*

Lady Phyllis blinked at him in surprise. "Wedding *Cleo?* Whatever gave you such an outlandish idea?"

"What's outlandish about it?" Smallwood demanded, thrusting aside his newspaper. "The two are courting, are they not?"

"Of course they're not. How can they be? Tris is betrothed to Julie."

"To Julie? You mean the Branscombe chit? How can that be?"

"What do you mean, how can it be? That's a silly question. They've been betrothed since childhood. Everyone knows it."

"Well, ma'am, *I* don't know it. And neither does Cleo."

"Perhaps I exaggerated about 'everyone.' But everyone here in Amberford knows it, even though it won't be officially announced until Julie and Tris are ready to set a date for the nuptials. Lady Branscombe and I are hoping to make the formal announcement very soon."

Lord Smallwood gaped at her, wondering what to make of this news. If Cleo learned of it, he dreaded to think what her reaction might be. There was sure to be a frightful scene, full of tears and noise and emotional excess. But above and beyond all that, Cleo would be heartbroken. She was sincerely attached to the Enders chap, more so than to any man she'd ever met. In truth, Lord Smallwood had grown rather fond of him too. This news was very upsetting. Very upsetting indeed. "Ridiculous," he muttered aloud.

Lady Phyllis stiffened in offense. "What's ridiculous about it?"

"Everything. Your son doesn't seem nearly as interested in Miss Branscombe as Lord Canfield is, for one thing. For another, he appears to be utterly enchanted with Cleo. Hasn't left her side for a moment since we arrived."

"Yes, but all that can be explained."

"How?"

"Well," Phyllis said thoughtfully, "as far as Lord Canfield is concerned, Madge Branscombe and I are convinced that Julie is using him to make Tris jealous and prod him into action."

Lord Smallwood sneered. "So he needs prodding, does he?"

Lady Phyllis looked troubled. "I know that sounds as if the boy's reluctant, but Madge says every man needs a bit of prodding in such situations."

"Hummmmph!" the old fellow snorted. "Tris doesn't seem to need any prodding when it comes to pursuing my Cleo."

Phyllis glared at him. "He's *not* pursuing her, I tell you!"

"Then what would you call his behavior?"

"I'd call it friendship. As a friend, and her host, he's obliged to squire her about, is he not?"

"Friendship, ha! There is no such thing as friendship between a man and a woman."

Phyllis drew herself up in defiance. "What folderol! Of *course* there is such a thing as friendship between the sexes. Why, just look at you and me. We're a perfect example."

"I would not be too sure of that either, ma'am, if I were you," the white-haired fellow muttered, reaching for his discarded newspaper. "You're too good-looking and good-natured to go about assuming that we men—I or any other fellow you know—have nothing on our minds but friendship."

Phyllis gaped at him. "Whatever do you mean by that?" she demanded.

He lifted the paper and hid his face behind it. "I mean nothing, ma'am," he said. "Nothing at all."

She stared in his direction openmouthed, but all she could see was newsprint. After a moment, she shrugged and reached for her knitting, for she knew by instinct that it was useless to pursue this interesting conversation. As far as Lord Smallwood was concerned, there was nothing further to be said.

20

The bimonthly Amberford Assembly was about to be held again. Like most rural assemblies, this one was usually anticipated with more eagerness by the ladies than by the gentlemen. Ladies were always excited by the prospect of dancing, flirtation and gossip, but gentlemen often chafed at the formality of the affair. This time, however, at least two gentlemen were looking forward to it. For very different reasons, both Tris and Peter were expecting this particular session to be a significant event, Peter because he was determined to dance with Julie in defiance of her mother's displeasure, and Tris because he suspected that Peter would use the occasion to offer for Julie.

Tris had completely regained his determination to see Julie married to the viscount of Canfield. The shock and abhorrence he'd experienced when he'd come upon them kissing was, he told himself, a momentary aberration. He couldn't really explain why he'd felt what he'd felt, but it was not a matter of importance. If an explanation had been required, he would probably have excused himself by saying that it had been merely a brotherly reaction, natural and protective.

But whatever the explanation, the feeling had passed. It was Cleo he adored, not Julie. There was no question in his mind that it was Cleo he wanted to wed. Cleo was more than beautiful; she was lively, witty and constantly, delightfully surprising. Julie, on the other hand, was drab, shy and held no surprises for him. So even though the scene in the library—the two embracing figures drenched in golden, mote-spangled light—sometimes recreated itself in his memory, it no longer disturbed him. He merely brushed it aside.

Thus, on the evening of the assembly, the gentlemen of two Amberford households—Enders Hall and Wycklands—prepared for the occasion with unwonted eagerness. And at Enders Hall, another gentleman was becoming interested in the event. Lord Smallwood, who had told his hostess earlier that he had no intention of participating in such "rustic folderol," was dressing himself in his evening clothes. When he later joined Lady Phyllis at the bottom of the stairs, she looked at him in surprise. "I thought, Smallwood, that you didn't want to attend this affair tonight. Didn't you say that this sort of evening would be a great bore for you?"

"Yes, but I changed my mind. I want to observe your son and this Branscombe chit with my own eyes before I take it on myself to inform my daughter that her expectations are hopeless."

"Don't be foolish," Phyllis said flatly. "You won't learn anything of that nature tonight. Tris and Julie are not the sort to make public display of their feelings."

"Don't underestimate my powers of observation, ma'am."

She shrugged. "In any case, whatever your reason, I'm glad you're going. Here, let me adjust your neckcloth. You've got it twisted around somehow."

"Thank you, ma'am," he said, offering himself to her ministrations. "It's a deuced nuisance dressing for a formal evening without a valet. If I'd known how long we would be here, I'd certainly have taken my fellow with me."

Tris came down at that moment. It gave him a gleeful sense of satisfaction to see his mother and the man he hoped would be his father-in-law apparently getting on so well. "Where is your daughter, sir?" he inquired. "It's getting late."

"Here I am," came a voice from the top of the stairs, and Cleo came wafting down in a flutter of copper-red silk chiffon. She was utterly breathtaking. Her short, dark curls framed the perfect oval of her face with a rakish charm, her bare shoulders gleamed in the light of the sconces on the wall behind her, and the diamond studs that glittered in her ears were not any brighter than the glow in her magnificent green eyes. "Oh, I say!" gasped Tris. "You *are* lovely! I'd wager our Amberford Assembly, in all the years of its existence, has never seen your like!"

Cleo paused in the middle of the stairway and gazed down at him. "Praise is even better when coming from someone who himself deserves praise," she said with charming formality. Then she threw him a beaming smile. "You look top-of-the-trees yourself."

His chest swelled with pleasure. He reached up a hand for her and drew her down the remaining steps. "The other fellows will be wild with jealously when they see you on my arm," he murmured in her ear.

She laughed in pleasure, a deep, velvety sound that seemed to go right through him. "Does that mean, you greedy boy," she asked, placing her other hand in his, "that you don't intend to let anyone else dance with me?"

"He'll have no choice about that," Lady Phyllis put in quickly, suddenly alarmed at the effect this coquettish London baggage was having on her son. "Our assemblies require that a gentleman may dance no more than three dances with the same partner."

"There's no rule that will keep us from sitting together through the rest of them," Tris retorted. He drew Cleo's arm through his and led her out to the waiting carriage. Behind the backs of their departing offspring, Lord Smallwood threw Phyllis a look that asked quite plainly, *And what do you make of that little scene, eh?*

Lady Phyllis said nothing, but when they approached the carriage she insisted that Cleo and her father climb into it ahead of her. Then, pulling her son aside, she grasped the lapels of his coat with a desperate urgency. "Be sure you dance with Julie, do you hear me, Tris? The first dance in particular."

Tris rolled his eyes heavenward. "If I must," he muttered in disgust.

This response did nothing to relieve Phyllis's sense of alarm. She climbed into the carriage with a decidedly anxious heart.

Meanwhile, Julie and her mother had already arrived at the hall. The girl's entrance had caused a pleasing stir, for she was in especially good looks. She was wearing, at her mother's insistance, a violet silk gown with a daring décolletage and a deep flounce that she'd not had the courage to wear before, and she'd brushed her hair into a single soft curl that fell over her shoulder. Her color was high, her skin glowed, and her eyes were alight with anticipation. The dowager onlookers put their heads together and agreed that Juliet Branscombe was having her bloom at last. And best of all, Lord Canfield, when he arrived some moments later, smiled across the room at her with unmistakable approval.

When the party from Enders Hall arrived, however, Cleo's entrance caused more than a stir. The reaction might have been called a gasp. While the dowager circle whispered disapprovingly of the daring color of her gown, the men in the room eyed her in awed delight. She was immediately surrounded by a crowd of eligibles who demanded a chance to dance with her. Tris reluctantly surrendered her arm and made his way to Julie, who'd already retreated to her usual seat in the shadow of her mother. "May I have the honor of the first dance?" he asked his childhood friend with a mockingly formal bow.

Julie rose and took his arm. "I should think you'd want to stand up with your Cleo," she whispered as they approached the dance floor, where a number of couples had already taken their places. "She is looking spectacularly beautiful."

"Yes, isn't she? But Mama ordered me to dance with you first. Besides, it will give us time to go over a few final instructions."

They took their place in a set. "What final instructions?" Julie asked with a frown.

"On your behavior tonight. If all goes well, it would not surprise me to learn that tonight is the night Peter will make his offer."

"Don't be a clunch," Julie said in annoyance as the music began. "He has no intention—"

They had to break for the first figure. When they came together again, Tris spoke to her through clenched teeth. "Don't waste time arguing with me, my girl. Just listen. I'm not going to suggest anything daring. You've been doing very well so far. Just remember to laugh at his quips. And to—"

They had to break again. When they came together, Tris tried to continue his instructions, but Julie cut him off. "You needn't go over the same ground again, Tris Enders. I'm quite capable of remembering your blasted instructions. And I don't see why you feel a need to remind me of them at all, especially when you've just said you think I've been doing so well."

"I just wanted to suggest one new tack. When he stands up with you tonight, he's bound to tell you how lovely you look—and, by the way, with your hair that way, you *do*—"

"Thank you for bothering to notice," she said dryly.

He ignored her interruption. "When he says it, tell him that praise is even better when coming from someone who himself deserves praise. And then add that he, too, looks very fine."

"Good God!" She peered at him in surprise. "How on earth did you think of *that?* It sounds like a stilted line of dialogue from a particularly bad play! You surely don't think a man like Peter would enjoy such—"

They had to turn away from each other again, but not before Tris threw her an offended glare.

"Cleo said it to me," he snapped when they came together for the final figure, "and I thought it was a particularly pleasant compliment."

Julie wanted to retort that she didn't need Cleo to compose conversational tidbits for her, but she held her tongue. The dance ended, she and Tris exchanged bows, and she quickly walked off the dance floor, not even waiting for his escort. She'd had more of Tris Enders and his deuced suggestions than she could bear.

She'd just taken her seat again when she looked up to find Peter standing before her. "May I have your hand for this dance?" he asked, smiling broadly at her but glancing sidelong at her mother. "I have it on good authority that it will be a waltz."

"I'd be delighted," Julie said, rising quickly to her feet in an attempt to forestall her mother's inevitable interference.

But Lady Branscombe was not easily forestalled. "I beg your pardon, my lord," she said at once, her voice loud and icy. "My daughter doesn't waltz."

"But of course she does," his lordship contradicted blandly, taking Julie's arm firmly in his. "She told me so herself."

Lady Branscombe's mouth dropped open at this brazen effrontery. She gaped, immobilized for a moment by astonishment.

Peter moved quickly. Before the shocked, white-lipped dragon could rally herself and think of a reply, he'd drawn Julie several steps toward the dance floor. "Don't look back," he muttered to the wide-eyed girl. "There's nothing your mother can do now. She's hardly likely to shout or to jump to her feet and dash after us, not with everyone's eyes on us."

They stepped on to the floor, where several other couples were also gathering for the dance, Tris and Cleo among them. Peter placed his hand on Julie's waist. "You *do* know how to waltz, don't you?"

"Not very well," she admitted in a shaking voice.

But he was not going to lose the battle for so insignificant a reason as that. "Well, don't worry, I do. We'll be fine."

She smiled up at him uncertainly. "Will we?"

"Take my word. Besides, you look so lovely tonight that you'll be the object of admiration no matter how you waltz."

A deep, gurgling laugh escaped her as she realized that

Tris had been right. "Oh, *Peter,*" she breathed, following Tris's instructions in her own way, "so will you!"

He didn't know why she'd laughed, but the sound of it delighted him. For the first time in many years, he found himself actually enjoying being with a girl on the dance floor. As the music began, he tightened his grasp on her waist and smiled down at her with real warmth. "Ready?" he asked.

She nodded.

"Good. Then just take a deep breath and follow me."

He started slowly. She took only a moment to understand how the hand on her waist was guiding her. Soon she was following easily. The waltz was not difficult, she realized, when one's partner was so expert. After a few moments, they were swinging round the floor as if they'd been partners for years. Julie, her feet almost flying and the flounce of her gown whipping about her ankles, was ecstatic. She felt lithe, graceful and utterly free. It was as if she, Peter and the music were all alone in the world and had somehow, miraculously, become one beautiful amalgam of music and motion.

Peter too was finding this dance a remarkable experience. The waltz was nothing new to him, but the girl was. It was not merely that she was light on his arm and completely responsive to his lead, for many of his partners in the past had been equally adept. It was Julie herself. He'd never known a young woman so fresh, so unspoiled, so open and frank in her responses, so unself-conscious. Julie Branscombe was more than beautiful, she was lively, witty and constantly, delightfully surprising. He looked down at her glowing face and found himself wishing that this moment would never end.

The excitement they both were feeling must have communicated itself, at least in part, to the others on the floor, for two by two they stepped aside to watch. But Cleo and Tris, watching with the others, had very different reactions. Cleo was irritated; she did not like watching another young woman take center stage away from her.

She knew the feeling was petty and ungenerous, and she hated herself for it. But she couldn't seem to help it.

She would have felt a great deal worse if she'd guessed what Tris was feeling. For some ridiculous reason that he couldn't understand, he found that he was furious. His emotions churned in his chest in an inexplicable, illogical turmoil. What right, he asked himself, had the damnable Lord Canfield to embroil Julie in such a crass, vulgar display? And why was Julie so lost to the rules of decorum as to smile so beatifically at her partner, looking for all the world as if this indecent exhibition were inspiring her with heavenly joy? If he had his way, he'd give her a tongue lashing she'd never forget! And as for Canfield, he deserved the trouncing of his life!

On the sidelines, watching every move, Lady Branscombe was experiencing emotions as livid as Tris's. How dare Lord Canfield behave in that high-handed way and take her daughter to dance in spite of her declared opposition? Had the fellow no manners, no proper upbringing, no respect for his elders? "I'd like to wring his neck, the impertinent coxcomb!" she muttered to her friend.

But on the other side of Lady Phyllis, Lord Smallwood was interpreting the scene in quite a different way. "I do believe you're right after all," he remarked to Phyllis sadly. "Your Tris is indeed in love with Miss Branscombe. Cleo has been wasting her time."

Phyllis stared at him. "Whatever drew you to that conclusion?" she asked in astonishment. "When Tris and Julie danced the country dance together, they seemed to be squabbling like cat and dog. And now that Julie's waltzing with Lord Canfield, she looks positively in alt!"

"Yes, but take a look at Tris. He's so riddled with jealously I fully expect his face to turn green."

Phyllis looked. It was true! No one could mistake the look on Tris's face. Could it be that Lord Canfield's interest in Julie might be the very factor that would bring her and Madge's dream to fruition? She leaned over to her friend. "Madge," she hissed, "take your eyes from your daughter and look at Tris!"

Madge looked. After a moment, her mouth dropped open. "Heavens!" she whispered back. "Does that mean what I think it means?"

"He's green as grass!"

Madge Branscombe's eyes widened, and a smile slowly suffused her face. "Dare I trust my eyes? Have Canfield's detestable attentions actually shaken Tris up?"

"It certainly seems so," Phyllis breathed, her gaze fixed in awed astonishment on her son's face.

"I can scarcely credit it." Lady Branscombe fell back against her chair and used her fan to cool her overheated cheeks. "Good God! To think that a moment ago I was ready to scratch his lordship's eyes out. Now I only want to take him to my bosom. The dear, *dear* man! Whoever would have thought—? I never dreamed I'd say this, Phyllis, but I do believe I shall live to bless the day when Lord Canfield came among us!"

21

THE NEXT EVENING, A HALF HOUR BEFORE DINNER, Lord Smallwood requested his daughter's company on a stroll round the rose garden. Cleo was perfectly aware that her father had no interest in roses (which, incidentally, were not yet in bloom), so she was quite prepared for a fatherly scolding. The April atmosphere, however, did not seem appropriate for scolds. The air was mild, the breeze gentle, the sky a glowing purple, and the setting sun, like a Midas, was tipping everything it touched with gold. But Cleo was too uneasy to enjoy the view. "Well, Papa, let's have it," she said as soon as they set foot on the gravel path.

"Cleo, my love," he began, his tone gentle and full of sympathy, "it's time for us to take our leave."

In spite of having anticipated this, the girl was not ready to face it. "I thought you were enjoying this rustication," she said evasively.

"That is neither here nor there. When you persuaded me to join you in this venture, you had a specific purpose: to determine the extent of Tris Enders's feelings for you. A fortnight has passed, during which you have been daily in his company. If you haven't determined it by this time, you are not the clever girl I take you for."

She cast a quick, guilty glance up at his face. "Perhaps I'm not very clever," she mumbled.

"You know better than that, Cleo. I would say, instead, that perhaps you're letting your wishes cloud your good sense."

She pulled her lace shawl more tightly about her shoulders, though there was no chill in the breeze. "You mean that I'm unwilling to face the truth, is that it?"

"I'm afraid so."

She stalked a few steps away from him, but then she paused. "I don't think so, Papa. If I were certain Tris loved Julie, I would depart at once. But until last night, he behaved in so adoring a manner toward me that I could not doubt him. He seemed as much in love with me as I could wish." She sank down on a stone bench, her head lowered. Her voice cracked on her next words. "Until l-last night."

"Are you saying that his behavior last night was an aberration?"

She nodded. "The evening started out so beautifully. You saw that for yourself. Then he watched Julie waltzing with Lord Canfield, and his mood changed. For the remainder of the affair, he was glum . . . and completely unresponsive to every attempt I made to distract him. I don't know what to make of it."

Lord Smallwood leaned on his cane for support while he peered at his daughter speculatively. Then, after a moment, he came to a decision. Seating himself beside her, he took her hand. "Did you know, my dear, that Tris is *betrothed* to Miss Branscombe?"

She swung round to him, her eyes wide with shock. *"No!"*

"Yes, it's quite true. His mother told me."

She gaped at him, her chest heaving. "It *can't* be true!" she cried, pulling her hand from his grasp and pressing it to her mouth. "We've been together every day, all of us. There was never the slightest sign—!"

Her father shrugged. "For some silly reason, they've kept it secret. But it's been in effect for years."

"I can't believe it! He even *told* me he loves me! He declared himself in just those words!"

"Did he? Then why hasn't he offered for you?"

She drew in her breath. "I don't know," she said, her lips trembling. "Do you think that's why? Because he's already . . . already—?" But she couldn't bring the word *betrothed* to her lips.

"Already committed to another? Yes, I do." He spoke quietly but with an unequivocal firmness. "What else is there to think?"

"There could be some other explanation," she said desperately.

"For instance?"

"I don't know . . . I can't *think!*"

"The most reasonable explanation I can find for his behavior," Lord Smallwood suggested in as kindly a tone as he could command, "is that he's chosen you—forgive me, my dear, but it's time to be blunt—as a . . . a . . . sort of last fling before he's launched into wedlock."

His daughter's eyes widened in horror. "A last *fling?*"

He could only nod and drop his eyes from the agonized look in hers.

"Oh, God, I *am* a fool," she muttered, white-lipped. "I, Cleo Smallwood, who had half of London at my feet! To have let myself be used so!"

They sat in silence for a while, she picking with nervous fingers at the fringe of her shawl, and he with his hands clasped on the head of his cane, his chin resting on them. They made a touching picture, with the setting sun behind them framing them in fire. But there was no one watching, no one either to admire or to sympathize. They were completely alone.

At last she lifted her head. Two large tears were making their way down her cheeks. "Oh, Papa, I do love him so!" she murmured. "Give me a few days more. A few days. Just to be sure."

"Of course, my love, if that's what you wish." He watched as she wiped away the tears with the back of her hand. She was so lovely at this moment, with the last rays of the sun playing heavenly magic with her curls, that he could hardly blame Tris Enders for being tempted by her. With a deep sigh, he heaved himself to his feet and pulled her to hers. "Come. We must make an appearance at the dinner table. Do you think you can face them with some semblance of cheerfulness?"

She turned to him with a sudden, completely brilliant smile. No one would dream it was utterly false. "There? Will that do?"

"Admirably," he said, patting her hand. "That's my plucky girl."

They started back up the path arm in arm. "I may be a fool," she said, throwing her shoulders back proudly, "but no man can say that Lord Smallwood's daughter is a coward."

22

Heavy rains poured down for two days, preventing any outdoor activities. And since no special indoor activities had been planned—no parties, no dinners, no festive teas—there was no intercourse among the three houses—Enders Hall, Larchwood and Wycklands. A kind of pall settled over them all.

At Wycklands, Peter used the time to work in his library, but every so often he found himself slumped down on a packing case with a book in his hand, staring into space. It was Julie he was thinking of, and his thoughts did not please him. He was reluctant to admit something in words that he'd known in his heart for some time: he'd fallen in love with the girl.

He'd been in love before, but lightly. This was different, much too deep and all-pervading, and he didn't like it at all. It was bad enough that the love was unrequited; what made it worse was that these feelings were, in a sense, a betrayal of her trust. He'd promised to help her capture Tris, her foolishly blind childhood sweetheart, not to attempt to win her away from him. But now that he'd become aware of his own feelings, it was becoming very painful to have to do what he'd promised. How could he hand her over to that superficial, self-absorbed Tris Enders, who didn't appreciate his marvelous luck one whit, when he, Canfield, wanted with every fiber of his being to keep her for himself?

He began to rue the day he'd ever encountered Juliet Branscombe and, even more, the impulse that had led him to promise to deliver Tris to her on a platter. But

Julie had given him to believe that she loved the deuced coxcomb—*that* was the rock on which the wave of his emotions broke. She loved Tris; there was no getting round it. And if she loved him, she would have him. That was his pledge, and he was honor-bound to keep it, no matter how it hurt him to do it.

But he had no intention of enduring this painful situation any longer than absolutely necessary. He had to get away, and the sooner the better. The only way, in honor, that he could do so was to bring Tris to his knees as soon as possible. If he was any judge of the signs, the poor fellow was already reeling. During the assembly, Tris had shown unmistakable signs of jealousy. He'd looked as if he would have liked to throttle Julie's waltzing partner with his bare hands. One more such experience and, Peter surmised, the battle would be won. And then he, Peter, could run away to London with a clear conscience and begin the arduous task of forgetting all about the lovely, dreamy-eyed Juliet.

At Larchwood, Lady Branscombe too was eager for Tris to endure another such experience as the one he'd encountered at the assembly. She was convinced that Julie's dance with Lord Canfield had shaken Tris up and brought him to realize how much he cared for her. Another such occasion might be the turning point that Madge and Phyllis had been waiting for.

Madge Branscombe wracked her brain to concoct some sort of plan—an outing or a gala of some kind—to bring the young people together again. She mulled it over in her mind at breakfast, continued throughout the morning, all during luncheon and even at tea. But it was not until Horsham, her butler, was removing the tea things that the solution came to her. Julie had already gone up to her room, and Lady Branscombe was on her way out when the butler chanced to ask if he might permit the maids and some of the footmen to take the next afternoon off. "The fair starts tomorrow," he explained.

Lady Branscombe paused in the doorway. "Fair?" she inquired.

"The Amberford Spring Fair. You do remember, don't you, ma'am? It's an annual event. I know it's not so important or grand as the Whitmonday Country Fair, but I do like to let the staff have a bit of a frolic whenever there's any sort of fair in town."

Lady Branscombe's eyes lit up. "The spring fair, you say? Isn't it a little early?"

"No, ma'am. It's usually held near the end of April."

"I must have forgotten. I haven't gone for years. Is it still as it always was, with booths and games and entertainments?"

"Oh, yes indeed, your ladyship. Mainly there's the cattle sale and the horse auction, but there's many other things going on. Games and sports and all kinds of shops, like cheese stalls and wine merchants and fruit sellers. And all sorts of delicacies you can buy. The men like the skittle alley, and the maids do enjoy the smockraces, for sure, and everyone likes to lose a penny or two on the games of chance. There's no balloon ascension like there is at St. George's field in London, but sometimes there's a magic show, and there's always a gypsy telling fortunes. The staff do love it, for certain."

"Tell me, Horsham, do any of the gentry still attend?"

"Oh, yes, ma'am, they surely do. Not on the first day, of course, when they mostly let the hired help have the day to theirselves, but every day after that you'll see the gentry hobnobbing with everyone else."

"I see. Well, thank you for the information, Horsham." She crossed the room to her writing desk, adding in as pleasant a tone as the butler had ever heard her use, "And you may certainly permit the staff to take the afternoon."

She smiled to herself as she pulled out a sheet of note paper. The spring fair, she thought, would not make the most exciting diversion one would wish for, but it would do well enough. She cut a nib, dipped it into the inkwell and dashed off a quick note to Lady Phyllis, informing her that she was arranging an outing to the fair for the day after tomorrow, weather permitting, and that she hoped (nay, *expected)* that Phyllis herself, her son, and her guests would attend. *I am also,* she added, *sending a note to Lord Canfield informing him of the affair and requesting his company.*

The weather continued to be depressing until midmorning of the appointed day, when, to Lady Branscombe's intense delight, the sun broke through the overhanging clouds. The entire party, including Lord Canfield, gathered at Larchwood just after luncheon. It was a very frolicsome, excited group that set off on foot to the town square, for after two days of enforced boredom, the prospect of a fair was a tonic to their spirits. With the eagerness of children let out of school, they romped, frisked and skipped down the hill and over the stone bridge to the town square, where the fair was taking place on the green.

A gaudily brilliant sight met their eyes. Dozens of tents and booths had been set up in two rows along the sandstone walkways that edged the green, each trying to outdo the other in the loudness of its colors. Yellows and oranges vied with reds and purples, as gaily garish as the penants and flags that floated over them in the breeze. A hundred or more villagers milled about the green, laughing and cavorting and bargaining with the merchants in loud voices. A great deal of shouting emanated from a tent where a wild cockfight was going on. A large group of children were surrounding a booth where a Punch-and-Judy show was stirring them to shrieks of laughter. Delicious aromas of roasting pig and frying pies rose in the air. Madge Branscombe was immediately heartened by the holiday atmosphere. "It's better than I dared hope," she whispered to her friend.

Unable to agree on which attraction to visit first, the group split up to indulge in their different likings. Lord Smallwood went off to wager on the cockfight. Phyllis made for the stall where a particularly famous local cheddar cheese was being sold, while Madge began immediately to haggle with a wine seller. Tris, who was interested in adding a horse to his stable, excused himself to attend the horse auction. And Peter laughingly challenged Julie and Cleo to a game of ringtoss. Cleo, who had been at considerable pains to hide her depressed mood, made up her mind to concentrate on the game, and she not only surpassed Peter in her score but bested every other participant who competed. By the time the proprietor of the booth awarded Cleo a prize for her skill—a huge doll with a painted porcelain face—she was ready to agree with everyone else that she was having a marvelous time.

The afternoon passed quickly. Tris, not having seen a horse to his liking, soon rejoined his friends and spirited Cleo off to see the magic show. On the way to the magician's tent, Cleo, delighted at his renewed attention, almost pranced as they made their way across the green. "I'm so glad you didn't spend all afternoon at the auction," she said.

"So am I. I'd much rather be with you." Tris glanced over at her and noticed for the first time that something was tucked under her arm. "What is that you're carrying?" he asked.

"A doll. Look at it, Tris. Hasn't it a charming face?" She peeped up at him with a grin. "I won it with my tossing skill."

Tris gazed down at her in admiration. "You, Cleo Smallwood, are amazing in your talents. Riding and billiards and now this! Top-of-the-trees, that's what you are."

It was a very happy young woman who took his arm.

Meanwhile, Julie and Peter strolled along the sandstone paths, stopping here to taste a plum pastry and there to watch a wrestling match. The sun was almost setting when Julie spied the gypsy tent, set off by itself a little way behind the row of booths and stalls. It was a shabby structure, its green-and-pink striped fabric so faded it almost looked gray. Julie was surprised she'd even noticed it, for it was almost hidden by a brightly painted booth bearing a sign reading "HOT BRANDY BALLS, TUPPENCE." "Look, Peter, a gypsy fortuneteller!" she cried.

"Where?" he asked, looking about.

"There, behind the brandy ball booth." She looked

down at the ground, feeling a bit shamefaced. "Excuse me, Peter, but I must go in. I know it's all foolishness, but I've always wanted to have my palm read."

"Then by all means do," he urged, pressing a gold coin into her hand.

She thanked him, walked quickly round to the shabby tent, hesitated for a moment and finally lifted the tent flap and stepped inside. The interior was very dark. It took a moment for her eyes to adjust to the dimness. When they did, she saw a wrinkled old woman sitting at a table covered with a long, colorful cloth that hung down to the floor. The woman was colorful too, with a striped bandanna covering her head and more than a dozen strands of beads hanging from her neck. "You wish fortune?" the woman asked in an exotic accent.

"Yes," Julie said timidly.

"Sit, then," the gypsy ordered. "Sit an' give me right hand."

Julie did as she was bid, her hand trembling slightly in the gypsy's tight grip.

"This," the woman said, feeling her palm with a knobby forefinger topped by a long, cracked nail, "is life line. Nice, long. Is good. But this . . . love line . . . is strange. Broken off."

"Broken off?" Julie asked, puzzled and somewhat frightened.

"Yah. Broken 'ere. But starts up again 'ere, see?"

"No, I'm afraid I don't—"

The gypsy shook her head impatiently. "Better we look at crystal ball, eh?"

"Crystal ball?"

"Yah. There." And she pointed to a large globe on the table before her.

Julie had not noticed it before, but now it began to glow with an eerie, flickering light. "Oh!" she exclaimed, staring at it in fascination. "Can you read my fortune in there?"

"Per'aps. For two silver coins."

"This guinea is all I have," Julie said, handing her the coin Peter had given her.

The gypsy's eyes brightened at the sight of the gold coin. She snatched it with her knobby, ring-bedecked fingers and tested it with her teeth. Satisfied, she cocked her head. "Ain't got no change," she muttered, pocketing it.

"That's all right," Julie assured her.

The gypsy smiled. "You good sort lady. I tell you good fortune," she said, leaning forward.

"How do you know it will be good if you haven't read it yet?" Julie asked.

The gypsy was not thrown by the question. "Good because true," she answered promptly.

The light in the crystal ball brightened, and as the gypsy woman passed her hands over it, the light seemed to move with the motion of the hands. Then clouds of smoke filled the globe, floating and shifting into formless shapes. "I see man . . . no, two men . . . ," the gypsy said in a low monotone.

"Where?" Julie asked, peering into the glowing orb but seeing nothing. "There in the ball?"

The gypsy ignored the interruption. "Men both dark. One tall."

"Yes?" Julie urged eagerly, nevertheless feeling quite foolish.

"They argue."

"Argue?"

The old woman peered closer into the light. "Then they fight. Terrible fight. I see blood." She looked up at Julie with a glittering, piercing gleam. "They fight for you."

"Oh, no, I hardly think—"

"Yes. They fight for you. Terrible fight."

"Not with . . . pistols!" Despite her skepticism Julie was completely caught up in the tale.

"No, no. With fists. Terrible fight. I see big crowd watching. Oh! The tall one down. Not get up."

"Oh, dear!"

The gypsy looked at her closely. "You wish other man to win? Tall one?"

"Yes! No! I mean, this is silly." She tried to think sensibly in a situation that made no sense. "I don't even know what men you're speaking of. You're the one who sees them, not I."

"Ah, that is so. I see, you not see. But tall man will not win, not ever, unless . . ."

She could not help herself. She had to ask. She had to know. "Unless . . . ?"

"Unless . . . unless . . ." The gypsy peered closer into the ball, but the light was quickly fading. "Oh . . . is going . . . is gone." She looked up at Julie and shrugged. "Sorry. Is all."

"All? Is it over? So soon?"

"Sorry. Crystal ball is ruler, not me."

"Oh." Julie rose from the chair, unmistakably disappointed, but ashamed of herself for feeling so. The silly tale was scarcely worth a gold guinea. "Well, good-bye," she said, turning to the flap of the tent. "That was . . . interesting. Thank you."

"Au 'voir," the gypsy said.

But as Julie reached out to lift the flap, another voice echoed through the tent. *"Unless you untie the knot you knit yourself."*

She whirled about. "What?" she asked, staring at the gypsy suspiciously. But the voice she'd heard was different from the old woman's and had had no trace of a foreign accent. Nevertheless she peered at the old woman accusingly. "What did you say?"

Again another voice, speaking in perfect English, reverberated through the tent. *"The tall man will not win unless you untie the knot you knit yourself."*

The gypsy woman had not spoken. When the strange voice faded, the old woman fixed her glittering eyes on Julie with an expression that was completely unreadable. *"Au 'voir,"* she said again.

It was an unmistakeable dismissal. Julie knew that those were the last words she'd hear from her.

23

MEANWHILE, OUTSIDE ON THE GREEN, PETER WAS passing the time watching the Punch-and-Judy show. The laughter of the children and the slapstick on the small stage so thoroughly amused him that when a hand grasped his shoulder and pulled him round, the smile still remained on his face. But there was no answering smile on Tris's face. Something about Peter bothered Tris of late. He'd truly liked the fellow when they first met, but now, inexplicably, the very sight of Canfield raised his ire. "Where's Julie?" he demanded rudely. "Don't tell me you were so buffleheaded as to let her go off by herself!"

"Cut line, man, she's perfectly safe," Peter assured him. "She's gone to have her palm read, there in that green-and-pink tent behind the brandy ball booth."

"You sent her to the *gypsies?* Alone? You must be mad."

"Don't be foolish, Tris," Cleo put in. "Gypsy fortune-tellers aren't a bit dangerous."

"Nevertheless," Tris said stubbornly, feeling a sudden prick of annoyance with her for interfering, "I'd better go and fetch her."

Peter realized that, in Tris's present mood, the time was ripe for the act that would propel him into Julie's arms. "No, you wait here with Cleo," he said, grasping Tris's arm to stop him from walking off. "I'll go." And before Tris could object, he ran off round the brandy ball booth to the gypsy tent.

"Wait, damn you!" Tris shouted and started to follow him. This time, Cleo caught his arm and held him back.

"Peter can find her easily enough," she said, taking his arm. "You needn't go chasing after him."

The little prick of annoyance Tris had felt toward her swelled up and became a tidal wave of irritation. "I don't need a managing female to tell me what to do," he snapped, abruptly shaking off her hold on him. This caused her to drop her doll. It fell to the ground, its porcelain face striking the sandstone slab with a clunk. The sound was enough to indicate that the porcelain had smashed. "I'm . . . sorry," Tris muttered in shamed reluctance.

"The doll needn't make you sorry," Cleo said quietly, glancing from the ruined plaything to his face. "It was an accident. But what you just said to me was no accident, and therefore more deserving of apology."

His expression hardened. "I'm concerned for Julie's safety. That needs no apology."

"I think it does. Am I a 'managing female' because I don't believe Julie's in danger? And because I pointed out that if she were, Peter was capable of seeing to the matter?"

"I don't agree. And I don't think this is the time to discuss it. I must go. If you'll excuse me for a moment—"

She felt a strange tremble at her knees. "If you leave me now, Tris," she said in a voice she herself did not recognize, "you will not find me waiting when you come back."

"It seems to me, ma'am," Tris retorted as conflicting paroxysms of rage, shame and impotence clashed in his breast, "that you gave me a similar ultimatum in London a few weeks ago. It was as unwarranted then as it is now." He turned on his heel and stalked off in the direction Peter had taken, leaving Cleo staring after him, aghast, her broken doll lying sprawled at her feet.

When Peter arrived at the gypsy tent, Julie was just emerging, looking distracted. But there was no time for him to investigate the cause. "Julie, listen," he said quickly, grasping her arms at the shoulder. "Tris is about to come storming round that booth. He's on the verge of falling into your arms. All he needs is a push over the edge. If he'd catch a glimpse of us kissing, I believe that would be enough to do it. So, please, don't struggle when I—"

Julie, blinking in the light and taken utterly by surprise, took a backward step. She only knew that Peter was completely mistaken in Tris's motives. "No, Peter, you don't understand," she said, deeply troubled. "Tris doesn't—"

"There's no time to talk," he cut in urgently. "He may come at any moment. He must find us embracing, or the moment will be lost." Without giving her time to respond, he pulled her close. His arms tightened about her, and he put his mouth to hers.

She didn't struggle. Her mind was too full of confusing impressions to think clearly. She'd not yet recovered from the shock of the mysterious voice in the gypsy tent when Peter had come upon her with this urgent demand. It was all too much to sort out now. She simply melted into his embrace and let herself enjoy the sensation. There would be time later, she thought, to figure things out.

Tris did not immediately appear, but Peter did not let her go. He was certain that Tris would follow him momentarily. Meanwhile, he too surrendered to the pleasure of the embrace. This would be the last time he'd hold this beloved girl in his arms, and he had no difficulty in convincing himself that he might as well savor every sensation while he could. He could not concern himself now about the difficulties he would encounter later, when he'd be trying to forget her. Yes, this would be a difficult memory to erase, but for now it was a taste of heaven to hold her like this. He would take what he could from the present; there would be plenty of time later, when the future was upon him, to pay the price.

In the pure joy of the embrace, Peter almost forgot why he'd done this thing. But as he'd predicted, Tris did appear. And, in Peter's view, much too soon.

Tris came striding round the brandy ball booth like an avenging knight. When he saw Julie and the dastardly Canfield locked in each other's arms, he exploded. "Good

God!" he swore in fury. "You damnable makebait, unhand that woman!" And he savagely pulled Peter around.

Julie tottered backward and almost fell. "Tris, what's the *matter* with you?" she cried, startled at his vehemence.

Tris ignored her. "Just *what* do you think you're *doing?"* he shouted at Peter.

"That's obvious, isn't it?" Peter replied coolly, determined to goad the fellow into action. "And what business is it of yours?"

"I'll show you what business it is of mine," Tris said through clenched teeth. And he swung his fist like a madman into Peter's jaw.

Peter went down like a stone. Julie screamed. A crowd began to gather, their eyes wide with curiosity and ribald delight. "A mill!" someone shouted. "There's gonna be a mill!"

"Why, it's young Enders," said a female voice.

"And that's the viscount from Wycklands," cried another in salacious pleasure.

"Get up, you blasted gudgeon," Tris shouted at the fallen man. "Get up and let me give you another!"

"Right," yelled a man in the crowd. "Get up, yer lordship, an' give 'im yer fives!"

Peter lifted himself on one elbow. A trickle of blood leaked from a split in his underlip. With a cry of alarm, Julie knelt beside him, agitatedly mopping up his blood with her handkerchief.

"Get away from him, Julie," Tris ordered. "I'm not finished with him yet."

"I'm not getting up," Peter said in rueful amusement. "I have no intention of engaging in fisticuffs with you."

"Get up, I say, or you're a damned poltroon," Tris insisted furiously.

But it was Julie who rose. She ran to Tris's side and clutched his arm. "What on earth's gotten into you, Tris?" she muttered into his ear in utter perturbation. "Isn't that kiss just what you *wanted* to happen?"

Tris gaped at her, arrested. What she'd said was true! He blinked at her for a moment like a man just awakening from a dream. Of *course* that was what he'd wanted. What *had* gotten into him? In his struggle to find an answer, the madness that had enveloped him during the last few minutes dissipated. His fists relaxed, his arms dropped to his side, and he shut his eyes in a kind of agony. Then, dazed and confused, he turned away from Julie's bewildered gaze and saw the mob. *Confound it, what have I done?* he asked himself. Awash in humiliation, he blundered his way through the crowd, ran round the intervening booth and disappeared.

The crowd, realizing that the fun was over, began to disperse. Julie helped Peter to his feet. "What was all that about, Peter?" she asked. "Did you *plan* to let yourself be knocked down?"

He licked his bloody underlip. "Well, I didn't expect to get a swollen jaw and a split lip, but, yes, I suppose I did. It was the only way I could think of to make him recognize his feelings for you. I think the young idiot knows them now. Go to him, Julie, and let him tell you himself."

Julie shook her head. "I think you *both* are idiots. But never mind that now. Let's go back to Larchwood and get your lip tended to."

"No, thank you, Julie. My wound is trivial. Your purpose now is to find your Tris. As for me, now that our goal has been accomplished, I think I'll take myself home and rest on my laurels." He looked down at her with a small smile, bowed briefly and set off for his home.

Julie's throat tightened in pain. "But Peter," she called after him, "you don't—! There's something I ought—"

He wheeled about. "Don't say anything, please! If there's anything I don't want from you, it's thanks." He took three quick strides back to her and lifted her hand to his lips. "Good-bye, my dear. I wish you happy." That said, he hastily walked away, leaving her staring after him in despair.

Just a few steps away, hidden by the brandy ball booth, Cleo stood leaning against its side, her cheeks white. It was there her father found her a few moments later.

"Cleo, my love," he exclaimed at the sight of her deathly pallor, "what is it?"

She lifted her head and peered at him as if at a stranger. Then she fell against his shoulder, as limp as a doll. "Oh, Papa!" she murmured miserably.

He stiffened in alarm. "Good God, girl, what's *happened* to you?"

She was silent for a moment. Then, with a slight shudder, she stood erect and straightened her shoulders. "Papa," she said in a muted voice, "let's go home."

24

WAT ENDERS HALL THAT NIGHT, DINNER WAS NOT served. No one wanted to eat it. Lord Smallwood had announced that he and his daughter were departing for London immediately and would not stay for dinner; Tris had not been seen since the fair had closed at dark; and Lady Phyllis, the only one left, had no appetite. So dinner was canceled.

The staff did not mind. They had quite enough to do, readying the guests for departure. On strict orders from Lord Smallwood himself, the maids and footmen had only one hour in which to ready their coach and bring it to the door, help Lord Smallwood and Cleo to dress, pack their bags and bandboxes, carry them down and load them atop the carriage. Why there should be such a great hurry all of a sudden, when the Smallwoods had been dallying in complete ease at the hall for more than a fortnight, was a question no one on the staff could answer.

Lady Phyllis, who had by this time completely forgotten that when the pair had first arrived she'd longed for their quick departure, was now quite upset by this abrupt decision to leave. It did not help in the least to hear Lord Smallwood's inadequate answer when she'd asked if anything was wrong. He'd only said that it was urgent they return to London at once.

Phyllis stood helplessly in the entryway watching the footmen rush in and out. Neither Smallwood nor Cleo made an appearance until the coach was ready to depart. They came down the stairs together, dressed for travel and looking strained. "I wish you will sit down and take a light repast before leaving," Phyllis begged.

"Thank you, ma'am," Smallwood said brusquely, "but we must be off."

"Can you not even wait for Tris to come home? I have no idea where the boy has gone for so long, but he's certain to come home at any moment. He'll be so dismayed at having missed seeing you off."

"He'll get over it," Lord Smallwood muttered.

Cleo threw him a quick, disapproving look. Then she threw her arms about Phyllis's neck and held her tight. "I shall never forget your generous hospitality," she said in a shaking voice. "Thank you from my heart, ma'am." And she ran out the door.

Lord Smallwood, using his cane to help the limp that had suddenly become very pronounced, hobbled across the floor to his hostess and took her hand. "I too will never forget your many kindnesses, ma'am," he said.

"Come now, Smallwood," Phyllis demurred, "we've surely become good enough friends to skip these formal thank-yous."

He smiled sadly. "Yes, I suppose we have. I only wish . . ."

"Yes?" she prodded eagerly.

He shook his head, dismissing the unspoken thought. "Well, no point in dwelling on wishes," he muttered as he limped to the door. "My mother used to say, 'If wishes were buttercakes, beggers would be fat.'"

She followed him out to the carriage and watched as a footman helped him climb up. Then the steps were lifted, the door was shut, and the coachman cracked his whip. Lord Smallwood lowered the window and poked out his head. "Good-bye, m'dear," he shouted against the noise of the horses' hooves.

"Good-bye," she answered sadly. "I also wish . . ." But the carriage was already moving down the drive. He probably hadn't even heard her.

25

DRIS CAME HOME REELING. HE TEETERED TOWARD the stairway, trying not to make any noise, for it was past midnight. But his mother, who'd been waiting in the sitting room, heard him. She hurried out to the hallway, took one look and gasped. "Tris! You're *drunk!*"

"Yes, ma'am. As a lord."

She glared at him, aghast. "How *could* you? Tonight of all nights, when I have such important matters to discuss with you!"

He blinked at her woozily. "Wha' important matters?"

"I can't tell you now. Not when you're in this indecent condition."

"Yes, y'can. I'm a bit mizzled bu' not yet seeing by twos."

"A bit *mizzled?* You can barely stand! I'm surprised you're not walking on your knees."

"Dalderbash!" He threw back his shoulders and tried to stride past her into the sitting room, but he stumbled and would have fallen if she hadn't caught him.

He shook her off, tottered into the room and dropped down on the nearest easy chair. "There, now. Wha'dye want t'say t'me?"

She shrugged and sat down on the sofa opposite him. "For one thing, your guests have departed for London."

He blinked at her, openmouthed. "Cleo? Gone?"

"Yes, with her father."

"Gone, eh? Hmmmmm." He thought the matter over for a moment. "I'm not . . . surprised."

His mother shook her head. "You look surprised."

"Well, in a way I am surprised. An' then again I'm not."

"That's a logical answer," Phyllis said sardonically. "For a drunkard."

"Cleo did indi . . . indicate t'me that she might leave," he managed.

"When did she do that?"

He wrinkled his brow in thought. "T'day, I think. This after . . . noon."

"Did you quarrel?"

"Yes. No." He put up a hand to steady his swimming head. "I dunno."

Phyllis eyed him in disgust. "Really, Tris, this is getting us nowhere. You should go to bed."

"Quarreled wi' Canfield, though. Remember that right enough. Gave 'im a facer. Knocked 'im off 'is pins."

"Tris!" She rose from her seat in concern. "Are you saying you actually engaged in fisticuffs? With *Peter?*"

"Knocked 'im right off 'is pins."

"But why?"

"Th' bounder wuz kissing Julie. Had no right t'kiss Julie."

Phyllis's eyes widened, and her heart gave a jump in her chest. Suddenly, in this useless and depressing exchange, she heard something to delight her. "Oh, *Tris,*" she cried, dropping to her knees before his chair and taking his nerveless hand in hers, "do you know what that means?"

"It don't mean anything. On'y means I floored 'im wi' my fives. Nothing at all nigsifigant . . . fignisigant . . . significant in that."

"But it *is* significant. It means you were jealous! And jealousy, my dear boy, is a sign of love."

He fixed his eyes on her blankly. "Is it?"

"It means you love Julie! Just as we've always wished!" She got to her feet and gazed at him fondly, her anger gone. "But never mind now, dearest. You need to sleep away your inebriation. We'll talk about this tomorrow. I'll ring for Livesey to put you to bed." She went to the bell-pull, her step almost dancing. "You dear, dear boy!" she chirped excitedly. "You've made me the happiest of mothers!"

Those words were the first Tris remembered when he awoke the next morning. Something in his head hammered painfully, preventing him from understanding the words' significance. It was a long while before he was able to think clearly, but when he could, he began to understand what it was that had made his mother so happy: she'd concluded that he loved Julie after all.

Perhaps it was true. He'd certainly been acting like Julie's lover these past few days. Ever since he'd seen Peter kissing her in the dappled sunlight of his library, he'd been like a man possessed. After plotting and scheming to encourage Peter to fall in love with her, he'd made a complete about-face. Now he seemed to be scheming, instead, to tear Julie from Canfield's arms. What did that mean? It was jealousy, certainly. But was jealousy the result of love?

What did he really know about love, after all? he asked himself. He'd truly believed he loved Cleo, but these last few days he'd barely noticed her, so blinded had he been with jealousy. And when she'd tried to interfere with him, he'd felt nothing but irritation. Had his love for her simply died away? Passed like a spring rain? Or had it never existed at all?

Perhaps love was a will-o'-the-wisp, like happiness, always floating just beyond one's grasp. Or perhaps it was a quiet, slowly developing emotion, made up of affection and loyalty and undramatic steadiness, like his feeling for Julie—a sleeping beast only roused to passion when driven to extremes of jealousy or lust. He wished he could discuss the problem with someone older, wiser and more experienced than he . . . someone like Peter. But passion had made him punch Peter in the jaw, thus precluding any possibility of engaging in friendly conversation with the man again. Passion had its price.

After another hour of head-hammering contemplation, he was still without a single answer to the dozens of questions his conduct and his muddled feelings had aroused.

There was nothing for it, he decided, but to go down and face the consequences.

His mother, who'd been eagerly awaiting his descent all morning, greeted him warmly. "Do you remember what we talked about last night?" she asked as soon as he sat down at the morning room table for a late breakfast.

"Yes, every word," he assured her.

"Then I think we should run over to Larchwood as soon as you've eaten, and tell Madge. And Julie, of course."

Tris paused in the act of bringing a muffin to his mouth. "Tell them what?"

"Tell them to set a wedding date, of course."

He set the muffin down on his plate unbitten. "Of course," he said at last. "What else could I have been thinking of?"

What else indeed? he asked himself as he slowly sipped his tea. His feelings for Julie were obviously very deep, much deeper than he'd dreamed, or else why would he have behaved like such a crazed buffoon these past few days? He would marry Julie, with whom he was always completely comfortable. They would live together in the blessed familiarity and fond affection that had been a constant condition of their lives. It was evidently meant to be. Their mothers had always known it. It was only childish rebellion that had made them oppose the idea all these years. Well, he'd grown up at last. It was about time.

26

JULIE HAD NO QUESTIONS IN HER MIND ABOUT THE nature of love. She knew what love was; she'd recognized it almost at once. Perhaps she hadn't quite admitted it when she'd first laid eyes on Peter at the assembly, but it hadn't taken her long afterward to acknowledge the truth. Though she'd never come face-to-face with that sort of love before, it was not in the least unfamiliar. Love was, to her, an instantly recognizable emotion.

As she lay sleepless on her bed the night after the disastrous fair, she was pondering a problem of another sort—how to win the object of that love. And that was a problem she had no idea how to solve. She'd gone to see the gypsy in the desperate hope of getting a clue, but the experience in the gypsy tent had been too confusing. Besides, it was ridiculous to take fortune-telling to heart. Crystal balls . . . mysterious voices . . . lines on the palm . . . they were all nonsense. Anyone who took such things seriously was a dupe, and she was no dupe. She knew perfectly well that someone had been under the table, holding a candle under the globe and blowing smoke into it. Perhaps that same hidden swindler was the one who'd said those confusing words. There was nothing supernatural about any of it.

And yet . . . and yet . . . Hadn't the gypsy said there were two men, one tall? Julie had known instantly that they were Tris and Peter. How could the gypsy woman have known that? And hadn't the old crone predicted the fight? The mill hadn't been as terrible as she'd said it would be, but there *had* been blood. And a crowd. And Peter had gone down and would not get up. That was a great deal to explain away by calling it coincidence. Perhaps there *was* something supernatural in the midst of all that flim-flam.

But of all she'd heard in the gypsy tent, the words at the conclusion troubled her most. *The tall man will not win unless you untie the knot you knit yourself.* What did it mean? What knot had she knit herself?

If she were honest with herself, she would admit that there was indeed a knot in the threads of her life. She could easily identify it. She'd foolishly admitted to Tris that she was attracted to Canfield, and she'd been a willing participant in Tris's scheme to capture him. If she'd never told Tris how she felt, and if she'd been brave enough to admit to Peter that she was not in love with Tris, the threads would never have tangled. She herself was the one to blame for "knitting" the plot. And that was the knot she had to untie.

But how?

There was only one possible solution: Peter would have to be told the truth. Once he knew that it was not Tris but Peter himself that she loved, the tangled threads would fall apart. The knot would not even exist. But she could not do it. Such a confession would take more courage than the shy Miss Juliet Branscombe possessed.

Besides, even if the knot were untied, there was no reason to suppose that anything would change. No substantial improvement would come of it. Peter didn't love her. If he did, wouldn't she have seen a sign of it? Of course, he *had* kissed her once, that afternoon in his library, but that had been because they'd both been drunk with poetry. Though it had been an unforgettable moment for her, it had not meant anything to him. There was, therefore, no reason to put her courage to the test. She would make no confession. There was no point in it.

The next morning, hoping that life would go on as it had before the altercation at the fair, she took out her horse as she usually did when the weather permitted. To her surprise, there was no sign of Cleo or Tris at their usual meeting place. She trotted along the river to the place where Peter generally joined them, but there was no sign of him either. She circled around for a while, hoping he might eventually appear, but he did not. She wondered if, now that he believed his goal for her had been accomplished, he no longer wished for her companionship. She was crushed with disappointment. Though they might never be lovers, she'd hoped they would still be friends.

Deeply depressed, she returned home. When she came in the door, Horsham informed her that her mother, Lady Phyllis and Sir Tristram awaited her in the upstairs sitting room. Without pausing to change her riding clothes, she hurried up the stairs to them.

The warmth of their greetings surprised her. Her mother was smiling broadly, and Phyllis too looked as if she were bursting with good news. But it was Tris who spoke. "Sit down, Julie, for we have something to tell you."

"Really?" She glanced from one to the other in puzzlement as she sank down in an armchair. "You all look as if you've a surprise present to give me. But it isn't my birthday."

"It's better than a birthday present," Phyllis said, giggling.

"Tell her, Tris," her mother ordered. "The suspense is becoming too much for me."

Tris perched on the arm and took her hand. "We're going to be married," he said, smiling down at her fondly. "I've made up my mind. We need only to set the date."

"Oh, Tris!" Julie exclaimed, her eyes brightening. "So Cleo has accepted you at last!"

"Cleo?" The shocked cry came from her mother, but everyone's face fell.

"No, you goose," Tris said quickly. "I meant you."

"Me?" The gladness faded from her face. "You want to marry *me?* Have you lost your mind?"

"What a thing to say!" her mother exclaimed, shocked. "Of course he hasn't lost his mind. He's regained it!"

Julie leaped from the chair, almost knocking him over. "No, he hasn't. He's mad!"

Her mother reddened in enraged disappointment. "You're the one who's mad!" she cried. "Oh, what have I done to deserve such a contrary daughter?"

But, Julie, who'd heard all that before, took no notice of her. It was Tris who troubled her. "What's gotten into you, Tris?" she demanded, glaring down at him. "Have you forgotten all about Cleo? And about all the machinations to get me wed to someone else just to clear the way for you?"

"I haven't forgotten," he muttered, abashed. "I just grew up is all."

"What on earth does that mean?"

"I grew up. I suddenly realized that our years of knowing each other, of closeness and friendship, made a sound basis for marriage. We've always been good together, haven't we? Then why wouldn't a marriage between us be good?"

Her brows knit suspiciously. "Cleo turned you down, is that it?"

"Not at all. Just the opposite."

"The Smallwoods have gone back to London," Phyllis put in gently. "You see, when Tris became insanely jealous of Lord Canfield, it became clear to everyone, including Tris, that he loved you."

Julie peered at Lady Phyllis in disbelief. "Are you saying that Tris—on his own, without coercion—decided to offer for *me* instead of for Cleo?"

"Yes. That's exactly what she's saying," Tris declared.

"So stop all this foolishness," her mother ordered, "and help us to plan the wedding we've been dreaming of all these years."

"No, I will not!" Julie cried, wheeling about to her mother, an uncontrollable fury overwhelming her usual cowardice in the face of her mother's imperiousness. Angry tears filled her eyes and began to roll down her cheeks. "I don't *care* about your dreams! Have you, or

Tris, or even Phyllis ever given one thought to *my* dreams?"

"Julie!" her mother exclaimed, appalled at this outburst.

"Oh, my dearest girl!" Phyllis clutched her hands to her bosom in anguish. "Don't you *want* to marry Tris? Are you trying to tell us you don't love him?"

"Tris knows *exactly* how I feel," the girl replied, wiping at her cheeks uselessly, for the tears continued to pour from her eyes. "And to th-think that he, who knows me so well, could possibly b-believe that I would accept this complete about-face without so much as a by-your-leave and agree to w-wed him is . . . is . . . the outside of enough!"

All three gaped at her, aghast. She looked from one to the other, hoping for a flicker of sympathy, but she saw only utter astonishment. Why, she asked herself furiously, were they so astonished at what she felt was a perfectly reasonable reaction to their high-handed assumption that she would jump as soon as Tris snapped his fingers? It was the last straw. She did the only thing she could—she fled from the room.

Out in the hallway, she came to a stop and leaned against the stair bannister, her chest heaving. Her mind was in a turmoil, but above the anguish and chagrin and all the other disturbing emotions, she felt a touch of pride. Never before had she been valiant enough to face her mother down, but she'd done it now. She'd spoken her mind, and in no uncertain terms. Where had that burst of bravery come from?

As she stood motionless, trying to catch her breath, a new thought came to her. Perhaps, while this heady infusion of courage still raced through her veins, she could do the other thing that required courage—courage that until this moment she didn't know she possessed: she could go to Wycklands and make her admission to Peter. *Yes,* she told herself firmly, *now is the time to untie the knot I made. With this feeling of pluck inside me, I can do anything!*

She brushed back the strands of wild hair that fell over her face, took another swipe at her eyes and started down the stairs. She would go now, this very minute, before anything would happen to change her mind. But she'd taken only three steps down when Horsham came round the turn of the landing. "I was just coming to find you, Miss Julie," he said, holding out a note. "There's four draymen downstairs carrying in a pianoforte. From Wycklands."

"What?" She stared at him in bewilderment. "A *piano?"*

"Yes, ma'am. So big they could barely get it in the doorway. I told them to put it in the drawing room, between the windows, which they're doing right now, but they'll hang about to see if you wish to move it somewhere else."

She still didn't understand. "What are you saying, Horsham? The piano is for me?"

"Yes, miss. P'rhaps the note will explain."

She took it from his hand and broke the seal. There were only a few lines written in a neat, firm hand. *Dear Julie,* she read. *By the time you read this, I will be gone and my house closed, so don't try to return my gift to sender. I realize that it is a bit early to send you and Tris a wedding gift, but since I'm not likely to be available at the time of your wedding, this seemed the best time to send it. An instrument like this needs playing. I hope that playing it will bring you many happy hours, and that married life with Tris will be everything you dreamed. Please accept the sincere best wishes of your humble servant, Canfield.*

By the time she finished reading, her hands were trembling. After a frozen moment, during which she stared at the butler with unseeing eyes, she came to herself, brushed passed him and ran down to the drawing room. The four draymen were placing the beautiful rosewood pianoforte at an angle between the windows so that the light would fall over the player's shoulder onto the music page. But Julie didn't care about that. "What does he mean, the house is closed?" she demanded of one of the draymen.

He knuckled his forehead. "Wycklands, ye mean? 'Tis closed, miss," he said. "The master an' staff's gone off t' Lunnon."

"To London? For a visit? When will they be back?"

"Dunno, miss. Not fer a long while, seems t'me."

"How long a while? A week? A month?"

The man shrugged. But another, who'd been kneeling to adjust the wheel at the bottom of one of the piano legs, stood up and wiped his hands on his apron. "I 'eard from 'is lordship's cook that they didn' think they'd be back fer a year'r more."

"A *year?*" Julie sank down on the piano bench, the color draining from her cheeks as all the energy drained from her body. *I'm too late!* she told herself in despair. *My courage came too late!*

"Is this place for the piano t'yer likin', miss?" the first man asked.

She didn't respond. It was as if she wasn't even there.

Horsham, peering at her worriedly, motioned for the men to go. Then, throwing her a last look of concern, he quietly followed them and closed the door.

She turned slowly on the seat, absently brushed back the strands of hair that had fallen over her face and ran her hand lightly over the piano keys. It was a lovely instrument, a magnificent gift. But it was all she would ever have of Peter Granard, Lord Canfield. She gasped in the agony of that realization. It was terribly painful to discover that no gift, however magnificent, could keep a heart from breaking in two.

She did not know how long she sat staring, unseeing, at the piano keys, but the sound of the door being opened broke into her revery. She looked up to discover her mother, Phyllis and Tris standing in the doorway, eyeing her—and the piano—with concerned bewilderment. "It's from Lord Canfield," she explained. "A wedding gift."

"A wedding gift?" Tris asked, amazed. "Good God!"

"At least *he* believes there's to be a wedding," Lady Branscombe muttered dryly.

"I must believe it too," Julie said with a small, sad smile, "for apparently I've accepted the gift. I suppose that means, Tris, that I've decided to marry you after all."

27

JULIE GAVE HERSELF A GOOD TALKING-TO. WITH her mother blissful, Phyllis walking on air and Tris declaring himself in love with her (though that was still very hard to believe), it would be ill-natured and mean to be unhappy. She could not, in good conscience, spoil the happiness of those around her by permitting herself to indulge in bad moods and crotchets. Whatever pain she felt in her heart had to be hidden. More than that, it had to be overcome. She was going to marry Tris, who was as dear to her as anyone in the world, and she was determined to make a good job of that marriage. True, she could never love him in that special way she'd loved Peter, but perhaps Tris was right when he said that friendship and loyalty and long years of familiarity were a better basis for wedlock than romance.

So she smiled at everyone, everywhere, whenever she felt anyone was looking. She smiled at the dinner party the vicar and Mrs. Weekes held in honor of the betrothed couple. She smiled at the assembly, when Tris stood up with her for three dances. She smiled when the banns were read at church, when she rode with Tris in the mornings, when Mama and Phyllis met with her to discuss wedding plans, when Mama's modiste came for the first fitting of her wedding gown. She sometimes believed that the contrived smile would be forever frozen on her face.

A month went by. The time had passed pleasantly enough, Julie told herself, what with everyone finding ways to celebrate the coming event and making her the center of attention. With the wedding set for the second week in June, only one more social event was looming up before it—Lady Phyllis's prenuptial ball. Other than the wedding banquet itself (which, if Lady Branscombe's plan came to fruition, would be the grandest ever held in the vicinity of Amberford), the ball was to be the most splendid affair of the prenuptial festivities. Phyllis had sent to London for champagne, three maids had been hired to assist in the kitchen, and no fewer than nine musicians had been engaged to provide dance music.

On the eve of the ball, it was not only Enders Hall that was the scene of excited activity. At Larchwood too, the servants were scurrying about madly. Lady Branscombe had found a crease in the sash of Julie's gown, a bead was missing from the trim on the neckline of her own dress, and the hairdresser who'd been specially hired to cut Julie's hair had not yet arrived. Her ladyship was beside herself. "We'll never make it on time!" she shouted at anyone who came near her.

The matter of the hair was troubling Julie. Tris had made a special request that she cut her hair short. "It's always getting in your face," he'd said bluntly, "and never looking as it ought. Why don't you just cut it off and wear it curled?"

Like Cleo? she'd almost asked, but on second thought she'd held her tongue. She'd agreed to the request because she'd made up her mind to be a generous, obedient girl and agree to everything. But in the matter of her hair she could not keep from feeling reluctant. She liked her long, unruly hair. It was a significant part of her. She knew that her habits of tossing it back, of twisting it round her finger when absorbed in thought, of letting it hang in a careless plait when she wanted it out of the way, were irritations to Tris, but she herself would miss all that when the hair was gone. It was a sacrifice she was making on the altar of wedlock. She hoped she would not live to regret it.

The hairdresser, who was Lady Kenting's abigail and had been recommended as a genius with a scissors, arrived an hour before the ladies were due to leave. "We 'as plenty o' time," she assured the nervous Lady Branscombe. "Time t'cut Miss Julie's 'air an' curl it too."

But when she lifted the scissors to the first strand, Julie cried out a resounding "No!" She was not prepared to sacrifice as much as that.

After considerable discussion, the hairdresser surrendered to the girl's insistence that she find some way to put the hair up without cutting it. A Grecian style, with the long hair bound into a tight chignon at the back of the head and a few strands hanging in curled freedom at the sides, was finally agreed upon. Lady Branscombe, who was waiting at the bottom of the stairs in nervous suspense, sighed in relief at the sight of her daughter. "It's very becoming," she assured the uneasy girl. "I'm glad you didn't cut it off."

"Tris won't be," Julie muttered as she covered her head with the hood of her cape.

"Yes, he will. You look too lovely for him to object."

Lady Branscombe proved to be right. Tris said very flattering things about her appearance when he greeted her. And so did everyone else. Julie was so relieved that she began to believe she was having a very good time.

When Tris presented himself to her for the last dance of the evening, Julie suggested that they go out on the terrace for a breath of air instead. It was a perfect night for a ball, with a clear, moon-bright sky and the mildest of spring breezes. "Everything was perfect tonight," she said, gazing up at the stars. "Your mother must be pleased."

Tris perched on the balustrade beside her. "Yes, she is. Did I tell you she's arranged for us to stay with the Contessa Dimanti when we get to Venice on our honeymoon trip? She's a distant relative, and has a house right on the canal."

"That will be lovely." She lifted her hand to one of the strands of hair hanging loose at the side of her face and twisted it round her finger. "Speaking of honeymoons, Tris, there's . . . er . . . something I've been wondering about."

"What's that?"

"I hope you won't mind my asking. It's rather . . . personal."

"Good God, Julie, don't be a clunch. You've known me forever. What can you possibly ask that would be too personal?"

"Very well, then, here it is. Did you ever kiss Cleo?"

There was a moment of shocked silence. Then Tris slid off the balustrade. "What sort of question is that?" he muttered in annoyance. "Why do you want to know?"

She dropped her eyes from his face. "I just do, that's all."

He remained silent for another moment. Then he threw up his hands in a gesture of disgust. "If you must know, I did. Of course I did. I kissed her. Several times."

"I see."

"It's nothing to be bothered about," he said in quick self-defense. "Kissing is just something that a man and a woman *do* when they go about together."

"We don't."

"What?"

"You and I. We don't kiss. We've *never* kissed."

He gaped at her, nonplussed. "Damnation," he muttered, taken aback by what she'd just said, "stop twisting your damned hair." He strode away a few paces, then swung about and stormed back. "We have *so* kissed."

"Have we? When?"

"Lots of times. Birthdays and . . . and special occasions."

She snorted. "Cheek kisses. They don't count."

"Why don't they?"

She tossed him a sneering look. "The kisses you gave Cleo weren't cheek kisses, I'd wager."

He rubbed his chin. "No, they weren't."

"That's what I thought."

"What are you saying, Julie? What's the point?"

"I don't know. Is there . . . something wrong with us?"

"Because we haven't kissed? There was a perfectly acceptable reason for that. We were like brother and sister. Brothers and sisters don't kiss."

She gave him a long look. "But we're not brother and sister any more. We've been betrothed for weeks now."

His brow knit as he considered the problem, but since the solution was obvious, his expression cleared almost at once. "Very well, you idiot, come here. I'll kiss you right now."

She held up a restraining hand. "No, not now. It doesn't feel appropriate right now."

"Yes, it does," he insisted, and he pulled her into his arms.

"Tris, no!" She turned her face aside. "I don't *want* you to kiss me now."

"Why not? Now is as good a time as any." He forced her face up and kissed her mouth. She struggled against him for a moment and then remained still. But there was no answering pressure from her lips, and after a moment he let her go. "I'm sorry," he muttered, deflated. "I shouldn't have forced you. It will be better next time."

"Will it?" She gazed at him quizzically.

"Of course it will."

"What if it won't?"

His eyes clouded over, but he didn't answer. With a slight, discouraged sigh, Julie turned to go inside. But she paused with her hand on the doorknob and looked back at him. "Perhaps, Tris," she said quietly, "it's something we ought to think about."

28

Julie let Tris think about it for a week. During that week he kissed her twice, once when he helped her down from her horse, and once when he brought her home after an evening musicale at the Kentings'. The first time, the surprise of it made the embrace seems a wee bit exciting, but the second time was as meaningless as the kiss on the terrace. It was quite depressing to realize that she felt no physical attraction toward her betrothed, but what was even more worrisome was her distinct impression that Tris was as unhappy as she was. He too seemed to be forever forcing a smile. Something about this betrothal was decidedly amiss.

When the week was over, she sent him a note asking him to meet her the next morning at the summerhouse. It was time to talk the problem over frankly and in private.

Tris was there first, as usual. She found him sitting inside on a bench, his shoulders stooped, his head lowered. He was taking no notice of the lush greenery and the vines bursting into bloom all around him. She went up the steps and dropped down beside him on the bench. "For a prospective bridegroom," she said quietly, "you don't look very happy."

He lifted his head and grimaced at her. "Happy? I've forgotten what the word means."

"Oh, dear," she murmured.

He took her hand. "It isn't working, is it?"

"No, it isn't."

He signed in despair. "I don't understand why."

"Yes, you do. You've said it often enough in the past. We just know each other too well. There are no—"

"No surprises," he finished. "But what have surprises to do with marriage?"

"I don't know. But I do know that we've been like brother and sister for too long. I, for one, cannot easily make the change from sister to lover. I can't even manage to kiss you properly."

"I know. Neither can I."

"Tell me the truth, Tris. Do you still love Cleo?"

He rubbed his forehead wearily. "I'm not sure. Sometimes I miss her so much that there's an ache right here in my chest. But if I love *her,* why was I so insanely jealous of Canfield when he kissed *you?*"

"I've given that some thought, Tris. It seems to me that you were reacting like a brother who didn't wish to see his sister being manhandled by an outsider."

"No, I don't think it's as simple as that. I've been giving it a great deal of thought as well. I think it's worse than that. I'm convinced that I'd become accustomed to your little-girl adoration of me, and I just didn't want to lose it."

"Even when you had Cleo to love you?"

"Yes," he said, shamefaced, "isn't it dreadful? I can't believe how selfish my feelings were. I wanted to be free to love anyone else I wished, but I wanted you to remain caring for no one but me."

"Like a child," she said, nodding understandingly.

"Yes, like a spoiled child."

"Well, if true, it's a sign of maturity that you recognize it now."

He shrugged. "For all the good that does. What shall we do, my dear? I, for one, am at wit's end."

"We must break the engagement, for one thing," she said firmly. "The longer we pretend, the harder it will be to come forward with the truth."

"Yes," he said, looking closely at her face, "but only if you're sure you really don't wish to wed me."

She lifted a hand to his cheek and patted it kindly. "I

would not wish to wed you even if you truly loved me above all others. You see, Tris dear, I too am in love with someone else."

He could not meet her eye. "I know. Canfield. I mucked that up for you too, didn't I?"

"Not at all. There was nothing to muck up. He never really cared for me."

"I don't believe that. I saw him kissing you!"

"He only did that to make you jealous."

"Nonsense. When he kissed you in his library, he had no idea that I was watching."

"Heavens!" she exclaimed, blushing. "Were you there?" The thought was disturbing. That Tris had been an observer poisoned a precious memory.

"Yes," he admitted ruefully, "I'd just stepped into the doorway and saw you embracing. You were drenched in sunlight, looking like a Dutch painting. It was the first time I ever in my life experienced jealousy. I wanted to grind Peter to dust under my heel."

She shut her eyes, as if the act would somehow block the memory of the scene from her mind. She didn't want to remember. But shutting her eyes did no good. She opened them and fixed them on Tris. "It was an insignificant event, you know," she told him firmly. "The kiss, I mean. A whim of the moment."

"It didn't look that way to me."

"You must take my word for it," she insisted. "I know better."

"Very well," he agreed, sensing her pain. "No point arguing."

"None at all. Besides, we have more pressing matters to discuss than my nonexistent romance." She stood up and paced about the wooden floor of the summerhouse. "If we're to break the engagement, we must gird our loins to tell our mothers."

Tris groaned. "The very thing I most dread."

"I more than you, for my mother is a growling bear compared to yours. But when it's over, we shall finally be free. And that, may I remind you, is what we've wanted from the first."

"Yes, to be free." He stood up and stretched out his arms. "Free to follow our own destinies, not a future decreed by our mothers. Let's do it! Today!"

"Yes, today!" She smiled at him as they pledged by shaking hands. "Won't it be grand? We'll be free to marry whom we please. Cleo for you, who-knows for me." But as second thoughts assailed her, her smile abruptly died. "Of course, what is most likely," she mused as they started down the steps, "is that I shall remain an old maid."

"Probably I shall never marry either," he said glumly, "for Cleo won't have me now. She'll never forgive me for what I've done."

"You won't know that until you try." She squeezed his hand in farewell and set off toward the stile.

"Oh, I'll try right enough," he replied as he marched off in the opposite direction, "but I probably won't succeed." Suddenly he paused and laughed ruefully. "Wouldn't it be poetic justice if we both remained single for the rest of our days?" he called to her over his shoulder.

"Justice for whom?"

"For our mothers, of course. What an ironic punishment for them *that* would be!"

29

If it were done when 'tis done,
then 'twere well It were done quickly . . .

Julie quoted those lines of Shakespeare to herself as she walked home. She would take Mr. Shakespeare's advice and do the deed quickly. Telling her mother the truth would be difficult, to say the least, but she'd pledged to do it today. It would be better to get it over with this very morning than to have the prospect of that dreadful confrontation hanging over her like the sword of Damocles.

She found her mother in the sewing room with her modiste, both of them laboriously stitching seed pearls onto the bodice of Julie's elaborate wedding gown. The sight of that gown increased Julie's already unbearable tension. In spite of all the labor and expense that had gone into its creation, she was now about to inform her mother that she had no intention of wearing it. Her mother would be *livid.* "Mama," she asked in a trembling voice, not daring even to step over the threshold, "may I speak to you for a moment?"

"Now?" Lady Branscombe peered at her daughter over her tiny, square spectacles. "We're in the midst of—"

"Yes, now, please, Mama. It's very important."

Lady Branscombe bit off a thread, thrust the needle into a pincushion and pulled herself to her feet. "I'll return shortly," she promised the modiste as she stepped out into the corridor. "What is it, Julie?" she demanded impatiently. "I haven't time to stand about gossiping. You know how much there is to do before the wedding."

"It's not gossip. Let's go into the sitting room." The girl

was so nervous her voice shook, but her purpose remained firm. "I think you should be seated when you hear what I have to say."

Her ladyship's eyebrows rose. She opened her mouth to object, but something she saw in her daughter's face stilled her tongue. Without another word, she turned and led the way down the hall. In the sitting room, she lowered herself upon the sofa, removed and pocketed her spectacles, folded her hands in her lap and looked up at her daughter. "Well, here I am, seated just as you asked. What is it you want to say?"

Julie, standing before her mother like a guilty child, clenched her fingers together and took a deep breath. "I'll say it right off, Mama. Tris and I have decided not to marry after all. I know this news will pain you. I'm very sorry."

Lady Branscombe stared up at her, agape. "What are you saying? I don't understand."

A flame of irritation flared up in Julie's chest. She'd had no expectation that this chore would be easy, but if her mother was going to resist even facing the bare facts, it would be impossible. "It's not hard to understand," she said with precise clarity. "The words are perfectly simple: *Tris and I are not going to marry.*"

"But—"

Julie burst out with "I know what you're about to say, Mama, so you needn't bother." Anticipating her mother's anger, she worked up an anger of her own to combat it. She turned away from Lady Branscombe's anxious eyes and paced about the room. "You will say I can't be serious," she said, continuing to storm. "That we've announced the nuptials to all the world. That I've been feted and congratulated by everyone in town. That Phyllis has given me the grandest ball ever held in these environs. That you are already preparing the wedding feast. That my blasted wedding dress is being made right down the hall. Well, I don't want to hear all that! I know it well enough. It can't be helped."

"I was not g-going to s-say any of that," came her

mother's voice, a voice so shaken with tearful regret that Julie could scarcely recognize it.

The girl wheeled about. Her mother—the stalwart, unbending, implacable, strong-minded Lady Branscombe—was weeping into her hands. *"Mama!"* Julie cried out, startled out of countenance.

"I knew it," the older woman sobbed, "I knew it. I just couldn't f-face it."

Julie had never seen her mother cry. Her anger seeped out of her like the air from a punctured soufflé. Nevertheless, she could not quite believe what was happening. It was not beyond possibility that her mother would use tears as a ruse. She crossed back to her mother's side. "Knew what, Mama?" she asked suspiciously.

Lady Branscombe wiped her cheeks and, taking hold of herself with an effort, gazed up into her daughter's face. "I'm your *mother,* Julie. Did you think I wouldn't notice your unhappiness? Did you think I'd be fooled by that pitifully false smile you showed the world? I knew something was wrong, but I didn't know what to do about it."

Her sincerity was evident. Julie, shamed to the bottom of her heart by her earlier suspicions, knelt down and took one of her mother's hands. "I shouldn't have snapped at you, Mama. Blame it on sheer terror. I was afraid of telling you the truth, knowing how much you desired this wedding. But, you see, the truth is that Tris and I don't love each other. Not in the way that's right for man and wife. We're fond of each other, like brother and sister, but we would be miserable if we were wed."

Lady Branscombe winced painfully. "Yes, I do see. I think I've always seen it. I just haven't wanted to admit it until now."

"I'm sorry."

"No, it's I who should apologize," her mother said miserably. "You were right when you said I indulged my own dreams, without thinking of yours. I've spent years dreaming the wrong dreams for you." Her tears began to fall again as she dropped her face in her hands. "I d-don't even know how to make amends. I hope, Julie, my love, that you can f-forgive me."

Julie, dumfounded by her mother's unexpected and complete collapse, cast herself on the sofa beside her mother and threw her arms about her. "Oh, Mama, don't cry! A mother can be forgiven for having dreams for her child."

They remained in the embrace for a long time, drawing solace from this unwonted display of affection. At last Julie spoke. "I know how hard it will be for you to let everyone know the wedding plans have been canceled."

"I shall manage it," her mother assured her. "It will be worth the effort, and even the disappointment, if it means I've won my daughter's affection back." She brushed aside a strand of her daughter's hair fondly. Then she rose from the sofa with a sigh. "Thank goodness the wedding gifts have not yet begun to arrive," she said as she prepared to return to the sewing room. The wedding gown came to her ladyship's mind as she walked slowly to the door. She would finish it anyway, she told herself, for it was unlikely that it would go to waste. *This* wedding would not take place, but her lovely daughter would certainly be married sooner or later.

"Wedding gifts?" Julie asked, not having thought of them before.

"They would have had to be returned, of course," her mother explained, "but I shan't be put to that trouble because none have yet arrived." Having been forced to give up her dreams of this wedding, she was ready to dream of the next. She glanced over at her daughter with a calculating look. "Except for that beautiful pianoforte. You'll have to return it, I suppose. It's really too bad. I know how much you've enjoyed playing it. Unless . . ."

Julie stiffened. Her mother's eyes had taken on a familiar gleam. It was the look she always had when she wanted to manipulate fate by manipulating the people under her influence. It alerted Julie's defenses. "Unless?" she prodded cautiously.

"Unless there is a reason for you to keep it." Lady

Branscombe cocked her head and asked innocently, "Wasn't there something going on between you and Lord Canfield?"

Julie jumped angrily to her feet. Her mother, it seemed, had very quickly recovered from her momentary show of affection. Peace with that woman, Julie realized with a pang, would probably never be more than short-lived. "You're dreaming again, Mama. There was nothing at all 'going on' between his lordship and me."

"It's not a bad dream, you know," Lady Branscombe went on, quite as if Julie hadn't spoken. "If you're not going to have Tris, then I'm willing to grant that Lord Canfield has much to be said for him: good looks, brains, charm, wealth. Not a bad dream at all."

"Really, Mama," Julie snapped in disgust, "have done! I don't want to hear another word on this head. There's to be no more dreaming on my behalf, do you hear? I hereby declare a ban on dreaming. Your last was enough for a lifetime."

30

PEACE BETWEEN TRIS AND HIS MOTHER CAME about more easily, although the scene was equally tearful. When it was over, Lady Phyllis regretfully accepted Tris's decision to call off the wedding and acquiesced in his determination to return to London. By the next morning, he was gone.

As soon as she'd waved good-bye to her son, Phyllis walked across the fields to Larchwood, hoping to console her friend for what she knew was an overwhelming disappointment. To her surprise and relief she found Madge in moderately good spirits. "Since a wedding between them is not to be," Madge said placidly as she poured her friend a cup of tea, "we may as well make the best of it."

Phyllis eyed her suspiciously. "I don't like the sound of that, Madge. You are being too sanguine. Have you some plot up your sleeve?"

"Of course not," Lady Branscombe said, dropping a generous spoonful of sugar into her cup. "A good general knows when to retreat."

"This is more than a retreat, my dear. It's a complete surrender." Phyllis lowered her eyes to her teacup as she added fearfully, "Tris has gone off to London to offer for Cleo Smallwood."

Madge Branscombe did not even wince. "Yes, I supposed as much," she said calmly. "I hope he will be successful."

This was too much for Phyllis to accept. "You can't mean it! Are you saying you *want* him to wed her?"

"Under these circumstances, I do. Since I am now convinced that he and Julie don't suit, I think Miss Smallwood is the next best choice."

Phyllis expelled a breath of real relief. "So do I," she admitted. Then, after sipping her tea thoughtfully, she broached the other subject that was on her mind. "Now if we can only see Julie happy with someone, I shall rest content."

Madge glanced at her from the corner of an eye. "What do you think of Canfield as a possibility?" she asked, nonchalantly stirring her tea.

"Canfield?" Phyllis brightened at once. "Yes! Of course! I should have thought of him myself. He's *perfect* for her."

"Exactly."

"But . . . isn't it too late? I hear that he doesn't intend to return to Wycklands for a long while. He's gone back to London, dash it all!"

Madge merely smiled. "London isn't the end of the world. In fact, my dear, I've been thinking that London is the very place for you to hold Tris's betrothal ball. As soon as he sends word that he's betrothed, we should all go down and join him in town to make the preparations."

Phyllis's eyes took on a sparkle of excitement. "By 'we' you mean—?"

"Yes, the three of us," Madge said, her smile widening to a mischievous grin. "You, of course, with Julie and me to help. It should take weeks. A month at least. Don't you think it possible that a great deal might happen to Julie in a month?"

Phyllis grinned back at her. "A very great deal. Madge, my love, I've said it before and I'll say it again. You are a genius!"

With that satisfying remark hovering in the air, Madge refilled their cups and the two of them contentedly drank their tea. But neither lady realized they had little cause for contentment, for Madge Branscombe's plan had a crucial weakness. It depended on Tris becoming betrothed to Cleo, and Tris was at that moment discovering that such a betrothal would apparently never come to pass.

31

Tris arrived in London in the late afternoon. After arranging for rooms at the Fenton Hotel, he immediately went to call on Cleo at the Smallwood townhouse. He was bursting with eagerness to get down on his knees and apologize for his strange behavior on her last day at Amberford. But the butler would not admit him. He was coldly informed by that high-in-the-instep personage that neither Lord Smallwood nor Miss Smallwood would agree to see him.

He spent that night lying awake in his dreary hotel room trying to think of a plan of action to overcome this first obstacle. It had to be overcome, for if she would not even see him, how could he convince her of the sincerity of his contrition? The next afternoon he purchased the entire contents of a street vendor's flower wagon and, tottering under the load, again appeared on her doorstep. Again the supercilious butler told him he would not be admitted. "Hold these for a moment," Tris begged the fellow. "I want to get something from my pocket for you."

The butler, no fool, guessed that Tris intended to bribe him. Not being opposed to bribes, he took the huge pile of blooms in his arms. Tris fished out a gold sovereign from his pocket. "Here, this is for you, if you will only bring the flowers up to her and come down and tell me what she says."

The butler did not take long to agree, a gold sovereign being worth almost three pounds and therefore only slightly less than a month's wages. "Wait there, sir," he said, backing into the hallway with his load and closing the door with his foot.

Tris paced about on the doorstep for several minutes. Then, to his delight, he heard a window being opened somewhere above him. He looked up eagerly to discover a cloud of flowers being flung down at him. They fell like a shower of arrows about his head and shoulders, one almost piercing an eye, and finally lay strewn on the doorstep, ankle-deep. In utter discouragement, he waded through them and went back to his hotel.

By the next day, he was furious. What right had she to treat him in this shabby way? he asked himself. He hadn't done anything to her that was so unforgiveable, had he? He'd only broken a silly doll and left her alone on the green. Was that so very dreadful? Did he deserve to be so callously spurned? In a rage, he stormed up to her door, brushed by the butler as soon as the fellow opened it, and demanded loudly to see Miss Smallwood at once.

"She won't see you," the butler said, not unsympathetically. After all, he'd been enriched by a sovereign, and with any luck some other bribes might be forthcoming. "I'd like to help you, sir, really I would. But I have my orders. I'm not to let you in."

"Well, I *am* in. So go and tell the lady I'm waiting."

"I can't, sir. You don't want me to get sacked, do you?"

"She won't sack you," Tris said, throwing him another coin. "Hop to it, man. *Now!*"

The butler pocketed the coin, shrugged and went up the stairs. In a moment he returned, followed by two footmen. Without a word, the footmen grasped Tris, one at each arm, and lifted him off the ground. "I'm very sorry, sir," the butler said as the footmen carried the protesting caller across the hall to the door.

"Then get Lord Smallwood," Tris shouted desperately, bracing his feet against the door frame to keep the footmen from ejecting him.

"His lordship knows you're here," the butler said, rather enjoying this opportunity to ride roughshod over one of the "swells." "He won't see you either." Then, with a grin, he nodded at the footmen to indicate that they were to get on with the job. Obediently, the footmen wrenched Tris away from the door frame, lifted him over the threshold, carried him out the door and deposited him unceremoniously on the pavement.

That night Tris wrote a note to Lord Smallwood, pleading for an interview. *I am at wit's end,* he wrote. *If you have an ounce of human kindness in your heart, meet me at White's at one tomorrow. I will be eternally grateful if you grant this request.*

At one the next afternoon, Tris was standing in the bow window of White's club, watching for Lord Smallwood. When a quarter hour had passed with no sign of him, Tris felt so discouraged he was ready to give up the entire matter. But at twenty past one, the Smallwood carriage drew up in front of him. It was with an overwhelming sense of relief that Tris watched his lordship climb down from the coach.

A few moments later they were ensconced in easy chairs in the club lounge, drinks in hand. Tris did not speak until Lord Smallwood had downed half his whiskey. Only then did he feel ready to broach the subject. "Thank you for coming, my lord," he began. "I'm exceedingly grateful."

"Yes, so you said in your letter," Smallwood said brusquely. "But I must be frank, my boy. I did not come to talk about Cleo. I only came to inquire after your mother."

"My mother?" Tris echoed, surprised.

"Yes. She's a fine woman. How does she get on?"

"She's very well, thank you. I'll tell her in my next letter that you asked for her."

"Good, send her my best regards. A very fine woman, your mother."

"Yes," Tris agreed. But discussing his mother's character was not the subject that interested him. He took a sip of his drink and plunged in. "I asked you to meet me, Lord Smallwood, to beg you to do a great favor for me."

"I know what it is, young man, so don't bother to ask. I

cannot intercede on your behalf because my daughter won't even let me mention your name to her. And, to be frank, I wouldn't even if I could."

Tris felt as if he'd been struck in the chest by a hard fist. "Why wouldn't you?" he asked desperately.

"Because I didn't care for your treatment of her, that's why. You won't get any help from me because you don't deserve it."

"I made a mistake, I admit, but surely it was not so dreadful as to be beyond forgiveness."

Smallwood threw him a look of disgust. "If you don't think your actions were dreadful, then you're a worse case than I thought. Any man who pursues one woman while being betrothed to any other is a cad."

"I was *not* betrothed to another," Tris declared so loudly that some gentlemen in chairs nearby turned to look.

"Then as near betrothed as makes no difference," Smallwood retorted. "And keep your voice down. I don't want my daughter's affairs bandied about in clubs."

"I'm sorry," Tris said sheepishly, lowering his voice, "but this matter is very important to me. I love your daughter. I want to marry her."

"You do, do you? Then what about Miss Branscombe, eh?" He leaned forward and jabbed at the air with a finger. "What would *she* think of this interview we're having?"

"She wishes me well in my suit, I swear it! She told me she'd like nothing better than to see me betrothed to Cleo."

"Hummmph!" his lordship snorted. "It didn't seem that way to me when I last saw you. You were so jealous of Miss Branscombe's admirer you wanted to slay him."

Tris looked down at his shoes. "I know. It was a mental aberration of some sort, too hard to explain."

"Then don't bother. Explanations won't help your cause with me in any case. Or with Cleo either."

"Are you sure of that, my lord? If she understands that my feelings for Julie were merely brotherly, and that I love her and no one else, couldn't she find it in her heart to forgive me?"

"No, she couldn't," Smallwood said flatly, putting down his glass. "She no longer has any interest in you." He used his cane to help him to his feet. "Do yourself a kindness, my boy," he said, frowning down at Tris, "and go back to Devon. Forget about my daughter. She wants nothing to do with you."

Stricken into discouraged silence, Tris watched Lord Smallwood make his limping way to the exit. "I won't give up, no matter what you say," he muttered under his breath.

At the doorway, Lord Smallwood looked back at him. "Don't forget to give my regards to your mother," he said. "A very fine woman, that. Don't know how she bore such a cad for a son."

32

THE MESSAGE JULIE RECEIVED FROM TRIS COULD not be ignored. *Cleo won't have anything to do with me,* he wrote. *I need your help, even more than you once needed mine. I know how you hate the idea of coming to town, but this is most urgent. I am at the end of my tether. Come at once. Please! Tris.*

With the note clutched in her hand, Julie went to her mother. "I must go to London at once," she said firmly, handing over the missive for her mother to see. "Today, in fact."

To her astonishment, her mother gave her no argument. "Of course you must," she said. "It wouldn't be right to ignore such a forlorn request. However, my love, I cannot permit you to go without chaperonage. London is not Amberford. A young woman cannot dash about town unescorted."

"I'll take one of the maids," Julie said promptly.

But that was not what Lady Branscombe had in mind. "I'll go with you, and so will Phyllis," she said with brisk finality. "We've wanted to take you to London for years. This will be our chance."

"But, Mama," Julie objected, "I'd prefer—"

"If you want to go to London, my girl, you will go with our escort. Like it or not."

Like it or not, that was how Julie went. And that was how, the very next day, she found herself standing in the lobby of the Fenton Hotel surrounded by the great number of bandboxes, trunks and portmanteaus that her mother and Phyllis had packed for the occasion. While the two older ladies made arrangements with the desk clerk for their accomodations, Julie looked about her with the fascination that a country girl feels in a large city. There were more people rushing in and out of the hotel lobby than she would see in the Amberford square in a week. And they were of many more varied styles, styles that seemed to typify London. Moving about among the potted palms were several elegantly clad ladies, with curled plumes on their bonnets and gold tassels hanging from the tips of their pelisses, details of adornment quite unknown in Amberford. Some of the ladies were accompanied by gentlemen so well dressed they would have won approval from Beau Brummel himself. But not all the women milling about were refined ladies, nor all the men nonpareils: there were overdressed dandies whose high-pointed shirts and tight-fitting coats were too ornamental to be comfortable; harried footmen whose uniforms bore more gold braid than a general's; housemaids and abigails in black bombazine dresses and white, frilled caps; draymen whose dark work clothes were covered with striped aprons; women of the "muslin company" whose loud, revealing gowns gave garish evidence of their trade; businessmen from the city in neat, conventional blue coats; and tradesmen whose ill-fitting coats were more practical than dandyish. Such color and variety, Julie thought, wide-eyed, could be found nowhere but in London.

She found herself looking more than once at a lady pacing about impatiently near the outer doors. The lady stopped after every dozen or so paces and peered out the windows that flanked the doorway, obviously watching for someone who'd not arrived on time. The woman was young—Julie estimated her age to be about twenty-two—and very beautiful. It was no wonder, for her eyes were green and framed by thick, black lashes, her hair was coppery-red and topped with a straw bonnet tied fetchingly under her ear with wide green ribbons, and her green jaconet gown, cut low across the bosom, revealed a figure both slim and seductive. What struck Julie as remarkable was that although everything the young woman wore seemed to call attention to itself, none of it could be called vulgar or lacking in taste. The gentleman for whom the lady was waiting so anxiously (for Julie was certain that only a gentleman could cause such impatience in a woman's step) must be, she thought, a very lucky fellow.

Julie's attention was distracted by a hotel footman who asked permission to begin carrying up the luggage. When she looked over at the doorway again, she was just in time to see the young woman cast herself into the arms of the newly arrived gentleman. Julie couldn't see the gentleman's face, for his back was to her, but the lady's face expressed an enviable joy. The sight of the happy embrace made Julie smile. She watched as the gentleman took the young lady's arm and led her out the door. Though she was not usually given to idle curiosity, this time she couldn't help watching for the pair to pass the window, just to glimpse the gentleman's face. When she did, however, her heart lurched in her chest. It was Peter! The man was none other than Peter Granard, Lord Canfield!

She felt a stab of pain so sharp it made her stagger. To avoid falling, she sank down upon one of the boxes and tried to catch her breath. Her mother and Phyllis approached her at that moment. "It took some doing," her mother was saying, "but we managed to cajole the manager into finding three adjoining rooms for—" She stopped short when she saw Julie's white face. "Julie? What's amiss? Good God, you look as if you've seen a ghost!"

"No, it's nothing, Mama," she said, forcing a smile and jumping to her feet. "Nothing at all."

Lady Branscome knew her daughter well enough to realize that *something* had occurred to upset her, but she also knew that Julie could not be coaxed to explain when she wanted to keep silent. Therefore, after exchanging a speaking look with Phyllis, she proceeded as if nothing had happened, directing an army of footmen in the disposition of the baggage and herding her friend and her daughter toward the stairs. "We must all lie down for a nap," she commanded them, pretending not to notice how shaken her daughter still was, "before we meet Tris for dinner."

After an hour alone in her room, Julie managed to recover her equilibrium, if not her spirits. She'd given herself a good scolding for her unwarranted reaction to what she'd seen. It was excessively foolish, she told herself, to be shocked at the sight of Lord Canfield with a beautiful woman. It would be shocking if he were not. Handsome and desirable as he was, he was probably never without a woman on his arm. The only thing that should have astonished her was to see him here, at this very hotel, on the very day of her arrival. *That* was a shocking coincidence, but nothing else she'd seen should trouble her. There was nothing between her and Canfield that would justify these feelings, so she had no choice but to rid herself of them. She had to try to forget the incident, and to forget him.

When Tris tapped at her door before dinner, in the hope of exchanging a few words with her alone before meeting with their mothers, she was able to face him with the appearance of normality. He perched on the window seat and gave her a brief account of what had passed—or, rather, not passed—between Cleo and himself. As he spoke, she studied his face. It was lined with sleeplessness and despair, and her heart went out to him. She gave the circumstances several minutes of serious consideration before suggesting that perhaps she herself should try to talk to Cleo. "Perhaps your defense will be more convincing coming from me," she said. The mere suggestion so filled him with hope that his spirits rose. As a result, he was able to be a charming host to the ladies at dinner.

The next afternoon, he drove Julie to the Smallwood townhouse himself. "I'll wait right here for you," he said, almost breathless with tension, "but talk to her as long as she'll let you. Don't worry about keeping me waiting. The longer it takes, the more hopeful I'll feel."

Julie mounted the steps and tapped at the door. When the butler invited her in, she threw Tris a smile of encouragement before stepping inside. After sending up her name, she was kept waiting an interminably long time before she heard Cleo's footsteps on the stairs. She looked up and almost gasped. Cleo, who'd always been a veritable fashion plate, was now pale and unkempt. Her once-bouncy curls lay flat, her eyes looked red-rimmed and without sparkle, and, though it was late afternoon, she was still wrapped in a wrinkled morning robe. "Forgive me for not being dressed," she muttered as she greeted Julie with a weak handshake. "I've not been feeling quite the thing today and decided to stay abed."

"I'm sorry," Julie said hurriedly. "If you'd rather not see me now, I'd be happy to come back at a more convenient time."

"No, now that you're here, you may as well stay and tell me what you've come to say. Let's go to the sitting room where we can be private."

Julie followed her down the hall. When they passed the open door of the drawing room, Julie caught a glimpse of Lord Smallwood looking up in surprise from the pages of the *Times.* But since Cleo did not pause to let her visitor and her father exchange greetings, Julie had no choice but to proceed without a word. She could only hope that Lord Smallwood would not think her rude.

When they were seated opposite each other on easy chairs in the sitting room, Julie looked about her. It was a small room with two tall windows that faced the street. The easy chairs faced a fireplace topped by a huge mirror. In it, she could see Cleo studying her with a penetrating stare. "You do not look like the blooming bride I expected to see," Cleo remarked bluntly. "In fact, you're almost as Friday-faced as I am."

"If you think that my 'Friday face' is caused by my not being Tris's bride, Cleo, you're fair and far off," Julie said, turning her eyes from the mirror and facing the other young woman bravely. "Tris and I have never wanted to marry. That's what I came to tell you."

Cleo crossed her arms and sat back in her easy chair, her posture clearly indicating her intention to reject anything she heard. "I didn't ever believe you wanted to marry Tris. It was plain as day to me whom you wanted to wed. But you cannot say the same for Tris. Not after what happened at the fair."

"Yes, I can. It took us—Tris and me—a long while to understand ourselves, but I think we do now. We were raised like brother and sister, you see, but we were never taught the difference between the brother-sister feelings and lovers' feelings. I believe it was our mothers' fault. Their hearts were set on our marrying. But Tris and I always knew that was something we didn't intend to do."

"Always? Even as children?"

"Always. And when he fell in love with you, that was the final proof. It was you he wished to wed, not me. That was why he tried so hard to get me married off to Lord Canfield. The trouble was that Lord Canfield, just like our mothers, decided that I loved Tris and ought to wed him."

"Peter?" Cleo's brows knit in disbelief. "Are you telling me that Peter was trying to marry you off to *Tris?*"

"Exactly. You don't believe me, do you? Tris never could believe it either. He convinced himself that Peter cared for me. It's hard to blame him, for Peter decided—not with my consent, I may add—to pretend to make love to me to make Tris jealous."

"Let me understand you," Cleo said, leaning forward with sudden interest. "Do you mean to say that while Tris was urging you toward Peter, Peter was urging you toward Tris?"

"Yes, just so! Do you know, Cleo, that I sometimes think men are quite idiotic?"

Cleo gave a hiccoughing laugh. "I've known *that* for years!" For the first time since she came down the stairs, her eyes took on a sparkle, and her voice was warm. "But, please, Julie, do go on. This is quite fascinating."

"There isn't much more to tell. When Tris saw Peter kissing me, he felt an unexpected and unexplainable anger. He and all the rest of us interpreted that anger as jealousy. If he was jealous, we all reasoned, he must be in love with me. That seemed a logical explanation, affecting everyone's judgment, even mine. We actually became betrothed."

Cleo's eyes fell. "Yes, I . . . I heard."

"But I knew almost at once it was a mistake."

"Of course it was a mistake," Cleo muttered. "You were in love with Peter. What's become of him, by the way?"

Julie was tempted to reveal what she'd seen that afternoon, knowing it would be soothing to share her pain with another woman, especially one who'd also suffered. But she'd come here to discuss Tris's problems, not her own. Dropping her eyes from Cleo's face, she fixed them on her folded hands. "Peter never cared for me in that way, you know," she said quietly. "His whole pursuit of me was a sham for Tris's benefit."

"So *that's* why you're looking so peaked," Cleo said with sincere sympathy. "I'm sorry, Julie. Truly."

"Thank you," Julie muttered, looking up again. "But I didn't come here to talk about me. May we return to the subject of Tris?"

"Yes, of course. I've already admitted being fascinated. You were saying that you knew the betrothal was a mistake. How did you know?"

"It's simple. You see, through all the days of the engagement Tris never kissed me. Even Peter, who doesn't care for me at all, once kissed me in a moment of spontaneous affection. But Tris never did."

Cleo gasped at that. "Never?"

"Not once. We both realized that was strange. So we talked it all out. Tris believes, and I agree with him, that it wasn't love but a kind of brotherly protectiveness that made him so angry with Peter. A strange man was mauling his sister, you see. That's all it was."

"Brotherly protectiveness?" Cleo frowned doubtfully. "That hardly seems an adequate explanation."

"Tris has a somewhat darker one. He thinks he *was* jealous, in a way. I'd always been his adoring little playmate, you see, and suddenly he was losing that adoration. He felt an unreasonable resentment toward Peter for stealing away that adoration. In some dark corner of his mind, he says, he quite selfishly expected me to go on adoring him and no one else, while he, on the other hand, could be quite free to love wherever he chose. He realizes now how childish those feelings were."

Cleo's eyes stared into hers, wide with astonishment. "I see," she said in a small voice. Shaken, she tucked her legs up under her and curled up in her chair, arms wrapped tightly about her as if she were protecting herself from the impact of this new information.

"He never stopped loving you, you know," Julie said gently. "The time of our betrothal was the worst of his life. I hope you believe that."

Cleo peeped over at her, tears filling her eyes. "I w-want to believe you," she said with a sob.

"You do love him, then?"

"Love him? I'm b-besotted!" She buried her face in her arms. "I haven't been able to get back to my old life since the day I left Enders Hall. I do nothing but m-mope about, whining and feeling s-sorry for myself, like the foolish heroines of silly romances. Yes, I'd say I love him! More than I want to. And much more than he d-deserves, the idiot!"

"Oh, Cleo, I'm so glad! He's waiting right outside, you know. With his heart in his mouth." Julie stood up and smiled at the tearful girl huddled in her chair. "Shall I tell him to come in?"

Cleo raised her head, her eyes flying up to Julie's face in sheer terror. "Now? No, I can't! Look at me, Julie! I'm a sight!"

"He will think you the most beautiful creature he ever laid eyes on, I promise. I'm like a sister to him, and I know."

Cleo got slowly to her feet, ran her fingers through her curls and gave a timid nod. Julie didn't wait for more but ran down the hall and out the door. Tris, whose eyes had been glued to the doorway all this time, leaped from the carriage and grabbed her shoulders. "Well?" he asked tensely.

"Go to her, Tris," Julie said with a tremulous smile.

The light of pure joy transformed Tris's face. He glowed like a just-lit candle. With a gulp, he took time only to press Julie's shoulders with intense gratitude before dashing into the house.

Julie climbed up into the carriage, wondering if she should wait for him or go back to the hotel by herself. It was getting late. The sun had set, and the street was darkening. She looked over at the Smallwood house as if she might find an answer in its facade. What she saw was the window of the sitting room. Inside Cleo was lighting a lamp. Julie could see her reflected in the mirror over the fireplace. As she looked, another figure appeared in the mirror. Tris had burst into the room. He said something brief. Was it her name, or the words I love you? Julie couldn't tell. But she saw Cleo lift her arms in response. Immediately, Tris took her into a fervent embrace. They held each other tearfully for a long time before he actually kissed her.

Julie turned her eyes away. Not only was it improper to watch, but it hurt too much. It wasn't jealousy, exactly. It was envy . . . the pain of realizing that she would never have the good fortune to experience just that sort of embrace.

After a quarter hour, Tris came out and opened the carriage door. His eyes were shining. "I'll never forget what you did, Julie. You're the best sister I never had."

"Am I?" she smiled.

"In every way. So, like the good sister you are, go on home without me. My lovely, forgiving, adorable Cleo would like me to stay here a while longer."

"I'm so glad for you, Tris. Go back to her. I don't mind waiting, really I don't."

"But I mind. I'll enjoy myself more fully if I don't have to think about you sitting out here in the dark."

"Very well, I'll go. But how will you get back to the hotel?"

He grinned as he shut the carriage door. "Don't worry about me," he chortled. "I'll float."

33

THAT EVENING, SINCE THE LADIES HAD NO MALE companions or social engagements, they dined modestly at the hotel and retired early. Though it was not yet nine, Lady Phyllis began to prepare for bed. She removed her shoes and took down her long gray hair, after which she brushed and plaited it. Just after her abigail finished unbuttoning the back of her gown, there was a tap at her door. The abigail answered. A hotel footman informed the girl that there was a gentleman down in the lobby who was insisting on seeing her ladyship. Phyllis, clutching her gown together at the back, pattered in stockinged feet to the door. "A gentleman? Is it my son?"

"No, ma'am."

"Then it must be a mistake."

"I don't believe so, ma'am. He asked for Lady Phyllis Enders."

"Well, whoever it is, tell him to go away. It's too late for me to see callers."

"He was very insistent, ma'am. In a high state of perturbation, I'd say."

"Oh, you would, would you? And did this gentleman in a high state of perturbation give you his name?"

"Yes, ma'am. Lord Smallwood, he said."

Phyllis started. "Smallwood? Why didn't you say so at once? Go and tell him I'll be down in five—no, ten minutes."

She put on her shoes and fidgeted nervously while the abigail did up her dress again. It was not a dress she would have chosen to wear when meeting Smallwood again, for the color was drab and the white tucker that reached up to her chin made her look like a governess, but since there was nothing to be done at this late hour, it would have to do. Her hair was a more serious problem. It hung down her back in a loose plait, fit only for sleeping. To dress it properly would require undoing the plait, brushing it again and pinning it into some sort of knot. Even the simplest style would require more time than she had. She and the abigail tried hastily to pin the braid up into a knot, but it was too heavy and kept falling down. With a helpless shrug, she decided to let it hang.

When she came down to the lobby, a mere fifteen minutes from the time she'd sent the message, she did not immediately see him. She walked about, peering round chairs and potted plants with no success. Suddenly, behind her, an angry voice said, "So there you are, ma'am! You've kept me waiting long enough, I must say!"

She swung about, her temper snapping. "Blast it, Smallwood, I should have kept you waiting longer. I was undressed!"

"Ridiculous," he snapped back. "It's only nine."

"Yes. Much too late an hour for civilized people to make calls."

"You are in London now," he pointed out icily. "We do not keep country hours here."

"Hummph!" Not able to think of a better retort, she merely glared at him. But as her eyes darted over him, she noticed that the hand clutching his cane was trembling. Her anger melted away at once. "Are we going to argue this way all night," she asked, letting a smile peep out, "or would you rather get to the point of this call?"

"You're right, ma'am. We are wasting precious time. Is there a private room where we may chat, or must we discuss personal matters right here where any passerby might hear?"

"I'm sure that an inquiry at the desk is all that will be needed to provide us with a private parlor," she said, and with a toss of her head that caused her long braid to flip, she marched off to make the arrangement. In a few moments they were ushered into a small, beautifully furnished room off the lobby. When the door was closed, she sat down on a red-and-gold striped sofa and looked up at him. "Won't you sit down, your lordship?"

"I will not sit down," he barked. "I have come to ask a question, ma'am. Do you know where your son is at this moment?"

The question surprised her. "I have no idea. The boy is of age, you know. He doesn't have to report to his mama on his comings and goings."

"Is that so? Well, then, let *me* tell you the answer. At this very moment he is at my house, in my sitting room, on my own leather chair, with my own daughter in his lap. When I left, they were kissing. It was a long kiss. I have no doubt it is still going on."

Her face took on a beaming smile. "Really? How *wonderful!* I was so afraid your daughter might not be willing to forgive him. I'm so happy for them both!"

"Happy for them, ma'am? *Happy* for them? I do not agree. It is a tragedy. You must take him away from London at once!"

Her eyebrows rose in bafflement. "Good God, why?"

"Because he will make her miserable, that's why."

"What utter nonsense! What makes you think so?"

"I think so because he's already done so. *Twice!*"

"I know that. But I don't see it as a portent of the future. He was muddled before, largely because of me, but he's seeing much more clearly now."

"He sees nothing clearly. He is a spoilt, headstrong, self-centered *cad* who—"

"Cad?" She jumped to her feet, furious, her braid slapping against her back in an angry reflection of her mood. "Tris? A cad? How *dare* you, Smallwood! That's my *son* you're maligning! He is most certainly *not* a cad. There's nothing he's done—nothing!—that warrants such unkind judgments!"

"Nothing, eh?" He came up to her until they were almost nose to nose. "From what I've seen of him, he's nothing if not scheming, manipulating, cocky and . . .

and . . . " He seemed to freeze for a moment before going on in almost the same voice, "And you are the most beautiful woman I've ever seen."

"What?" She was sure she hadn't heard properly, for the words did not suit the tone at all.

"I said you are beautiful." He looked at her belligerently, as if he would defend the statement with his life.

She took a step backward, agape. "Are you *mad?*"

He shrugged as if madness were of no concern to him. "You must know how beautiful you are."

She shook her head at his insanity. "Smallwood, you poor, crazed fellow, I'm fifty-eight years old."

He nodded. "Yes, a lovely age for a woman."

"Oh, yes, quite." She had to laugh, for she was suddenly beginning to enjoy herself. "A lovely age indeed. I shall be fifty-nine in three months, and *sixty* shortly after that. Are those lovely ages too?"

"For you, yes. And so will sixty-eight, and seventy-eight and on and on."

Since he was not smiling, she had to assume he was serious. She sank down upon the sofa in bewilderment. "Surely you didn't come here to give me foolish compliments. Try to be sensible, man! What is it you really want of me?"

"I thought I *was* being sensible," he muttered, limping to the nearest chair, sinking down on it and putting a shaking hand to his forehead. "I left my house for the purpose of enlisting your aid in an attempt to separate our offspring. But the sight of your face has completely undermined me. It now occurs to me that perhaps my aim in coming here had more to do with seeing you again than with separating Cleo and Tris. I have ached to see you again, you know."

"Have you really? How lovely of you to tell me." She gazed across at him tenderly. "I've missed you too."

He smiled. It was only a small, rather wan smile, but it was the first one since his arrival. "How lovely of *you* to tell *me.*"

"Perhaps so," she said, "but that does not mean I can

ignore your insulting comments about my son. Are you serious about wishing to wreck his affair with your daughter?"

He thought about it for a moment and then sighed. "No, to tell the truth, I'm not. Hang your son and my daughter! Let them take care of their own lives. Let's you and I get married."

Her mouth dropped open, but only for a moment. Then she snapped it shut and got to her feet. "I've had just about enough of your foolishness, Smallwood. I'm going to bed."

"Don't you *want* to marry me?" he asked plaintively.

She tossed her head. "I've never given the question a moment's thought."

"Then think about it now. We get on well, don't we? We spent every day for a fortnight in each other's company, and enjoyed every moment, didn't we? Without ever disagreeing or arguing?"

"There were several disagreements, as I recall," she reminded him, but even as she spoke she was remembering their days together quite fondly.

"All right, yes, we had disagreements," he granted, "but they were more in the nature of spirited fun than real arguments."

"Yes, I suppose they were."

Sensing his advantage, he leaned forward eagerly. "And we miss each other when we're apart; you just admitted that. And we are neither of us in the flush of youth, which means we haven't so very many years to waste in fiddling about making up our minds. Of course there is *one* problem . . ."

"Oh? And what, pray, is that?"

"I cannot spend the rest of my life hearing you call me Smallwood. My intimates call me Harry."

"Do they, indeed?" She gazed down at him speculatively, head cocked. "It doesn't suit you. You should have a dignified name, like Gerard, or Cuthbert or Sebastian. But I suppose I could call you Henry, if you like."

"I like Harry."

She put up her chin. "It's Henry or Smallwood, take your pick."

He rose from the chair and came toward her, his spirit so much revived that he barely used his cane. "Except for Cuthbert, you may call me anything you like. Now that that's settled, will you marry me?"

"My dear Henry," she said, both amused and bemused, "the leap from the first use of your given name right into the bonds of wedlock is a very large leap to make all at once."

"I know. Loving you has made me agile. No, more than agile. It's made me daring. I've always been a timid, pedantic sort of fellow, but suddenly I'm ready and eager to make this very large leap. I know it's true for you too. I can see it in your eyes."

She lowered them at once. "Can you, indeed?"

"There's a man at my club whose brother is a bishop. He can get me a special license. We can be wed tomorrow morning."

She lifted her hand to his head and brushed back a lock of white hair from his forehead. "You *are* mad, you know. As Tris would say, upper works completely askew."

Ignoring her remark, he reached for her hand, lifted it to his lips and kissed the palm. "Are you heeding me, ma'am? Tomorrow morning. It's an order. I'd like you to wear your hair just as it is now, but if you must wear it up, I'll forgive you. There's a bonnet I've seen you wear—yellow straw with roses along the brim—that will look bridal, I think. I'll bring yellow roses for you to carry. I shall call for you at ten-thirty. Be ready."

She stared at the palm he'd kissed. "Henry, you fool," she murmured in a choked voice, "I can't be ready for a wedding overnight." Then she lifted her eyes to his face. "Give me one day more."

34

Lady Branscombe couldn't help but wonder why her friend Phyllis was behaving so strangely. For one thing, she had forgotten their plans to shop at the Pantheon Bazaar and had disappeared for an entire day. Then, when they met at dinner, Phyllis didn't make any explanation. Madge had too much pride to press her, but she fully expected that Phyllis would offer one freely. To her disappointment, however, none was forthcoming. Furthermore, Phyllis excused herself after dinner and left the hotel under the escort of Lord Smallwood. Madge surmised that they wanted to discuss plans for a betrothal fete for Cleo and Tris, but she didn't quite understand why she herself was not included. Helping Phyllis plan the fete was one of the reasons Madge had come to London in the first place.

She intended to say as much to Phyllis when they met in Madge's room for breakfast the next morning. But when Phyllis arrived looking particularly pink-cheeked and bright-eyed in spite of it being a rather rainy morning, Madge decided that a scold would not be in order. "You look very pleased with yourself," she said instead. "You and Smallwood must have come to a happy agreement about the betrothal party."

"As a matter of fact, we did," Phyllis chirped. "We're going to hold a small champagne breakfast right here in the hotel on Saturday, for us and the Smallwoods and a few of our London acquaintances. Probably no more than twenty."

This was too much for Madge. She would have to speak

out even if it drove the pink bloom from her friend's cheek. "Good heavens, Phyllis, have you forgotten all our plans?" she cried. "We were to hold a ball, and invite a crowd! How else can we manage to inveigle Canfield? In your excitement over *Tris's* good fortune, have you forgotten all about *Julie?*"

Phyllis reached across the table and grasped her friend's hand. "Of course I haven't. Julie's situation hasn't been out of my mind for a moment. We'll simply invite Canfield to the breakfast. The chances of their being thrown together are much greater at a small party than at a ball."

Madge's brows knit. "Perhaps you're right. But must the breakfast be held so soon? I was hoping Julie and Canfield might meet at the theater or at some evening gala *before* the betrothal celebration, to give that meeting a little momentum."

Phyllis smiled complacently. "I've arranged for that too. You see, Smallwood's friend, Lord Chalmondeley, is hosting a ball for the prince, and Smallwood's arranged for the three of us to attend under his escort. He says it will be a dreadful squeeze, but for one thing, it will give Julie a chance to meet Prinny!"

"Yes, she will certainly enjoy that," Madge muttered, "but what has that to do with—?"

"Wait! I haven't told you the best part." Phyllis looked across the table with a triumphant grin. *"Canfield will be there!"*

Madge gasped in pure ecstacy. "He *will?* Are you sure?"

"Positive. Chalmondeley said so."

"Oh, my goodness! Tomorrow?" She clasped her hands to her bosom in dismay. "How can we possibly—? I haven't yet had time to order a new gown for her! And she hasn't a decent pair of gloves! We can't possibly be ready!"

"Yes, we can," Phyllis said serenely, rising and gliding to the door. "She can wear the lilac gown she wore to the last assembly. Canfield himself admired it, remember? And as for gloves, she can have mine."

Thus, on the following evening, Julie, dressed in her lilac silk and wearing Phyllis's gloves, found herself making her way up the crowded stairway to the Chalmondeley ballroom, her mother ahead of her and Phyllis and Smallwood following. She'd been told that the prince was expected to attend, but no other name had been mentioned. Although the prospect of meeting the prince face-to-face was certainly exciting, she was otherwise not looking forward to this evening. She knew no one in the huge crowd, and she wondered if any young man at all would ask to stand up with her. It would probably turn out to be an affair not unlike the Amberford Assembly, only larger. She would be a wallflower in London just as she was at home.

She took a seat in her mother's shadow, as usual, and sat miserably through three dances. She glanced into the corner where a large clock bonged quietly to mark every passing quarter hour. Forty-five minutes had still to pass before Prinny was to make his appearance at midnight. To Julie, convinced she'd never been so miserable, it was an eternity. Suddenly, however, Lord Smallwood appeared with a young man in tow. "Miss Branscombe, may I present the Honorable Horace Chalmondeley, who earnestly desires to stand up with you?"

The fellow was probably not more than twenty years old, but he was quite good-looking and marvelously dressed. Julie jumped up and took his arm without even glancing at her mother for permission, so grateful was she to escape her role as wallflower for a little while.

The Honorable Horace did not say anything as they walked to the dance floor, but once they took their places in the set, he began to speak. "I've been watching you all evening," he said with an assurance beyond his years, "and I can't determine why you've been hiding away back there. Girls as pretty as you usually station themselves where they can be seen."

"Yet you managed to see me, didn't you?" she answered flippantly, thinking that Tris would find that retort saucy. He'd be proud of her.

"Only because I'm more observant than most," the cocky young fellow said. "You weren't hiding away because you're spoken for, are you?"

She was about to give him another saucy retort, but the music started. It was a lively selection called "Mutual Promises." She very much enjoyed the opportunity to expend some of her pent-up energy. She laughed at the Honorable Horace's every quip, swung on his arm with spirit and was almost sorry when the music stopped. Just as they left the floor, however, she was accosted by two other young men, each requesting her company for the next dance. As she hesitated, not knowing how to choose between them, a third man came up. "Sorry, gentlemen," he said, "but this dance is mine."

"Pete— Lord Canfield!" she gasped, the blood freezing in her veins.

He smiled down at her. "You can't refuse me, my dear. The next dance is a waltz."

"N-No, I couldn't refuse that," she said breathlessly, managing to smile up at him.

He took her arm, and they started back to the dance floor. "It's good to see you, Julie," he said warmly. "What are you doing so far from home?"

"Tris sent for m—" she began and then realized that the words might give him the wrong impression. All she wanted him to know was that Tris was betrothed, and *not* to her. However, she couldn't just blurt it out. "I mean . . . ," she began again, blushing, "that Mama and Phyllis decided to . . . to . . ."

He sensed her embarrassment, though he couldn't explain it. "Where *is* the lucky dog, anyway?" he asked. "I haven't seen him here."

She sighed in relief. Now that he'd asked, it would be perfectly proper for her to tell him that Tris was just where he ought to be, with this betrothed, Cleo Smallwood. "He's not here," she said eagerly. "He's spending the evening with—"

The music began at that moment. Peter placed his arm round her waist, causing her voice to fail her completely. *I'll tell him after the dance,* she promised herself. *There's plenty of time.*

They quickly got into position and started to dance. They'd taken no more than three steps, however, when the music stopped abruptly. After a brief pause, the musicians struck up the "Rule, Britannia." Peter looked down at her, his face showing real chagrin. "Dash it," he muttered, "that means the prince has arrived. We shall have to—"

He was cut short by the arrival of a young woman who'd run across the floor to him in a flurry of jade-green flounces and who now grasped his arm. Julie recognized her as the same young lady he'd met at the Fenton. She now looked even more spectacularly beautiful. "Peter, he's here!" the lady cried excitedly. "You promised you'd introduce me! Come quickly!"

Peter's look of chagrin deepened. "Julie, this is Miss Catherine Marquard. Kat, I'd like you to meet Miss Juliet Branscombe. The Branscombes are my neighbors in—"

"A pleasure, Miss Branscombe," Kat Marquard said in breathless and uninterested dismissal, not even giving Julie a second glance. "Peter, please!" She pulled at his arm urgently. "If we don't hurry, he'll be surrounded by a crowd and we won't get his attention!"

Peter looked down at Julie miserably. "Excuse me, Julie, I must go."

"Yes, of course," Julie said numbly. "Good-bye."

With one backward look, he let the girl hurry him away. Julie was left standing alone on the now-deserted dance floor. Her knees shook as she started back to where her mother had been seated. But her mother was on her feet and approaching her, looking white-faced and agitated. "Were you just conversing with Lord Canfield?" she asked Julie tightly.

"Yes. Why do you ask?"

"Why? *Why?*" Her face reddened in agitation. "Because he doesn't deserve your attention, that's why!" She looked about her to make certain no one was close enough to overhear, but the area where they stood was completely deserted. Everyone who hadn't managed to squeeze out to the reception area to greet the prince was crowded round the door. "Canfield is an unprincipled scoundrel and shall henceforth be beneath our notice."

"How can you say that, Mama? He is a neighbor of ours, is he not? And a friend."

"He is no friend of mine! And not of yours, either."

Julie was baffled. "I don't understand you, Mama. Not more than a fortnight ago you said that he was handsome and wealthy and charming—a gentleman a girl could dream about."

Lady Branscombe waved her hand dismissively. "You must have misunderstood me."

"Come now, Mama, your words were perfectly unambiguous. You sounded as if you would have liked him to *offer* for me. And now you say he's unprincipled. How can you make such a complete about-face? And how, may I ask, can you say he's unprincipled?"

"He *is* unprincipled. He told me in Amberford that he was a suitor for your hand. Now I'm reliably informed that he's about to be betrothed to someone else."

This caught Julie off guard. "B-Betrothed?" she stammered, her chest contracting as if from a blow.

"Yes, betrothed to a Miss Marquard. If that isn't unprincipled, I know not what is!"

Julie, shaken as she was, nevertheless felt impelled to defend him. "He was never a suitor for my hand, Mama," she said, trying to speak calmly despite the fact that her throat burned and the floor seemed unsteady under her feet. "It was all a pretense to entrap Tris. Lord Canfield has every right to attach himself to Miss Marquard . . . or to anyone else who suits him."

"Well, if he's not to attach himself to you, there's no point in giving him any further thought. Besides, if he's foolish enough to leg-shackle himself to that flibbertigibbet, I'm glad to be rid of him! Did you *see* the girl in that vulgar jade-green costume? I'd wager she damped the underdress, the ostentatious creature! I would have thought the man had better sense."

"Please, Mama," Julie begged, her emotions stretched to the breaking point, "have done. She seems to me to be a lovely young woman." Her knees gave way, and she sank down on the nearest chair. "He c-calls her Kat," she added miserably.

Her mother peered down at her, taken aback by those pathetic words. Only now did it occur to her that her daughter was truly smitten with the fellow. Her heart was stricken with sympathetic pain. But she knew that if she showed it, they would both dissolve in tears. In this public place, that would not do. They had no choice but to be strong. She squared her shoulders. "Come, my love, I think we should go home . . . that is, back to the hotel."

"I wish we could go home," Julie muttered under her breath as she got to her feet. Home in Devon was where she wanted to be. Home was the best place for nursing wounds. But this was not the time for self-pity, she reminded herself. They'd come to London for Tris's sake, and here they would stay until their duties were over. She too squared her shoulders. "What about Phyllis and Lord Smallwood?" she asked her mother. "I can't see them in that crowd, can you?"

"Let them stay. We can go home in a hack."

She glanced at her mother curiously. "But don't you want to see the prince? I thought that was why we came."

"It's not why *I* came. But I'll stay if you wish. He's the reason *you* came, after all."

"I suppose he is," Julie said dully, "but I find I'm not as eager as I was earlier. You're quite right, Mama. Let's go home."

35

MADGE BRANSCOMBE WAS ALMOST ASHAMED TO admit to herself that she had little stomach for the wedding breakfast that Saturday morning. After learning that Lord Canfield was to be betrothed, her enthusiasm for London and everything in it had considerably waned. Although she was glad that Tris was embarking on what would undoubtedly be a happy marital voyage, he was leaving her Julie behind, alone on the shore of spinsterhood. It was enough to dishearten any mother.

Nevertheless, Tris was like a son to her and Phyllis her closest friend. She had to put a good face on it for their sakes. That being the case, she dressed herself that morning in a new tiffany-silk gown in imperial purple and topped it with a silver turban bearing half-a-dozen plumes in a color that matched perfectly. When Julie saw her, her eyes lit with admiration. "I say, Mama, you look positively regal."

"Thank you, my love. And you are looking very fine as well. I might not have chosen sprigged muslin for so important an occasion, but it does look charming on you. And it is almost summer, so I suppose you may be forgiven." With that motherly compliment Julie had to be content.

The betrothal breakfast was already in progress when Lady Branscombe and Julie joined the party in a private room on the hotel's main floor. The room was bright with sunshine and so massed with greenery it looked like a conservatory, its white walls and green-and-white painted chairs adding to the cheery atmosphere. A long buffet table had been set up along one of the walls, and a few of the guests were already partaking of the hot cheese buns, smoked salmon, lobster au gratin, scrambled eggs with truffles, tiny apple soufflés, tomatoes hollandaise and all sorts of pastries, jellies and creams. In the center of the table a large fountain gave forth a steady stream of champagne. It was a sparkling sight, but not nearly as sparkling as Cleo, who stood near it. Her curls bounced, her cheeks glowed, and her gown—a soft, filmy rose-colored creation twinkling with gold threads and tied just below the bosom with a wide gold band—set off her figure and her eyes to perfection. Tris, standing beside her, beamed with pride. "I think, Mama," Julie whispered, "that I've never seen Tris looking happier."

Phyllis came up to greet them as they entered. "Julie, my love," she said as she embraced the girl, "how very lovely you look. That sprigged muslin couldn't be more perfect for the occasion."

Julie threw her mother a taunting grimace before going off to greet those guests she knew and to meet those she didn't. Two hours passed with much eating, drinking and merriment. Finally, however, Lord Smallwood tapped on his wineglass for order. "I believe it behooves me at this time to make a toast," he said in his precise, scholarly way. "I shall save my wittiest bon mots for their forthcoming nuptials, but for now it will suffice for me to say: here's to my beautiful, foolish and headstrong daughter and the charming scoundrel she loves. May they always be as happy as they are today, and may they present their devoted parents with many bouncing grandbabies!"

"Hear, hear!" his friend Lord Chalmondeley shouted, and as Tris kissed his blushing betrothed, everyone cheered, applauded and downed more champagne.

Lord Smallwood tapped his glass again. "May I have your indulgence for another announcement? It is only a small bit of news, but a very happy one. I think it will surprise you all. Two days ago, a very lovely lady and I were married quietly by special license. Therefore I would be obliged if you would lift your glasses to my wife, the erstwhile Lady Phyllis Enders." While everyone gasped in astonishment, he crossed the room to where Phyllis stood smiling at him and raised his glass. "Phyllis, my love, to you!"

Shock had frozen everyone into immobility. The room was absolutely silent. Suddenly there came a sound between a groan and a gasp, followed by that of a glass crashing to the floor, and Lady Branscombe, her purple plumes waving madly, took a step forward, declaring, "This is . . . too much!" in a strangulated voice. Then, with everyone's eyes fixed on her in horror, she stalked across the room and out the door.

"Mama!" Julie cried, appalled, and started to run after her.

But Phyllis stopped her. "No, dearest, let me," she said quietly. "Please, everyone, go on with the party."

Phyllis found Madge in the lobby, leaning on the back of a chair, breathing heavily. She came up behind her and laid a soft hand on her shoulder. "Forgive me, Madge, dearest. It's all my fault. I should have told you. Prepared you."

Madge threw her an angry look over her shoulder. "Yes, you should have. I thought we were friends. I never had an *inkling* of something like this going on between you and Smallwood."

"I wanted it to be a surprise. I thought it would be a happy one. I should have realized how difficult the news would be for you."

"Difficult is hardly the word," Madge said, turning her back on her friend. "I am flabbergasted."

"I know. I've said I'm sorry. But when the shock is over, you will be happy for me, won't you?"

Madge wheeled about furiously. "Happy for you? How can I be?"

Phyllis looked stricken. "But, Madge, you *must* be. Henry and I love each other, you see, although we didn't admit it until just a few days ago."

"Why didn't you tell me?"

"I don't know." Phyllis, troubled by the realization that

there was some justification for Madge's anger, sank down upon the chair Madge had been using to support her. "It was all so ridiculously sudden," she admitted, half to herself. "I thought . . . I suppose I was afraid you would disapprove."

"I *would* have disapproved," Madge retorted sullenly. "I *do* disapprove!"

Phyllis turned in the chair. "But why, Madge? Do you think Henry and I won't suit?"

There was a silence. "I have to think about that," Madge said slowly, her mind switching from consideration of her own offended feelings to those of her friend. "I suppose, on consideration, that there's no reason you and Smallwood shouldn't get on together," she admitted reluctantly.

"Then can't you forgive me, and be happy for me?"

"How can I?" She walked round the chair and looked down at Phyllis more calmly. "Even though, now that I've had time to think about it, I can see that Smallwood may be right for you, the fact remains that I'll be losing you."

"Losing me?" It was Phyllis's turn to be surprised. "Why on earth do you think that?"

"You'll be living here in London, won't you? In Smallwood's town house?"

"Heavens, no! Henry loved living in Amberford. He'll be moving into Enders Hall as soon as we return from our wedding trip. Tris and Cleo may be intending to settle in London, but Henry and I are not."

An expression of real relief brightened Madge's face. "Is that true, Phyllis? You're not just offering a sweet to a bawling baby, are you?"

"Madge, you idiot," Phyllis scoldly fondly, jumping up and taking her friend into a warm embrace, "after all these years, how can you think I could ever move far away from you?"

Madge returned the embrace, surrendering to the necessity of accepting and adjusting to those changes with which life is ever surprising us. The two women sat down together, and Phyllis told her dearest friend every detail of her husband's astounding five-minute courtship. "And now," she concluded, "we are off for a honeymoon in Scotland, where we will come to know each other while admiring the lochs."

"And I," Madge sighed, "will return at once to Amberford, where I will try to find some way to mend my daughter's broken heart."

"Why don't you remain here for a fortnight?" Phyllis suggested. "You've always wanted to give the girl a little town bronze. Now is the perfect time. You can take her to parties and routs and theatricals and all that London has to offer. I'm certain the Chalmondeleys will see that you are invited everywhere. Who knows what may transpire in a fortnight? And by then, I shall be back, and we can all return to Amberford together."

Madge considered the idea but then shook her head. "I don't think Julie will agree. She wants to go home."

"Since when have you ever let Julie make such decisions?" Phyllis teased. "Don't tell me, Madge Branscombe, that you are growing soft!"

"Everyone else around me seems to be changing," Madge sighed as she pulled herself to her feet, "so why shouldn't I?"

36

MADGE BRANSCOMBE DID NOT CHANGE NEARLY AS much as Phyllis had thought, for she remained as firm with her daughter as she always had, hardening herself against Julie's heartfelt desire to go home. "We *must* stay, for a little while at least," she told her daughter. "With Phyllis and Smallwood gone off to Scotland, Tris and Cleo have no one left to help them with their wedding plans but us."

"But Mama," Julie objected, "the wedding will not be held until fall. Phyllis will be back in plenty of time to make arrangements."

"You don't understand, my love. These matters cannot wait. Weddings, especially fashionable ones of this sort, must be planned months in advance. I promised to help Cleo choose a pattern for her gown. And Phyllis has asked me to make the decisions regarding the date, the guest list, the menu, the wines and all sorts of details. Don't look so stricken, dearest. I promise we won't remain in town one day longer than necessary."

Julie, as usual, surrendered to her mother's pressure with as good grace as her depressed spirits permitted. She did everything her mother suggested without argument. She shopped for gloves and bonnets at the Pantheon Bazaar. She allowed herself to be fitted for two new gowns. She went to the opera at Covent Garden, to the theater at the Haymarket, to a dinner-dance at the home of Lord and Lady Hertford and an excursion to Vauxhall Gardens under the escort of the cocky young Horace Chalmondeley, all in one week. She was sampling all the delights of London social life and feeling absolutely miserable.

Tris and Cleo, on the other hand, were enjoying themselves immensely. Besides being feted by all their acquaintances every evening, they spent every day together in pleasurable activities. They rode in the park, drove to the country for picnics, visited the Elgin marbles, went to the races and shopped for the dozens of items—such as china and linen and plate—that a betrothed couple would need in their new lives. Tris had never before realized that London offered so many delightful things to do.

It was on one of these shopping expeditions that Tris ran into Lord Canfield. He and Cleo had gone to a linendraper's to choose fabric for the bed hangings in their bridal bedchamber, but Tris, bored with this feminine chore, had excused himself to go outside and stretch his legs. He was strolling down the street, whistling cheerfully, when he saw Canfield coming toward him. He had not seen him since he'd landed the fellow a facer at the fair. "I say, Peter, old man," he shouted in excited greeting, "what a piece of luck! I've been hoping I'd run into you."

"Have you?" Peter asked, shaking his hand. "Why is that?"

"To apologize, of course."

"Apologize? Whatever for?"

Tris made a rueful face. "You know what for. For making a deuced cake of myself that day at the fair."

"There's no need for apologies," Peter assured him. "I goaded you into it, you know. Besides, the whole incident is ancient history . . . of no importance now."

"You're right, of course," Tris said, falling into step beside him, "especially since everything's turned out so well. Have you heard the news? We're betrothed at last."

"I supposed as much." Peter offered his hand again. "Congratulations, Tris. You're a damned lucky fellow."

"I know it very well. I say, Peter, would you care to come and give your best to the bride-to-be? At this very moment she's choosing fabric at the draper's, right there up the street."

Peter, tempted to catch a glimpse of Julie again, hesitated for a moment. But then he thought better of it and shook his head. "No, I'd better be getting along. Besides, I gave her my good wishes when I saw her at the Chalmondeleys' the other night."

"At the Chalmondeleys'?" Tris blinked at him, puzzled. "But she didn't attend—"

At that moment, however, Cleo came running up to him, a fabric sample in her hand. "Tris, wait," she said a bit breathlessly. "What do you think of this pattern for the—?" Then she looked up. "Goodness!" she exclaimed. *"Peter?"*

Peter tipped his hat and bowed over the smiling girl's hand. "Cleo, my dear, how very nice to see you! Are you helping the happy couple choose their trousseau?"

"Couple?" Now, Cleo too was puzzled. "What couple?"

"Why, Tris and—" All at once Peter stiffened and stared from one to the other. "Good God! Can I have been so mistaken? Are *you* the bride-to-be?"

"Yes, of course she is," Tris said, laughing at Peter's discomfiture. "Didn't I say so?"

"No, confound it, you didn't," Peter said, a pulse beginning to throb in his temples. "I simply assumed . . ."

"That it was Julie?" Cleo asked, her smile broadening.

"Yes." His brow furrowed as he tried to adjust to this startling revelation. "I should have known better than to make assumptions."

"Well, now that you know," Tris grinned, "don't you think you should offer my betrothed your good wishes?"

"Yes, of course," Peter said somewhat absently. "You know you *both* have my best wishes." Forcing himself to concentrate on the present moment instead of the confusion in his mind, he bent down and kissed Cleo's cheek. "I am truly happy for you, Cleo. Truly."

"Thank you," the glowing girl said. "I know you are."

Tris slapped him on the shoulder. "Come and join us

for a luncheon at Gunther's. We can reveal all the lurid details of our rocky courtship over one of their chocolate pastries."

"No, thank you, Tris. Much as I'd like to hear the tale, let's make it another time. I must be off." With another tip of his hat and another murmur of congratulations, he started down the street. The betrothed couple, looking after him, saw him pause at the corner as if uncertain of his direction.

"She's still in town, you know," Cleo called after him, a smiling glint in her eyes.

Peter stopped and turned. "Is she?"

Cleo nodded. "At the Fenton."

A slow grin suffused his face. "Cleo, you're a peach!" he said. "Thank you. I'm on my way."

37

PETER'S HIGH SPIRITS DID NOT LAST LONG. WHEN HE arrived at the Fenton, he learned that the Branscombe ladies were out. He had to wait for them. This delay gave him time to think. As he sat in the lobby impatiently tapping a foot, he began to realize that there was less reason for rejoicing than he'd first believed. True, Julie was not betrothed; that was the news that had sent his spirits aloft. But whatever made him conclude that she would be happy about it? If she truly loved Tris—and he'd long ago convinced himself that she did—she would now be heartbroken. She might, of course, turn to him for consolation, but was that the sort of reaction he wanted? Could he accept being second choice?

He was mulling over the answer to that question when the ladies walked in. They were carrying parcels, so they'd evidently been shopping. They both looked tired. Peter, whose cogitations had left him feeling decidedly ill at ease, rose and approached them. "Good afternoon," he said, removing his hat. "Lady Branscombe, how do you do?"

Madge quickly recovered from her initial surprise. "Well enough," she said coldly. "You aren't here to call on *us,* are you?"

"On your daughter, yes," he said, smiling down at Julie, who was regarding him, white-faced.

"My daughter has nothing to say to you, my lord," the protective mother declared. "Please excuse us."

Lady Branscombe was acting the dragon again, Peter thought in irritation. How many times would he have to fight her before he could win the girl? "I hope you won't find me rude, ma'am, but I'd rather learn from Julie herself whether or not she'll speak to me."

"Julie will do as I say," Madge Branscombe snapped. "Come along, girl. I'm much too weary to be standing about."

"Then go upstairs, please, Mama," Julie said with quiet decision. "I'd like to visit with Lord Canfield. He's given me no reason to refuse to speak to him."

The dragon reddened in chagrin. "See here, Julie—!"

Julie faced her mother firmly. "Mama, do go along. I'll be up shortly."

Madge glared at her daughter in a fury. Julie met her eyes in a speechless battle of wills. Then Madge's eyes fell. "Very well, do as you wish," she muttered in defeat and marched off to the stairs.

Peter grinned down at Julie. "Good for you," he cheered. "You've learned how to battle the dragon yourself, I see."

She returned his smile with a small, rueful one of her own. "One has to grow up sometime, I suppose," she said.

"No, that's not so. Not everyone manages to do it. I'm very proud of you." He took her elbow and guided her to a sofa. "Shall we sit here? That potted plant will shield us from view."

She nodded and seated herself nervously on the edge of the sofa. He took a place beside her. "I had to see you, Julie. I just learned, this very afternoon, that you and Tris are not betrothed after all. Needless to say, I'm astounded."

She looked down at her hands. "I tried to tell you at the ball the other evening . . ."

"Yes, I realize that now. I'm sorry I had to be so abrupt that night."

"Not at all. You had a promise to keep. I completely understood."

"But that's beside the point. What troubles me, Julie, is *your* situation. I can't help wondering what happened to our plans. I thought that Tris would surely offer for you. I still have a stiff jaw to prove it."

She tried to laugh but couldn't. "Nothing untoward happened," she explained dispiritedly. "We discovered we didn't suit, that's all."

"I see." But he didn't see at all. He tried to look at her face, but with her head bent, the brim of her bonnet hid it from him. "I'm truly sorry. I thought you suited very well."

"Yes, everyone did. We were all mistaken."

"I hope . . ." He hesitated briefly and then plunged on. "I hope you're . . . er . . . reconciled to the outcome."

"To Tris's betrothal, you mean?" She turned her head and looked up at him with convincing sincerity. "Of course I am. I'm very happy for him. For both of them."

He was more than eager to believe her. With a wave of hope surging through him, he took her hands in his. "Are you sure, Julie?" he asked earnestly. "You've had only a very short time to recover from what must have been a painful experience."

She pulled her hands from his grasp and turned her face away again. "Please believe me, Peter, there was *nothing* to recover *from.*"

Nothing to recover from? What did she mean? He stared at her, taking in her bent head with its shrouding bonnet, the graceful line of her neck and shoulders turned away from him, the clenched hands in her lap. Everything in her posture seemed to indicate withdrawal from him. He did not know what to make of her. She seemed to be telling him she hadn't cared for Tris at all, but if she was, why was she so distant, so detached? He wished he could find some way to penetrate these defenses she seemed to have erected between them. "In that case, Julie," he said, forcing himself to sound cheerful, "perhaps you'd agree to come driving with me tomorrow. We could ride up north toward Isling—" He stopped abruptly, for she'd thrown him such a startled, offended look that his tongue was stilled by it.

"The . . . the two of us, you mean?" she asked awkwardly.

"Well, yes," he answered, baffled. "Unless you'd like to take your mother along."

She didn't smile at the quip. Instead, she rose slowly and looked down at him. "Lord Canfield," she said in a kind of trembling formality, "you've been a good friend to me, and I hope you will continue to be. But you surely must understand that it would be improper for me to accept any such invitations from you."

He got to his feet, more bemused than ever. "But I *don't* understand. In what way improper?"

She shook her head, unable or unwilling to reply. "I'm very tired," she said, turning away, "so let me wish you good day. It was kind of you to come, but now please excuse me."

He followed her and grasped her hand. "Just a minute, Julie, please! May I call on you tomorrow? I'd like to speak to you again. There seems to be a great deal I don't understand."

Again she removed her hand from his grasp. "I think it would be best," she said, not meeting his eyes, "if we don't meet again like this. Good-bye, my lord." And she hurried off to the stairs.

He stared after her, dumfounded. Something about her remarks had seemed strangely askew, but he couldn't put his finger on what it was. But one thing was glaringly clear. Though she'd suggested that she no longer loved Tris—and perhaps never had—she certainly didn't care for Peter Granard, Viscount Canfield. She wanted him to remain her *friend!* Remembering those words of hers, he gave a derisive, self-deprecating laugh. For the first time in his life, he'd been soundly rejected by a woman. *I hope you'll always remain my friend.* Weren't those the words every woman used to rid herself of a suitor she didn't want?

Julie, meanwhile, ran up the stairs, brushing away the tears that she'd managed to hold back during the interview. How could he have behaved in that intimate way, she asked herself, when he knew he would soon be betrothed to his "Kat"? She would have liked to fling that question in his face, but she'd been too reticent. Besides, if a betrothal had not yet been officially announced, did it officially exist? One couldn't even mention it except in whispered gossip. Perhaps that's why he felt justified in seeking her company—because the betrothal was not yet official. But from her point of view it was quite wrong of him. To show attentions to one woman when you are betrothed to another is the act of a . . . a cad.

Already in pain from the fact of his attachment to that beautiful red-headed creature, Julie now found herself in greater pain because of his thoughtlessness. And the only way she could think of to ease the terrible ache inside her was to throw herself across her bed and sob her heart out.

But even that sad solace was denied her. Her mother was sitting on her bed waiting for her. "What did he want?" she asked, still angry at Julie's disobedience. And then she saw her daughter's tearstained face. "Julie!" she cried in alarm.

"I'm all right, Mama, you needn't worry," Julie said, dashing the wetness from her cheeks with the back of her hand and speaking as resolutely as she could. "But I do have something to say to you. You may stay here in London and help Tris and Cleo as long as you like. But as for me, I'm going h-home. Today!"

38

THE FIRST THING JULIE SAW ON HER RETURN HOME was the pianoforte. His pianoforte. The very sight of it troubled her. He'd given it to her as a wedding gift, but she was not going to have a wedding. On the other hand, he was. Hadn't her mother learned, on good authority, that he was going to marry Miss Catherine "Kat" Marquard? His deuced Kat was the one who should have the instrument. Julie had possession on false grounds.

Besides, she, Julie Branscombe, no longer wanted it. Every time she saw it, her heart constricted achingly in her chest. When she sat down to play, she sooner or later found herself crying. The pianoforte, magnificent as it was, had become a symbol of rejection and grief. She had to rid herself of it.

After dwelling on the matter for several days, she decided that as soon as his engagement was announced in the *Times,* she would send the piano back to Wycklands and, in a congratulatory letter to him, inform him of it. Every day, for the next three weeks, she pored over the announcements in the newspaper, searching in vain for his name. She wondered why, if the betrothal was as certain to come to pass as her mother had said, it was taking so long to make it public.

She even wondered if she should write to the brash young Horace Chalmondeley to ask if he'd had any news of the betrothal. Ever since she'd danced with him at the ball, the silly young fellow had been besieging her with love letters. She'd never answered a single one, but her curiosity and suspense regarding Peter's impending nuptials were so great that she was tempted to contact the boy. But of course she did not.

After three weeks, however, her mother came home in a state of considerable excitement. She'd been visiting Phyllis and Smallwood at Enders Hall, as she'd done every day since their return, and had heard some news. "He's back," she said to her daughter as if announcing a catastrophe.

"Who's back?" Julie asked, not particularly curious.

"Canfield. He's come to pack up his library. Evidently he's decided to sell the property." Unmindful of Julie's immediate stiffening, she babbled on. "I, for one, am delighted he's giving it up. Perhaps now we'll get a new bachelor at Wycklands, someone with better sense, who'd appreciate a true gem when he saw her."

"And perhaps," Julie said as she fled from her mother's diatribe, "it will be bought by a huge family with a drunkard of a father, a whining mother and seven noisy children all under the age of ten."

"Really, Julie," her mother shouted after her, "I don't know what's come over you lately. You are becoming a positive hoyden."

The "hoyden" ran up to her bedroom and shut the door. She had to think about this new development. If Peter had truly returned to Wycklands, perhaps this would be the proper time to send back the piano. Why not? she asked herself. He himself would be there to receive it. What better time would there be?

She sat down at her writing table to pen a note. She started and discarded three before she wrote one she considered acceptable. *To His Lordship, the Viscount Canfield,* she finally wrote. *I have never felt deserving of the magnificent pianoforte you were generous enough to bestow upon me on the occasion of what you believed was my imminent marriage. Since that marriage never came to pass, I feel that my continued possession of it is under false pretenses. You, on the other hand, being yourself anticipating an imminent marriage, will no doubt wish to present it to your bride. I am therefore sending it back with my best wishes for your happiness. Yours most sincerely, Juliet Branscombe.*

That done, she went back downstairs and asked Horsham to arrange for four men and a cart to transport the instrument (and her note) to Wycklands that very afternoon. She hoped she could handle the matter quietly on her own, but when the men came to remove the piano, her mother heard the commotion. She came running down from the upstairs sitting room where she'd been reading, demanding to know what was going on.

"I am returning the pianoforte to Canfield," Julie explained. "You yourself told me that any wedding gifts I'd received had to be returned."

To her relief, her mother made no objection. "It's the right thing to do," she sighed as she went back upstairs, "though it's a lovely thing to have to part with."

Julie watched the carters carry it away with a strange feeling in her innards. It was relief, she told herself. Decided relief. She was truly glad to see it go. Truly. Then why, she was forced to ask herself, were these tears coursing down her face?

Self-pity was a quality she scorned, so she tried to shake away the doldrums that this business with the piano had brought upon her. A vigorous ride along the river might be, she decided, the very thing to lift her spirit. She ran upstairs to change into riding clothes. As she started down again, in her old, shabby skirt and with her hair loose, she was startled to discover that an angry Lord Canfield was brushing past the butler and storming in. *"Peter!"* she gasped, freezing into place halfway down the stairs. What rotten luck, she thought, that he should see her looking so deucedly unkempt.

But he was too out of temper to take any notice of her appearance. "What, ma'am, is the meaning of this?" he shouted, waving a crushed piece of notepaper at her.

"Is that my note?" she inquired, her knees a-tremble.

"If this gibberish can be called a note, then I suppose it is. It has your name on it."

"I don't see why you call it gibberish. I thought I'd

written it in plain English and, if I may be a bit immodest, that it was rather felicitously phrased."

"Felicitously phrased? Are you completely *shatter-brained?*" He took several angry paces about the entry hall to gain control of himself before turning back and looking up at her again. "In the first place, ma'am, you know perfectly well that I wanted to give you the instrument before there was any talk of marrying Tris. So this business of possessing it on false pretenses is utter nonsense."

"Well, you did write in your note that it was a wedding gift."

"A mere excuse, as well you know! And what is this idiotic jibber-jabber about *my* imminent marriage and giving the piano to my bride?"

Her legs were so unsteady she had to cling to the bannister. "Well, I know you haven't officially announced it as yet," she explained uneasily, "so perhaps it was not in the best of taste to mention it, but—"

"Mention *what?*" he roared. "I don't know what you're babbling about."

She drew herself up angrily. "Dash it, my lord, I don't babble! And I don't like being shouted at, either. I am speaking of your . . . your almost-intended, Miss Marquard."

"Who?" He gaped at her, befuddled. "Do you mean my cousin Kat?"

"Your c-cousin?" Julie stammered, taken aback.

"Catherine Marquard is my nuisance of a cousin whom my aunt in Yorkshire insists I must escort about town on her once-a-year visit. *Why* would I want to give her a *piano?* She doesn't even play!"

"But . . ." Julie took a gulping breath, almost afraid to go on. ". . . Are you not intending to . . . to marry her?"

"Marry *Kat?*" Peter gave a snorting laugh. "I'd sooner wed one of those whirling dervishes from the east! I can't abide the chit more than half an hour at a time." Then, with a quick, gasping intake of breath, he gazed up at her, a light of comprehension dawning in his eyes. Suddenly a number of pieces of the puzzle of Julie Branscombe were beginning to fall into place. "Is *that* why you behaved so strangely at the Fenton? Because you thought I was getting *married?*"

She felt her heart jump right up into her throat. "Aren't you?" she asked, choked. "Have we perhaps . . . gotten it wrong? That is . . . can we have heard the wrong name?"

He didn't answer for what seemed an eternity. He merely continued to gaze up at her with a look of intense speculation. Then, when she thought she could not bear the silence a moment longer, he spoke. "Julie, come down here," he said quietly. "Please!"

She started down, slowly and unsteadily, as he came round to the foot of the stairway. When she reached the third step from the bottom, he held out his arms. Without knowing quite what she did, she leaped into them. He held her in a crushing embrace, her feet high off the ground, and kissed her, long and hard, with the intensity that comes from passion long restrained. When they had no breath left, he set her down. "I love you, Julie," he whispered in her ear. "Almost from the first moment I laid eyes on you. I could *never* wed anyone else. I want to marry you even if it means taking second place to Tris in your heart."

"Second place?" She broke from his hold and stamped her foot. "Dash it, Peter, I could wring your *neck.* I've been trying to tell you from the moment you started to push me into Tris's arms that it's *you* I love, not Tris."

Even now he couldn't quite believe it. "That can't be so," he said, peering at her suspiciously. "You and he were so . . . so close. It seemed to me you could almost read each other's minds."

"Balderdash. Neither of you could read my mind. He was trying to teach me how to win you, just as you were trying to teach me how to win him. And I, fool that I was, tried to follow the advice of both of you. I was like a marionette, with two idiotic puppet masters pulling the strings."

"My poor darling," he exclaimed, appalled. "And when in the course of this farce did you decide you loved me and not him?"

Somehow the question infuriated her. He still didn't understand her feelings. But as usual, it was hard for her to express them, especially with his eyes fixed so lovingly on her face. "Peter, you . . . you buffleheaded fool," she said, turning and addressing the newel post, "why won't you *listen* to me? I've never loved anyone but you. Not anyone. Not Tris, not Ronny Kenting, not even the Honorable Horace Chalmondeley, who's been importuning me by post to marry him ever since I danced with him at the Chalmondeley ball."

Peter snorted. "Good God, *Chalmondeley?* I should hope not, indeed. The fellow's a looby."

She laughed and turned back to him. "The truth is, my lord," she said shyly to the buttons of his coat, "that you took hold of my heart the night you sauntered into the assembly and I got my first glimpse of you. I've tried to tell you so many times in every way I could think of—except to say the words."

He pulled her into his arms again and brushed back her wild strands of hair. "My sweet, beautiful Julie, you *should* have said them. A buffleheaded fool like me needs to have things said plainly, I'm afraid."

"I was . . . shy."

He lifted her chin and made her look up at him. "I hope, my girl, that you'll never be shy with me again."

"I think I'm much improved in that regard. In fact, I'm almost growing bold. Almost bold enough to ask . . . but perhaps I'd better not . . ."

"Go ahead, girl, be bold and ask it," he insisted.

"Well, then, my lord," she said, tossing him a daring grin, "how long is it going to be before you kiss me again?"

It took no time at all for him to comply. They were in the midst of a shockingly close embrace when Lady Branscombe's voice came to them from somewhere close by. "Julie, where on earth are you?" she was calling. "Horsham tells me that that clunch Canfield has sent the pianoforte *back again!*" Her step came closer and then stopped altogether. She'd caught sight of the embrace. "Oh, good *heavens! Canfield,* you cad, release that girl at once! Or . . . perhaps not. If someone doesn't tell me what has passed, I shall positively *swoon!*"

Julie lifted her head but didn't take her eyes from the face of the man who still held her in a crushing grip. "Don't be so silly, Mama. You never swoon. And as for you, my lord"—she held him off and, with eyes full of laughter, regarded him with head cocked—"*did* you do something so quixotically idiotic as to bring the piano *back?*"

He shrugged sheepishly. "Well, how was I to know the altercation I'd embarked on this afternoon would conclude with you in my arms? And since we're going to be wed anyway—and very soon too if I have my way—what difference does it make where the blasted piano stays?"

Coming back in print
in January 2005

A Grand Deception

by Elizabeth Mansfield

Turn the page
for a thrilling preview!

"To make an advantageous marriage is the goal, the purpose, the sum and substance of our existence," Lucy Traherne declared firmly, tying a satin, pearl-spangled sash on her henna-washed curls and observing herself fatuously in the dressing-table mirror. "Do you think this sash is too theatrical for a hairband?"

Her friend, Georgianna Verney, shook her head. "That," she declared with a firmness equal to her friend's, "is disgusting!"

Lucy stared at her reflection in surprise. "Good God, Georgy, does it look as bad as that?"

"Not the sash, you idiot. I'm not talking about your blasted hairband. It's your view of a woman's purpose that's disgusting."

"It is *not* disgusting. It is the way of life." She leaned toward the mirror and peered at her curls dubiously. "Are you certain this sash is not too . . . too *Babylonian*?"

"*You,* my dear girl, are too Babylonian! How can you sit there and speak as if women were nothing but chattel, to be bartered to the highest bidder?"

"What else were we raised for?" Lucy rejoined, turning her head to the right and left in an agony of indecision. "Are you going to give me an opinion on this hairband or not?"

The two friends, sitting in the upstairs dressing room of Lord and Lady Denham's townhouse (in which they'd deposited their wraps and were making final adjustments to their attire before descending the stairs to the ballroom where the final rout of the season was taking place), were a decided contrast to one another. Lucy Traherne, at twenty years of age, was a little younger than Georgianna Verney, and would have been considered the prettier of the two if one looked quickly. With her dyed red curls and light eyes, she was more obviously pretty than her taller, more striking friend, and was a great deal more ostentatious. Lucy's blue eyes were underlined with blacking, her azure gown was tucked and flounced wherever possible, her décolletage emphasized by a double strand of pearls, and her hair (now bedecked with the jeweled hairband) was a curled, pomaded testament to her hairdresser's art.

Georgy, on the other hand, was the model of restraint. Only a keen observer could discover that her auburn hair, pulled back from her face with almost prudish severity into a tight bun, was thick and lustrous and that her features, completely unemphasized by any touch of rouge or eyeblacking, were almost Grecian in their sculptured perfection. She was taller than her friend, but seemed even more so by her proud carriage and the confident lift of her chin. That chin was square and perhaps a bit too pronounced for current tastes (which required that female features be softly rounded), but her nose and high cheekbones could not be faulted. Most noticeable, even to the unobservant, were her hazel eyes—wide and lustrous and sparkling with humor and intelligence. They did not require blacking to attract admiration.

But Georgy's beauty was more subtle than pronounced, and she refused to use cosmetic arts and feminine decoration to make that beauty obvious. Understatement was her style. In addition to the understatement of her coiffure and her lack of cosmetics, her neck, ears and arms were bare of jewelry. And most understated of all was the gown she was wearing. She'd chosen (over her mother's emphatic objections) to dress herself in a lilac jacquard so subdued in color that it was almost gray. Only those who looked closely tonight would decide that she was, in her way, as eye-catching as her gaudy friend.

At the moment, Georgy's eyes were flashing fire. "Is *that* what you believe, Lucy? That we were raised merely for the purpose of attaching ourselves to men of wealth? That our minds and our characters were molded for no other purpose?"

Lucy gave her hairband a last pat and stood up. "What other purpose *can* there be?"

"What other purpose? I should think that being useful to society in some way is *one* possible purpose. Or becoming learned or wise. Or developing a talent. Or doing some *good* in the world."

"Do you know, Georgy," her friend said, shaking out the flounces of her skirt, "that sometimes you sound like an Evangelical?"

"If you're saying I sound like a wild-eyed preacher, you're right," Georgy admitted with a shame-faced grin. "I do sermonize a bit, don't I? I'm sorry, Lucy. But I hate the thought that making a good match is all we can accomplish in this world."

"There's nothing wrong with making a good match. If we can catch ourselves a pair of rich husbands—someone, say, like the famous Lord Maitland, who, by the way, Mama tells me, is expected to put in an appearance tonight—we can spend the rest of our lives doing exactly as we like."

"Is that why you've been adorning yourself like a crystal chandelier? To catch this Lord Maitland's eye?"

"Yes, why not? They say he's rich as a nabob, and

attractive, too. There's nothing I'd like *better* than to catch his eye."

"But for the sake of argument, let's suppose he's not attractive. Let's suppose he's gross and vulgar—the sort who makes suggestive little winks and takes surreptitious little nips at your buttocks when no one is looking. Would you *still* wish to sell yourself to him?"

"Frankly, Georgy, my love, I don't much care *what* he's like, if he's as rich as they say. Once one is wed, you know, one can go one's own way—if one is discreet."

Georgy raised her eyebrows. "What do you mean, go one's own way? Do you mean . . . are you trying to make me believe that you'd be like Lady Whitbrough and that sort? Go about town with escorts not your husband? Invite gentlemen into your rooms to watch you dress? And . . . and have *affairs*?"

Lucy giggled. "I might. If one is rich enough, one can do anything, and people only think it stylish."

Georgy glared at her. "Now, that *is* disgusting!"

"There's nothing disgusting about it," Lucy declared defensively. "Letty Denham, our hostess, married advantageously, and everyone says she's the happiest creature in the world. But of course, why shouldn't she be? I certainly would be happy with a charmer like Lord Denham, who could give me clothes and jewels like that magnificent emerald her ladyship always wears. And Maitland is another such. Every unmarried female who's come tonight would barter her *soul* to engage Maitland's attention. And you'll never convince me that you don't have the same desire. You'll never make me believe, Georgianna Verney, that you don't want to catch Maitland's eye yourself, in spite of the fact that that dowdy jacquard you've chosen to wear isn't likely to turn *anyone's* head."

Georgy, caught off guard by her friend's abrupt attack, couldn't help laughing. "This gown *is* dreadful, isn't it? I only wore it to convince Mama that I won't be forced to 'exhibit my wares' on the Marriage Mart. She coerced me into attending this rout, but she'll never coerce me into playing this matchmaking game. I shall not agree to an advantageous match, even if one should ever be offered me."

"You're joking. You can't prefer an *un*advantageous one."

"If you want the truth, I don't want to marry at all. But you may take my word that, whatever I do, I shall *never* marry for money."

Lucy snorted. "You may think you're an idealist, Georgy, but I think you're a fool."

Georgy shrugged and rose from her chair. "Perhaps. But in the meantime, you may be missing the arrival of Lord Catch-of-the-Season Maitland. Are you ready to go down?"

Lucy bent down to the dressing table mirror for one last look. "Are you certain this sash is not *de trop*?"

"It may well be, my love, but surely you don't care, do you? So long as everyone notices you?"

"I don't care about everyone, only about Maitland. Do you think *he*'ll notice me?" Lucy asked hopefully as the two girls strolled to the door.

Georgy stopped, ran her eyes over her friend's beads, flounces, necklaces, bracelets, dangling earrings and jeweled headband and gave a ringing laugh. "How could he possibly help it?" she teased.

Lucy, satisfied, walked out the door. Georgy hesitated, took one last glance at herself in the mirror and sighed ruefully. "One thing sure," she muttered as she followed her friend and closed the door behind them, "is that he'll never notice *me*."

Signet Regency Romance

An Encounter with Venus

by Elizabeth Mansfield

"One of the enduring names in romance."
—*Paperback Forum*

When he was seventeen, George Frobisher caught a glimpse of his sister's best friend emerging from a bathtub...*naked.* In the ten years since that fateful day, however, the now Earl of Chadleigh hasn't heard a word about the dazzling venus—until now...

0-451-20997-4

Also by Elizabeth Mansfield:
The Girl with the Persian Shawl
0-515-13414-7

Available wherever books are sold or at www.penguin.com

s009